The
Book
Binder's
Daughter

BOOKS BY JESSICA THORNE

The Lost Girls of Foxfield Hall
The Queen's Wing
The Stone's Heart
Mageborn
Nightborn

JESSICA THORNE

The
Book
Binder's
Daughter

bookouture

Published by Bookouture in 2021

An imprint of Storyfire Ltd.
Carmelite House
50 Victoria Embankment
London EC4Y 0DZ

www.bookouture.com

ISBN: 978-1-80019-857-9
eBook ISBN: 978-1-80019-856-2

To all the fantastic libraries
and library staff everywhere

Prologue

I dreamed about the tree again last night. I've had the dream for as long as I can remember. Not every night, not every dream. In fact weeks can go by, sometimes months, without it rising from my subconscious to torment me. But it's frequent enough and vivid enough that the after-image haunts me for days. Weeks. Months.

When I was little I would excitedly tell my mother every detail and she would sit and listen in that indulgent, solemn way parents listen to the ramblings of a three-year-old. She'd hold my hands together, wrapped in hers, and smile. When I'd finished she would breathe out slowly, as if I had reached the end of translating some ancient epic, or performed a feat worthy of a hero, and she'd smile.

'Well,' she would say. 'That's something, isn't it?'

And I'd be happy with that.

But that was before she vanished. Everything changed after that.

I never told my father. He wouldn't want to know. I understood.

The tree is taller than a redwood. Taller than a mountain. As tall as the sky. I'm certain that there are clouds threaded through its branches while the uppermost golden leaves are tangled with stars. It stretches beyond understanding, and so very far beyond my dreams. It feels eternal.

But for something so tall, it is strangely fragile. The trunk is slender, knotted with a million old black scars. Its branches twist like a contortionist, like the end of a corkscrew, or the whorls and spirals carved on a standing stone. And the bark is pale silver, opalescent, peeling away from the tree like paper. It's so fine, so delicate, that it crumbles if touched with even the gentlest caress.

The shadow beast flits around the base of the tree, in and out of the mighty roots which plunge into the ground, rise again and then dig even deeper. It leaps from the great flat rock at the foot of the trunk to the earth. I can never quite see it, but I know it. I'm not afraid of it. I never have been. It's a guardian, that's all. It was created to protect the tree. I'm no threat to it.

It is always the leaves that entrance me. They're golden, not merely yellow. They shine. They dance in breezes I can't feel, moving and whispering, singing a strange sibilant song that winnows its way inside my mind and becomes my ear worm for the rest of the day. It's a tune I know like my own heartbeat, like the rushing of my blood, but I can never quite capture it. All the same I find myself humming snatches of it for days afterwards.

The leaves that fall, twisting like a girl on a flying trapeze, glimmer with light, with fire. The sunlight eats into them and I can see markings on them. Words perhaps, although the little crow-scratch symbols are not in any language I, or anyone else on the earth today, might know.

Or perhaps I do.

They're familiar, like something half forgotten. They glow with their own life, capturing the eye, lines of fire which eat away at the leaves' surfaces even as they appear, devouring the very thing that supports them. But no matter how much I run and leap and try to catch them, the moment I do the glow dies away and the leaf, that shining glowing perfect thing, turns to ash in my hands.

My mortal, earthbound hands.

I wake up sobbing, my face silver and wet.

With ashes on my hands.

Chapter One

The cream envelope felt thick and heavy, that sort of cotton-rich, handmade paper sold in the most expensive stationers. It lurked on Sophie's hall table, waiting to be read.

The address was written with that kind of elegant penmanship learned only as part of the most exclusive education. A deep red-brown ink, such a contrast against the cream paper. Like old blood. Sophie couldn't take her eyes off it. As she carefully put on her coat, tucked her necklace beneath her scarf, and made sure she had everything ready for work, it drew her eye back to it.

'Haven't you opened that yet?' Victor asked, walking by her on his way out of the door.

'Not yet,' she admitted.

'Looks posh. Could be an invitation or something.' He lingered there, obviously hungry to find out what it said. 'Want me to read it for you?'

It sounded like a kind offer, which was how he always made things sound. He said he liked to watch out for her. Which was true, she supposed. He had stopped her making some terrible mistakes in the early days of their relationship.

She saw the gleam in his slate grey eyes, and the twist of his mouth. She knew she ought to say, 'Yes please, Victor.' But somehow she couldn't.

He had never gone so far as opening anything without her permission, she knew that. Nor would he. He respected her privacy.

He just liked to know.

Sophie picked up the letter, the paper soft as a caress on her fingertips, and slid it carefully into her handbag. 'I'm sure it's nothing. I'll deal with it later. I don't want to be late for work. What would Dr Bellamy think?'

But as she moved to go by him, Victor wrapped his arms around her, holding her in place. His voice was unbearably gentle.

'You shouldn't have gone back so soon. You weren't ready. Take the day off. They'll understand. You're still grieving.'

Was she? It didn't feel that way. It had been months and she felt numb. She was happy to be back at work, to be honest. She couldn't stay away forever, not even if Victor thought she still needed time. She had already managed a couple of weeks.

Normality, that was what she needed. The Academy offered it and the library there was her safe space. It always had been.

'No, I'm fine, I just—'

'Of course, of course. I understand. Whatever you think is best. But if you keep hiding from your loss…'

Her loss. Yes, it was her loss. After her father had died, she had barely left the apartment. But she couldn't keep staying home, staring at the ceiling, at the photos, cooking for Victor and cleaning like an obsessive. The kitchen had never sparkled quite so much. She knew he liked the apartment to be clean. It was easier to do it herself, and so she'd let the cleaner go. She had been at home anyway.

But now… now…

She breathed in carefully and rested her head on his shoulder. His arms tightened a bit too much but she didn't complain. He was trying to look after her.

Victor was grieving too. Sophie's father had been his mentor, his friend. And the source of a thousand painstakingly restored rare books to sell.

'*Take a break,*' he'd say. And then, '*Why not set up a little studio here on your own? I could sell your work for a fortune.*'

And he could too. He had the contacts. She had the expertise. They had gone over it a thousand times. But if she did that, he'd never want her to go back to work.

'It's all right,' she told him. 'Don't worry. I'm fine.'

It was a normal conversation. Just a normal conversation. Why did she feel the need to second-guess everything? He was being nice.

'I'll come and meet you for lunch,' he replied with an annoying grin.

Sophie hesitated. The girls at work had been planning to go out for lunch but she hadn't mentioned it to him. Nothing special. A sandwich and a picnic in the park near the Academy, but he'd hate that. Outside like peasants. And Victor didn't exactly get on with her co-workers. Silly, he called them, frivolous. *Not like you, Sophie. You're so much more responsible. So much more sensible.*

She chose her words with care. She didn't want to upset him, and it was a kind offer really. 'It's such a hassle for you to come all the way across town, and you're so busy right now. Why don't I come and meet you for a coffee this evening? Then we can come home together. Like we used to.'

For a moment she thought he might argue, or say something cutting, but he relented, smiling in delight. 'What a lovely idea. Let's do that.'

Sophie kissed him demurely and fled out of the apartment before he could change his mind. She was most of the way down the street outside before she could breathe evenly again.

*

The fine tissue paper felt like butterfly wings, delicate and easily torn, but strong when treated correctly. With a light layer of glue and the gentlest brush it could bring pages back to life, repairing them and making them stronger than ever. It had to be used sparingly. Too much and it would overwhelm the original page and drown it. Too little and it wouldn't be strong enough. But in the right hands, with the right skill, it worked wonders.

Sophie laid the piece down on the glue, and then found a large soft brush to smooth it out, chasing away any bubbles and creases with a determined but gentle hand.

'Are you busy?' Lucy asked.

Sophie blinked as her concentration broke and she tried to focus on the interruption instead of the work.

'Almost finished. Is everything okay?'

Lucy shifted from one foot to the other and twisted her fingers together. It wasn't like her to be so nervous. As the personal assistant to Sophie's boss, Dr Bellamy, Lucy guarded the studio like a lioness. No one gained access without an appointment. The Conservation Department was a restricted area. The Academy's damaged children deserved the greatest of care and the strongest of security. And the work ought to be uninterrupted.

Even Victor couldn't bully his way in here.

It was Sophie's refuge.

Fragile and delicate volumes came here to be repaired, from torn pages and cracked spines, to new covers and re-stitched text blocks. One lecturer had told Sophie's class they were training to be the trauma surgeons of the book world. The Academy championed both the arts and science, and the collections in its library were extensive – and old. Sophie and her colleagues kept those pieces intact and preserved them for the future. She would never lack for work rebinding, repairing, restoring the works housed here. The Academy was hundreds of years old, and everything about it made her feel like she was standing on a rock securely anchored and safe. The staff were an important part of that.

If Lucy looked so agitated, it had to be huge.

'There's someone here to see you. He says he expected you at a meeting two hours ago. That you have an appointment.'

Sophie didn't try to hide her confusion. 'I do?'

She was fairly certain she had nothing on her schedule for the day. Or for the week. She never missed a work appointment. It was unprofessional and her father would never have stood for that. So who was demanding her presence?

'He's from the Special Collection. In *Ayredale*. He's…' She leaned in, her face flushing. 'It's Dr Talbot. Sophie, what on earth is the Head of Acquisitions of the Ayredale Special Collection doing here, asking for you?'

'Dr Talbot?' That wasn't possible. 'Dr *Edward* Talbot? Are you sure?' She laid down her brush, pushing herself back from the workbench.

'Sophie…' Lucy paused, clearly flustered. Then she made some kind of decision and pressed on. 'He says he's your uncle? And that he sent you a letter.'

Uncle Edward. She hadn't seen him in years. Her mother's brother. He and her father had fallen out around the time her mother vanished.

She closed her hand around the pendant that hung from her neck. Her mother's. The only thing she had left of her.

Sophie didn't know much about what had happened. Her father didn't talk about the Special Collection. Or her mother. Or her family, the Talbots.

For hundreds of years the Special Collection had held a place at the heart of the library and archival world. It was *the* library. The rest of the world might not know it, but the fact remained inviolate. Everyone Sophie had ever met, at the Academy and other institutions, wanted to work there, if only for a few weeks on a placement. There were precious few permanent roles and it was a place where open competition never applied: invitation only. The rivalry for the single six-month internship there which came up when she had been studying conservation had been extreme. She was the only one who didn't apply for it and the rest of her year thought she was insane. None of them got it anyway.

People stared when they found out she had grown up there. At least for a while. Then the questions came in an avalanche, few of which she could or would answer.

The frustrating thing was, she could barely remember the place. There was just a sense, an echo, like a dream that faded the moment she woke up. She knew it must be trauma. It had messed with her memory. Well, that was her explanation, her excuse. What she told everyone because then, finally, they stopped asking.

In the world of libraries and archives, the Ayredale Special Collection was up there with the Library of Alexandria or the Vatican Secret Archives. A legendary place, with a thousand stories surrounding it and very few facts. In Sophie's memory it was the place she had grown up. And a huge, gaping hole of loss.

Suddenly Sophie remembered the letter in her bag. The one she hadn't wanted to open in front of Victor. The one she hadn't wanted him to touch.

Rich, cream, handmade paper. Oxblood red ink. Exquisite penmanship.

There had been birthday cards, once upon a time. They tended to have scenes from literature or classical art rather than anything frivolous, with an entirely handwritten interior. Sometimes there were famous quotations or snippets of poems. Nothing as light-hearted as 'Happy Birthday Sophie'.

And the man who'd written them, her uncle, was here now, all the way from Ayredale. Waiting to see her.

'Damn,' she said, too loudly. Several of her colleagues were looking, fascinated, earwigging. She grabbed her bag and her coat, but didn't pause to put it on. Instead she bundled everything together and tried not to run out of the Conservation Unit with Lucy close behind her.

'Please tell Dr Bellamy I'll be back as soon as I—'

'He'll understand. It's *Dr Talbot*. Sophie, what was in the letter?'

Sophie glanced at her friend. Lucy seemed breathless with excitement. The news was going to be all over the Academy in no time. They'd all be gossiping about her by lunchtime.

Sophie Lawrence is related to Dr Edward Talbot. Why would she keep that quiet?

Why? Because it was never a thing. Because she didn't see him or speak to him and hadn't in years. She didn't really know him. She didn't know any of them. Her father had been clear.

Don't, whatever you do, get involved with that place. It will destroy you. Eventually it destroys everyone.

She barely remembered the Special Collection at Ayredale. After her mother vanished, she'd been traumatised. At least that was what the various therapists had said. Sophie herself tended to be more blunt about it. She'd had a breakdown. Though she had been fifteen when they left, she had only a hazy memory of Uncle Edward – a young man then, in a perfectly tailored suit, with a sweep of dark hair and a smile. Such a smile. It promised wonders. He'd made her laugh. He'd reminded her of those heroes in old black and white movies, suave and elegant, a gentleman from a bygone age. She remembered thinking he could do magic.

But that was almost fifteen years ago. Half her life.

Except, when she followed Lucy around the corner and burst through the doors out to reception, she recognised him in an instant. Her uncle had not changed at all.

He got to his feet as she approached, smiling, that same incorrigible smile that she used to love. He was a tall man, with a presence, not quite in his fifties, and he didn't really look much older than she remembered. He'd have been just a little older than she was now.

In her small world of academia and libraries, there were few people so well known as him.

The suit wasn't the patched and tattered, smudged and sagging fabric of half the male library world, or the starched things that lived on hangers, in the wardrobes of men who didn't wear suits except for interviews and funerals who made up the rest of them. This suit probably cost more than her monthly salary. It looked like it had been made for him, hand-sewn.

For a moment Sophie thought he might spread his arms wide and hug her. But she hesitated, a little too long, and instead he thrust one hand out as if that was what he had always intended to do. She had to juggle her bag and coat to free a hand of her own so she could shake his.

'I'm so sorry,' she babbled, suddenly panicking. What did you say to a relative you hadn't seen in years, let alone one who was as important as he was and you had just inadvertently snubbed? 'I never got around to opening the letter and then I—'

'Sophie!' His voice was rich and tender with affection, so deep it sent ripples of recollection through her mind. 'Sophie, I'm here now. No harm done. Where can we talk?'

Where? She didn't have a clue. The canteen maybe or—

'The tutorial room is free,' Lucy cut in, seamlessly. 'If you'd like to follow me. Shall I arrange some tea or coffee?'

Sophie shot her a grateful glance.

'Tea would be delightful, Miss Harding. Thank you,' Edward said and ushered Sophie into the room ahead of him. He pulled out a chair for her to sit in, as if entirely familiar and at ease with the place. 'Well, Sophie, my dear, where have you been hiding all this time? And what exactly do you think you have been hiding from?'

Chapter Two

Sophie stared across the expanse of the oval table in front of her. She hadn't answered her uncle. Not because she didn't want to but because she couldn't think of an answer. Not one that wouldn't paint her father in a bad light, or reveal her to be the coward she was. Abruptly her vision swam and tears stung her eyes. She blinked them back hurriedly. Her uncle's gaze was still on her, but it had softened.

'I was sorry to hear about your father's passing,' he said gently, as if she had managed some sort of reply after all.

Sophie dipped her gaze again, back to the table. Her father hadn't spoken to her uncle in years. Not since her mother vanished. They had never exactly been friends anyway, she suspected, going from the way her father would clam up when Edward or anyone connected to the Ayredale Special Collection was mentioned.

They had lived there – her mother, her father and Sophie. And her mother had vanished there. It had been 2006, in the winter. Sophie would never forget that. When you had forgotten so much, you clung to the smallest details. There had been a search. A police investigation. But it was a cold case now. Elizabeth Talbot-Lawrence had never been found. And as far as her father had been concerned, the Special Collection had closed ranks, hadn't done a single thing to help. He had never forgiven them.

'Thank you,' Sophie replied, hiding behind formality. 'It was quite sudden really.' What would her father say if he saw her here, now, sitting with Edward as if... as if they were family?

Which was crazy because they *were* family. She just hadn't seen him in almost fifteen years. Hadn't heard from him. Hadn't even tried to contact him. And yet here he was. Come to find her.

Clearing his throat, he tried again. 'I wrote to you when I heard. Several times.'

'You did?' She hadn't received any letters from him. All she'd seen arrive was bills, and Victor generally dealt with them. 'I'm sorry I didn't get them. Did you have the right address?'

Edward smiled softly, a little too knowingly. 'I did. I made sure of that. I found your home number and tried ringing that.'

That surprised her. 'You rang me? At home?'

'Yes. Ah...' He paused, picking his words carefully. 'Your... um... friend, Victor Blake, informed me not to telephone again. He was most insistent.'

Oh. She dropped her gaze to the table again. Victor. He hated it when the telephone was tied up in any way. He paid for it, after all. What if there was a work call for him? An important deal? Of course he had a mobile as well, but still. His work was important.

It didn't matter. People didn't tend to ring her anyway. She often switched her own phone off and forgot to put it back on, if she was honest.

'Oh,' she said. 'I... I'm sorry.'

How many times had she said that now?

Her uncle shook his head. 'Don't be sorry. It isn't your fault. Victor is... well known.'

'You know Victor?'

'Everyone in this business knows Victor. He's grown quite the reputation as a finder of rare and valuable things, for a price.' That was true. And people often said it in a lot less flattering terms. Victor was a rare books dealer. One who didn't really care too much about how he got the things he sold.

Her first urge was to apologise again. Or maybe try to explain. But Edward was looking right at her and she felt so awkward. Like she would be lying to him.

'I should have phoned you when Dad passed away. I just…' There wasn't an explanation. Not really. If she was honest, she had never been able to work up the nerve. What would her father have thought? What would he think now?

'Your father and I didn't exactly part on the best of terms,' Edward said, ignoring the way her voice trailed off. 'Well, we never exactly were on the best of terms to begin with. I was Elizabeth's little brother and, to be honest, I wasn't exactly thrilled that she married him at the time.' His voice softened and he smiled at her. Sophie felt the warmth of affection in that smile wash over her. 'But then there was you. Do you remember Ayredale? I don't imagine so. It was a long time ago. I managed to keep an eye on your career, made sure you were doing okay. Not that I needed to worry about you. I hear only the very best things. Now, do you have any questions about the letter?'

The letter. She'd completely forgotten about the letter again. She pulled it out of her bag and placed it on the table in front of her. Edward glanced at it, clearly taking in that it was unopened.

He rubbed the bridge of his nose. 'Right. I see. Well, why don't you read it and I'll go and help that sweet girl with the tea.'

'That sweet girl'? Lucy? He'd better not try to refer to her that way in person. Mind you, judging by the star-struck way Lucy had acted around him, he would probably get away with it. He had all the charisma Sophie remembered.

She remembered that, and so little else about Ayredale. Funny what the trauma did. But how did Edward know that? He must have had some contact with her father if he knew about her patchwork memory.

Sophie picked up the envelope, turned it over in her hands, once more relishing the quality of the paper. There was a seal on the back, still intact, heavy red wax with a crest bearing the image of a tree pressed into it. She peeled it back carefully and unfolded the letter.

It was addressed to her, Miss Sophia Lawrence, and it was a job offer.

There it was, written in that same blood red ink, in the same beautiful hand. Why they didn't type like everyone else was a bit of a mystery, but still…

Usually handwriting would be a bit of a trial for her. Dyslexia made it that bit more difficult, like everything. Usually she contended with that by working harder, forcing herself to focus. She'd even studied the palaeography of old manuscripts. But for some reason the writing seemed perfectly clear to her. It was a joy to behold.

As was the offer it conveyed.

Conservator and specialist binder at the Ayredale Special Collection, at a salary twice what she was paid now, and two grades up from her current position within the Academy. Not to mention accommodation and board included.

She stared at it in disbelief. It was the offer of a lifetime. A chance to escape. A chance to get some answers about a part of her life which had been wiped away.

And maybe, just maybe, to find out what happened to her mother.

If she dared to seize it.

That said, she could imagine Victor's face. She could imagine her father's. A chill crept through her at that thought.

She hadn't been back there since she was a teenager. Traumatised, ill, broken…

Dad hadn't so much resigned from Ayredale as fled, wiping it from his résumé and refusing to talk about the place, or ever to allow Sophie to ask questions. Still, it had followed him, as such places always did, whispered about by his colleagues, clinging to his reputation. For anyone else, they would consider it an honour, an enhancement, but not Philip Lawrence.

He hated the Special Collection and everything about it.

This was the place where her mother had last been seen, leaving behind a man who adored her and their teenage daughter. She had vanished one night, when Sophie was sick with a fever. Philip had been away at a conference.

That hadn't mattered. Police always suspect the partner first. The rumours had followed her father too until the day he died.

All those whispers.

The paper shook in her hands and she had to put it down.

They had barely talked about it, certainly not for years. If the subject of her childhood or the events that had taken her mother from their lives came up, Sophie's father would close down the conversation abruptly. And she couldn't remember anything on her own.

Memory loss was common enough after bereavement, or so her doctors told her. The feeling that she was going crazy, the way her remaining memories showed impossible things and the subsequent breakdown were not. After they moved, all she wanted to do was go back to Ayredale, to find her mother. She had been absolutely adamant she could find her, that she could bring her back. She just… didn't know how. Or why she thought that. After the second time she tried to run away from the miserable house in Islington her father had moved them to, only a month later, he sought professional advice.

Sophie remembered the hospital, and the special clinic where they had tried to get her to talk about what had happened the night her mother vanished, where they had tried to get her father to share his grief in order to help her express her own and oh, how that had backfired.

He'd sent her away to boarding school shortly after she was discharged, and then she had left for college. They'd carefully emotionally distanced themselves from each other to avoid ever having to talk about the Ayredale Special Collection, two planets in orbit around the black hole of their loss. It was always that way, even when she followed in his footsteps and dedicated herself to rare books and their bindings. He might have taught her everything, every trick of the trade, revelling in her skills, but they never spoke about her mother or her childhood. The books were all that mattered, the only subject to discuss. They worked together day by day, spending time together by appointment rather than chance. It was like having a tutor instead of a father. What little still remained of Ayredale had simply drifted out of her conscious memories.

Her leaf pendant swung free of her blouse. She closed her eyes and caught the dangling piece of old yellow gold, closing her hand around it tightly until the metal bit into her skin. A solid, constant reminder that her mother had been real. Elizabeth had always worn this necklace but Sophie had never known where her mother had got it. Nor when she had passed it on to Sophie. Only that she had.

It was all she had of her mother. Elizabeth Lawrence had been wiped from her life. Sophie's father reacted by pretending she had never existed, by removing all traces of her from their lives. In his unguarded moments he claimed he was protecting Sophie.

No one talked about it. No one dared.

Sophie hadn't realised how badly her father was doing until the call came from the hospital. There was a brain tumour, they said. There was nothing they could do.

When she tried to talk to him about it, tried to reach him, he raved about the library again. *They did this to me. They did this. They stole her from me and they caused all of this.*

And then her father died…

There were tears on her face when she heard the door and the clatter of the tea trolley that Lucy had liberated from the kitchens. Uncle Edward held the door open for her and followed her back inside.

'Here we are,' Lucy said with uncommon brightness. She didn't miss a trick. Sophie wiped her face with her sleeve and tried to make her voice sound even. She knew it wasn't a good impression of a functioning human being but, all the same, she had to try.

'Thank you, Lucy.'

For a moment Lucy just stared at her, obviously seeing her distress. She hesitated, fidgeted and then dug a pack of tissues out of her pocket.

'Are you sure you're okay?' she asked softly. 'I can sit in, if you—'

Sophie shook her head, but took the tissues gratefully. 'It's a family matter,' she replied and Lucy nodded although she still looked reluctant to leave.

'I'm right outside if you need anything.' That remark was a little more pointed than perhaps Lucy would have normally sounded. It might have been for the benefit of Edward Talbot. A warning.

And with that, she was gone.

Sophie fixed her attention on her uncle, who had settled himself in the chair across from her. He sat back, gazing up at the ceiling, waiting for her, his fingers interlocked over his waistcoat. He had a watch chain, hooked in a button hole and running to the pocket, thick, made of old gold, that kind of rich, buttery metal you didn't see any more.

It wasn't unlike the necklace.

'What do you think, Sophie?'

'You're offering me a job? Isn't that nepotism?'

But Edward Talbot just shrugged. '*We* are offering you a job because you are one of the most highly skilled experts in your field. And you learned from the best. Whatever our differences, I never doubted your father's skill. Anyway, you aren't going to be working for me. You'll work alongside Professor Hypatia Alexander, our Keeper, so you can count that as continued professional development too. The things that woman can teach you... well, there isn't a university to compare. Besides, Ayredale tends to run in families. Legacies, we call it. Like your mother and myself. We aren't the only ones, but the Talbots have worked for the Special Collection from time out of mind. And if it isn't to your taste long term, it will be the jewel in the crown on your résumé. Our former staff members have their pick of positions with the world's universities and libraries. More than that, Sophie. They run them.'

Sophie frowned at him, trying to work out if that was meant to be a joke.

It was too big, too much. She needed to think. She needed to talk to Victor. And part of her simply... didn't want to tell him. She knew already what he would say.

'I'll... I'll have to think about it. It's quite a move.'

But it was also an amazing opportunity, one her peers would glee-fully commit murder for. She knew that.

'That doesn't sound like you,' her uncle replied, giving her a shrewd look. How did he know? He had no idea what she sounded like. Problem was, he was right. When she said it, apart from the hesitancy, it didn't sound like her at all. It sounded like Victor.

'All the same, I need to talk to… to my… to Victor about it.'

He leaned forward, his gaze suddenly intense. 'I would hate to think you would pass up this opportunity for someone who might not give you the same consideration, Sophie. We all deserve to have the life we want, to be with people who deserve us.'

What did he mean? She could guess, but she couldn't admit it. For a long time now she'd known that Victor wasn't any good for her. She just didn't know what to do about it. And how could Edward know that?

'I don't understand,' she whispered. Lying.

Edward Talbot tilted his head to one side, examining something she couldn't see.

'Of course.' He didn't approve, but he didn't challenge her on it again either. 'It's a big decision. Take your time. I'm sure it will all become clear soon enough. Sleep on it and let me know.'

'I… I see.' She didn't. But what could she say? There was no way she could take this job. Victor would never agree to move away from London and a long-distance relationship wasn't going to work. He laughed at people who even tried. And she wasn't sure the powers in charge of Ayredale would actually want Victor Blake, or anyone associated with him, anywhere near their precious collection. She knew her bosses at the Academy had raised eyebrows when they found out about her relationship with Victor. They called him unprincipled, a conman, even a thief. Not in front of her, of course, but she knew the rumours. He sought out rare books for collectors without scruples, no matter the legality of acquiring them. Only Sophie's own reputation saved her. Hers and her father's.

She couldn't do it. Could she?

Then there was the past, everything that had happened at Ayredale. Her father would roll over in his grave. She would be giving up everything. Her job, her home, her life.

But…

She had *some* memories of Ayredale – vague, inoffensive things, the gardens and the village beyond with its cluster of cottages, a couple of shops, the church, and the school she had attended over in neighbouring Kingsford. The memories were hazy and distant, but always tinged with a feeling of home, belonging, friendships.

Edward was here, her uncle, her family. And this was a chance… a chance to finally ask the question.

'Uncle Edward, what happened to my mum?'

The look that passed over his face was one of such guilt and pain it stole her breath away. For a moment he didn't answer. She could see the sorrow fill his eyes.

'I wish I had an answer for you,' he said at last. 'I truly do.'

It was more than she had ever heard from her father.

*

The closer Sophie got to home, the more she convinced herself that this would never work out.

Lucy had been the one to suggest she leave for the day. 'You look shaken. Go and talk it over with what's-his-name.'

She knew his name, Sophie thought. She just didn't like him. Victor had said as much and he was rarely wrong. Lucy didn't bother to hide her feelings or be polite.

'Victor won't be there. He's at work. He has a big sale coming up.'

'I'm sure he does. Told some grandmother her priceless family collection is worth peanuts, no doubt.' She rushed on before Sophie could protest. 'Well, take the day off anyway and think about it before he gets home and complicates everything.' She laughed, but it didn't sound entirely like a joke. 'You've got about a million days saved up in leave anyway. HR will thank you. You deserve a day off, Sophie.'

Sophie wasn't sure she did. But she took it anyway. She needed space to think. Room to breathe.

It was surely all a massive mistake. Uncle Edward had done this because he remembered her as a girl and felt sorry for her. He was now her only living relative and probably felt as guilty about that as she did. It wasn't like they were close. He was blinded by familial affection, he had to be, and if she actually took the job she would let him down immediately. He'd see through her as soon as she got there. Oh, she was good, she knew that, but she never felt she was good *enough*. Her father had always said how tough it could be at the Special Collection. His stories made Professor Alexander, the Keeper at Ayredale, sound like a monster. He had trained under her, worked alongside her. She was legendary.

That woman, he had called her. *That place*, he called the library, and ghosts would fill his eyes if it was mentioned.

He'd never mentioned Edward Talbot at all.

And yet the Special Collection clung to its place in legend. And the memories of it never left him. Not like they had left Sophie.

Once, when she visited the nursing home towards the end, he had called out for her mother. *Elizabeth! Are you down there again? Elizabeth, where did you go?*

Sophie had made her apologies and fled from the room, sobbing all the way to the Tube station which would take her home, those words ringing in her ears. His voice still haunted her. She heard it in her nightmares.

When she left work it was early enough that she got a seat on the Tube but that didn't help her mood as much as it would normally have done. All the way home, Sophie fretted. She took out the letter a few times and read it again, before stuffing it back in her bag. It still didn't seem real. She walked quickly, head down, all the way home from the station, her mind caught up entirely in the ramifications of the contract, of the possibilities. She even checked the letter one last time in the elevator up to their floor.

She opened the door, stepped into the apartment and heard—

Two people. Low laughter. A gasp, a grunt.

Unmistakable.

The sound of the kitchen table legs scraping on the tiled floor.

Sophie pushed open the door to see Victor and a woman together. Mouth to mouth, half undressed, legs entangled, sweaty…

She was never going to be able to eat at that table again.

'Sophie?' Victor gasped, staring over his PA's shoulder. 'What the hell are you doing home?'

*

He was back to yelling by the time she'd packed her bags. The poor woman had fled, mortified by the whole affair, and all Sophie wanted to do was emulate her. She didn't know what to take with her, so she shoved as much as she could into a case and a holdall and hoped for the best. It wasn't like she had a lot of personal belongings anyway. All that her father had left her was in storage, or at least everything that they hadn't sold after probate. Most of her own things, other than some clothes, were there too, stored away, her life before Victor labelled, packed into boxes and consigned to the grim confines of a warehouse on the outskirts of the city somewhere. She paid the bill monthly and never thought about it. She had the papers for it in the file holding her birth certificate, qualifications and official documents, now shoved in the bottom of her case.

Her tatty bric-a-brac had never gone with any of Victor's lovely, stylish furniture. It had no place in his chic apartment. And it had never bothered her because she knew he was right. And as for her father's things… her so-called inheritance…

Victor had made her give up everything. And for what?

He barged into the lift with her at the last minute, seething and berating her the whole ride down. The doors opened and she stepped out into the expanse of the foyer.

'Sophie, will you stop being hysterical?' Victor yelled at her, drawing glares from their concierge, a terrifying woman in six-inch heels.

But Sophie wasn't being hysterical. She was perfectly calm. He was the one being hysterical. It wasn't the first time she had seen it, but it was the first time she recognised it for what it was. She eyed him warily over her shoulder and kept going across the marble floor, avoiding the exceptionally ugly sculpture dominating the middle. She hated this place. She always had. But Victor wouldn't dream of living outside Zone 1.

'Where are you even going to stay?' he protested.

She didn't care. She had money. Mainly because the one thing she had never given up for him was her own bank account. A mercy now, she realised. He had tried so hard to convince her that she didn't need it and she had almost believed him. She barely used it except to pay her share of the bills. So her wages went in and built up.

'What are you even going to do?' he yelled. 'I know where you work. I'll ring them up and tell them all about you.'

What was there to tell? Anyway, it didn't matter now.

'I have a new job,' she said, and walked away.

He stalked her all the way down the road, barefoot and cursing, his shirt still undone, until finally he called her a bitch, and told her he was well rid of her.

'And you know why?' he said, in a cold, calm voice that was so much worse than when he shouted. She knew that voice. It was deliberately cruel, wrapped with enough barbed truth to really sink in deep. He didn't use it often. But when he did, it was designed to hurt. 'You made me do it. A man's got to get affection somewhere. You're a frigid cow who'll end up on her own with only a manky cat for company. I mean, *look* at you. Scrawny, old and useless. Dropping everything like this? You'll end up homeless and jobless. Who'd want you now?'

Sophie sucked in a breath and forced herself to keep going. It didn't matter what he said.

Who'd want her now?

Well, Ayredale Special Collection for one.

And that would have to do.

Chapter Three

The hotel room had floor-to-ceiling windows looking out over the Tower of London, Tower Bridge and the Thames. It had been a whim to walk in and ask for a room, a dare to herself. Sophie hadn't really expected to get one. She handed over her credit card and didn't even allow herself to flinch at the thought of what it might cost. It didn't matter. Not tonight.

She treated herself to room service, a glorious dinner cooked to perfection for her by someone else without a thought for what anyone would say about calories, fat and carbs. She ran a bubble bath and lingered in it, enjoying it without anyone knocking on the door demanding that she hurry up. She slept a dreamless sleep in a bed so big she could stretch out however she wanted to. It was like sleeping on a cloud.

She woke up to a text message on her phone from an unknown number.

Train booked for midday, ticket & directions at reception. Contact numbers & itinerary included. I'll have Will Rhys collect you from Kingsford station. Uncle Edward.

She hadn't signed the contract, hadn't even managed to get around to contacting her uncle, hadn't done anything except finally leave Victor.

But he knew.

How did he know?

And how had he got her number?

Wish for something without thinking about it, her father had said, *wish hard enough, and it may happen. And then you may wish it hadn't at all.*

But it wasn't a wish. Edward had prepared for this. He had known she would take the job. He'd left tickets and instructions at reception, even though she hadn't told him she was here. Strange. Had he known about Victor's affair as well? The thought tripped her up. That made no sense and she hated the idea.

Why hadn't he told her?

Not that she would have believed him. No, he couldn't have known. Could he?

A feeling crept over her, like a memory, that once she had believed everything Edward told her. She used to hang on his every word, she recalled. He'd babysat her. He told her stories when she was little, such stories...

About two librarians who trapped a demigod who would have destroyed their library. They broke him in two and made him human. From then on he became their guardian.

'Was it magic?' she'd asked.

'Of course it was. All librarians can do magic.'

Her mother laughed, that wild, infectious laugh. 'Don't wind her up, Edward. You're incorrigible.'

Sophie adored him. He could do magic, Uncle Edward could.

Sophie forced her suddenly rapid breath to calm. It took a few minutes. The doctors had tried all sorts of things to trigger her recollection, but nothing had ever worked. She had never remembered that before, and so vivid a memory... it had to be because she'd met

Edward again. It had dredged up memories from long ago, things she had suppressed. From before her mother had gone.

She barely remembered anything from that time and she had grown to accept that. But her mother, that laugh... It was so real, so powerful. A memory she'd thought lost.

The sound of it still ringing faintly in her ears told her one thing. She needed to find out what had happened to her mother. That was the real reason to go back to Ayredale, to finally know the truth. She wasn't just running away from Victor. She was running home.

Sophie sat on the massive bed and read the message again.

Will Rhys. She remembered him, too. Will, with the solemn green eyes, who had played in the gardens with her, under the tree, that endlessly tall and beautiful tree. Will, who had grown into a young man alongside her, just a year older than her, who had been, if she was finally being honest with herself, her first love. Not that anything had really happened, had it? A kiss, perhaps?

God, why couldn't she remember that? Everyone remembered their first kiss, didn't they? He'd lived there too, someone's son, or stepson, or something. Memories of him flickered through her mind like old, degraded video. Memories rekindling even as she reached for them. They had been inseparable, best friends. And then... His lips brushing tentatively against hers, his scent, his warmth...

His fingers tangling with hers as they looked up at the tree, the impossibly tall tree.

And he was still there now. Like a ghost from her broken past. All those things she had thought lost and gone. Blocked out. Swallowed by grief.

But the library lingered in the corners of her mind, stubborn and insistent.

Like Will Rhys.

What was she doing? She was giving up everything and going back to somewhere she barely knew. She was walking away from her life. But then... it wasn't like Victor was a reason to stay any more.

Sophie got dressed and went down to the hotel dining room for breakfast, stopping by reception to pick up another envelope of the same heavy cream paper with her name written in oxblood ink in the same elegant hand. She took it into the dining room and ordered a full English breakfast with all the trimmings.

The instructions were far more detailed than Edward's text message and contained contact numbers for the Ayredale Special Collection and his personal number, even though she had already saved it in her mobile. The train itinerary was meandering and would take hours. There wasn't a direct line that went anywhere near Ayredale apparently, so she had a number of changes. Instead of printing it out, Edward had written it all by hand. Like he had a kind of personal vendetta against technology.

Checking out of the hotel she discovered that Edward had already paid for her. Something in her bristled a little at that. It was the type of thing Victor might do, if he was feeling generous or wanted something. She pushed that thought away. Edward was family. That was different. Or so everyone said. He was also the only family she had left so what did she know? She wondered for a moment if anyone would notice she was gone, except for Victor. Maybe her colleagues in work, and Lucy. Maybe.

Lucy! She hadn't even handed in her notice. She couldn't take off without explanation, could she? She tucked herself into a corner of the vast reception and fished out her phone.

When she rang, Lucy answered with the crisp efficiency Sophie expected.

'It's me. I'm… I'm taking some time off. Personal reasons.'

Lucy paused a little too long. 'Sophie? Everything okay?'

'Fine. I'm fine. I'm… I have a family thing.'

Lucy was not fooled. 'A family thing? Like a *library* family thing?'

She knew, didn't she? Well, Dr Edward Talbot of the Ayredale Special Collection had waltzed into her workplace and upended her entire life. People noticed things like that. Especially clever people who read the currents of office politics like Lucy.

And it was a library family thing. Ayredale and her mother…

'Kind of. I think… I just left Victor and I stayed in a hotel and… They want me to go to Ayredale. I don't really have anywhere else to go so…'

Lucy sucked in a breath. 'Jesus, about time, Sophie! Don't worry about anything. I'll let Dr Bellamy know. I reckon you have about a year's worth of leave saved up anyway, don't you?'

Did she? Despite the promises of a sun holiday, she and Victor had never quite gotten around to it for the last few years. They could never agree on where to go. There was never time.

'Maybe? Could we call it a sabbatical?' Sophie asked.

Her friend sighed as if Sophie was being particularly dense. 'You're meant to apply for them in advance, you know? Don't sweat it, Sophie. They can't say anything, not when the Ayredale Special Collection summons you. I'll sort it out, I promise.'

Or maybe Uncle Edward had taken care of that for her too. She wouldn't put it past him. 'I owe you, Lucy.'

'You owe me nothing. I'm over the moon you finally left that creep. Stay in touch, and stay safe, okay?'

A taxi took her to Waterloo Station where she made her way through bustling crowds and out onto the platform.

The ticket was first class, which she hadn't expected. Was this treatment because she was Edward Talbot's niece or did they indulge all employees this way at the Special Collection?

What if this was all a terrible mistake?

And then she'd have to head back to London. Homeless and jobless. Exactly as Victor had predicted. It didn't bear thinking about. She huddled in her seat and closed her hand around the leaf-shaped pendant.

She was going back to Ayredale. She was going to spend time with people who'd known her mother – her uncle, the Keeper, maybe some of the other long-standing staff. And she was going to ask them questions she'd never been allowed to ask.

*

The train rocked her all the way out of London. Grey gave way to suburbia, which gave way to empty fields and barren hedgerows. A winter landscape flashed by her. There were delays to the service, of course. And when she had to change, there was another wait, a rather sad sandwich and a lukewarm coffee. She huddled in a draughty platform café and prayed for the train to hurry up. Her anxiety was building now. But it didn't matter. She just had to keep going.

Rain streaked the windows as the light faded. She made another change, this time standing on the platform because there was no café. Twilight came early. The train did not.

When it finally did arrive she was frozen to the core and gratefully found a seat in the warm carriage.

Sophie didn't mean to doze off but there was something of a relief to being on her way somewhere, to travelling away from Victor. She hadn't even realised she was so tired, or perhaps she had been like a coil of wire, too tightly wound for too long, and she had finally let go.

She dreamed an old dream, one of paper and leaves, of a tree reaching up to the heavens, its golden leaves falling in sweeping spirals towards her.

On the leaves characters glowed, like a burning trail which drew words in sweeping lines, words she couldn't read. It was no surprise to her. With her dyslexia, words were always difficult and she had learned early to disregard them. There were ways around them and her work was with the books themselves anyway. When she was little – before, she always reminded herself, before he changed – her father had sat her down, when she had tearfully tried to read and failed yet again, and told her that the words didn't matter.

She listened to stories instead, and remembered everything. Her phenomenal memory, her father told her, was her greatest asset.

A huge irony now, that was what it was. She had near perfect recall of things she managed to read, or things she heard. Just not her own life.

'It doesn't matter,' her father reassured her time and again. 'One day, my love, you'll find the words that *do* make sense to you, the ones you were meant to read.'

That had been before, too. Before they left. Before he changed.

The books themselves, their bindings, the beauty of their very nature… that was what mattered to her. Not so much the words inside them. The diagnosis of dyslexia helped, but it didn't really change anything.

So she used audiobooks, radio plays and, more recently, podcasts. She listened in silence and drank in those words like songs. They sang her to sleep. Sleep gave her dreams, wondrous dreams.

In her dream now a shadow with terrible teeth and glowing eyes wound around the base of the tree, guarding it. But it wasn't dangerous to her. Perhaps it was *her* guardian. That was what it felt like. Not a threat at all. She looked up again. The leaves sang to her as they fell, their words burning like embers, like molten gold eating through their surfaces. Ash rained down on her and covered her hands.

Sophie awoke with a start as the announcer garbled the name of her station, Kingsford, as the next stop. She had to scramble to grab her belongings and reach the doors.

She spilled out onto the platform into near total darkness.

The contrast was a shock, sudden and terrible. She turned back but the lights of the train were already receding into the night, down the line, under the bridge and far away.

There was not a soul to be seen anywhere. Nobody else had disembarked. By the light of her phone, she fished out the instructions again and tried to read them. Will Rhys should be meeting her here. Somewhere. She hadn't actually read it all that closely. Now she was in the middle of nowhere on her own, in the dark.

Sophie dragged her bags out through the open side gate of the station – unmanned of course – and found a car park without a single car to be seen. Train delays were all very well but after all the planning surely they would have made adjustments for that?

She piled up her belongings on the pavement and dialled Uncle Edward's number, but it rang out.

Sophie had thought herself so lucky this morning. Now it was all starting to resemble a massive disaster. Or maybe a huge practical joke.

She rang a taxi company instead. The wait time was an hour. So she stood there staring at an empty car park with the flickering lights far overhead. There was no sign of any other buildings, no staff, no sign of life at all. Kingsford was a halt rather than a proper station, no more than a platform and a ticket machine in the middle of nowhere. Fields stretched out beyond the station, hedgerows looming over the road which trailed off into the black.

Abruptly, her eyes burned with tears. This wasn't fair. This just wasn't…

'Miss Lawrence? Sophie?'

Sophie turned, caught between running and using her handbag as a weapon, and failing to do either.

A man walked towards her from the far end of the car park, passing under a flickering light which seemed to spring into life just for him. He was tall and slim-hipped, his shoulders broad, just a silhouette.

'Hello?' she said, trying to keep her voice steady and pretty sure she was failing.

He came closer, his stride long and easy, a man her own age in jeans and a T-shirt with a wool coat that skimmed his thighs hanging open and a red scarf looped about his neck. His black hair was a little too long, overdue a cut, but framed a high-cheekboned, handsome face with soulful eyes, a deep and dark green. Sophie stared a bit too long and he cleared his throat.

'Miss Sophie Lawrence?'

There was something familiar in his voice, in his eyes. Something she hadn't seen in years.

'Yes?'

'I'm here to collect you. From the Special Collection. Are those your only bags?'

He didn't say anything else but picked up her belongings and walked back to a sleek black car she hadn't even seen at first. It was as dark as the night, and parked away from the remaining uncertain light. He loaded the bags deftly into the boot.

When he opened the passenger door for her, the interior light came on and a sensor pinged insistently.

But Sophie didn't move, couldn't move. Her feet were frozen to the spot and something in the back of her mind, something buried deep in the most primordial part of her brain, an instinct, a primitive urge, said whoever he was, he wasn't... right. She didn't know what it was but she couldn't deny it or pass it off as a funny feeling.

'Who are you?' she asked. Not what she actually wanted to say. Not, *What are you?* She couldn't bring herself to say that. It would be rude.

He smiled, a brief, self-deprecating smile which was, in and of itself, devastating. 'Will,' he replied, his voice so soft he could be whispering in her ear, his breath playing on the sensitive skin of her neck. Except he wasn't that close. 'Will Rhys? You might not remember me. It's been a while.'

She shivered, staring at him. Edward had said Will would collect her. She remembered Will, of course she did. But he had been a boy. And this was a man. A stupidly handsome, darkly dangerous man.

'I'm an assistant librarian at the Special Collection now. The Keeper asked me to collect you. Dr Talbot should have mentioned it.'

Well, of course he had. What was wrong with her?

And now she saw Will himself, tall, dark and slightly unreal, she didn't know what to think. He was watching her expectantly, waiting for a reply.

Will had grown up into the most handsome man she had ever seen. God, why did she keep thinking about that? He had been her friend. She hadn't seen him in years. He probably – no, looking at him he *definitely* had a girlfriend. Or a boyfriend. Or a spouse. Something, anyway. He couldn't be single.

'Yes… I guess… I guess he did. I'm sorry. I just—'

Her face turned hot with embarrassment. She was cold and tired, and everything ached. Everything was so strange. And Will was right in front of her. She hadn't seen him in so long and now…

He tilted his head, the way a crow would, watching her. 'Would you rather stay here?' There wasn't a trace of humour in his voice.

Obviously not. But all the same, she hesitated, frozen in place. Another memory wrapped its greedy fingers around her mind.

Will, sunlight falling on his upturned face, his eyes so bright a green… Will's lips brushing tentatively against hers…

Will gave an impatient sigh, tinged with frustration – so unbelievably familiar –and something in her finally seemed to unwind itself enough. 'Please get in the car, Sophie. It's freezing out here. And it's going to rain any minute.'

It was. She could smell it in the air. Heavy clouds threatened snow and the wind had turned biting.

'Fine,' she sighed, hoping for the best. 'But I'm ringing my uncle.'

'Could you do it *inside* the car? I have Bluetooth and everything.'

And in the end, there wasn't much else she could do.

He wasn't the boy she had known all those years ago, and she didn't know him at all. But seeing him there meant one small link to the past, to a time when she had both parents and a home.

*

Will drove with practised ease along the narrow lanes that passed for roads here. The headlights picked out their way through the thick hedgerows and the effect was dizzying but Sophie tried not to show it. The call to Uncle Edward had been brief.

'Sophie, is Will not there to collect you?' His voice boomed around the car interior.

Will had winced but said nothing, letting her answer.

'No, I mean yes, he is. I mean, I wanted to check...' She trailed off, her face heating to an unbearable degree again. She was glad that it was dark, but she was still sure he would be able to pick up on the waves of embarrassment rolling off her regardless. 'I wanted to let you know we're on the way. I'm so sorry about the delay. The trains—'

'Don't think twice about it. It's no bother. See you soon.'

He hung up and she glanced at Will whose expression was fixed on the road ahead. No bother for Uncle Edward, perhaps. Will had been the one waiting for her at the station in the cold.

'Were you waiting there long?' she asked gently.

'Not too long. I checked the times online.' Of course he did. That was what anyone reasonable would do in the modern world. It's what she would have done.

'Have you been at the library all this time? Since I left?'

For the longest, strangest moment he didn't answer. He glanced at her and a small, attractive smile flickered over his lips.

'Not as long as *some*,' he said as if it was an admission. Or a secret code between them that she didn't get any more. 'I went away to school too, not long after you left. And then uni. But I came back. We always do, I guess. That's what Tia says. It's that kind of place. Strange.'

Strange enough to steal her mother away from her.

'Tia? Is she your partner?'

He laughed, a great bark of a laugh which almost made her recoil.

'God no. Sorry. Don't you remember Tia? She's the archivist. She's something of a permanent fixture. I would have thought she'd burn herself into anyone's head.'

'It was a long time ago,' she told him. 'I don't remember anyone much. I was ill after we left.' That was an understatement but she didn't want to go into details. Breakdowns were a bit more serious than a cold or the flu and sometimes when you were put back together, all the bits didn't fit properly.

'What? No one? I bet Edward loved that. How did his ego take it?'

She carefully corrected herself. 'Apart from Edward. And Mum. Not what happened to her but, you know... And you, of course.'

But even the memory of Will was a bit hazy, like a dream that didn't quite survive past breakfast.

Sophie couldn't help but feel uncomfortable about that. It seemed rude. She remembered enough to know there had been more to their friendship. But not everything. The facts of it were there, but the emotion was hollowed out, leaving a shell.

They fell back into a slightly awkward silence. After a moment he began to slow and turned into a long, wandering driveway. Gravel crackled underneath the car wheels.

Long perfect lawns fell away on either side of the road and the building rose from the ground like a living thing. It was huge, much bigger than she had thought. And old too. She knew that right away. It resembled a country house, one of those grand things from period dramas, neo-Palladian or Georgian or something, all symmetry and elegance executed in a soft yellow sandstone. In daylight it would surely be stunning. But it was dark and cold, the sky overhead thick with winter clouds. The library loomed over her like a giant, made entirely of threat and shadows.

It wouldn't be out of place in a horror movie either.

A light illuminated the door beneath the impressive portico with four thick columns on either side. Steps led up to it, a puddle of illumination in the darkness. The door itself had eight carved panels and she longed to study the details, to see what they depicted.

Sophie stared, trying to dredge up memories of it, actual memories from her childhood. She ought to be able to recall this place but all she could think of were the photos she had found online last night while frantically searching the internet to assure herself she wasn't going mad. That it was real. But she couldn't recall this austere place. Not at all.

She didn't know why. Looking at it now, she couldn't imagine ever being able to forget it.

Will parked the car and got out, immediately opening the boot and dragging out Sophie's pitiful bags. She struggled with the passenger door and only remembered her handbag at the last minute so when she turned back, he was standing right beside her. Towering over her more like. He was so tall she barely came up to his extensive shoulders.

He had to work out. And God, he smelled so good.

What was *wrong* with her?

'Here we are. Home sweet home.' He glanced down at her, as if waiting for a reaction. It shouldn't feel like home to her. Not after so long. But it did.

And Will was still here. At least she remembered that they had been friends.

'Will? What do you do here now?'

'Assistant librarian,' he said. He'd already told her that. Damn. Now it seemed like she hadn't been listening. 'Not general dogsbody, honestly, although it might look that way sometimes. It's good to have you back, Sophie. Come on, let's get inside.'

'Do you… do you live here full time as well?'

'We all do, more or less. It's easier than trying to find accommodation nearby anyway. Ayredale village is about a fifteen-minute walk that way.' He pointed off through the grounds, the opposite direction to the road. 'But there's not much there, besides a pub, the church, and a couple of shops. Nice place though. Quiet. Average village really. There's more in Kingsford. The grammar school – you've got to remember the grammar school, with that awful cafeteria and the gym falling down? They built a new one, by the way. The train station… well you saw that, and some high street shops and that's it really. But yeah, it's quiet. Definitely not London.'

Well, she'd wanted a getaway. Somewhere quiet. Until she'd looked at the photos last night she hadn't expected a stately home. Or a haunted mansion. She eyed it warily, trying desperately to shake that impression.

Will smiled. It was a surprisingly good smile. An unexpected comfort. 'There's loads of room, and it's very private. You'll see. I know it isn't what you'd normally expect, but think of it like a university residence. We hardly see each other half the time. It's big enough to avoid people, if you want to.'

If she wanted to? Perhaps her reputation as someone shy and reclusive had made it here ahead of her. Perhaps Will remembered more about her than she did herself. Perhaps he thought she wanted to avoid him.

Will stalked off towards the door on those long legs, leaving her with little choice but to follow him, sure that she had insulted him somehow and not sure what to do about it.

She stopped by the door as he unlocked it, and her gaze fell on the brass plaque. It had been polished to a gleaming shine.

Ayredale Special Collection.
By Appointment Only.

It wasn't much bigger than an A4 sheet but it seemed to carry the weight of something far greater with it.

What was she doing here? She was miles away from anything resembling a city and she liked city life. Well, she corrected herself, she was used to it. She didn't exactly like it. She hadn't told anyone where she was going apart from Lucy, not that there was anyone really to tell. There was only Victor and she didn't want any contact with him. She was yet to sign any sort of contract, or get the full details of the job. Some of it was in the letter but to be honest she'd struggled to make it all out. It was so elaborately written, so detailed, and used the kind of language that she was more accustomed to seeing in documents from the Middle Ages.

She still wasn't entirely convinced this wasn't Edward's idea of a hilarious joke.

What would the conservation studio look like in this place? Would she be up for the job? What had she let herself in for?

She stood there, still clutching her bag as the huge doors, carved and ornate, swung open and Will stepped back, sweeping his arm out to invite her to enter ahead of him.

A black cat sat on the floor in front of her, staring intently at her with the largest green eyes Sophie had ever seen, except perhaps for Will's. She stared back, bemused. It wasn't actually blocking her way. Not as such. But she was going to have to step around it. And she had the feeling it might move into her path if she did.

'Let her in, Villus,' said Will. She could hear the amusement in the warmth of his voice. 'She's one of us. Remember?'

With an indignant sound somewhere between a meow and a huff, the cat turned around and strode away, pointedly. For a moment all Sophie could do was stare at the animal. Then she glanced up and her breath was stolen away.

The Rotunda beyond extended to the height of the whole building and above her was a glass dome like a rainbow of petals in the ceiling. It was lit by a chandelier, and numerous wall sconces. The tiled floor spread out before her, a mosaic starting at her feet. It depicted a tree.

Sophie stared at it, frozen again as she saw it.

The branches stretched towards the split staircase, and off towards the doors on either side, as ornately carved as the entrance. She could make out creatures amid the leaves of the mosaic, some birds, some mammals, some… other things entirely. She had the strangest feeling that she knew it. She knew it all.

The same way she knew the cat.

A memory stirred, of sitting on this floor, leaning on the bottom step of the left-hand staircase, drawing the creatures in the branches of the tree in a tattered sketchpad while, behind her, two people argued. *She hated it when they argued…*

But Villus… that wasn't his whole name, but… *Villus purred, pushing up against her arms until she let him on her lap and cuddled him. Her crayons made a soft scratching noise against the thick paper sheet her mother had given her from the bindery.*

But that was impossible. The cat she had seen couldn't be that old. Cats didn't live that long, did they?

The door closed with a decisive bang, making her jump, and Will stopped beside her.

'Are you all right?' he asked, his voice softer now, a gentle rumble that found its way deep inside her and made her shiver. Almost like the purr of her memory.

'Fine. It's just…'

'Impressive, isn't it?' He smiled then and for the first time she saw him properly in the light – a breathtakingly handsome man, with a smile that lit up his green eyes from inside. He had been gorgeous as a boy. But now…

'It's beautiful,' she whispered, and then blushed again. What was she thinking? What exactly was she referring to? Him or the building?

'Do you remember it? We used to slide down those banisters. I almost broke my neck more than once.'

Another memory. *Laughing wildly, the wind tearing past her, she was sure she would never fall, that the library building wouldn't let her. It would never hurt her. This place was safe. It was home.*

It left her breathless. Her smile wavered as she looked back at Will.

'I think so. Didn't you actually break your arm?'

He lifted his left hand and waved at her. 'My wrist. God, the Keeper was furious. Do you remember—?'

'Sophie, there you are at last!' Uncle Edward's voice boomed around the Rotunda, amplified by the natural harmonics. She almost jumped out of her skin, turning as if under attack. He smiled at her surprise. The suit he wore looked just as expensive as the one from yesterday, a charcoal grey this time, teamed with a pale blue shirt which made his eyes even brighter. 'I was afraid he'd lost you entirely until you rang. Come along, I'll show you to your room. Will can bring your bags.'

What else could she do? Uncle Edward headed off up the left-hand staircase and she cast an apologetic smile at Will before hurrying after him.

Chapter Four

Well, she wasn't what Will had expected. Sophie. Edward's niece. Elizabeth's daughter.

Her mother had been fierce, a firebrand. Even when everything fell apart for him, Elizabeth had been there holding the last scraps of his life together. And Sophie, beautiful, laughing, reckless Sophie… Nothing like this scared mouse of a woman.

She wasn't the girl he remembered. The girl who lived life at full speed, who never showed fear. His Sophie. It was like she had been broken and put back together wrong.

But from what Edward had said, she was running from something in London. Something or someone. Everything perhaps.

'*Escaping*,' Edward had said with a laugh, as he sat there with the Professor and Arthur over dinner. She was escaping. '*Running right back to us here. Thank the gods.*'

Someone had made her like that, Will thought bitterly, sapped all the joy out of her, made her suspicious and scared. Philip Lawrence, her father, he supposed, and everything that had happened to Elizabeth.

It wasn't fair. Or right.

He felt something dark and vengeful stir in him and hurriedly pushed it back down. This wasn't the time. It was not his place.

'What's she like then?' Tia stepped out of the Reading Room, her voice unexpected.

He paused a moment, picking his words carefully. It usually paid to do that with Tia. She loved a bit of gossip. And she knew how to make a knife blade twist. Even if she didn't really mean to.

'Not like you'd expect.'

The archivist shook back her glossy red hair. 'Time changes people. Even the people we wished would never change. And what did you think would happen? That you were getting your childhood sweetheart back? You know it doesn't work like that, Will. She's been away too long.'

Will frowned at her. 'That's not fair, Tia.'

She shrugged, nonchalant to the last. 'Life isn't fair, my darling boy. It never has been. Anyway. Margo's making hot chocolate. Do you want some?'

'What are we? Children?' But the desire to spar with her wasn't strong enough right now. He felt… deflated somehow. Like he had been filled with hopes and dreams and now they were all gone. They had been all that had been keeping him going. Sophie didn't remember him. Not really.

It shouldn't have hurt quite as much as it did.

'Well, you can top it with marshmallows and cream if you want but I for one am planning to add a large amount of liquor,' she replied. 'Each their own. There's a party about to start in the lounge for that paper O'Neill published as well. I mean, there wasn't meant to be a party but all the scholars are in there drinking so it should get interesting in about…' She thought about it for a microsecond and shrugged. 'Half an hour? Come on, Will, don't abandon me to them. Edward doesn't have time. He's all distracted.'

He lifted Sophie's bag, showing it to Tia. 'Time to fetch and carry, I'm afraid. She's going to need her belongings if she's staying.'

He hoped she would. Because the library needed her.

And yet, he was afraid she'd run from this. He would, given half a chance.

If she remembered even a fraction of it she'd never have stepped back over the threshold.

She had been his friend once upon a time. His only friend. But she left. She hadn't had a choice, but she left just the same and never came back. Just like everyone. It was the way of things. Everyone else left and he stayed here. Because he really didn't have a choice either. He had nowhere else to go.

Tia looked intrigued, reading his expression as she always did. At least Will hoped it was just his expression she could read. 'Don't you think she'll stay this time, Will?'

He didn't answer, but glanced up the stairs where Sophie had vanished overhead with Edward. Few people stayed. Not for very long. Even when they were desperately needed. Apart from the legacies.

He had to think of the library. That was what mattered here. That was his job, to protect it. The hope inside him died and he heaved out a sigh. 'I don't know.'

Tia laughed then, an unexpected sound. There were moments when Will thought she was somewhere else entirely, drifting in time and space, in memories. She said she got lost in her work, but there was more to it than that.

That was the thing about Ayredale and the Special Collection. There was always more to it than anyone thought.

Researchers came and went. Temporary staff shook things up from time to time, but eventually the library took over and it all settled down into its same old self again.

What would Sophie Lawrence find here? What was she in search of? That all remained to be seen. Because he knew that look. She was in search of something. And as for staying...

No one stayed for very long unless they really and truly belonged here. And people like that were few and far between.

But Sophie did, didn't she? Philip and Elizabeth's daughter... if she didn't belong here, who did?

Philip had been the kind of father Will had always wanted. Kind, strong, with a wicked sense of humour. And then... then he wasn't.

After they left, Will, overwhelmed with remorse and missing them terribly, had gone to London to find both of them, to see them. Philip had slammed the door in his face.

Losing Elizabeth had changed him. That was what the Professor had said.

It had changed all of them. Especially Sophie.

'Will,' Tia said softly, calling back his attention. 'Don't be sad. It's a good thing, her coming here.'

'Is it?'

He climbed the stairs, leaving the red-haired woman to watch him with her dark eyes. The bags weighed nothing at all but it felt as if he was carrying a great burden and he wasn't sure why.

Edward was still talking when he reached the room. No, not just talking. Lecturing. That was what he did best. Charming, enthusiastic, able to convince someone that black was white given enough time, but gods, he did like the sound of his own voice. Acquisitions meant being out in the world, acquiring things, and for that he sometimes needed the fox-like cunning of a conman. Or probably more often than sometimes, Will suspected.

And there was no denying he had the skills he needed.

Not like Elizabeth. Because Elizabeth had been everything – Edward's sister who they had all adored – a shining light. The Keeper, Professor Alexander, had seen her as a potential successor. When Will had first arrived here, a lost and frightened child without any clue what was happening or why his world had just been turned upside down, Elizabeth had been there for him. With a child of her own a year younger than him, she'd let him slot into her life. He'd more or less spent all his time with Sophie, and with her family. Until…

He still had nightmares about it.

The light around them raged, a maelstrom of blinding colours, the sound of a hurricane.

'You did everything you could, Will,' Elizabeth said. 'I always knew you would. Our guardian. Let go, love.'

Elizabeth had vanished. That was the last he saw of her.

Fifteen years she was gone, and it might have been yesterday. But even if she was able to come back, everything would be different now. She would be different.

Sophie had been gone just as long and she had changed. She definitely wasn't the girl he used to know.

God, what had happened to her?

When Will cleared his throat pointedly before stopping in the doorway, she turned and smiled. There was something like relief in that smile, Will was sure of it. Maybe listening obediently to her uncle drone on wasn't her idea of fun either.

And that was more like the Sophie he knew.

'Your luggage, ma'am,' he said with an easy grin which hid his own disquiet. It helped to put others at their ease, to think he was no threat. Sophie covered her mouth as she laughed, so soft a laugh you'd barely know it had happened, but he could see it in her eyes. For a moment he *did* know her again. There was the girl who had befriended him. Then she blushed, looked back at her uncle who, Will realised a moment later, was glaring at him with murder in his eyes.

Yeah, jokes weren't Dr Talbot's thing either. And he definitely didn't want Will befriending his niece again. He had never wanted Will here at all.

Luckily it wasn't his library, much as he would have liked it to be.

Will grinned impudently at him and then offered Sophie her bags.

'Should I give you a tip?' she asked. Her voice was little more than a whisper. But it was a joke nonetheless. Either she didn't see her uncle's reaction or she was ignoring it. That was interesting.

'Does it involve horse racing? Because I've never been lucky there.'

It was worth Dr Talbot's even darker glare to see her smile again. The smile hadn't really changed then. It had just become a rare and special thing.

'Sophie, you should unpack,' her uncle interrupted them. 'Then come down. I'm sure there will be some supper for you. See to it, will you, William? I need to talk to the Professor. It looks like I'm going to be called away again sooner than I thought.'

Will waited until he was gone. Sophie was still standing there, a little lost in the middle of the room where she had just been abandoned again.

He felt sorry for her. She looked so forlorn. Not the girl he remembered maybe, but still someone who right now needed a friend. Even if it was a friend she didn't really remember.

'Did he give you any idea where you were *coming down* to?' he asked, carefully keeping his voice soft and non-threatening. At the sound, she seemed to remember that he was there and wrapped her arms around her chest, trying to paste a brave smile on her face. It was all defensive.

She shook her head.

'I thought so. Do you want to freshen up and I'll show you around?'

'That would be… very kind. I'll only be a moment.'

He nodded, and stepped outside to wait. To wonder about Edward's behaviour, and his motives for bringing Sophie here.

Because Edward Talbot always had his own reasons for everything.

*

Sophie was as good as her word, fast and efficient. While Will waited in the corridor outside, staring at the stained-glass window which dominated the far end, she did whatever she needed to do and joined him a few minutes later. She had taken off her jacket and now wore a crisp white shirt over a pair of jeans. Her outfit shouldn't have been quite so attractive as it was.

A pendant hung against her chest, nestled above her cleavage, and it caught his eye immediately. It was delicate, expertly crafted to resemble a golden leaf. A thousand questions choked the base of his throat as he stared at it.

Elizabeth's. It had been Elizabeth's. He remembered it. She had always worn it.

Elizabeth laughing. Elizabeth calling his name and handing him a sandwich. Elizabeth wiping away his tears when Arthur had been… well, Arthur…

Elizabeth, turning her fiery gaze on him that final time, her hands spread wide, holding the world together for them, just long enough. 'You did everything you could, Will…'

Will shook his head, scattering those already scattered memories further, banishing them. Well of course Sophie would have it. It had belonged to her mother.

Sophie frowned, staring at him, and he remembered himself. Realised he was staring back at her in far too intimate a way, he forced himself to look off towards the stairs, to carry on as if this was a totally normal situation.

As if nothing had happened to her mother fifteen years ago.

'So, we're on the second floor in the west wing. Hardly even a president around though. This is your room for as long as you're with us. The key's in the door and it has the room number on it.'

They all did. It was about the only way to keep track of them all. Even then, it didn't always work. The doors always got mixed up. So did the keys. Someone would have to explain that to her, but it certainly wasn't going to be him. Hopefully there wouldn't be a need. Or if there was, she'd already have remembered and accepted the odd ways of the library.

Like him.

Sophie had spent her childhood here. Her family had an apartment on the first floor, but that had all changed in the renovation. It was accommodation for visiting scholars now. He didn't want to tell her that but she didn't ask.

'It's such a lovely place,' she said as they made their way back towards the staircase. 'But strange too. Like time has stood still here.'

'You have no idea,' he muttered on a breath. Because she didn't. She was talking about the appearance, wasn't she? Not everything else. She couldn't know. And he was certain Edward wouldn't have told her anything. Because if he had she wouldn't be here, would she?

She seemed a little puzzled but didn't press. Perhaps she felt it too.

'I thought I dreamed what it was like. Or made it all up as a kid. I only remember bits of it. How old is the building?'

'It's mostly Georgian. About 1750, I think. But there was a smaller building here before, mid-1600s. The library was built all around it, swallowing the original, and it's been added to over the years. The stained glass is original, and the woodwork. There's a test later, by the way.'

'A what?' She stopped and gave him a startled glance.

'I'm only joking.'

And once more, that fleeting, flickering smile, a smile that wanted to be accepted, that wanted to shine, but didn't quite feel safe enough to do so. As if she was afraid she'd be mocked for it a moment later.

He'd have to be careful of that.

No one should be scared of smiling. She never had been, not the Sophie he remembered. She'd had the most beautiful smile.

He shook himself.

'Scholars' rooms are on the first floor. They're the researchers. They come from institutions all over the world to study here, only a few at a time. Bed and board is part of the deal with most of the academic placements. Margo takes care of that. The rest of us have rooms up on the second. If you need a study, I'm sure that can be arranged, but the conservation studio is all yours for your binding work. It's over in the other wing, behind the library itself. There's more accommodation up on the third and that's where the Prof has her rooms. She has a warren of them. Your uncle too but he's hardly ever here. There's a general lounge on the ground floor for staff and residents, the ref, and the kitchens too. That's still Margo's domain, but she doesn't mind if you ever want to cook something for yourself.'

'The ref?' she asked.

'Refectory.' She didn't look any more enlightened. 'The dining room. It's closed up at the moment but you'll see it in the morning. You need to sign in for lunch and dinner but Margo will assume you're here for breakfast unless you're away. It's old-school monastic around here. But don't worry about Margo, she's a pet.'

'And Margo is—?'

'Our housekeeper. Definitely the person to get onside if you want the best snacks. She was here when we were kids, Sophie. Don't you remember? She'll mother you to death given half the chance.'

'I think… I think I do…'

As they reached the bottom of the main staircase, Sophie looked up at the dome with its coloured glass and the night sky beyond it, her face glowing with wonder. For a moment all was still and the library was silent around them. He hardly dared to breathe.

When a roar of laughter came from the lounge, Sophie jumped like a startled cat and turned with an expression of horror on her beautiful features. Tia's promised party was kicking off.

'It's okay,' he said, but she didn't look certain. 'Come and meet everyone. They don't bite. Well, most of them don't anyway. Promise.'

Sophie nodded and Will felt that strange discomfort again. He wasn't lying. Not exactly.

Chapter Five

Will opened the door before Sophie could say a thing to stop him. Not that there was anything she could say, not without looking like a total fool. A coward. But the thought of walking into that room rocked her back on her heels. Despite the hunger gnawing in her stomach, she would rather have stayed on her own without food than walk in there, right into the middle of a group of people she didn't know. It hadn't been so bad with just Will. And to be honest she'd thought he was going to show her the way to the staff kitchen where she could heat something up or make something simple like toast before retreating upstairs. She took a step back, ready to flee for safety.

'Aha, there she is,' someone's voice boomed from inside. 'And Will. Get in here, Will. Has anyone seen Tia?'

Sophie's stomach dropped like a skydiver who'd discovered there was no parachute. What had she been thinking? Leaving everything she knew in London to come here. Edward might be family but she didn't know him from Adam. And while she might have lived here as a child she couldn't remember anything or anyone now. It was a terrible mistake and she should have known better. Besides, Edward wasn't even in there. Just a load of strangers.

Victor would have laughed at her. He would have told her she was an idiot and swept into the room ahead of her, shielding her from it all. Or better yet, he would have taken her back home.

But Victor wasn't here.

'Sophie?' Will said, in that voice like the ripple of shadows. 'It's okay. Really.' It grounded her, brought her back to reality. Victor wasn't here and she didn't want him here. She was standing on her own. She had to take the reins of her own life.

She couldn't run away, much as she wanted to. She was here now, standing in front of a room full of expectant faces. She swallowed hard and then made her way inside, trying to smile. There followed a flurry of introductions which didn't do anything to enlighten her as to who was who. Or what was going on. She felt lost.

Stepping through the crowd as politely as she could, she sought out a quiet corner where she could fade into the dark green wallpaper and mahogany panelling.

An older woman watched from an armchair in the corner, a large sherry to hand. Noticing her, Sophie had such a shock of... not recognition, not exactly. But she knew her. She was certain of it, and the woman clearly knew Sophie.

Her raptor-like features tensed and she nodded slowly, acknowledging Sophie in a formal manner. Her hair was slate grey and her eyes were sharp as blades.

'Miss Lawrence,' she said at last, her voice clipped and refined, the accent beneath it impossible to place. 'What a pleasure to have you back. Welcome home. I do hope you will settle in easily.'

Sophie remembered her now. Professor Alexander, the Keeper of the library. Because places like Ayredale weren't content with just a librarian. There were things, her father used to say when he'd had too much to drink and sat by the fire, sleepy and maudlin, that needed to be kept in places like this. Kept safe, kept secret, kept locked up. They needed a jailor, a Keeper.

Sometimes she'd wondered what he meant. Now she wondered *who* he meant. *Her*, it had to be.

'Professor,' she murmured and knew she was right from the gleam in the woman's pale grey eyes. Her hair, now so silver, must have been jet black once upon a time, but to Sophie she had not changed in fifteen years. The memory rippled through her whole body like a chill. There wasn't a trace of softness anywhere about Professor Alexander. She wore a closely fitted tweed suit without a single button undone, even sitting by an open fire.

Sophie knew she needed to talk to her but didn't know what to say. The Keeper had been here for years, had known her mother. She wanted to ask about what happened all those years ago, but she couldn't think of how to start. And this was not the time. Too many people around them. Too many listening ears.

She didn't want to spill out her family history in front of a room full of strangers. Even though they must already all know the rumours.

The older woman set down her empty glass. 'I hope your trip down from London wasn't too arduous, my dear.'

'No, it was… it was fine.' It really hadn't been but that was hardly the point now.

'And I expect you have a plethora of questions. We should sit down together and talk. Perhaps tomorrow?'

Sophie nodded, feeling more than a little foolish. 'That would be… great,' she finally managed to stammer out. She had so many questions. More by the second.

'Well, I shall take my leave for the night. Early start in the morning. I just wanted to welcome you.' With that she rose from the chair. The Keeper swept from the now silent room, shutting the door behind her.

The crowd closed in, talking to each other all at once, and Sophie hung at the edge of it, hopelessly out of her depth.

She backed away.

'The problem is…' said a skinny blonde girl beside her, offering Sophie a large glass of wine. She barely looked old enough to drink. 'You forget she's there, she's so quiet. Like a shark.'

Her companion laughed, her teeth very white against her dark skin.

'Hannah, don't be a brat,' she replied, meeting Sophie's gaze. 'She means the Professor. Not you.'

'Meera and Hannah,' Will supplied. 'Both of them brats. And interns, so don't worry too much about them. They'll be gone soon.' Hannah stuck out her tongue at him, which Will ignored with effortless good humour. When he glanced back at Sophie, he seemed to catch the panic on her face and nodded to the right. 'Kitchen's this way. Come on.'

Sophie didn't care what it looked like. She put her head down and hurried after him, out of the door on the far side of the room.

She was almost hyperventilating by the time she closed the door behind her, struggling to control a mounting panic attack.

'They're all right, Meera and Hannah,' Will said softly. 'They have good instincts. But gods, they make me feel old sometimes. You don't handle crowds, do you?'

Her face turned hot and she pulled out a chair at the kitchen table, sitting down heavily. 'I'm just… it's just that…' Just that Victor would have led the way in a situation like that, and laughed about her shyness, would have introduced her with a backhanded compliment, would have ushered her around like a prize pony. She couldn't seem to get the words out, not in any order that made sense. She'd been really rude to her new colleagues and there was nothing she could do to fix that now.

'It's okay.' The voice of another woman came from the corner. 'I hate people too. Present company excluded, of course.'

Will laughed and Sophie stared, mouth open as the most beautiful woman she had ever seen stepped out of the shadows behind her. Had she been hiding in here as well?

The woman was dressed in black trousers and a silky top, slim and elegant, her head crowned with a fall of red hair. Not just red, wine – the shade of claret or burgundy – her lips painted a matching colour. The woman could be a model. It was impossible to tell what age she might be. Hers was the kind of beauty that defied age. She could be Sophie's age, or more than twenty years older. She didn't look like she belonged in a library, not even a special one like this.

And certainly not in a homely kitchen. The tiles on the floor were shades of red, yellow and gold, rather than uniform terracotta, and felt old, really old. The cabinets were old too, painted a warm cream quite recently by a careful hand.

'Tia,' said Will. 'This is Sophie. Sophie, this is Tia, our archivist.'

She definitely didn't bear a resemblance to any archivist Sophie had ever seen.

The large table which dominated the middle of the room was oak, a thick slab of wood which had to have come from a single tree. Sophie sat down and ran her hand across the smooth, polished grain. Ancient, worn, loved. So many people must have sat here, worked here, ate here, touched the same wood as she did now.

She remembered this, sitting here, eating, drawing. A child, a girl.

Snatching back her hand she looked up to find Tia watching her, head tilted slightly to one side, eyes keen. Will placed a bowl of fragrant stew in front of Sophie, along with a napkin and cutlery. Tia pulled out a chair opposite them, turned it around and sat astride it. 'Sophie Lawrence,' she said. 'I knew your parents well.'

'You don't look old enough,' Sophie replied, before she thought about how that would sound. 'I mean... I...'

Tia grinned, a hungry, vulpine look. 'Flatterer.'

Will sat down with them and gave Tia a long-suffering stare. 'Oh stop it, Tia. Not everyone wants to shag you. Why are you hiding in here anyway?'

She rolled her heavily kohled eyes. 'Better than being out there. Edward has already made a break for it. I don't blame him either. Rude though. He could have at least stayed to help you settle in.'

Another rush of panic seized Sophie by the throat. Edward was already gone? Gone where? Then she remembered they were both watching her and she couldn't bear to see their pity. Or whatever else they might see.

'I didn't realise he was leaving so soon,' she muttered and pushed the stew around in the bowl.

'He hung on to make sure you got here safely but he never sticks around,' Will replied. 'Too busy. Acquisitions is that kind of job. He probably has an early flight. He brings things here, and then he's off for the next thing.'

'Things like me?' she asked, and paused, horrified at herself. Victor would sulk for days if she talked to him like that. Especially in front of other people.

Tia laughed, loud and delighted. Will gave Sophie a look of panicked apology. 'That wasn't what I—'

'Oh no, you don't get to wriggle out of that one,' Tia interrupted. '*Things* indeed.'

'I'm sorry,' he said, as solemn as a priest. 'I didn't mean to imply you're a thing.'

He was apologising? To her? Victor would never have done that.

Now she felt bad. Tia was winding him up. Or at least, she assumed so. They had that easy-going interaction of long-time friends. Would she and Will have been like that if Sophie had never left? She couldn't imagine it, but the lure of it was fascinating. She longed for that kind of friendship. She always had.

Sophie decided to put him out of his misery. She owed him that much. 'Apology accepted.'

He blushed a bit and turned to clatter about the cooker in the corner. Sophie forced her attention to the stew, which was as delicious as it smelled.

'Oh, you'll be fine here, Sophie.' Tia rose like a prima ballerina preparing for her solo. 'But if you have any problems I'm sure our Will would be more than happy to help out.' She winked suggestively. 'He's so good like that.'

The door to the lounge opened with another burst of noise, making all three of them turn. Sophie dropped her spoon in the bowl with a clatter as she rose to her feet.

'There you are,' said the man who entered. Older than herself and Will, but younger than Edward. His dark hair was swept back from a hawkish, clean-shaven face. He looked familiar but she couldn't place him. He wore chinos and an expensive-looking shirt. The sleeves were rolled up to the elbows in a neat, affectedly casual way which wouldn't fool anyone.

'Arthur.' Tia sat back, her long legs stretched out in front of her defiantly. Her glare was a challenge which Arthur ignored completely.

'I wanted to check that Sophie had everything she needs?' He grinned. 'Sophie? You don't remember me either? I should be hurt.'

'I'm sorry,' she whispered, mortified. For a moment she had an urge to explain about what had happened when she left here, about her breakdown, and she *never* told people about that. She wasn't even sure why she had the urge to tell him. Because she didn't really want to. She really didn't. She hadn't even told Will – she'd just said she'd been ill after she left Ayredale – or Edward. All the same the urge was palpable. 'I just…'

'Arthur,' he said with a broad smile. 'Arthur Dee.'

Arthur Dee – their idol, their role model, only about three years older than them which practically made them the same age in the Special Collection – cracked open a can of cider and offered it to Sophie. She took a mouthful of the cloying sweet liquid and passed it to Will. He looked nervous, something which seemed to amuse Arthur more than anything.

'Don't just stare at it, kiddo,' he said with a laugh. 'Liquid courage. Go on, I dare you.'

Neither of them could ever resist a dare. Even though Sophie knew her dad would kill her if he caught her down here, let alone drinking. But mostly just being down here. Under the library. Where none of them were meant to go.

The music sounded soft as a whisper, playing against her ears, and the pale wood of the locked door felt warm against her hand. The sound definitely came from the other side. But how?

'We shouldn't,' Will said again, but even he didn't sound very convinced. He could hear the same enticing song as she could. Sophie hesitated.

'Go on,' Arthur whispered.

He seized her in a strong pair of arms, pulled her out of the chair and hugged her close, the resurgent memory leaving her too stunned to evade him. His scent… expensive, exclusive, surrounded her and choked her. He released her moments later and Sophie stood there, shocked, turned to stone in panic. Will appeared beside her and looked ready to hit something. Even Tia stood up.

Arthur Dee had filled out since then, his muscles defined, his build strong. He obviously worked out. He was good-looking, in that clean-shaven, public-school kind of way. In other company, she'd call him handsome. But not beside Will.

Will spoke first. 'I'll see to everything.'

Arthur didn't so much as glance at him, but Will was still bristling. There was something else going on there. Something far beyond her. They really did not get on, that much was clear.

Sophie forced herself to smile, to calm the situation, make sure no one got upset. 'I'm fine, really.' She was aware she was saying it to both of them but she didn't know if they were listening.

'It's so good to have you back, Soph. We'll have to grab a drink some time. Once you've settled in. Just like old times. I'm not around that much but I'll make a point of it now you're back.'

'I…' What could she say? Not that he shouldn't call her *Soph* because she hated it with a passion. Not that he sounded unnervingly like Victor when he did. She shook that idea off as quickly as possible. Victor and any thoughts of him had no place here.

Tia waited until Arthur had gone. Barely. The door had only just closed. 'Just like his father. Sweeps in, assumes everyone's world centres around him, and thinks everyone is desperate for his company. He never changes.'

'Do any of us?' Will asked with a bitter laugh. He looked calmer now, a little sheepish. Tia shrugged.

'Speak for yourself. Where's the wine? I'm taking it to bed with me, since Edward's gone. You okay, Sophie? Want a glass?'

Sophie nodded, trying to work out exactly what Tia meant about that. If Edward was here she'd stay up longer? Or... if he was here, she'd take him to bed instead?

It wasn't any of her business. Edward wasn't that old. And Tia could be older than she appeared. And anyway, they were consenting adults. Even as colleagues, maybe the rules here didn't mean they couldn't date, or whatever it was they were doing. Her parents had met here after all, fallen in love and married... *Stay out of it, Sophie. Just mind your own business.*

She was rattled enough by Arthur. How had she forgotten him? Well, not forgotten exactly, but he had faded in her memory. Just a name really.

Tia fetched three huge glasses and filled them with a red wine almost as dark as her hair. She tapped her glossy nails against the glass as she held it up to the light and examined it, before lifting it to her equally red lips. She drank deeply and then her gaze met Sophie's once more.

'I think you're going to fit in just fine, pet. Don't mind Arthur and Will. They have history. Take your time. Things will come back to you eventually. That's the way of it.'

That was the problem. Things were coming back. And she didn't like it. Each of those snippets of memory left her unaccountably shaken. It ought to be a good thing, but it wasn't.

As Tia sauntered off through another door, which led into the silent hall, Sophie wondered... how did Tia know she'd forgotten everything? And how did she know things would come back? What was 'the way of it'?

Sophie sipped at her wine as she finished her meal and made small talk with Will. She didn't ask what Tia meant. And she was pretty sure Will didn't want to talk about Arthur either. They reminisced in that vague way people did when they were trying to catch up but didn't know what to say, skirting around the edges of a conversation. She told him about her work in the Academy, and they shared college stories. Where she had focused on conservation and bookbinding, he preferred cataloguing and indexing, working with the researchers who came here and fielding enquiries. They hadn't led so different lives after all. Except that he had come back here eight years ago after college and she had not. It was easy to talk to him, to slip back into an old camaraderie that made her want to linger.

Sophie's smile became gentler and he made her feel at ease for the first time in ages. She wasn't able to remember the last time someone else had been able to do that for her. Certainly not Victor. He liked her to be on guard, she realised, on her best behaviour. At his beck and call.

It was so strange. How had she never realised that before? She thought of what he'd say if he saw her now, talking to Will so easily. He wouldn't like it, that was for sure.

Are you trying to make a fool of yourself, Sophie? The voice in her head sounded suspiciously like Victor's. *I mean, look at him. Why would he be interested in anything you have to say?*

But he had been, once upon a time.

'Are you okay?' Will asked, interrupting her thoughts.

'Yes,' she told him, and for the first time she realised that she actually meant it. She was okay. More than okay. She was home.

No one else joined them in the kitchen, although the party clearly carried on with some enthusiasm in the lounge. It was almost as if they were shielded here, protected. It was a warm, homely place, with a range and a deep Belfast sink. It carried the lingering scent of baked goods, and a sublime feeling of safety. For the first time in an age, Sophie felt the knots in her shoulders begin to unwind.

Eventually, too tired to keep her eyes open much longer, Sophie made her reluctant excuses and said goodnight.

Will got to his feet. 'I'll show you the—'

But Sophie shook her head. 'I'm sure I'll find it. Don't worry. I don't want to take up your evening.' She had to do something on her own. She had to start making a stand.

Sophie used the door Tia had left by and the corridor led her back towards the Rotunda at the main entrance to the building. She found the stairs with no problem and made her way back up to the second floor. The corridor stretched out in front of her and she had to take out the key and check the room number a couple of times before she located it.

The door opened with a soft click and moonlight spilled over the room. For a moment she stared. It felt so right, as if she was meant to be there. Like coming home.

The bed nestled in the corner, with a bedside table and a lamp. It was covered with a beautiful patchwork quilt in soft pastels which looked handmade. Beneath the window, which sat into an eave of the building itself, there was a desk and a chair. There was a wardrobe and a chest of drawers too. On the far side was a comfy-looking armchair. The en-suite was bright and cheery, with pretty tiles circling the shower.

The room had everything she could possibly need.

'*Sophie?*'

The voice was a whisper, a sigh. A woman's voice that came straight out of the deepest depths of her memory. She knew it. She was sure she knew it.

There were no recordings of her mother's voice. Her father had made a point of destroying everything linked to her, no matter how much Sophie had cried and begged. Nothing remained. Not a single photo, video or recording.

As if she had never existed.

But she had. She had been Sophie's mother.

'*Sophie?*'

She turned around, glancing back down the corridor towards the stained-glass window. It was dark outside and the colours were muted, leaving a mere outline of an angel holding a sword.

'*There you are, Sophie,*' her mother whispered, from memories long buried and put away, from somewhere across the years. '*Off to bed now.*'

It was another memory. She knew that. Only a memory. Coming back here was stirring them all up. The therapists had suggested it years ago, but her father had flatly refused. And Sophie had never dared to defy him.

Now she was back, she was tired, overwrought and she'd had wine to drink. There was no one here. She stood, all on her own in the doorway, caught in the liminal space between here and there, then and now. And for a moment, just a moment, she was sure she heard her mother's voice, reaching out from the past.

An echo, a memory, a dream. Her overactive imagination.

'Hello?' she whispered. But no one answered. Sophie waited but there was nothing else. Just the sounds of an old building at night, of wind in some tree outside, and perhaps the faintest murmur of the party downstairs.

She closed the door behind her and let her breath escape in a rush. The stillness of the room closed over her.

As she settled down to sleep, she listened to the sounds of the library more intimately, the soft whispers in the walls, the fluttering noises that echoed through the roof, the rise and fall of a building settling around her. There were no other voices, real or imagined.

The smells, the air itself, the building around her, cradled her and kept her safe.

She could not shake the sensation that someone, or something, watched over her and for the first time in years, it seemed, she slept without a care.

Chapter Six

It was late when Will could finally head to bed. The party had gone on for some time and he didn't like to leave them down there without at least one of the permanent staff around. Usually him. The researchers were fine, but they were often young, or away from a family home, and things happened. Especially when there was alcohol and high spirits involved.

He had a responsibility to the library. *His* library.

Except it wasn't his library. However much it might feel like it. Will had never known anywhere to feel so much like home. While he had loved university, he had always felt a longing to come back. He'd never had anywhere else to go. He had no family, not in the normal sense of the word, and no home. Not a real home. Just here. And the people he had here weren't what you'd call an incredibly functional family, but they were all he had.

Will pushed that thought away as he turned off the lights and shut the door of the lounge.

It felt good to have Sophie back. When he was young, they had been so close. Now she seemed vulnerable, lost. He only wished he knew what to do to make it easier on her.

Hannah was still singing to herself as she meandered up the stairs to the first floor. She had that sort of sweet, soprano voice that carried through the silent building. Haunting.

Well it wouldn't be the only thing haunting the Special Collection, would it?

Will finished locking up and put out the remaining lights downstairs. Then he headed up himself.

He passed the portraits lining the staircase, silently greeting them all in turn. Elias Ashmole the antiquary, the philosopher Francis Bacon, and Mary Sidney, the Countess of Pembroke, famed for her poetry. The astronomer John Dee came next, and Paracelsus, the physician. All of them alchemists, all connected to this library. He passed other pictures too, other librarians, less well known or completely forgotten. The School of Night, they were sometimes called. Their heirs still managed the place. The modern School of Night weren't quite as illustrious as their forebears, preferring to keep to the shadows. They had learned not to stand out quite so much.

The slow sighs and creaks of the building murmured to him as he made his way to his own room. He paused at the door, glancing down the long corridor towards Sophie's door. She was skittish as a racehorse, and had that rangy air to her, as if she might bolt at any moment. That came from bad experiences, didn't it? He knew that look.

Such a difference from the girl he had known. The girl who had made anyone else a poor substitute without even trying. Before he even knew what love was.

Edward assured them all that she was perfect for the library, 'born for it', but Will wasn't sure. She didn't seem the kind to settle anywhere. Rather she looked like she would keep running, or step back in a vain attempt to fade into the background forever.

Few people stayed here very long. He knew that and accepted it. The Prof, Tia, Margo and him. They were the only ones who lived here full time now. Delphine too, although he figured she'd move on eventually. Arthur came and went, at the beck and call of the School of Night and the Ministry of Defence. He was their intermediary. Meera and Hannah were too new to tell yet. And while Edward kept coming back, it was only in the way you returned home out of obligation. Tia pulled him back, but sometimes Will wondered if she deliberately pushed him away as well. She had been hurt so many times and Will worried about her. Edward was already showing the signs of bolting. With Sophie here, he'd thought surely her uncle would want to stay to help her settle in.

That was what actual families did, wasn't it? Watched out for each other? But then again, what did Will know about actual families? He had a father who had acknowledged him only because he had no choice, and managed to make it mean nothing at all. A mother who didn't seem to realise she was actually a mother. And a brother who couldn't bear to be in the same place as him for more than a few days.

Once, he'd felt more a part of Sophie's family than his own. And look where that had got them all.

But there was something about her. Something that drew him to her, drew his gaze to her whenever he stopped making an effort to not look at her. He didn't want to be that creep who stared but, at the same time, he couldn't help it. Perhaps he was trying to find the girl he had known within her, to find out where she was hiding.

Sophie made him feel something… something he hadn't felt in years. Not like this. Not really. Arthur would have laughed at him, but then Arthur laughed at everything he did.

She'd blushed when he kissed her, so many years ago. He still remembered the way her skin had glowed. She'd blushed and laughed, but she'd kissed him back. They had interlaced their fingers, twining their hands together. He had breathed her in and she was all he could think of. She had been everything. Everything.

No, she was a different person now. She didn't even remember. He'd known that from the moment he saw her at the station. She'd forgotten it all.

Tia had warned him that might have happened. The pity in her eyes when she realised she was right had torn right through him.

Nature of the place, as she always said.

Shower, he told himself. Sleep. That was what he needed. He was worn out.

He stripped off the moment the door closed behind him, and folded his clothes on the chair. A draught from the window felt like a ribbon of cold wintry air but he didn't care. The chill in the room was a relief. He felt warmer than he should and he knew he wasn't sick. He didn't want to think about what might be causing it.

Or who.

A shower would help him sleep. It usually did, warm water massaging tired muscles, steam surrounding him and a moment to wind down.

Pushing his ridiculous thoughts away, he turned on the water and waited. It gurgled, reluctant, and for a moment he thought the pipes were going to make some sort of protest which could wake up everyone on the floor. Then he'd be popular. It didn't make sense. Modern plumbing had replaced the ancient system, and it still managed to sound like something from the nineteenth century if the mood took it. He pictured Sophie, bewildered and sleepy, standing in the corridor outside her room trying to work out what was going on and why the walls were making that noise. In a nightdress which did little to disguise the body underneath.

His imagination was definitely not helping. Not helping at all. He leaned forward, pressed his forehead to the tiles, and groaned.

'Come on,' he whispered. 'Give me a break.'

Freezing cold water gushed over him, a flood of it, stealing his breath and at the same time almost making him scream.

He fumbled madly for the controls until he managed to turn it off.

Somewhere, he was sure, he heard echoes of laughter.

Serves me right, he thought. It serves me bloody right.

He towelled himself dry, all thoughts of risking another shower gone now. Shivering, he pulled on a pair of pyjama bottoms and a hoodie before getting under the duvet to continue shivering until he warmed up again.

That was when he heard a knock at the door. A quick, frantic knock from someone trying desperately not to be heard by anyone else.

'Will?' Tia hissed. '*Will!*'

He struggled to his feet and lurched for the door, wrenching it open.

'What is—?' He didn't get any further.

Tia grabbed his arm, dragging him out into the corridor. 'Will, it's Sophie! Come quickly.'

Chapter Seven

Sophie dreamed. She walked the corridors of the library, and while the world around her was still and silent, the carvings that edged the wood panelling and the glowing stained glass were alive. They flowed from shape to shape, figures scurrying through the carved woodland. The glass moved, rippling like water, glowing with colour and light. Singing filled the air and as she reached the staircase and the window looking over the garden, she was finally able to see outside.

The sky was alight, bright as day. Behind the library, in the garden it embraced with its long, elegant wings, she saw a tree. It was almost as tall as the building itself, and its leaves were made of gold. They shone as if the sunlight had been trapped within them and instead of photosynthesis a very different kind of alchemy had taken place. On the leaves she could make out words.

No, not words. Not exactly. Symbols.

'*You can read them, Sophie,*' said her mother. '*They're written on your soul. It's the language of the birds. Remember?*'

Elizabeth stood at the bottom of the stairs, her hand held out as if to a child, and Sophie froze, staring at her. She didn't know how she knew it was her mother, but it was the figure who had always featured in her dreams in that role. A memory she didn't even remember having, a ghostly image who lingered in her dreams, waiting for her.

This isn't real, she thought, and knew she was right. It was a dream. It had to be.

'*Come along then*,' her mother sighed, as if talking to a recalcitrant child. As if she had said those words a thousand times already. Perhaps she had.

Sophie had dreamed the same dream for as long as she could remember. Her mother, the library... and the tree. But it had always been distant, half remembered, like something from long ago. This was different, like a picture finally coming into focus.

The voice called her. Not her mother's voice now. Not a human voice. Not recognisable words. It was the song of a siren, full of longing and need, full of desire that hooked itself into her heart and dragged her forwards.

Sophie followed it. She had no choice, descending the stairs step by step. The figures in the glass moved like ghosts, drifting with her, beckoning her onwards. She couldn't name them or place them. It didn't matter. They were ancient and ageless. They wore a thousand faces, none of which she knew. Some shone like gods, others were terrible to behold.

Beneath the twin staircases a small door stood open and golden light spilled across the mosaic floor of the Rotunda. It rippled like sunshine. But outside, all around Sophie, it was still night.

The song called her out into the darkness, into the garden. The library rose behind her like a hawk, mantling the formal grounds, wings spread wide, protecting the thing Sophie now saw in the centre: a tall and slender tree, its golden leaves aglow with light.

It towered over her, stretching to the sky, the full moon tangled in its upper branches. But it was like staring at the sun rising. She had to squint her eyes, even though all around her the night pressed close, dark and cold. The light of the tree, its burning leaves... that was everything.

And slowly, so slowly, the leaves began to fall. They drifted down, waltzing around her as they did. Sophie reached up, ready to catch them, her heart thundering at the base of her throat with the thought of touching them, holding them.

Her hands shook.

'Sophie?'

A man's voice. It didn't belong here. Not in her dream.

'Sophie? Are you okay? Sophie, answer me.'

It echoed strangely, as if heard from far away cut by a storm, but there was no storm. The air was still.

All the same, everything felt charged with ozone, as if a storm was indeed gathering.

The leaves fell gently, floating around her. Where they touched the ground, the grass ignited. Where they landed in the bushes, the foliage burst into flames. Fire, hungry and terrible, devoured the garden all around her. But she didn't feel the heat.

The tree shook, the leaves fell, and the world around her burned. Fire wrapped her in an embrace, ran fingers over her skin, pressed burning lips to hers.

'*It's okay, love,*' her mother said. '*I'm here.*'

And the other voice didn't go away. Deep and insistent, *his* voice...

'Sophie. Please answer me. Sophie!'

*

Sophie's eyes snapped open and she dragged in a ragged breath. Cold. It was cold. And dark. There was no fire, only the night. She could feel the touch of a winter storm in the offing.

She was standing outside in the garden behind the library in her pyjamas, shivering. And she wasn't alone.

'Sophie,' Will said. 'Answer me.' He didn't touch her, but he stood close, behind her. She was sure she could feel the warmth emanating from his body.

She turned so sharply she staggered and, before she knew what was happening, she felt him reach out to steady her. His touch was warm and gentle, but firm. He held her up and she shook in his hands. Slowly, he righted her and she stared into his face. His hair was wet, curling darkly against his skin.

Once upon a time he had kissed her. They had been teenagers. They had been under a tree. Like this...

Only it hadn't been like this. The cold made her tremble. It was the cold. It couldn't be anything else. Will wore a black hoodie over a pair of loose pyjama pants and he was barefoot.

'What are you doing out here?' he asked.

It didn't make sense. She had been in her room, asleep. She had dreamed. Dreamed of the tree with golden leaves. The tree that burned.

She glanced over her shoulder and froze.

There was a tree. It was real.

Its upper branches didn't reach the moon and the stars, and it didn't have leaves right now. Not in the heart of winter. The boughs and twigs were bare sticks, tangled together in the darkness. She was standing in the cold, wet garden, beneath an old aspen tree, the maiden aunt of the slim and elegant thing she had dreamed of with peeling silver bark and a fall of golden leaves. The one in front of her was still huge. This tree had to be a hundred years old, if not more, the bark knotted and scarred with black lines.

'Is she okay?' Tia asked, still wrapping herself in a dressing gown as she came outside from the library building, the door standing open and the lights on inside.

Will answered, although he didn't turn away from Sophie. She couldn't shake the way he had studied her face. She didn't know what he was looking for, and she didn't want to ask. She had the feeling she wouldn't like the answer. 'Sleepwalking, I think.'

'You're not meant to wake someone up when they're sleepwalking, Will,' Tia warned.

'I'm not. Not any more,' Sophie told them and wriggled out of Will's arms. She had to. The sensation of being so close to him was unnerving. 'Not sleeping anyway. What – what happened?'

The night's air bit with the promise of snow not far off. The breeze cut through her skin like razors.

Will frowned at her, glanced back at Tia and then answered. 'We saw you out here, at the tree. We should get inside. It's cold.'

That was an understatement. She clenched her teeth to stop them chattering. What was going on? What had just happened to her?

She pointed at the tree. 'How long has that been there?'

Confused, Tia shook her head. 'I don't know. It must be pretty old. A hundred years or something like that? It must have been there when you lived here before, when you were a child. Wasn't it, Will?' When she turned to him, he nodded, but only slowly, his concerned gaze still fixed on Sophie. Tia was less patient though. 'It's just a tree. An old tree. Come on, Sophie. It's freezing. You'll catch your death. We all need to go inside.'

The tone of her voice was a slap. Oh God, what was she doing? Sophie hadn't found herself sleepwalking for years. She thought she'd grown out of it. Victor would never have put up with it for one thing.

But the tree... *that* Tree... she knew it. She had dreamed of it all her life. That was the same tree.

The one she had always been told did not and could not possibly exist.

She drew in another shaky breath.

Well, not quite. But near enough. This tree was real, a living thing. It didn't glow or sigh, or shed leaves that burned. At this time of year the leaves were all gone. It was a skeletal hand reaching for the stars overhead.

A square of light fell on the ground in front of them, and they twisted, looking up at the window above them. A silhouette stood there watching them. Sophie couldn't tell who it was.

'The Prof knows all and she sees all,' Tia groaned. 'Well, at least she won't gossip. Your secret is safe with her.'

'What secret?'

'We all have secrets, pet.'

Sophie frowned, ready to ask what Tia was talking about but she didn't get the chance.

'Come on,' Will told her firmly, cutting Tia off. 'Let's get you inside before anyone else turns up. You're freezing. Tia's right. We'll all catch our deaths.'

Sophie let him usher her back inside. She didn't even know what to think now and didn't have the strength to argue. It took her breath away.

The tree. The Library Tree.

It was a real tree. A normal tree. But she knew the shape of it, knew the curve of every branch, every bump of bark. Knew it with the intimacy she had known Victor's body when she had thought she adored him.

The moment she stepped back into the library building, and Will ushered her back into the warmth of the kitchen, her legs almost gave way. She grabbed the counter, forcing her arms to lock so she wouldn't betray herself but it was too late.

Forget the Professor. Will and Tia saw all.

'I'll call the emergency doctor,' Will said. 'They can be here in no time.'

'No,' Sophie interrupted. 'I'm fine. I'm sorry. I'm just tired. Overtired. And it's… I had a dream, that's all. I didn't mean to disturb you. I'm so sorry.'

He didn't look convinced. 'You don't have to apologise,' he said at last.

'But I…'

'You don't. Not here. That's kind of the point of this place. We're good with weird shit. Can I get you anything? Tea, maybe?'

Weird shit. Great. Was that what he thought? Did he think she was crazy or something?

'No, I'm… I'm fine. I should…' Her face felt hot and uncomfortable. She couldn't believe this was happening. She had only just arrived here and already her stupid brain was making a mess of everything, making a fool of her. And in front of her new colleagues. This wasn't fair.

She felt the familiar sting of tears beneath the bridge of her nose. She couldn't cry, not here, not in front of them. Not on top of everything else. The anger that welled up inside her, her self-disgust, made it so much worse. Her breath caught in her throat and she barely managed to smother the sob. This wouldn't do. Not at all.

'Excuse me,' she said, and fled. There was no other word for the way she ran from the room, back up the stairs and to her room, where the door stood open, and the bedclothes spilled across the floor. Where she had left them presumably.

Sleepwalking.

They had called it prolonged grief disorder or, sometimes, traumatic grief, all those experts her father dragged her to. He hadn't liked that answer. Bereavement was something to get over. He hadn't liked hearing post-traumatic stress either. There was nothing to cause that, he insisted. He dismissed it. And Sophie was left to deal with it alone. Behind a locked door, on her own. She was still dealing with it.

An incredible start to her job here. Wonderful.

Will and Tia had turned out of their own beds in the middle of the night to stop her. Or out of their bed.

Oh God, she realised. They'd been together, hadn't they? They'd arrived together, in nightclothes. Not that it mattered if they were sleeping together. Maybe they had been a couple for years. What did she know? And why should she care? She'd known Will fifteen years ago but she had no memories of Tia at all.

Sophie sat on the bed and tried to make her breathing calm down again.

Victor would have held her, wrapped her in his arms and pressed his body to the whole length of her, winding around her until she went limp once more.

'See?' she could imagine him saying. '*It was only a dream. I'm here. I'm real. Not that wretched tree. I've got you, Sophie.*'

And now she was on her own once more. Broken, with no one to help hold the pieces together. She was a plain, scrawny woman, pushing thirty, a nervous wreck. And she had left the only person who could help her keep everything together. Without Victor, she was already falling apart. Pathetic really. Her throat closed on another sob and the tears stung her eyes. She had always been broken. She just didn't know why.

Her mother had dropped out of her life. She had been torn away from everything she ever knew. She had lived here. She had gone to school in Kingsford, the next town over, and had friends there. She had Will here, and Arthur, although he was older and less inclined to indulge them. She had her mother, her family, and this place. A wonderland.

And suddenly it was all taken away, replaced by boarding school and a distant father, grief and pain and…

She glanced out the window. She hadn't even realised it had a view over the garden. She had arrived in darkness and it had showed only her reflection when she turned on the light. She had closed the curtains against the night, but now she drew them back and stared. The world outside blurred and swam as she cried but she forced herself to look.

The tree she'd sleepwalked to was there, under the light of the moon. A normal tree, no golden leaves or silver bark. But it was the tree she'd dreamed of all her life.

All these years, she had been dreaming of the gardens of Ayredale.

Chapter Eight

Hiding from Will Rhys wasn't going to be an option, no matter how embarrassed she might be feeling. Not when he was waiting for her the next morning for orientation. He even had a folder full of paper for her to sign, contracts, non-disclosure agreements and probably something involving her soul. But he was brisk and businesslike, eager to get on with it.

'How did you sleep?' he asked, as if it was the most normal question in the world.

'Fine.' She didn't mean to sound brusque. He was just being kind. 'I'm sorry I disturbed you and Tia.'

'You didn't,' Will replied. And that was that.

Sophie had brought her roll of tools with her, the soft leather a familiar bulk under her arm. And while she was sure there would be access to whatever materials she wanted here in Ayredale, bookbinding tools were personal. Most of them had belonged to her father. They were the closest thing she had to a security blanket.

She clung to the roll now, and tried not to glance out the windows at the tree. It wasn't quite the tree in her dreams, but it was close enough. Its mortal incarnation, perhaps, ungilded by her sleeping mind. But it was real. She couldn't quite believe it. And yet, there it was.

The library itself was accessed through the Reading Room on the ground floor, a beautifully restored or more likely preserved Victorian room of wood panelling polished to a shine, filled with wide desks with emerald glass lampshades and forest green leather chairs. It wasn't as grand as some of the reading rooms Sophie had seen through work, and certainly not as large as the one in the Academy, but it was a beautiful space of peace and all-enveloping silence. Several researchers were at work and a young woman Sophie had not seen before manned the desk, working on something herself. She looked up when they entered, pushed back the long fall of golden hair over her shoulder and smiled.

At Will. She only smiled at Will. Sophie noticed that straight away. She might as well not be there. The woman sat up a little bit taller as he approached, that perfect smile beaming out.

So confident, so pretty that it was probably hard not to be confident about anything. Her skin was freshly tanned, and her blonde hair had that sun-kissed sheen.

'Hi Will,' she said in a soft, low voice. 'Did you miss me?'

Several people looked up from their studies and Sophie found herself blushing. They were interrupting the work going on here and she felt their nascent irritation as well as the discomfort of being the cause of a disturbance. Back at the Academy, Dr Bellamy would have gone nuts over researchers being disturbed.

This is not the place for idle chit-chat, ladies. Take it elsewhere.

'Delphine, welcome back. This is Sophie. She's our new conservator.'

Delphine finally graced Sophie with her attention and clearly wasn't terribly impressed by what she saw. 'Oh. Hello. Is Will showing you around?'

Sophie nodded, not seeing how this conversation was likely to be improved by her input.

'He's so good that way. Aren't you, Will?' And like that she had turned that smile on Will again, all careless flirtation and a somewhat suggestive use of her lips on the end of her pencil. 'I had a fab holiday by the way. Beach every day and parties every night. I have so many photos. Are we still on for Friday night? I'm really looking forward to it.'

Will frowned for a moment as if trying to remember what on earth she was talking about. Sophie saw the moment it came to him. He didn't seem thrilled. 'Oh, sure. Friday afternoon really. It's only an appointments review. I wouldn't want to keep you late or anything. You probably have plans. Coming, Sophie?'

If Delphine was put out, she chose not to show it. But still, Sophie caught the glare before she turned away. Directed at her.

Great. That was just what she needed.

And Will had clearly noticed nothing. He was Captain Oblivious.

Or maybe he chose not to notice.

Will opened a door behind the desk, one with a brass 'Staff Only' sign displayed prominently on it. Sophie pursed her lips, wondering if she should say something. She didn't know him. She might think she did but it had been years ago. They had been kids. Perhaps he was having it away with every single woman here. Who knew? He was attractive enough and clearly didn't lack interested partners. Maybe not Tia, but Delphine hadn't left any doubt.

Sophie did not need complications like that in her life. For the first time ever she was standing on her own feet. Kind of.

All she had was a vague memory of a childish infatuation from another lifetime, a world away from where she was now. Of their fingers tangled together, the warmth of his grip. His lips smiling against hers.

Did he remember the same things she did? Did he remember that last summer? That kiss? It haunted her now, had drifted through her dreams last night when they weren't full of trees and leaves, teasing her. For something she had forgotten, now it wouldn't leave her alone. Every time she so much as glanced at him.

They were different people now. Had to be.

A troublemaking part of her wanted to ask what he was actually doing on Friday afternoon with Delphine that she was trying to turn into something more. But then she turned to see where they were and all conscious thought left her body.

How could she have forgotten this?

It wasn't just a library. It was magnificent. It was a work of art.

From the ground floor where they stood dwarfed by the immensity of it, the library stretched up to the roof of the building. All three upper floors were lined with balconies, each full of shelves, and all those shelves were full of books. High about them, dizzyingly high, the ceiling was painted as elaborately as the Sistine Chapel. Figures which probably were meant to represent schools of thought and philosophies lounged amid clouds and scattered around the edge she saw buildings from all the ages. There was a tower with a light at the top which was clearly meant to be Alexandria, and a desert palace which could have been the Royal Library of Ashurbanipal. Perched on top of a cliff, overlooking an azure sea, that had to be Pergamon. And over there on the left, nestled in a valley of dust, that definitely reminded her of Saint Catherine's in the Sinai Desert. Beautifully painted, the details clear even from so far below. Libraries. It was like a cathedral dedicated to libraries.

She couldn't name everything up there. She was too busy trying to take in what she was seeing.

On the ceiling was another tree, the pale trunk running right up the middle along the central beam. It incorporated the curving beams of the vaulted roof as its branches and its leaves gleamed gold. Like the mosaic in the Rotunda at the entrance. Like the one outside. And the one in her dreams.

Sophie caught her breath and dragged her gaze away from it because it made her dizzy, standing there staring up at it.

The shelves stood perpendicular to the windows to avoid light damage to the spines of the books they housed. Though they were tall, they were still dwarfed by the structure itself, the sense of the library. The windows on the lower floors were all stained glass, depicting figures and events from throughout history, but she'd never have had time to identify them all even if she had the background knowledge needed.

She glanced down to the gleaming, polished floor and struggled to maintain an even breath. To ground herself.

In the centre of the room was another staircase, the opening surrounded on three sides by a gleaming brass railing designed to look like intertwining brambles. From that, the stairs spiralled down into darkness. So strange, right there in the middle.

Something in her chest tugged at her, a lost memory or a desire, and she wanted to run to it. At the same time the dread it evoked in her made her take a step back. Pulled there and repulsed at the same time.

It was like a mouth, a gaping wound…

'The Great Hall,' Will said, his voice rich with affection and pride dragging her back to the wonder of the place. Who wouldn't be proud to work here, to have access to this? It was breathtaking. 'It's better to see it from here and get the full impression first, isn't it?'

Sophie had read about the great libraries of the world, followed blogs full of photos, and pored over their websites. If there had been space for her to do so in Victor's apartment she would have bought endless books just for the glossy pictures and obscure details. True, she had never visited all those wonderful places herself, but she knew them intimately nonetheless – Spain's Royal Library of San Lorenzo de El Escorial, the monastic library of St Gall in Switzerland, the Klementinum and the Strahov libraries in Prague, and the Long Room in Trinity College Dublin. She had dreamed of going to visit them, even to Berlin so she could see what remained of ancient Pergamon, reconstructed there in the 1930s, just to get a taste of what Ashurbanipal's library might have been like. She had gazed longingly at the tablets and cylinders in the British Museum. There were so many spectacular, famous and beautiful libraries she had dreamed of seeing. Planned trips she would never have the nerve to take.

This single room put them all to shame.

She couldn't breathe. It was as if something had grabbed her heart and was squeezing it with an invisible fist. She had such a sense of homecoming here, of belonging to this place, feeling the rightness of standing here deep inside her that she would never be able to articulate it.

Slowly she turned around, trying to take it all in. She knew this place and it knew her. She knew the smell, the taste of the air, the sounds.

'Need a moment to take it in?' Will asked gently.

A moment? She'd need a lifetime. She barely noticed as he walked away, humming gently to himself.

Sophie turned around slowly, feeling so very small in this vast room. She didn't know where to look, where to start. It was all so beautiful.

How had they ever managed to keep this secret? She could imagine it topping every one of those 'Most Beautiful Libraries in the World' lists.

A wild giggle worked its way up through her body and she clapped her hand over her mouth to silence it. Unprofessional. What would her father say?

And just like that her good mood fled like morning mist.

What *would* he say? He'd be furious with her for just being here. She imagined the weeks of passive aggressive comments she'd have endured. Living with him had never been easy. No wonder she had been so keen to move out.

'Miss Lawrence, here you are,' said the Professor. She was sitting at a desk by the window, light falling across the various tomes spread out before her. She stood up with some difficulty, an old woman, older than she had looked last night. Will already stood beside her, waiting for Sophie. 'Come and join me.'

'Thank you.'

She took the offered seat opposite her and Will started taking out the paperwork but the Professor waved him away.

'Oh, you and Arthur can deal with all that. Sophia and I have other things to discuss. You have questions, I expect. We have a conservation studio for the actual binding work, but much of your other responsibilities will be here as well. Simpler repairs. Assessment and such. I trust that is agreeable.'

It was unexpected. As a conservator Sophie would rarely work in the actual library. But her father, while cursing Professor Alexander's name, would still refer to her as a master craftswoman. '*I learned it all from her*,' he would say.

When Sophie didn't say anything, the Professor spoke again. 'You won't disturb anyone. Researchers only ever use the Reading Room, and the others bring the materials to them there, where they can be properly supervised. It's usually just me in here.'

Sophie's mother had been here then. Her mother had done this job. And all of a sudden, it came out.

'Professor Alexander,' she said, surprising even herself. 'You worked with her. You knew her. What happened to my mother?'

There was a long silence. The hushed and expectant library seemed to hold its breath around them. Suddenly Sophie wished she'd never opened her mouth. This wasn't what she had intended. She was going to get to know these people again, see what she could find out first. But instead, she just blurted it out the first chance she got.

The Professor finally spoke, her voice soft and so very gentle. Almost like the voice of someone else.

'Did your father...' Professor Alexander paused, choosing her words. 'Did he ever talk to you about his work here?'

'No. Not really.'

Not at all, was closer to the truth. But that would sound strange to them, to be erased from someone's life, the way he had attempted to do.

The Professor pursed her lips and glanced at Will. 'Don't you have somewhere to be?' she asked.

'I was just... I...' Flustered, he glanced back at Sophie as if she was a book on display and then at the Professor. Something seemed to pass between them. Sophie didn't know what but the old woman smiled.

They must know each other so well. And she knew, with a sudden bitterness, that her father had robbed her of such intimacy.

'I'll go and sort these out then,' he said, waving the file at them. 'It won't take long. I still need to show Sophie the studio and...' The Professor gave him another pointed glare. Will rolled his eyes, as if he was fifteen again, and then he was gone, leaving Sophie sitting there with someone who might finally be able to give her some answers.

Chapter Nine

The Professor steepled her fingers together in front of her face, studying Sophie intently from behind them.

'Your mother was a great talent. One of the finest binders I ever had the pleasure of training. We worked together, here at this very desk, you know.'

Sophie pressed her hands against the wood and breathed in the sensation. It was as if she could feel Elizabeth's presence. Unexpected tears stung her eyes and she fought to hide them. If the Professor noticed she gave no indication.

'She and Edward were always... special. Yes. Special. I thought she would succeed me, one day. And when she fell in love with your father we all celebrated. He was a fine binder, so talented.' She shook her head in regret and suddenly Sophie wondered how it had felt for the Professor when he rejected them all. To be a teacher and have your student turn against you so completely. 'As we did when you were born. You were happy here, the three of you. You and Will became inseparable. It was a blessing none of us had expected.' For a moment she seemed distracted, dwelling on other things, other times. Then she pressed on. 'It was shortly after your fifteenth birthday. There was a terrible storm. You were unwell, if you remember, a fever? Your father had gone to a conference. And, in the middle of the night, you woke us all. Standing here in the library, screaming for her. And Elizabeth was simply... gone.'

Here? She glanced back at the stairwell in the middle and a chill passed through her. Why didn't she remember that? If she'd been in here, why didn't she remember it?

And then she realised, when faced with that cold darkness inside her, perhaps she did. Perhaps that was what her mind had blanked out. And all this with it.

'Gone?'

Just like that. There must have been more. There had to be.

'There was no trace of her. No sign of her leaving. No sign of anyone... taking her. You couldn't say what had happened. Your father... well, he blamed us. All of us.' She sighed and pinched the bridge of her nose as if trying to dispel a headache. 'When he returned, and the police were swarming all over the place... I believe there was an argument. Philip and Edward were at odds and... well, perhaps that's something you should ask Edward, if he's willing to talk about it. He might, with you. You're family, after all.'

'She... she might have just left. Run away from him. He was... he was difficult.'

Once again, the Professor frowned and Sophie feared that with those few words she had revealed far more of her personal life than she wanted to.

But what was this conversation if not personal?

'He wasn't always like that, my dear. Besides, I don't believe she would willingly have left you, Sophia, do you?'

That should have been a comfort, but all it did was tear open that terrible, gaping hole in Sophie's chest, the one which had always lurked there but she occasionally managed to believe she had papered over.

'So where did she go?'

The Professor shook her head, having no answer to give.

'I always wondered…' Sophie began, her voice no more than a whisper. It was not something she wanted to say out loud, but here she was, sitting with one of the few remaining people who could possibly answer. She had to be brave and ask. 'I always wondered if she took her own life.'

The Professor took a moment, though if the statement shocked her she gave nothing away.

'I find that hard to believe. Elizabeth had so much to live for. No…' But she didn't sound completely certain. Sophie studied her carefully, trying to see some clue, some way past the mask she wore. 'Like your uncle, she was a fixed point in the library, a legacy, as you are.'

'A legacy?'

She smiled. 'One whose family line is tied here. There are a few of us.' That explained a lot. About her job, and the others here too. Had Edward mentioned that? She couldn't remember.

'Will and Tia as well?'

The Keeper tilted her head to one side. 'Will and Tia are… special cases.' Her lips flickered, though whether in amusement or something else it was impossible to say. 'No, your mother… I couldn't believe she would take her own life. It wasn't in her nature.'

'But my father was…' How did she begin to explain her life with him, what it had been like? Boarding school had been bad enough, but it was better than being at home. His increasingly controlling nature. His rules and strictures. The very things that had seen her running to Victor. And finding herself in the same position all over again.

A look of understanding crossed the older woman's face.

'Ah. I feel I should explain… Your father was not always the man you knew, the man he came to be. I know how he changed after he lost her. He did not simply love your mother. He worshipped her. He would do anything for her. To lose her like that… it broke him. It was too much for him. And when he pulled himself together again, he was very different. He cut us all off. Refused to talk to us and removed you from everything you had ever known. We reached out, tried to help, in the years after he left us, but he rebuffed all attempts.'

He'd never mentioned that. He had never spoken of the place again, even when she tried to ask questions or share her own fragmented memories. She tried to picture him as a man in love, a man with a wife he adored and a teenage daughter. A man who was ever happy.

She couldn't.

The father of her childhood had vanished too.

'He was ill,' she said, trying and failing to keep the bleakness out of her voice. 'Early onset dementia, that's what we thought. Three years ago. But then… they diagnosed a brain tumour. There was nothing that could be done about it. He never had treatment and hid the symptoms too well. Before I knew what was happening, it was too late.'

For a long moment Professor Alexander said nothing, just gazed at Sophie like she could read all the other secrets, the fact that life with her father growing up had been a nightmare, that they had next to no relationship to begin with apart from that of teacher and student, that Sophie had barely visited him in the care home in the last few years and when she did he would fly into a rage until it was easier not to go at all.

'He was fifty-eight,' Sophie prompted, because nothing else seemed likely to break this awful silence. 'When he died.'

'I wonder if it started then,' the Professor said, almost to herself. 'I wonder if...' Then she seemed to wave the thought away. 'Well, we cannot change any of that. But before he was ill, he was a talented bookbinder, a master craftsman, and he loved your mother and you so very much. I want you to know that.'

Loved her mother but not her, Sophie was tempted to retort. Perhaps Sophie reminded him too much of Elizabeth. And that was too painful. He'd sent her away and distanced himself from her even when she came home again. He was her mentor, her teacher, but less like a father every day. The only good memories she still had of him were of his studio, during holidays from school or university, and later, when she began her professional life, the person she went to for advice and particular techniques. But it wasn't a family relationship.

'I was hoping there would be something here, something to tell me what happened. Something to jog my memories. The doctors told me... that I'd blocked a lot of things out.'

'What do you remember?'

Sophie glanced at the tree through the window before she could stop herself. It was different, changing the moment she had woken up. Just a tree. Old, huge, but nothing magical.

Leaves falling, golden and beautiful. Burning. Her hands reaching up to catch them. The air trembling around her, and a wave of energy building within her, ready to tear itself free. Burning inside her too. It hurt. Oh God, it hurt so much. But she couldn't stop. She couldn't let go.

Her mother's voice.

'It's okay, love. I'm here.'

She shook the thoughts away. They didn't make any sense. None at all.

'Fragments,' she replied. 'Snippets, like bits of dreams the next morning.'

'And the tree?'

She stiffened, and snapped her attention back to the Professor. Nothing got by her. She'd have to watch that. She remembered her father's warnings.

'Yes… I mean… I'm not sure. It's not… not like *that* tree but… you know the way dreams are.'

The older woman smiled gently. 'Yes. Indeed I do. You often played in the gardens when you were little, you know? She loved to sit out there with you, in the afternoons, especially in summer. Then you and young Will spent so much of your time there. Escaping us, I presume, as teenagers do. We have some records on Elizabeth in the archives. There is not a lot, but as you are her next of kin I can make them available.'

'Please.' It was something. She had been hoping for more, but there might be a clue in whatever papers they had. There had to be. Or failing that, something – anything – about the mother she'd once had. What her handwriting had been like. Her favourite pen. A picture. 'Please' didn't seem to be enough to say in reply. 'Thank you.'

The door to the library opened and Hannah made her way silently to them. 'Professor? Your appointment is here,' she said brightly. 'Will I show them to the office?'

Sophie flinched at the interruption, but there was no one else here, no one to be disturbed beyond the Reading Room.

'Yes, Hannah. Thank you. I won't be a moment.' The girl gave Sophie a grin and left. No hard feelings there after last night, Sophie thought with relief.

The Professor got to her feet and laid a hand on Sophie's shoulder when she made to do the same. Her grip was firm and a ripple of something flowed through Sophie's body. It should have been comforting but Sophie shivered.

'Don't dwell too much on the past, Sophie. It helps not one bit and it can harm us. You need to live in the now. And look to your own future.'

Will was back, advancing up the length of the library on those long legs, a wild animal in his natural habitat. She smiled before she even realised what she was doing and he returned the expression. The Professor saw that too.

'Now, Will can show you the studio and we'll get to work tomorrow, you and I,' the Professor murmured and Sophie blushed, returning her attention to the Keeper. The Professor saw that as well. *The Prof sees all.* They really weren't joking. 'I wish I had a different answer for you, my dear.'

'It's okay. I've thought for a long time that she had to be dead. I just… I always wondered if she had run away from him… from us… or… or something else.'

'Something else,' Professor Alexander echoed her and turned to look out at the tree. 'Indeed.'

*

Sophie's studio was on the top floor of the east wing, an airy room with a bank of high windows which let plenty of vital natural light in. They looked out over the lawns which rolled down to the river. Not over the gardens and the tree, which was frankly a relief. Her mother had worked here once, as had her father, in this very room, and somehow echoes of them seemed to linger. Something in the fine layers of Japanese paper, the reels of linen thread and the scent of beeswax in the air. The regulated shelves of supplies, well stocked and waiting to fulfil every binders' need, sang to her of her father's studio at home. All the finest quality, the very best.

He had always complained about the costs of materials, even though he charged the highest fees of any of the conservators in the business. People had begged him to work on their books. And he had taught her everything she knew. Where other families had holidays, they had visited libraries and examined binding techniques. Where other families had love, they had... what? Professional respect?

Victor had been in awe of him and his work. When he first came into their lives, he'd gushed about her father's work. Then about hers. Before the nit-picking and the many criticisms had begun.

But to her father, nothing had ever been as good as what he had left behind at the Special Collection. He would mutter about it whenever there was an issue, even something small. Oh he'd never say it to her, but she couldn't help overhearing. Now she was beginning to believe he had not been exaggerating.

Despite everything that had happened, he had loved working here once. Just as she had loved living here. Before her mother vanished.

Book presses of varying sizes stood there like something out of the Victorian era or a steampunk dream. The lightboxes, on the other hand, were pure twenty-first century, newly brought in for her. Her workbench was a U-shape, at right angles to one of those windows, perfectly positioned, with a height-adjustable section depending on whether she needed to sit or stand. The computer was brand new too. It had run through a final set-up process as soon as she turned it on. She couldn't have asked for anything more. Everything was either state of the art or time-honoured and it was all so beautiful. But there was just her, working here alone. The room was large enough for four or five conservators, and surely the Special Collection could afford to employ more. But no.

Just her.

'Is it okay?' Will asked.

'Okay? It's perfect,' she replied.

He was standing in the doorway, watching as she explored the space, clearly enjoying the wonder that must have been playing out on her face.

'It's mainly repairs,' he said, almost as if it was an apology. Some binders might turn up their noses at that, but Sophie didn't. She loved repairs, that sense of rescuing a book, of giving it new life for another generation or more to enjoy. 'Some cleaning. But some items will need to be rebound completely. Especially some of the pieces Edward brings in from other libraries, collectors or auctions. Sometimes I think he just digs them up out of the ground. The Professor has been doing it since your father left but she could do with the help. Not that she'd admit it.' He lingered by the door, as if loath to leave her.

It wasn't like he made her nervous. Or at least not in a bad way. 'It's beautiful, the Great Hall. I don't really remember it. The library itself, I mean. I suppose we weren't allowed in there when we were kids, were we?'

Will frowned, and she wondered what she'd said. She could have sworn, for that moment, he was genuinely distressed. Or maybe even guilty. Perhaps Will had snuck in there anyway. She couldn't remember doing it, which, given her memory, meant nothing.

But the Professor had said, the night her mother had vanished they had found her in the library. Had he been the one to find her?

'It's fine. Not forbidden but… There are valuable books so security is tight. The vaults can be a bit… it's an old building and the stairs are steep. There have been accidents. Best stay up here, okay?' But even as he said it, he smiled as if it wasn't a big thing. Accidents? That did not sound good.

Will's smile was a thing of beauty. It lit up the green of his eyes and made little lines form around their edges. He had the longest, darkest eyelashes she had ever seen on a man. Beautiful.

This was a complication she really didn't need. But it was suddenly far too late to think about that. She had fallen in love with him when she was a teenager, before her mum vanished, before her dad took her away. She was beginning to suspect she had never actually fallen out of love with him.

He'd been lost in the chaos that followed leaving Ayredale. In her broken mind and shattered memories.

She wondered about telling Will that she wanted to find out more about what had happened to Elizabeth. He'd known her. He clearly had fond memories of her. Everyone here seemed to hold her memory in such awe.

The cat slipped in the doorway behind him and leaped up onto the workbench beneath the window.

'Titivillus,' Will admonished him. 'You aren't meant to be in here.'

Sophie smiled. 'I don't mind.' She stretched out her hand but the cat just glanced at her and then sat down to wash himself.

'Sorry, he takes time to warm to people.' Will came closer and leaned against the workbench.

'Sensible,' she replied and he grinned. 'Was there another cat here? When we were kids?'

The smile faded. 'Maybe. I don't know. Lots of cats around really. There used to be a story about a big cat in the area, a huge thing, like the Beast of Bodmin Moor. You used to make up ghost stories about it. Frightened me half to death saying it was inside the library some nights.'

She blinked, trying to wrap her mind around that. 'I did?'

'The guardian of the library, you called it. I think you got it from your mother.'

That black shadow in her dreams, circling the base of the tree, weaving its way through the roots... like a great cat. She stared at him. 'I don't remember.'

She wished she sounded firmer than she felt.

He scratched Titivillus behind the ears and the cat began to purr so loudly even Sophie could hear him.

'Lucky for us, there's only this guy.'

Will headed off, closing the door behind him, leaving her to the silence of the studio. Her studio now.

Sophie tried to push away the strange dream of last night but she felt closer to her mother at last. Just being here. Working where she worked.

When Sophie thought about it logically, the studio had clearly been redone in the last few years. And the Professor had said they mainly worked in the Great Hall anyway.

But some of the equipment was older. Some of it would have been hers, wouldn't it?

She could ask Will. Maybe.

If she could muster the nerve to bring it up.

'*Never talk about it*,' her father had said, his voice cold with suppressed fury. '*Never. I don't want to hear about that place or your unmitigated nonsense ever again.*'

That had been one of the worst days.

He hadn't meant it, she had assured herself. It had been the illness talking. But had it?

A shadow passed over the sun outside and the room dimmed, cold and empty. Sophie suppressed a shudder.

Professor Alexander had been frank and open with her, hadn't she? But the nagging doubt remained that she hadn't been telling Sophie everything. There had been far too much all in one go. Like she wanted to get it all out of the way as quickly as possible, put her version of events in Sophie's mind before anyone else said anything. Was that why she had dismissed Will while they talked?

Since when had she been so suspicious? Maybe this place was getting to her. She could hear her father's voice in the back of her mind, warning her, chiding her, telling her to beware of trusting any of them.

And at the same time, underneath it, there was another voice, a song, a whisper.

Calling her.

Chapter Ten

Will's office nestled on the lower ground floor, a sort of half-submerged basement if you got technical, with narrow windows right at the top of the back wall which let in a basic amount of light. Some rooms in the library were known for the views. His view was mainly of ankles as people came and went via the main door.

But it was cosy and quiet. He spent most of his time cataloguing, fielding calls or doing paperwork. When, Tia often reminded him, he wasn't doing everything else, everywhere else for everyone else. She called him the firefighter, the guardian of the library, forever running around, taking care of problems, putting out the proverbial sparks. He told her that naked flames weren't allowed in the library.

'Tell that to Alexandria,' she sniped back. 'Tell it to Ashmole. Fires and libraries go together in the worst possible way, Will…'

He had been surprised that she hadn't made a comment about the nakedness being *de rigueur* rather than the flames.

It had been a few days now since Sophie's arrival, but nothing untoward had happened. He wasn't sure what he had been watching for – Sophie sleepwalking again or something more. He felt constantly on edge, waiting. But the library was still and quiet.

And the girl – *the woman*, he reminded himself – seemed to be settling in happily enough. At least he hoped so. It was so hard to tell.

She was quiet, studiously polite, and she had absolutely no idea what the library was like, what this place could do. He could feel it stirring, gathering its strength, preparing. He passed the temporary stacks. The books waiting there murmured on as he walked by and he hushed them, running his fingertips gently along the edge of the functional metal shelf. The hum from them subsided but not entirely.

The cat waited for him, sitting on Will's desk, right on top of some of the paperwork he had left there, washing himself studiously as if he had never done a single thing he shouldn't. Will lifted him off it, gathered him into his arms and held him close. Villus nuzzled into his neck and made noises like an engine.

'What are you doing up there?' Will asked, his voice so soft it was almost drowned out by the purring.

'Up where?' Edward asked from the doorway and Will nearly dropped the cat in shock.

Titivillus hissed, wriggled free and strutted out of the room, tail high in indignation. Edward sidestepped to avoid the cat, because there was no way the cat was going to avoid him. The cat belonged here and as far as he was concerned Edward Talbot was not welcome.

Will forced himself to ignore that and be pleasant. 'Dr Talbot, I didn't see you there.'

'That little demon really doesn't like me,' Edward commented, glancing over his shoulder after the retreating cat. 'The feeling is mutual though, so I suppose it's fair. I was looking for you. You're a difficult man to track down all of a sudden, William.'

'I was working. I didn't know you were back already. Tia will be delighted. Sophie too.'

Edward gave him a speculative glare. 'How is my niece settling in?'

Will certainly wasn't about to share everything that had happened with Sophie, certainly not with her uncle. If nothing else, he didn't want to get on the bad side of Dr Talbot. Or possibly land Sophie in trouble.

'She's fine. I think. Maybe you should ask her? I think she was a bit surprised that you had to leave so suddenly when she arrived.'

'I was gone for three days, William. Not exactly an age. Duty called. You know how it is. There was a find in Heidelberg and a host of collectors swarming.'

'But you got there first.'

Of course he had. Otherwise he wouldn't have mentioned it.

Edward pulled out Will's chair and settled himself in it. The suit was another new one, or at least Will had not seen it before. Expensive, definitely, and tailored, probably by that guy he liked in London. He wore it with a waistcoat and a silk tie which were probably worth more than Will had ever earned. But then, there was family money, wasn't there?

He wondered if Sophie knew that.

Will was comfier in jeans and a T-shirt. Plus they didn't cost as much. Which was lucky because he had next to nothing to his name.

Family money. He should be so lucky. Half his family didn't want to know about him anyway. And the other half could easily forget he existed as well.

Edward Talbot cleared his throat. 'I wanted to talk to you about Sophie, actually. She left a rough situation in London, William. She needs our help. We want her to stay, after all.'

With nowhere to sit, Will perched on the corner of his own desk.

'What sort of rough situation?' he asked, in spite of himself. Yes, it was none of his business, and he waited expectantly for Edward to tell him that.

But instead the suave Head of Acquisitions leaned forward like a gossip blogger with the biggest scoop ever. 'Her boyfriend. Ex-boyfriend now, thank goodness. Gods, it took some Art to peel him off her. But, I had to get her down here somehow.'

'*Art?*' Will knew what that word meant. Nothing good. 'Edward, what did you do?'

But Edward beamed self-satisfaction. 'Ensured my niece's safety, of course. Dreadful man. Controlling. Vile. Narcissist extraordinaire.'

Well, thought Will, takes one to know one. But he had enough survival instincts not to say the quiet bit out loud. Oh, Tia would laugh at him. She might dote on Edward, but she knew how Will felt too. Sometimes he wondered if she was playing them off against each other for her own ends. He also wondered if Edward was aware of the full situation. He had to be. He knew everything.

He sighed, pushing towards the point, whatever that was. 'So, why are you telling me this? It's none of my business.'

No matter how he might want it to be. It explained so much. And if Sophie was coming out of a bad relationship he needed to tread carefully.

Edward, it appeared, had other ideas. 'I want her to be happy here, settled. The two of you were close when you were younger.'

'And?'

'Gods, William, were you always this dense? Anyone would think you were made of clay.' He reached into his pocket, taking out his wallet and unfolding some notes. He slid them across the table. 'I can't be here all the time. Someone needs to make her feel part of the family. Take her out. Make her happy.'

Will didn't take the money. He stared at it, mildly affronted. But he couldn't exactly tell Edward to fuck off, no matter how tempting.

Edward was still Will's superior. Only the Professor and Tia had been here longer.

Which left him in a quandary.

'I don't need to be paid to take someone out.'

Pushing himself up to his feet, Edward dusted off his suit without thinking. 'It helps though, doesn't it? Don't overthink it, William. Drinks, dinner. Nothing else. *Definitely* nothing else. Understand?'

Suddenly it made sense. This wasn't a bribe to take her out. It was a bribe to make sure nothing else happened. There was no way he could make Will avoid her. Besides, that wouldn't be possible here. But the rest was perfectly clear.

A warning. *She's been through a lot.* A bribe. *Stay away.*

'I see,' Will said, because he did. Any other words lodged in his throat.

'You're very different people, William. From very different backgrounds. I know you were close as children. But that has to stop now, do you understand? She is my niece, Talbot blood, a legacy. You know what Talbot means, don't you? Where the name came from? And our link to this place. It's delicate but here we are. Both of us. I won't see her used, Will. Not by anyone.'

Used? He had no intention of using anyone.

The Talbot family had served the library longer than anyone. Will knew that. Tia had a thousand stories about them. Some of them were dark indeed.

No more needed to be said, apparently. That was that, as far as Dr Talbot was concerned. At the door, he paused. 'I've left a new Agrippa for you. It'll need cataloguing. Now, I have an appointment with Tia in—' He checked his pocket watch. 'Five minutes, if you'll excuse me.'

An appointment. Will rolled his eyes. So that was what they were calling it now...

'Dr Talbot—'

'Just get a few people together and take the girl out to the pub or something, William. I'm sure you can manage at least that. We need her to stay here. All of us. She's important to the library and should never have left in the first place. Philip was a fool to take her away but then he *always* was a fool. I shouldn't have expected anything more. And look what it got the two of them. Utter misery. I want her happy, contented. She needs a friend. But that's all. Understand?'

Before Will could tell him where to go, a delighted cry interrupted them.

'Edward! You're back!'

Tia launched herself at him from the corridor outside, kissing him extravagantly. If Edward was initially taken aback, he recovered quickly enough, scooping her up in his arms.

'I missed you too, my love,' he murmured. His face transformed, as it always did when she came into view. Smitten, bewitched. Will knew the look. It made his stomach twist.

Tia giggled. 'What did you bring back for me?'

'Oh, just you wait and see.'

'It's my office, you two,' Will said in jaded tones. 'You have rooms of your own.'

Tia smiled, a brilliant joy-filled smile that broke his heart to see. Because Will knew that Edward would leave once more and she would be devastated all over again.

'Spoilsport,' she teased. '*Apparently*, we have rooms of our own, Edward. Why don't we go and explore them. After you show me my present.'

In response he laughed, a low, suggestive laugh, and Will felt like he might throw up in his mouth.

'Edward, about Sophie,' he interrupted, before they forgot about anyone else entirely. 'You're going to have to talk to her, tell her what's really going on here. Before anything happens. If you don't want her scared off entirely.'

Because it certainly was not going to be his job. Not this time.

But if Edward heard him, he didn't let on.

They were gone before Will remembered the money. He cursed softly to himself and shoved it into the drawer. At least there, he didn't have to look at it.

Because when Dr Edward Talbot gave an order, Will didn't have much choice but to obey.

Take Sophie out. But don't get any ideas. Edward knew what Will was and he would never ever be good enough for his niece. Message received loud and clear.

He grabbed the Agrippa off the shelf outside and brought it back to the desk, beginning his careful assessment of it before he unlocked the computer screen and got to work.

Around him the library whispered and sighed, and he knew why. Even if no one else wanted to admit it.

Chapter Eleven

Working with Professor Alexander turned out to be an unexpected joy. She had so many stories. Every book she pulled from the shelves had a history and the way she told them had Sophie hanging on her words. There were tragedies, lives lost and fortunes squandered. There were happily-ever-afters as well. Some of her tales were so funny Sophie ended up laughing herself to tears.

Most of the books from the vault that had to be assessed for repair were still in their phase boxes. These were made of blue-grey board, cunningly designed around the book they housed. They opened like the petals of a flower and closed over to be secured with a loop that hooked around a small button. Each one had been made by hand and she couldn't help but wonder if one or the other of her parents had created some of them.

Phase boxes were so called because they were meant to be the first phase of restoration. Over time they had become the norm and restoration rarely went further. They cradled their contents in non-invasive, acid-free wrappers which delayed the deterioration of a volume. They'd first come into use in the 1970s in the US Library of Congress, but some of these, strangely, looked older. They were everywhere now. There were videos detailing now to make them in under five minutes online and courses you could take. In college they had debated which were the best designed and the best materials but Sophie had always gone with her father's method.

The boxes had been labelled, but some of them were so old the ink was faded to a ghostly scrawl. She wrote up her assessments of ten volumes, mostly superficial repairs, although one needed a new cover and the spine was going on another.

A whisper rippled around her, a sigh, one of those half-heard voices that seemed to linger on the air in Ayredale. But there was no one there. She was alone in the Great Hall of the library, the Professor having been called off to one of her many meetings.

It was an old building, Sophie knew that, and she knew about the way old buildings settled and the noises they could emit, the way they changed from day to night, the strange way sound would carry. The library had already enchanted her but she also worried it was playing with her too.

The great vault of the roof overhead, with its frescos and wooden beams, always made her think of a church. No, a cathedral. Row upon row of shelves which seemed to lean in to peer at her, to whisper behind her back, to shiver when she passed. She could catch their scents on the air, the books the library wanted to show her, wanted her help with...

She knew she was being fanciful.

'Hello?' she called, in case someone had come in without her knowing. It was a big enough space, after all. Someone could be down the far side of the shelves, or on one of the upper balconies.

A faint laugh drifted down to her.

No, up. It came from beneath her, rippling up from the stairwell.

Sophie's throat went dry. She drew in a breath, slowly, carefully, feeling her chest contract even as she tried to breathe evenly.

And then she saw it. A book, an old, beautiful book, on the desk where Professor Alexander worked. The Professor had obviously taken it out earlier, ready for display perhaps.

It was cushioned by foam blocks, waiting to be examined. It looked like it should be locked away somewhere. Not left out like this.

But then the Great Hall was closed access. Only staff were allowed in here.

'You can examine it if you want.' Professor Alexander's voice rang around the library, even though she hadn't raised her voice. Sophie turned sharply to see her approaching, the door to the Reading Room closing silently behind her.

Sophie didn't have to be asked twice. She picked up the book with all the care she could muster.

It was old.

She knew that much simply by touching it. She could feel it, that weight of ages haunting it, threaded through it, lingering on the pages.

The cover was made from wooden boards, with a plain leather exterior that definitely wasn't goat or anything so simple. Not pig skin either. She smoothed her hand over the surface and tried to gauge what it could be. Too fine for vellum. She opened the book carefully, checking the structural integrity as she did so.

It wasn't damaged. In fact it was perfect. Excellent preservation in every aspect. She couldn't even see any previous repairs. Immaculate. Almost as if it was made only yesterday. So why was it here?

The Professor said nothing, just watched her.

Sophie ran her fingertips over the end papers, the exquisite marbling on thick cotton-rich paper, so soft to the touch, such a contrast to the austere cover. The text block was an entirely different material, one she didn't know.

Her touch as careful as it could be, she turned to the ornate title page, the whole thing covered in a swirl of lines and colours intertwining. In the centre she made out the words, *They who can read this know the language of the birds for it is written in their soul.*

It wasn't a title. More like a colophon, but it was at the beginning of the book instead of the end, and didn't give any information on who had created it as they normally did. What was it? An introduction, maybe? An invitation?

The language of the birds…

The phrase was strangely familiar but she couldn't say why. A memory. An echo. Little more than a feeling. She laid her fingertips against the page, felt the surface.

She expected vellum but this was more like paper. Or…

No. The pages inside weren't paper. Or at least not traditional paper. It was more like…

Leaves fluttering down in wide circles, leaves made of gold with letters that glowed with an inner fire, in a script that, when she tried to read it, when she squinted at it…

Sophie turned another page, a few of them, but while beautiful, the words were unknown to her. Until, all of a sudden, they weren't. She couldn't say in what tongue they had originally been written, but the words seemed to flicker through about a dozen different forms, ancient scripts she couldn't hope to translate, through Greek, Latin and finally resolved into English.

'*You can read them, Sophie,*' said her mother. '*They're written on your soul. It's the language of the birds. Remember?*'

That was it. The phrases her mother had used in her dream.

They read like instructions, but written as poetry. It was manuscript, rather than print, which made this even more precious, an archival item. Unique. Each section had a title and a series of subtitles, each picked out in red. Rubrics, she recalled.

Of the Divine, read one.

A prayer book, perhaps? It was beautiful enough. Not a Book of Hours, but something similar.

She turned the page. An illustration of a leaf unfurling and hidden in the lines were words. Terrible, beautiful lines of text.

To Wake.

The next page showed thorns coiling around more words, each one tipped with gold. The vines were the vivid green of malachite, rather than the brown tones of ancient verdigris.

To Bind.

Another page turned with a soft whisper. Not a prayer book. This was something different. It read like poetry, fluid and beautiful.

To Unbind.

She knew what this was. Not because she recognised it or had seen anything like it before. But she just knew, deep in her soul. This was a spell book. A grimoire, they were called.

Another page whispered as it turned. This page depicted a figure wreathed in flames of red and gold, with a tree made of flames behind them. Red ochre, the same hue that coloured the earliest cave paintings, as old as humankind, and gold, its most treasured metal, applied in leaf form and polished to a shine. An incredible example of true illumination, with no base metals mixed. It was lavish. Truly priceless.

To Undo.

Sophie frowned. Words of power, words which had the power of creation and destruction, words of coercion and release, wove between images so beautiful she felt them rather than simply saw them. Everything about this book felt odd, different... magical.

'It's skin,' said Tia blithely. Sophie hadn't seen her approach either. She must have come up the stairs from the vaults. The two women stood watching her now. Waiting. 'The binding, I mean.'

Sophie closed the book gently, put it back in the cradle of its cushion, and then turned, forcing herself to breathe calmly, to face the archivist and the Keeper.

'Leather tends to be.'

'Animal skin perhaps. But this is different. This is human.' The amusement in her voice made Sophie smile. She didn't want to. She wanted to be filled with indignation and tell Tia all about it. The other woman was trying to shock her, to frighten her, to make her recoil in horror. But she met Sophie's smile with her own and Sophie couldn't be angry. It felt like a game. 'You must have worked in more interesting places than I thought.'

Sophie glanced at the Professor, but her ancient face was unreadable. A test then. Well, two could play at that.

Yes, Sophie knew about books bound in human skin. They were not common, but not as rare as people believed. Nor had they been created for any particularly nefarious purposes. They were only books, and the people who made them and paid for them, only people. And there were always people who wanted to shock and horrify others, who wanted to be edgy. So accounts of murders were bound in the skin of the man executed for the crimes, most famously the grave-robber Burke. They called it anthropodermic bibliopegy.

But it didn't disgust or frighten her. Why should it? They were dead. Long dead. There were worse things to be afraid of.

'Really?' she replied as lightly as she could. 'Whose skin was it?'

Tia laughed. If she had hoped to get a dramatic reaction she didn't seem disappointed in any way. Or maybe this was what she wanted, to see what Sophie was made of. She walked her fingers along the edge of the nearest shelf, as if they were little legs.

'Oh, probably someone who used to work here. What else are we going to do with the dropouts? We can hardly release them back into the wild. Waste not, want not, as they say.' Her walking fingers reached the edge and she tipped them off, like someone falling from a great height.

'You know this book then?' Sophie asked.

'Oh yes,' the archivist replied. 'Intimately. Are you planning to read it?'

She picked up Sophie's bone folder from the table where she'd been working, the familiar white tool, so useful for rescuing creased pages, transforming in Tia's hands to something else. Pale as the bone it was named for, the point like a weapon.

Sophie's throat went dry. A flutter of panic rose again, but then it was followed by a surge of indignation. What was she playing at? The Professor still said nothing, but she was still watching. Watching the two of them, their interaction.

'No. I'm not great on reading to be honest. Dyslexia.'

The book was also far too old and far too rare to be sitting out here all alone. Or to be part of the elaborate practical joke on the new girl.

'What are the leaves?' Sophie asked.

Tia stared at her, and Sophie got the impression she was waiting for something else. And that Sophie had somehow surprised her. 'The leaves?'

'The leaves of the book. It's not paper. It's not vellum.'

From the corner of her eye, Sophie saw Professor Alexander smile.

Tia on the other hand looked aghast. 'You were reading it, weren't you? You aren't interested in the contents? Or in the binding?'

Back to her game of trying to scare the new girl. 'If it *is* human skin, it happens. There's a book called "*Des Destinées de l'âme*" that a friend of the author Houssaye deemed so beautiful a meditation on the nature of the soul, he bound it in a woman's skin. The most beautiful woman he knew.'

Tia rolled her eyes, coming closer now. 'The Victorians were so melodramatic. "*A book on the human soul merits that it be given human clothing*", that's what he wrote, Dr Bouland. He didn't kill her or anything. She was his patient in an institution. She was insane. Or so they said. I mean, you could get committed for reading too many novels at the time so who knows? Hysterical women, wandering wombs, repeat *ad nauseam*.'

'Could you put the bone folder back please?'

Tia pointed the sharp end towards her. She made it resemble a weapon instead of a tool, just by the way she held it. 'This?' she teased. 'Whose bone is it though? That's the question.'

'It's not real bone, Tia,' Sophie replied. 'They make a lot of them from plastic these days.'

'Plastic,' she pouted. 'Such spoilsports.' She set it down on the desk. '*Mine* isn't plastic.'

'Your bone folder is made of real bone?' Sophie asked. Tia swung back towards her, like she had almost forgotten Sophie was even there.

'Of course. Human bone. The very finest.'

It had to be a wind-up. Like the book. Tia was watching her, waiting for a reaction. The threat was gone from her eyes. Back to the game.

'So whose bone was it?' Sophie asked, as clearly that was what was expected.

One perfect eyebrow rose in an arch and the perfect, scarlet smile widened, as if delighted that Sophie was finally playing along with her.

'One of your predecessors, a binder. Such a pretty young man, he was.'

'Oh hush, Tia,' said Professor Alexander at last. She came forward and took the book from Sophie. It was just a book again, and the words of the page were now entirely illegible, just beautiful loops and squiggles. No more than decoration. Had she imagined it? Was that possible?

'The Mortlake grimoire,' she said and carefully looked at it herself. Sophie admired the way she handled it. Cautious, but secure, decades of experience in every touch. She didn't fuss around with gloves, thank God – that could cause more harm than good. No pair of gloves could be as sensitive as human touch. It was better to have clean, dry hands and take your time, being aware at all times of the actual materials, feeling it give or resist, to make sure it didn't tear.

'What is it?' Sophie asked.

'An alchemical text from the 1500s. Possibly a copy of an earlier work. We don't really know what it says. The code hasn't been cracked.'

Sophie glanced at Tia who was wearing that knowing grin again. 'Maybe you should check that, Professor,' she said and the smile broadened. 'Things may have changed.'

Turning away, Sophie fought to quell the roiling sensation in her stomach. She didn't want to tell them what she had read, or thought she had read. What if she was wrong? What if it had just been her imagination? She'd make such a fool of herself. She was only just starting out here. It could ruin everything. Besides, she couldn't read it now. Perhaps she had imagined the whole thing. Her mother used to tell her stories so maybe this was just another fragment of memory sidling back into her mind. No. She had to get control of herself, calm her imagination and focus on reality.

Professor Alexander gave Tia a stern look, as if she had said something she shouldn't. 'I will. Arthur requested it for his own research. He's the expert. I thought it might make a nice display. Perhaps it needs some time locked up where we can keep an eye on it. And control access a bit. Don't worry about this one, Sophie. It doesn't need work.'

The 1500s. Of course, working with rare books gave you a twisted view of what constituted 'old'. Sophie had once had to stifle a laugh when someone quite senior in the Academy described a 1920s print as ancient. Her father had barely counted anything from the eighteenth century as worth his attention.

And this one was perfectly preserved.

'I'm not sure I'd be willing to touch it unless it was an emergency anyway.'

Tia gave her another odd look, that piercing glare. 'Why not?'

A strange question. An archivist should know the answer already. But if this was some kind of test, Sophie supposed she needed to give an answer.

'Because I might damage it. A lot of conservation is knowing when not to meddle, you know? If it's inert, with no risk of deterioration, why risk interfering? Half the time a new binding is just vanity on the part of the owners, or someone wanting to drive up a sale price.' Someone like Victor, for example, she thought bitterly and then pushed memories of him away. He had no place here. 'Fixing lightly damaged bindings or shabby leather, nothing serious, superficial stuff, but people still want it to look like new. Besides…' She shivered, remembering the way it had felt when she touched it. The strangeness of it. The weird materials.

The Professor slid it expertly into a phase box, binding it up with string. 'Besides?'

The Ayredale Special Collection housed some of the most unusual books in the world, and Sophie had been handling one of them. She dismissed Tia's wind-up about human skin. That didn't matter one way or the other.

'It's beautiful. But the materials *are* unusual. The text block.' She didn't know how to articulate it. The strangeness. The familiarity. The way the two warred with each other.

'Ah,' the Professor sighed. 'Yes. It's not paper, not in the way we know it today. Well spotted. Its text block is made from leaves.'

Leaves. That was it. Sophie felt that same shiver, one that was starting to become so familiar since arriving here. She could feel the echo of touching the pages on her fingertips, the delicate scent that had come with the sensation, so unlike the dry and dusty smell of old paper. This was fresh and subtle. Like life itself. Like spring.

'Leaves made from leaves,' Sophie murmured and the Professor smiled.

Leaves that fell in slow, inexorable waves, glowing with a light, burning, turning to ash...

She forcefully shoved the dream back into the recesses of her mind. Not now. This wasn't the time.

'It is a rather enchanting idea, isn't it? But not that uncommon. The Javanese palm books are probably the most famous, and it is common enough in Vietnam of course, but then paper, particular Western paper, has a relatively short history. And before Cai Lun mixed hemp with mulberry bark and rags in water, crushed it into a pulp and pressed out the liquid, leaving the result to dry in the sun, there was papyrus. Before that there were clay tablets. But leaves have always been used. In one form or another.'

'What type of leaves are they?' Sophie asked before she could stop herself. This was like talking to her father again, the depth of knowledge, the way the subject would flit onwards. Before he had become ill, on the days when bitterness didn't consume him. Like he had been when she was little, when they were here. Before... before it all went to pieces.

Had he had conversations with the Professor like this? Had her mother?

'Do you know...' the Professor paused, as if mulling Sophie's question over. But it felt like an act, as if she was pantomiming all this for Sophie's sake. 'I'm not entirely sure. Maybe they don't have a name. The trees that produced them could be extinct. Now, time for a coffee break, I think.'

A break. As if everything was perfectly normal.

But Sophie couldn't help but feel as if she had just been set some kind of test. She was not entirely sure if she had passed or not, or what assessment the two of them had made of her in the wake of it.

Chapter Twelve

The book went on display in a glass case in the Rotunda. It was locked, and probably alarmed. Will had muttered about it darkly, and every time he passed it Sophie saw him casting suspicious glances at it. Almost as if he bore some personal grudge against it.

On the other hand, she just felt drawn to it.

Of the Divine.

The words were back. Some of them, anyway. They filtered in and out of intelligibility, like looking at it through water. Sophie still didn't dare tell anyone. She really wasn't certain it was real. Some of the phrases were Latin, some other, older languages and she didn't so much understand them as intuit. She didn't want to test this magic and find it was a lie.

And maybe it was just her memory playing games with her again. Maybe she wasn't reading the words at all but – the frustration was unbearable, and it kept pulling her back to check.

Someone turned a page each day and each day she read another spell, hidden in the script and decoration, surrounded by gold, cinnabar, malachite, red ochre and lapis lazuli, with animals and birds entwined in marginalia like a wild tangle of undergrowth.

It was only after the third day that she saw someone else there before her. Arthur Dee.

His hands were folded behind his back, pushing in against the soft pastel pink of his shirt, perfectly cut for him, like the pale cream chinos. His dark hair was swept back from his intent face, and he leaned slightly forward, his brow just a little furrowed as he studied the book.

Sophie was about to leave quietly when he noticed her. She wasn't sure what she did to give herself away. She hadn't made a sound. Maybe he just saw her reflection in the glass.

'Sophie,' he said in that rich, pleasant voice. 'Another fan of the Mortlake grimoire, I believe.'

'I wouldn't say a fan,' she protested. Definitely not. It intrigued her, but it scared her as well. And yet… 'It's just… it's beautiful.'

Arthur smiled. 'It certainly is. My obsession, to my shame. I think Professor Alexander has locked it up here to keep me from requesting it. Perhaps she's rationing what I can see. I could stare at it all day.'

'Can you read it?' she asked, fascinated. If Arthur knew what it said, she wouldn't feel quite so strange about it. Or about the idea that the book itself was trying to make her read it.

Some of the words ran around her head, invaded her dreams, and on occasion her waking mind as well.

O divina numen, splendida, lucidissima stellarum…

'Oh no,' said Arthur with a laugh. 'I'd give anything to know what secrets are locked in here, although I've cracked bits and pieces based on other derivative works. A spell of binding and such. Similar to the Thomas Allen one.'

A spell of binding, she thought, a vivid image of the vine-decorated page flaring up in her mind… *Of the Divine, To Bind…*

Arthur pressed his hand to the glass, as if reaching for the book, his gaze intense.

'Some people think it's Sumerian, or perhaps Akkadian. Can you imagine an Elizabethan scholar, even one as brilliant as John Dee, knowing the languages of ancient Mesopotamia?' He laughed at the thought but Sophie couldn't join in. 'No, it's a code. It has to be. Do you know the book's history? It was rescued from Mortlake, after fire gutted the library there.'

She shook her head. 'Where's Mortlake?'

'You've heard of Dr John Dee, the Elizabethan astrologer, the alchemist, haven't you? Spy, polymath, codebreaker, and magician... He was a favourite of the Queen, for a time anyway. He was the Keeper of the Special Collection when it was at Mortlake. He moved it there, and lost it when he went on his travels. The School of Night betrayed him. They stole it all, took it to London, destroyed anything that wasn't of value to them. A travesty, really.

'They were a... secret society, for want of a better word. And in the Elizabethan age they were powerful indeed. They still run the Special Collection, our bosses as it were. The members at that time were famous. Sir Philip and Mary Sidney, Sir Walter Raleigh, Christopher Marlowe, any number of other luminaries of the court. And Dr John Dee had been its head. Its guiding light.'

She racked her brains for the only thing she knew about Dr John Dee. 'He communicated with angels.'

Arthur's eyes darkened. 'He communicated with something. Not angels. Not as people understand them today. Something else. Perhaps the spirit of the library itself.'

'Seriously?'

'Absolutely. We don't know where it came from but I believe the book tells how he did it. But he was a master at cyphers, you see? A lot of people think he wrote the Voynich manuscript as well.'

'The what?'

'Another book full of gibberish,' Will's voice cut in sharply. She hadn't seen him approach. He stood on the bottom step of the staircase, Titivillus winding between his legs.

Arthur twisted towards him, the good humour in his expression fading to a blank hardness. 'This, however, is the real deal. There's no comparison. The Voynich is an ugly scribble beside the Mortlake grimoire. Look.' He waved his hand towards the gleaming pages on display. 'This is a work of art.'

Will shrugged his shoulders. 'Maybe. At least we know it definitely came from Mortlake, but that's about it. Nothing about who wrote it or why, how Dee got it or what he made of it. Or if it is indeed real.'

'It has survived the destruction of Mortlake and the Great Fire of London,' said Arthur. 'Countless wars and natural disasters… It's special.'

'That just makes it lucky, not special.'

Arthur shook his head. 'If we could just crack the code, who knows what we could do. Dee could work marvels. You'll have to forgive him, Sophie. My half-brother has no soul.'

Sophie was looking straight at Will when he said it, so she couldn't miss his expression faltering as if Arthur had slapped him in the face.

'Half-brother?' she asked.

'Different mothers,' Will said quickly, obviously uncomfortable.

That was when Arthur's phone started to ring, a strident tune completely out of keeping with the library. He dug it out of his pocket, checked the screen and grimaced, almost comically.

'Minister,' he said in expansively familiar tones as he answered. 'How are you? No, not at all. Happy to talk. What can I do for you?'

Arthur threw his gaze up towards the glittering dome above the Rotunda. Then he put his hand over the phone, where a thin voice piped out some long and convoluted answer. 'You'd think they couldn't do anything without me. Honestly. I'd better go. Later.'

He strode off, still listening to the phone and making occasional noises of interest.

Will had found something fascinating to study at his own feet.

'Sorry,' he said into the silence closing in on them.

He met her gaze at last, and she smiled apologetically. Then immediately, she blushed. She felt so foolish. Will was a grown man now and she was a grown woman. He was no longer the boy on who she had doted. And she was no longer a little girl.

'I... I'd forgotten he was your brother.'

'*Half*-brother, as he's so fond of pointing out. It doesn't matter. We aren't exactly close. We're both legacy employees, like you, that's all. Anyway, enough about him. How are you?'

'I'm fine,' she said, not sure she was telling the truth. She stared at the book again. She hadn't asked the Keeper or Tia. She had been too nervous. No one else could read it and suddenly she could. Sometimes anyway. When the book, or the library, or something wanted her to. She would sound insane and she could not put herself through that again. But this was Will. She trusted him. 'What's the language of the birds?'

Will's whole body froze, every muscle tensing. The sinister shadow she had seen in him before rose like a threat. All around the two of them everything went silent. Everything, as if the library held its breath.

'*What* did you say?'

But he had heard her. She could tell. How could she doubt it? The words had hit him like a static shock.

'It was on the first page. In the illustration, threaded through it.' Doubt suddenly assailed her. She'd read it but words had a habit of jumbling themselves up on her. Maybe she was wrong, or it was all part of her feverish imaginings, not real at all. 'I'm not great on… on scripts but…'

The flowing, coiling lines had resolved until they were as clear as day. The words had seared themselves into her mind. And those words… The same words…

In the dream, her mother had used those words.

You can read them, Sophie. They're written on your soul. It's the language of the birds. Remember?

'But…' Will came closer, studying her now like she was some sort of weird exhibit in a museum, a curiosity to be unpicked and examined. There was something almost feral about his movements, not quite human. She remembered thinking that when she first saw him at the station, there was something… Not *wrong*… not exactly. But *other*.

She took a hurried step backwards and Will stopped, reading the fear she couldn't hide.

His demeanour changed, right in front of her, a ripple passing through him until she saw a man thoroughly ashamed of himself. 'I'm sorry,' he whispered. 'I didn't mean to… but Sophie, how do you know what it says?'

Was he still messing with her? Were they all in on it? Was this going to be her whole life now? God, it was unbearable.

Tears welled up in her eyes, stinging inside the bridge of her nose and blurring her vision, making Will a vague and indistinct shape. She blinked furiously, trying to push them back before she consolidated her position as a hysterical female.

'I read it.'

'You can *read* it? That book? That one right there?'

'Well… yes. I mean, not easily. It just sort of comes to me.'

'"Comes to you…"' he murmured. She didn't know how else to describe it. That was how it worked. The words resolved themselves as she stared at them, as she let her eyes rest on them and relax. Like an optical illusion. It was how she imagined reading might be for other people. And then, if she looked away, they were gone again.

Will stared at the book for a long moment.

'Sophie,' he said at last, and his voice almost sounded normal again. 'Listen to me, don't say anything about it to Arthur, do you hear me? Don't say it to anyone. Except maybe the Keeper. But seriously… what else did you read there?'

She squirmed a little, uncomfortable now. 'It's not… it's not really like reading.'

'What else?' His tone hardened, determined, angry.

'O Divine Goddess, brightest light of heaven, I summon and bind—' she whispered.

Will surged forward, his hand closing over her mouth, his other arm pulling her against his hard body. She gave a cry of alarm, and then fear stole her breath.

'Stop,' he hissed, his voice frantic, his hands shaking against her. 'Please, Sophie, you have to… how do you know those words?'

How could she answer with his stupid hand over her face? She struggled free, glaring at him, and though he released her, he stayed close, poised to leap on her in an instant if she started speaking the wrong words again.

'I'm sorry… I just… just don't say it out loud, understand? Not here. Not anywhere. Where did you hear it?'

'I told you. I read it. They're just words, Will.'

'Words have power. Have you told Edward?'

'He'd have to be here for me to tell him, wouldn't he? I know he's been back but I can't keep track of him. He comes and goes all the time. Besides, it's just…' She sighed. 'That phrase. It was on the title page, but also… it's something I think my mother must have said, years ago.'

She had, hadn't she? The words lingered in Sophie's memory, drifting echoes from her dreams. *The Tree will tell me. It's the language of the birds.*

Sophie knew she was trying to rationalise the impossible. And so did Will, that was clear from the expression on his face.

'Elizabeth said it?'

'It's one of the few memories I have of her. It started coming back, when I got here. Lots of things did but they don't make sense.'

Now she'd started talking to Will, it was all coming out. She couldn't help it. So many questions, so many things she didn't understand.

'My doctors said…' She paused, realising what she was saying. But what did it matter now? He could think she was crazy if he wanted to. She couldn't do anything about that. 'My doctors said it might if I ever came back. Years ago. But Dad didn't want me to. Like he didn't want me to remember her at all. Nothing makes sense. What happened to her, Will? I dreamed of a tree. The tree in the garden but it wasn't the same tree, not really, and…'

Suddenly a sob rose up from within her chest, completely unexpected and unheralded. She covered her mouth but tears began to spill from her eyes instead. Sophie tried to plough on.

'The leaves were falling but they were on fire. There was ash everywhere, all over my hands. And she said… she said… it's the language of the birds. And that she needed me to be strong, to run, to get help.'

She could still hear the voice. Her voice. It echoed through her head endlessly. But now it said something else and pain threaded through each word.

I'll try to hold it here until the Keeper comes. Together we can stop it. Now go. Run.

She couldn't keep talking. The words turned into a sharp pain in her chest, her own body crushing them inside her bones, trying to push them down, make them stop. Because if she didn't say them... if she didn't say them out loud...

Will folded his arms around her again, so gently this time. Something unhitched itself and breath rushed into her lungs. She felt herself lean in against him, press her face to his chest and sob. She hadn't cried like this in years. Not since they had first left Ayredale. Not since that first night. Because she had known there was no point. Her father didn't want to know, didn't want to deal with whatever had happened, whatever she had seen. He'd closed himself off emotionally and taught her to do the same.

'Come on,' Will said in his deep, soothing voice. 'Let's go outside. Fresh air does wonders.'

Did it? She didn't know. All she could think of was the madness of coming back here. The strangeness of the library. Her vanished mother, her dead father, and the elusive uncle who was meant to fix all of the broken things in her life.

And why did she even think that of Edward? What had he actually done besides bring her back here and then bugger off, abandoning her again?

Perhaps it had just been a vain hope. The dreams of a child. She hadn't been a child for a very long time.

Will was right, of course. The fresh air did help. It was a cold but bright winter's day. The sun was low in the sky, turning it golden and orange, but there was still some warmth in it. She drew in breath after breath, trying to gain some sort of control over herself.

'I'm sorry,' she said at last.

Will didn't seem in a hurry to let her go. He kept his arms around her lightly and she leaned into his warmth. He had the softest jumper on, and his scent was intoxicating as ever.

What must she look like right now?

Desperate, possibly insane, hysterical?

'Don't be sorry,' he murmured. Hesitantly. He frowned, silent for a moment, as if trying to decide what to say. 'The book is special. And what you're feeling is real. And your reaction. We'll find Edward, make him explain it all to you. He was here earlier. I'd try but I… it's really not my place, Sophie. The Special Collection… it's special for a reason.'

'Special.'

'Yes. You know that. Somewhere. You have to remember.'

'Dreams. Broken memories. What goddess is it talking about, that… that poem?'

She couldn't say prayer. She just couldn't. Or worse. Spell…

The words had lodged themselves in her mind. They had appeared, she had read them and now she couldn't cast them out again. *O Divine Goddess…*

'There's an old story about the Special Collection. They say she was the first goddess,' he said, his voice soft, almost hypnotic. He sounded like someone telling a fairy tale, filled with childhood certainty. 'She was chaos and wildness, and all the madness of creation. But she knew that creativity, thought and invention need order and stability which she couldn't provide. So she sacrificed her power to give mankind that opportunity, and created the library. It's a story, just a story. The Special Collection has existed for generations. It moves occasionally, when it must, when chaos and destruction get too close. But it endures, feeding thought and creativity all over the world. Without it…'

'No one would have a creative thought again?'

He shook his head and his hand came up to cup her face. 'Maybe?'

She pressed her cheek against the palm and sighed. He attempted a wavering smile, which she tried to return. For a moment she thought he might lean forward, bend down and kiss her. She wanted him to. She couldn't remember ever wanting anything quite so much. Will was magical. If she knew nothing else for sure, she knew that.

It wasn't just the ghost of teenage infatuation. Not any more. She was a woman grown and he was a man now. She had always loved him, from before the time she knew what love was. They had been torn apart when her father took her away from Ayredale. That didn't mean she had stopped loving him.

Even in those moments when she wasn't sure what he would do, or felt that first tingling of fear, she knew there was something about him that defied logic and reason. And about the way she felt about him. Just like the library.

She wasn't sure what he saw in her eyes. She couldn't read his thoughts and emotions.

'You know what, why don't we go out?' he said, changing the subject abruptly. 'Go and get a drink in the pub? Away from the library? We could ask some of the others if you like. Tia likes it there.'

'Do we need a chaperone?' she asked. They kind of did. They were standing there in each other's arms, wrapped together like they had never been apart. But at least she felt halfway normal again. She needed to cling to that now.

Which seemed to mean clinging to him.

He looked completely confused for a moment. 'No, I just... I don't... you're upset and I don't want to rush you or...'

Affection made her lean her head against his chest. It felt so good. So right. It was what she had been missing for so long. She couldn't tell him that, but as she rested her ear against him she could hear his heart. It seemed to echo her own.

'A night out would be wonderful. Thank you.'

'Tonight?'

She smiled. The rush of pleasure was more than she could articulate. 'Tonight.'

Chapter Thirteen

It preyed on Will's mind all afternoon. Not the prospect of going out somewhere with her. Although that was there too, tempting him, teasing him, warning him it was all going to go wrong. Because he always screwed that side of things up.

No. It was the grimoire. It wasn't possible. It simply wasn't possible. The Mortlake grimoire. Will couldn't say how many times he had stared at the pages of that book, trying to decipher it. He wasn't alone either. He knew Arthur regularly requested it from the vault, obsessed with his ancestor. *Their* ancestor, he supposed. So did any number of the researchers who came here frequently. They studied it, time and again, but he'd never known anyone to crack the code.

He hadn't wanted to leave Sophie alone but he couldn't exactly follow her about the place. No matter how much he wanted to. It wasn't safe. *She* wasn't safe. And neither, he feared, was the library with her wandering around. *Reading things.* Just like that.

He'd never asked Tia what was in it, and she wouldn't answer him anyway if he asked her. And he didn't have the courage to ask the Keeper. Professor Alexander would wonder why he needed to know.

And he didn't want to reveal Sophie's secret.

He'd tell them too. He couldn't help that. He told them anything they asked, even if he didn't want to. That was the way things were. The way they always had been.

He owed them everything. He couldn't lie to them.

And then he would have to tell them about Sophie being able to read a book that *no one* could read. An impossible book, a secret kept for generations, locked away. If Arthur found out he'd be unbearable. He wouldn't rest until he'd made her translate every last word.

And then what? Will wasn't sure.

If Sophie had confided in Arthur while they had been standing there, talking about it. If she had even let slip for a moment that she could read it…

It didn't bear thinking about.

Tia sat in one of the chairs in the bay window at the far end of the lounge, staring out at the gardens as the late-afternoon shadows crept across the paths.

When Will entered the lounge, Tia didn't stir. She'd finished up early. Sunlight gleamed off her ruby red hair and she seemed distracted. If her eyes had not been open he might have thought she was asleep. Even then…

'Tia?'

She turned around sharply, her mouth open, and he saw her expression fall when she recognised him. 'Oh Will, it's you. Where have you been?'

'Working.' He wasn't about to admit he'd been hiding out in his office trying to figure out what to do about Sophie. Tia dropped her gaze again, hardly listening. Will frowned. 'Are you okay?'

'Yes, I… I'm fine.' She didn't look fine. Her eyes were red-rimmed, as if she had been crying. She looked away quickly when she saw him notice. 'Margo's made some lovely ginger biscuits. Do you want one? The tea's still warm in the pot.'

There were two places laid. Only one of the cups had been used.

'Were you expecting someone?'

She dragged in a breath. 'Yes. Edward. But he had to leave. Again.' She let the air out again, measuring it so as to stay in control. There was a sob buried under her words. 'Such a pity. We had plans. We were going out tonight.'

But Edward had done a flit and she was left on her own again. Same old story.

'I'm sorry,' he murmured as he sat down beside her. Bloody Edward. Running other people's lives and leaving them in the lurch. It didn't surprise Will, not after so long knowing him. He was stunned that Tia still expected him to change somehow. Surely she knew better at this stage. She had known him even longer.

'Not your fault,' she whispered and stared out of the window at the tree again. 'He was back for two whole days this time. It was nice.'

'That's a record, isn't it?'

She tried to laugh but he knew that she was forcing it. The world of the Special Collection was small and everyone knew Edward had pursued Tia for some time before she'd relented and agreed to a relationship. And then… he seemed to drift away. Narcissist that he was. Suddenly she was the one doing all the running. He liked it that way.

'That's how he is. It's not his fault. The job calls him away and… He forgets me, when he leaves, did you know that? Doesn't mean to, of course.' She sounded so miserable. 'That's the way it is. The way *I* am. I slip out of the memory too easily.' Maybe that was the reason for the bright hair, the flamboyant clothes and the outrageous behaviour. To make herself lodge in someone's memory a little longer. Because the way this place worked, she was always the first to go. 'It's all right,' she told Will when she noticed his expression. 'When he comes back, it's like falling in love all over again.'

It sounded awful, but he couldn't say that. It was too close to how he was feeling about Sophie.

'Why don't we go out?' Will asked, trying desperately to cheer her up. 'I promised to take Sophie to the village.'

'The three of us?' she asked.

'Why not?'

'Wouldn't you rather… you know… go with just her?'

She sounded so tentative, afraid. That was what made him furious about the whole situation.

'No.'

Tia gave him a glare which said he was a liar and she could read him like a book.

'Yes you would. And you have history. Childhood sweethearts. She's totally your type.'

'I have a type?'

'Of course you have a type. Everyone does. Unfortunately mine is total bastards with too much charm. Known for it. Come on then. I'll give you an excuse to take Sophie out for a pint.'

'I thought we'd have a meal.'

'One step at a time, Romeo. What she needs right now is a good night out.' She sighed. 'I think we all do. Besides, Margo's cooking is much better than anywhere else. And it's pizza night. I can't miss pizza night.'

Well, she had a point. Especially about Margo's pizza. But something was still bothering him, something else he needed to ask.

'Tia, did you leave the Mortlake grimoire out for Sophie?'

'No, that was the Keeper. Testing her, I think.'

'Did she pass?'

Tia peered at him closely, suddenly alert and interested. 'Why do you ask?'

He couldn't tell her. He couldn't lie. But… he could bend the truth. 'Just… just worried about her. She's fragile.'

'I hope you didn't tell her that. Honestly, Will. You never learn.'

'I didn't do anything.'

She got to her feet and then leaned over to ruffle his hair affectionately. 'Oh sweetie, you always do something. Enjoy the tea. And you'd better eat enough pizza before we head out. I don't want to have to carry you home yet again. And I imagine Sophie would be less than impressed at what a lightweight you are.'

'Drinking is not a competition, Tia.' She drank too much. But how could he tell her that? She wouldn't listen anyway. He worried about her.

'Says you,' she replied and sauntered away. 'That's why you always lose.'

He couldn't for the life of him think of a witty retort. Instead, he sat there, drinking the tea, staring at the tree in the gardens. The ginger biscuits were good, homemade and expertly spiced. No one could beat Margo's cooking. Tia was right about that.

As he sat there, he saw Sophie in the garden. She walked up to the foot of the tree, pressed her hands to the trunk, and tilted back her head so she could look up into the branches. She stood there for a moment, frozen, and then she seemed to wilt, stepping back.

Defeated.

What was she looking for? Will could guess, but he didn't want to be right.

By the time he made his way out there to find her, she was gone. Back inside, he presumed, back to work. Will tightened his jaw. She hid in her work, he understood that. He did the same thing, if he was feeling honest. Not that he would admit it out loud.

Hiding your real feelings was easier when you hid yourself away.

Everyone here did it in one way or another. Sometimes he thought that was what the library was for. To hide things.

All of them were hiding something. Tia, Sophie, even him.

Chapter Fourteen

The village was far prettier than Sophie had remembered, caught in a valley on a frosty night beneath a cloudless starry sky.

After dinner – which was a lavish buffet of the most delicious pizza Sophie had ever eaten – she grabbed her coat and bag from her room and met Tia on the stairs, heading to the door. The archivist had wrapped herself in something sleek and designer, the coat perfectly cut, and she balanced on a treacherous pair of high heels. Sophie paused, glancing down at her own preferred going-out ensemble of jeans and a nice top.

'Oh, don't worry about that,' said Tia, reading her mind. 'I overdress. I'm known for it. It's only a pub, Sophie. People spit on the floor.'

'Really?'

The red-haired woman pulled a face. 'No, not really. Not any more. It's rather nice actually. They did it up a few years ago but times change, don't they? Now it has a cocktail menu and everything. Where has that boy got to?'

Will was waiting outside, wrapped up in an overcoat, with that red scarf around his neck. He had no right to look that handsome. And he wasn't alone.

Meera and Hannah stood with him, bundled up for the winter's night.

'There they are,' Meera hooted as they came outside. 'Come on, ladies. It's freezing out here.'

'I didn't realise you were invited, children,' Tia said, revelling in the teasing. 'Isn't it a bit past your bedtime already?'

'Will said—' Hannah began and then Sophie saw the slow realisation spread over her face that Tia was playing with them. 'Oh you.'

'Yes, *me*. Haven't you learned yet?'

The walk down didn't take long but they didn't have a pavement for a lot of it and Sophie picked her way carefully. Hannah and Meera laughed and yelped, talking loudly all the way, while Will was silent as the grave.

'Did you mean to invite them?' Tia asked softly, only Sophie close enough to hear her question.

Will shrugged. 'It just sort of happened. They asked what I was doing and I said going for a drink and then…' He glanced at Sophie. 'Sorry.'

She shrugged. It wasn't like this was a date or anything. And she didn't mind Meera and Hannah. They were sweet. Young. She just didn't know what to say to them half the time. They were so full of life and excitement. They made her feel old. Like Will had said.

'It's fine. It'll be fun.' She tried to make her voice sound like she meant it. She had been on nights out like this before where she didn't know anyone and it was all awkward. She tended to end up in a corner on her own, nursing a single glass of wine before making her apologies and leaving early. Especially if she knew Victor was waiting for her.

The pub was as postcard-perfect as the village itself. There was a beer garden outside, and possibly another at the back, which would have been lovely in the summer, but tonight was only going to result in hypothermia. Inside, low beams, white walls and a roaring fire seemed to transport them back to another age. Tia waved to the barman, who turned scarlet and rushed to find them a table. Sophie and the rest of them followed, watching as the young man nearly fell over himself to serve her.

Tia settled into her seat and shrugged off her coat as if it was a cloak. 'Oh I do like it here,' she purred. 'Now, some wine for me. Anyone else? Sophie?'

Sophie nodded and Tia had ordered a bottle before she knew what was happening. The others were having pints of a local ale. The girls spoke about their courses, and the placement that brought them both there. Will and Tia traded stories of previous interns and where they had gone on to. Tia poured her another glass of wine and Sophie realised she hadn't even noticed she'd finished the first one.

'I'm a bad influence,' Tia said with a wink. 'Didn't they tell you?'

'They've told us so many stories about your escapades,' Hannah replied. 'It's hard to know what's true.'

'Oh, it's all true.' She laughed at them. 'But if it's stories you're after… Will, tell them the one about the guardian of the library.'

His face froze just for a moment and he swallowed. Sophie saw his Adam's apple move in his throat. 'That's just a fairy tale,' he said.

'Well they're all fairy tales,' Tia told him. 'Doesn't mean they aren't true. In some way. I like fairy tales. Now…' A glimmer entered her eyes and she lowered her voice. Everyone leaned in to hear her story. You couldn't resist.

'Long long ago, when the Special Collection was somewhere far away from here, somewhere hot and dusty, *sandy*,' she said the word with such distaste, Sophie had to smile and she thought of Pergamon, in Turkey, and St Catherine's, in the Sinai Desert, both sites of legendary libraries. 'It was dangerous and difficult, enemies at the gates and all that. So the Keeper summoned a creature from the shadows to guard the library for all eternity. A great cat, or a wolf or, well, *something*. But the guardian longed to shed its immortality. Longed to be human. It longed to love.'

Will pushed himself up from the chair. 'Right, pints? My round.'

Tia paused as she watched him go, a strange smile on her lips.

'What happened?' Meera asked. She'd taken Hannah's hand and squeezed it tightly. The other girl smiled, curling in against her. 'To the guardian?'

The archivist turned to look at her and didn't answer for a long moment. When she did speak, it was like she was reciting something Sophie felt she should know.

'*He went ahead to save his comrade. He knew the route to protect his friend. He took the road to the Tree.*' She sighed. 'He left when those he loved were gone. That's the problem with immortality, isn't it? You need someone to share it with.'

Not just a problem for immortals, Sophie thought as she watched Will waiting at the bar. It was all too easy to lose love of any kind. But to hold onto it… 'That's real magic, I guess,' she murmured, more to herself than anyone else.

'Quite,' said Tia softly, a darker glimmer in her eye now, so Sophie couldn't tell if she was still being playful or deadly serious. 'You should remember these stories, Sophie. You grew up on these fairy tales. You and Will both. Your mother told them wonderfully.' Sophie blushed, unable to stop herself. Of course, she didn't remember. She just had snatches. Glimpses. Snapshots.

Tia glanced at the two other girls and gave another wicked grin. 'Another story then. Another guardian. Gather round, children.'

They did, all three of them, wide-eyed and enraptured, just like children. It was impossible to ignore Tia's voice, the sweet cadence and soft falls, as she spun out her tale. Like magic, Sophie thought again, just like magic.

'Once upon a time, not so very long ago, a goddess fell in love with a mortal man and had a child, a demigod. Oh but he was wild and dangerous, a monster of chaos. Libraries don't do well with chaos. They're kind of the antithesis. So two librarians scoured through all their books, studied all the secrets in the Special Collection, and they cast a spell. The same spell, in fact, that the Keeper had used all those years ago to call forth the guardian. A great working of Art, they called it, those cunning men and women, those scholars. It divided the creature, separating the god-part from the man-part, and they gave him a new life, a new purpose. But they left his heart torn between them so he could never find peace, except at the Special Collection. He was the guardian as well. Or at least, he took on that role.' The girls leaned in against each other, waiting for more, hanging on Tia's every word. She glanced up at the bar and smiled. 'And then there's Will.'

The spell broke suddenly, like a string had snapped. Meera gave a nervous laugh and Hannah shushed her.

'Will?' Sophie asked, surprised. What did she mean? What about Will?

For a moment Tia looked immensely guilty, as if she had said too much. 'It's just what I call him. The reason he doesn't like the stories. Guardian of the library. You know,' she waved her hand in the air, 'the way he does everything. Don't tell him I said it. He gets embarrassed. So, who's next? You two,' she said to Meera and Hannah. For a moment they looked at her as if they didn't quite understand. Then

Meera flushed, a warm glow in her golden skin, and Hannah blinked at Tia, as if she didn't quite understand what was being asked for her. Whatever storytelling spell Tia had woven, its effects lingered for a few more seconds, sending shivers down Sophie's spine. 'What scandalous college stories do you have? There have got to be some.'

Hannah was first, then Meera. College life, undergraduate pranks, broken hearts, the time someone's car ended up in the lake… Nothing as strange and intriguing as the stories Tia had told. How could they be? Sophie watched her carefully, the beautiful archivist clearly enjoying listening as much as she had enjoyed speaking, her face animated and alive, her laugh infectious. It was as if she thrived on the stories the girls told, lived for them.

Sophie glanced up as Will returned, a guarded expression on his face. He set down the drinks he had been buying and gave her a rueful smile, but said nothing to interrupt Hannah's tale about a fancy dress ball one summer evening where someone had pretended to be someone else's boyfriend and everything had gone to hell. He sat beside her and Sophie tried to shake the thought of him as the guardian of the library. Tia might tease him about it, but it kind of fitted as well.

'Sophie?' Tia's voice called her attention back to the conversation. 'Your turn.'

Before Sophie knew what was happening she was telling stories about the Academy, and about college. Even a story or two about the last couple of years she spent in boarding school. Nothing earlier. Nothing relating to her parents. Because she couldn't. She knew she spoke haltingly, her own shyness making her feel awkward. But she tried nonetheless, not wanting to be the outsider here, needing to be part of this group.

Tia launched into a long, convoluted tale about a book that a knight wanted to buy from a local lady landowner who had some pretty unusual demands by way of payment. It was bawdy and medieval, and soon all of them were laughing together.

When Tia went to buy another round Sophie realised she was reaching her limit, but she nestled back in her seat, free to look around the pub, watch the world and not feel obliged to force herself to perform. It was busy, but then Friday nights usually were the night people went out, weren't they? There were some old men sitting nearer to the fire, silent and content. On the other side of the main room, clustered around the bar, was a group of young women who celebrating something, loud and giddy. They kept eyeing Will, who looked anywhere but at them. He seemed so uncomfortable that Sophie wanted to reach out and take his hand to comfort him, and perhaps even to warn them off. She'd never do it though. The urge shocked her. She wanted to protect him.

Realising that staring at him herself wasn't going to help either, Sophie looked away, studying the people in the pub again, the old men, the young women, the barman…

And over there, buying a vodka and tonic, she saw a tall man in a suit and an expensive shirt, his hair styled in exactly the same way Victor preferred. His back was turned to them, but the resemblance was uncanny. He took his order and left for a snug in the corner where someone else was sitting, waiting for him.

Sophie's whole body went cold. She stared. It couldn't be him. He couldn't be here. A ripple spread over her skin, a sense of alarm and fear. Tia arrived back, clattering a tray of shots onto the table, and blocked her view.

'Are you okay, Sophie?' Will asked.

'I just thought I... I saw someone, over there...'

'Who?' The tone of his voice changed, like he knew who it was. But she hadn't talked to him about Victor. She hadn't told any of them. 'Is that Arthur?'

'It is!' Tia exclaimed. 'Wonders will never cease. What's he doing here? Far too lowbrow for him, surely. They can't possibly have enough varieties of champagne for a Dee here.'

It was him, though. Arthur Dee sat in the snug, staring at them as if they had just walked in on him rifling through the petty cash box. And the man with the vodka and tonic was making right for him. Victor's drink. Victor's walk.

Slowly, grudgingly, Arthur lifted a hand and waved at them. Or more specifically, she felt, at her. The air seemed to twist and warp around them, suddenly cold, then warm again.

The other man turned to look.

It wasn't Victor. It was someone else. He didn't actually look like Victor at all.

Sophie's stomach lurched as if she was about to throw up.

'Excuse me.' She pushed her way out of the seat. She picked out the sign for the toilets and fled, wondering if they were all staring after her or if they didn't notice at all, with the spectacle of Arthur Dee in the pub to entertain them.

No, that wasn't fair. She glanced back and Will was still watching her, a look of concern on his handsome face. He glanced towards where his brother was sitting and the shadow in his face was back, darkening his green eyes.

The large bathroom area was accessed via a corridor off the main room, about as far from the snug as she could be. The lights inside were brighter and, as she glanced in the mirror, Sophie saw her own face, washed out and pale. A shadow of herself.

She sat in the tiny cubicle and forced herself to breathe, and to bring her nausea under control. She had sensed something, she was certain of it, something in the air right after Arthur waved. And for a moment she had been absolutely certain that man was Victor. But he couldn't be. Was this what was going to happen now? Would she see him everywhere? Live a life haunted by him? No. She was not going to do that. She refused. She could make her life her own again.

Her churning stomach almost revolted at the thought. She stayed there for another five minutes, counting to herself, making herself breathe, trying to bring some form of equilibrium to her life. Finally, finally, she felt like herself again.

Sophie washed her hands with her usual meticulous attention, avoiding eye contact with her own reflection.

'Sophie?' Tia's voice pulled her out of her contemplation and the door banged shut behind her. 'You okay? You look like you've seen a ghost.'

'I'm okay. Sorry. I just…'

'Worse, was it an ex?'

The flush of shame made her face heat. 'Yes. I mean, it wasn't him. It just…'

'Oh, you poor love,' Tia said and hugged her, a huge expansive gesture that should have had her squirming and trying to get away. If anyone else had tried it, she would have. But somehow, with Tia, it was so genuine and heartfelt, she couldn't help but accept it. Besides, it was a comfort. 'Was he a bastard? I bet he was a bastard. Has to have been to have you in this state.'

Sophie was about to answer, when three of the women from the bar spilled by her in a rush of raucous laughter.

'He's well fit, isn't he?'

'Way out of your league.'

'No he isn't!'

'Well go and talk to him then. He's just sitting there. His mates have all— oh!' They saw Sophie and Tia and collapsed into helpless laughter. They almost fell into the cubicles, slamming the doors behind them.

Tia pulled back, taking Sophie's arm in hers and drawing her away from them. 'Come on, we'd better extract Will before they come back and make a move.'

'They're talking about Will?'

'Well, of course they are. Who else? Happens every bloody time. It's like he has special pheromones or something, poor sod.' Still Sophie hesitated. She didn't want to go back out there. 'Come with me, there's a shot with your name on it.'

'I'm okay. I think I've had enough for one night.'

'Oh god, was it Arthur? Don't mind him. He's just pissed off we're intruding on his whatever it is.'

She allowed Tia to draw her back out to the bar. Better that than listen to the giggling and suggestive, not-terribly-quiet whispers about Will happening in the toilets right now.

'Do you think he's on a date?' Sophie asked.

'Not him. Straight as the poker up his own arse, that one. And a bit of a prude if I'm honest. No, he's probably just meeting a mate or something. Who knew Arthur had mates outside of London?'

But Arthur and his friend had gone, moved elsewhere, out of sight. Sophie could breathe once more.

Will stood up as they got back, his face coloured with concern. 'Are you okay?'

Sophie tried to smile. 'Yeah, sorry. Just needed some air.'

Behind them the gaggle of girls re-emerged, and locked eyes on him standing there. To Sophie's amazement, Will seemed to shrink in on himself and she felt instantly sorry for him again.

No one needed to be objectified like that.

'I think maybe I should head back,' she said. 'Sorry... I just...'

He seized the opportunity she was offering.

'I'll walk back with you,' Will said softly and held out her coat for her.

*

The library sat still and dark beneath the full moon. A single light was on over a side door. Everything else seemed silent, closed. Will fished out his key and unlocked the small red door. The light above picked him out of the darkness, his breath misting in front of him. He seemed to unwind as he stepped inside and flicked on the light, his shoulders softening beneath his jacket, the tension she had seen in him draining away since they left the pub.

Had it just been the girls ogling him that had soured his mood? Or seeing his half-brother there? Or something else?

They hadn't spoken the whole way back. Not deliberately. At first she kept checking behind her, to see if there was anyone following them. There wasn't. She knew that really. And it hadn't even been Victor. It *hadn't*. She knew that too. The sensation of dread just wouldn't go away.

'Are you okay?' Will asked.

She stood outside in the darkness, staring in at him. Standing there, in the boot room that led to the kitchen, back in his library, he finally looked comfortably at home in a way he hadn't since… actually, for all the conversation and cheer, he hadn't looked comfortable for the whole evening. Perhaps he had just been expecting something to happen, if, as Tia said, it invariably did.

Well he was handsome. Unbearably handsome. He always had been, but the beauty of his teenage years had matured to so much more. Like something from Greek legends. How ridiculous to find someone like that working here, in a specialist library in the middle of nowhere.

The cat appeared, Titivillus stalking across the tiled floor of the kitchen and then stretching out like a long black line of ink at Will's feet.

Will bent down, lowering his hand, and the cat lifted himself, pushing his head into the librarian's palm. The rumbling purr was cut with a meow that sounded like a question. Will laughed softly, under his breath, and she wondered if the cat had said something in a language only the two of them understood.

His cat. She realised that now. Couldn't doubt it. She should have seen it all along. Titivillus adored him. The cat merely tolerated anyone else.

The light around Will warmed, embracing him, and he in turn seemed to fuel it, turning it to gold. But there was something else, something about the way he was standing, the way the light hit him.

'Will? How did you come to live here when we were kids?'

He smiled at her, that devastating, brilliant smile. 'Family,' he replied. 'You know how that goes. Legacies. Come on inside. It's freezing. You're letting all the heat out.'

Sophie relented, even though she knew he hadn't answered her question. Nor would he. She understood that now, and why. They walked through the kitchen and the lounge, out to the main hallway and the stairs.

'Do you remember when we snuck out, that last summer?' he asked softly.

And like that, suddenly, she did remember. The heat of the night. Their giggles. Her own unwavering confidence.

'We went to the village. You were convinced you could snag some beer off someone. Arthur ended up buying it. It was foul.'

'Do you remember afterwards?'

She couldn't forget it. Never could. He'd been so nervous when he'd kissed her that she hadn't realised what was happening at first. They had spent the rest of the night talking, as well as some more kissing. A lot more. It hadn't gone further but her father had been furious when they finally got back around four a.m. He'd waited up all night.

No one had been waiting for Will, had they?

'I remember the shouting,' she admitted.

'Before that,' Will said and stepped a little closer. She didn't retreat, not this time. She could feel the heat from his body, the warmth of him, emanating out to her. His scent made her head spin and suddenly she was fifteen again and he was everything. Absolutely everything.

It's like he has special pheromones or something, poor sod.

Maybe Tia was right.

Will lifted one hand to her face, tracing a finger along the line of her jaw, and Sophie felt her lips part for him. She wanted him, everything he had to give her. And she didn't care about consequences or anything else. Just him. She felt drunk on him.

'Sophie, I missed you.'

Just like that. So easy an admission. Her eyes burned.

'I missed you too. I always did.'

His lips brushed against hers and a shiver of desire went through her like electricity. It stole her breath, made her gasp for air. He gave a soft groan, a noise of need and surrender, and suddenly he was holding her against him. Sophie sank her hands into his hair, pulling him closer, lost in him.

For the longest while he was all she knew and all she wanted to know. Eventually, Will was the one to pull back, out of breath, his green eyes dark with longing.

'Sophie, I…'

She tried to calm her breathing. Her lips tingled and all she wanted to do was pull him back to her again. 'I'm sorry. I shouldn't have…' What was she doing? What was she thinking?

'No.' He laughed softly, a sound that did interesting things to her insides. 'It's wonderful. You're wonderful. And I want nothing more than to keep kissing you, and more. So much more. But maybe we should take it slowly. I don't want to rush you. I know things have been… rough, haven't they? Why don't we try a date? Just the two of us?'

He was right. She knew he was right. But she didn't want logic right now. She hadn't felt like this since…

She had *never* felt like this.

'I'd like that. I'd like it very much.' And even though there were a lot of other things she would like at this moment. She had just left a terrible, manipulative relationship. She couldn't just plunge into this. She needed to be careful.

'Well then.' He kissed her again. Gentler this time, but just as passionate. The same longing surged up within her and she was lost. Lost in him. When he pulled back again, he sighed, resting his forehead against hers and closing his eyes. As if, should he look at her, he wouldn't be able to pull away again. She thought of those paintings of martyrs, of the suffering of saints, doing something they dreaded for a higher cause. 'Will we say goodnight? And talk about this in the morning? I have a couple of things to do down here. Besides, if I follow you up there I won't want to leave.'

It took everything she had to walk away.

She glanced down the stairs and her last glimpse of him was of a man standing in the middle of the ornate Rotunda with the little black cat weaving between his legs. He gazed up at her, thoughtful now, but he was smiling, such a fond and loving smile. It made her treacherous heart speed up again.

Chapter Fifteen

Sophie woke in the night to a song. It rang through the air, trembled through the walls of the library building, made the floorboards shiver with its haunting rhythm. At first she was sure she was still dreaming, she had to be. Reaching for her phone she checked the time… three a.m. And still the song went on, just on the edge of hearing.

Around her neck, her mother's pendant felt warm, tingling against her skin. She slipped out of her bed.

The whole place was deserted, silent. She opened the door but the music was still just out of reach.

And at the end of the corridor she saw the figure, just as she had in her dream. It was indistinct, and she wouldn't have sworn to it in the light of day, but she was sure it was her mother.

A dream. Or a memory. But it wasn't a dream this time.

Elizabeth beckoned her forwards and began to descend the stairs. Sophie followed, leaving her room, only half sure she was doing so of her own volition.

Outside, the corridor lay in darkness but at the far end she saw the stained glass alive with light. Sophie frowned. She had dreamed this, countless times. Most recently on her first night here.

The library was calling her, summoning her. In this half-waking state, she had to know, had to find out what had happened.

Sophie felt the tug within her chest, the vibration lurching forward. Like the sleepwalker she sometimes was, she allowed the sensation to guide her. It almost felt like a hook buried deep inside her, drawing her forward, something far off and unknowable reeling her in.

The images in the stained-glass windows moved and glowed, alive and vibrant, even though there was no light falling on them. It was like watching a film from underwater, the distortions in the ancient glazing rippling. She saw a tower rising out of a rocky landscape, figures moving towards it, and she could hear them whisper. Faces pressed up against the glass straining to get out, but she couldn't have reached them even if she stood up against it. She knew she wasn't looking at something from her own world, but from somewhere else.

Carefully, she walked forwards, the song that vibrated through the whole building guiding her now. She descended the stairs, into the darkness below.

At the foot of the stairs, the cat was waiting, curled up on a chair near the display case holding the Mortlake grimoire. The book added its own whispers and enticements, but the library was more powerful now. She knew where it wanted her to go.

Titivillus opened his green eyes, the only indication she had that he wasn't just another patch of shadows. As she approached, the hum that hovered beneath her skin rippled with a new tone and he uncoiled himself, slipping down to the ground and padding silently towards her. When she stopped, he rubbed against her leg, coming up on his hind legs to reach her hand. He was silky and warm, his purrs almost drowning out the music for a moment.

She remembered… long ago, the cat slept at the foot of her bed. She'd had a cold or possibly the flu. She'd lain there weak and shivering and Titivillus had curled up beside her, purring like an engine, watching over her until she got better. How was that possible? Cats didn't live that long, and he didn't act like an old cat.

'Hello, Villus,' she murmured. She half expected a reply. It was that kind of situation, where she wandered around in the darkness, led by silent music, and cats spoke to her in English.

Thankfully nothing like that happened. Or perhaps it would have been better if it did. Then she would have known it was a dream.

The thought made her pause. It made sense, didn't it? That this was another dream. Maybe she wasn't awake at all.

Villus trotted away from her and stopped at the door into the Reading Room. He stood there, waiting for her, and when she didn't move, he came up on his hind legs again, his front paws pressing to the wood. The meow was plaintive, insistent.

'It's locked,' she told him. 'I don't have the key. I'm sorry.'

She pressed her hand to the closed door. And then she heard it.

'*It's okay, love. I'm here, I'll deal with it, Sophie. I need you to be strong now. For me.*' Her mother's voice, soft but stressed, cut by the sound of a storm, trying so hard to be strong, to be calm while the world tore itself apart around them. Sophie could hear branches cracking, leaves tearing through the air. She could smell the fire as it consumed everything.

Sophie snatched her hand back in alarm and instantly all was still again. The library was silent. The cat watched her. She could hear her own breath, her own heartbeat.

And then the music swept through her again. A dream. It had to be a dream.

But since this was a dream…

She pushed the door and it opened for her.

The Reading Room was empty as well, and all along the walls, above the reference bookshelves, the carvings flowed with life, creatures tumbling over foliage, branches and each other as they followed her path across the silent room, her footsteps the only sound, echoing around her.

She reached the door to the Great Hall of the library, the one marked 'Staff Only'. This time when she reached out to touch it, sure it would be locked, her hand trembled. The wood was cool and smooth, but inside it she could feel something reverberating. It felt like life itself.

And there were voices.

'You were born for this, Soph. I know you can do it. Go on, I dare you.' A young man's voice, one she knew but at the same time didn't know. Not any more.

'We shouldn't,' said another. Will's voice this time. How could she ever have forgotten Will's voice?

'Scared of getting caught?'

'No, it's just… it's the Axis Mundi. The Keeper said—'

'I don't care what the Keeper said. We were born for this, Will, the three of us. We can wake it. We can control it. This is all going to be ours one day. Why wait? Why not now?'

'I'll do it,' Sophie said. Not Sophie now, but another Sophie. Another person in another life. A fifteen-year-old girl who had no conception of the cost involved. Her older, battered heart hammered in her chest as she heard the stupid bravado, the reckless self-confidence, and even though the blank space in her mind was just as complete, Sophie felt the sickening dread gnawing inside her. *Don't do it*, she wanted to shout. *Don't*.

But she didn't even know what *it* was. Just that the cost would be far too great. It still was. She would never finish paying for it.

Sophie swallowed hard. This was the past. She was hearing the voices of the past, of a time she couldn't remember any more. Her own past. It was happening just on the other side of that door, an echo, a ghost.

She shoved the door with all her might. The library opened up to her. But there was no one there. No one at all.

As she entered Sophie heard murmured sighs, whispers, the rustling of paper, the library itself awakening all around her. It was like standing in a vast cavern home to a colony of bats. Alive and watching, restless, intrigued.

Her every step was marked.

Was it a dream? It felt dreamlike. And yet, Sophie knew she wasn't asleep. This felt nothing like sleepwalking. She was aware of everything, every breath, every heartbeat. She made herself keep moving. The enormity of this place rose in the back of her mind like a wave. Magic, endless, ageless… But the song was still in there too, stronger than ever, the books assembled here adding their harmonies to the chorus. They drew her on, called her forwards. And she could do nothing but keep going, keep following, keep walking.

Step after step, she made her way to the centre of the library, beneath the glorious fresco of the tree. In the middle of the library, the opening like a gaping wound in the polished floorboards, a spiral staircase led down into darkness.

From the shadows other pieces of her history here filtered through to her.

'*I love you,*' Will whispered. '*I will always love you. No matter what. I promise.*'

Not Will now. This was Will of fifteen years ago, Will of that fateful, beautiful summer. He whispered the words and his breath played on her face. But when she glanced over her shoulder he wasn't there. No one was.

There was no gate, nothing to bar her way. She stood at the precipice, looking down, a vertigo-inducing drop into nothing, as far as she could see. The tug in her heart was more insistent now, more desperate, the music almost maddening. The metal rail warmed against her skin, vibrating, and she knew she had to keep going.

Dream or not, this was a mystery she needed to solve. There was something down there she needed to see, something calling to her. It had been from the moment she had set foot back in the Special Collection.

The song surrounded her, the murmuring of the library insistent, and her foot took the first step on the stairs.

But she knew it wasn't a dream. It was the library calling her, its magic driving her, making her attempt this descent.

The stairs wound steeply down, turning around and around four or five times. She saw doors off on each level and she stopped on the first floor of the vaults, as voices shouted from behind a closed door.

'*This is madness, Elizabeth. You don't know what you're doing.*' It was Edward, her uncle, shouting at his sister.

But her mother didn't shout back. Her voice was reasoned calm, insistent and unswerving in her intent.

'*It's the only way. If he's to survive, we have to do this. Two parts, two lives, and a guardian to protect this place. Otherwise who knows what will happen.*'

'*You're risking too much.*'

'*It's mine to risk.*'

'*What about Sophie? What about your husband? What about Tia?*'

'*Edward, put your own feelings aside. We can't leave him like this. It isn't fair. Not to anyone. No matter what else, he's just a child. We can't abandon him to this. It's our duty. Now help me. Or get out of my way.*'

Sophie pressed her hand to the door. Her mother, magnificent, determined, a force of nature… The door opened but, once again, there was no one there. Just a dark room with shelves stretching back, holding who knew what books, and countless memories.

What had they done, her uncle and her mother? Who were they talking about?

The library wanted her to go deeper, right to the bottom, and she knew she had to follow. Not that she could say why. The song was powerful and the fragments of memories led the way. Not her memories, not now. This was something else.

Was it an enchantment? Were such things real?

How could she doubt it right now, following a feeling, listening to the music of the library?

She paused at another door, hearing laughter, joy, two people in love. '*I'd do anything for you Elizabeth. You know that. Anything.*' It sounded like another version of her father, a version who didn't know pain and madness, hadn't lived a life of bitterness and regret.

Down another level, another door. And this was a voice she didn't know, couldn't hope to know. An earlier time. '*We can turn the tide of this war and you know it. You can't keep these secrets locked away here, not when they can serve King and Country. Damn it, Talbot, this is our duty.*'

Door after door. She heard sounds of the building, the creation of the very vaults through which she descended. Her hand pressed against countless doors, and the memories that permeated the whole building spilled out their history to her. Not enough so that she could understand everything. Just soundbites, fragments of the past, like her own scattered recollections.

The sound of a fire, people screaming, running, great buildings collapsing in ruin and destruction.

A man sobbed, as clearly as if he sat on the other side of the wooden panel from her, his head banging against it as he threw it back in despair. '*Damn it all, Elias. It should have been a simple enough affair, just moving the damn Tree. Why did it come to this? Why?*'

She was almost halfway down the stairwell. Names screamed through the air. She didn't even have to touch the doors now, just follow the song and let it harmonise with these sounds of the library's past. She could sense the heat of fire, or of sun, she could smell river water, feel the frustrations and terror of those who lived here, the wonder as well. A thousand lives, thousands of years.

It wasn't just here in Ayredale. It was everywhere. The heat of the desert sun, the cold of an arctic waste. The stench of blood and death. She heard laughter, wild and insane, and the crazed ramblings of madmen, listing out spells and incantations. Sobs and cries, the sting of death and remorse. Endless lives all tangled up in the song of the library.

She followed the stairs all the way down until there was nowhere left to go. She stood at the bottom of a well without water, in the heart of the library. The floor beneath her feet felt ancient, some kind of mosaic in tiny cream and terracotta tiles. Behind her, the metal staircase rose like a spiral of smoke into the night, and in front of her there was another door. Just one.

It was made of an old silvery wood, one she didn't recognise, heavy and ancient, the hinges made of wrought iron which curved in extravagant patterns, reaching across it like branches. The black handle and lock seemed to drink in the light, blotting it out forever. It had the soft curve of a Romanesque arch, and when she touched it, the wood felt warm, alive. The metal on the other hand sucked the heat from her skin. She snatched her fingers back as the kiss of it turned to pain.

There was a symbol in the middle inlaid with gold of that rich, buttery tone she knew so well. The pendant hummed against her skin, the shape matching it exactly, a leaf or a feather, something else instead, something lost so long ago. Sophie closed her hand around it, feeling its familiarity, staring at the image replicated here on the pale wood. Sunbleached in the darkness. Impossible.

Inevitably, as if by its own will, her hand reached out for the door. And she heard a voice. The words were as old as time.

'*O divina numen, splendida, lucidissima stellarum...*'

Sophie sucked in a breath and her head fell back as something swept through her, something new and powerful, far greater than she would ever be. The urge to give everything she was to it, to surrender completely to the power behind it, was too great to resist. There was no fear in this, only desire, only joy.

O divine Goddess, most wondrous, brightest star in the heavens...

There was a goddess, Will had said.

She was chaos and wildness, and all the madness of creation. But she knew that creativity, thought and invention need order and stability which she couldn't provide. So she sacrificed her power to give mankind that opportunity, and created the library.

The force behind the door was endless, wondrous. That was what she could feel. All the madness of creation.

Sophie couldn't help herself. She pushed at the door and felt it begin to give.

A grip like iron closed on her wrist, dragging her away. The light snapped off, the song fell abruptly silent, and shadows swallowed her up.

'What the hell do you think you're doing?' Will growled, and his green eyes blazed in the darkness.

Chapter Sixteen

Will towered over her, shadows wreathing his whole body, and his hand tightened like a vice. Sophie opened her mouth but no voice came out of it. She could barely manage a gasp.

He kept his grip on her wrist, holding her away from the door.

'Sophie.' He couldn't keep the fury from his voice. 'What are you doing down here?'

'I don't... I don't know...' She tried to tug away from him but she wasn't strong enough to break free.

'Only a Keeper can access that room. It's forbidden. Completely forbidden. Don't you remember that at least? You can't have forgotten what happened when—'

'Let her go, Will.' Arthur descended the stairs. 'You're hurting her. Scaring her.'

Will's head snapped around to face him, but he didn't let Sophie go. He bared his teeth like an animal.

'What are you doing here?' Will snapped at his half-brother.

'I'm on duty tonight.'

'Then why were you in the bloody pub earlier?'

Arthur gave him a flat glare. His voice was quiet and calm, focused. 'Let the girl go, William.'

'Please,' Sophie whispered, her voice very small, still trying to pull free of him. He turned again, as if ready to kill her there and then. And whatever he saw in her face struck him like a physical blow. She saw it ripple over his handsome features, horror and revulsion.

He released her as if her touch scalded him, his voice and his glare abruptly softening with shame.

'Sophie,' he said and trailed off, as if he didn't even know what to say to her. She shrank back from him, retreating towards Arthur. His brother opened his arms and ushered her behind him while Will stood between them and the door. He sank back, blocking the approach.

Only hours ago he had been kissing her.

Arthur pushed Sophie further behind him, back up the stairs. He tensed all over, ready to run or fight.

'You aren't thinking, Will. Just letting the old instincts take over again. If Sophie found her way down here, she was called. You know how this works. It wants her down here. Now step aside.'

Called? What did he mean 'called'? Sophie didn't know and she didn't dare ask right now.

'I can't do that. You remember what happened before. We were almost killed. We lost Elizabeth.'

'Wait, *what*?' Sophie gasped, finally finding her voice again.

'In there,' said Arthur. 'Something wiped it from your mind, I see that. But she came in after us and—'

'You ran,' Will yelled at him. 'You persuaded us to come down here, persuaded Sophie to try to wake it, for the gods know whatever reason of your own, and then you ran.'

We were born for this, Will, the three of us. We can wake it. We can control it. This is all going to be ours one day. Why wait? Why not now?

That was what she had heard – Arthur's voice. All those years ago. Down here, at this door. *Why not now?*

Arthur shrugged. 'You agreed. You both agreed. And I was right, wasn't I? Come on, Will. You know I'm right.'

'You can't make her,' he growled.

But his brother spread his arms wide again, a barrier, a shield. 'I would never do that, and you know it. It's Sophie's decision. It always had been. Tell him, Sophie. He'll listen to you. Tell him to stand aside and let you through. Well?'

'We were here and my mother came after us? And… what happened to her, Arthur?'

'Don't you want to find out?' he asked, his voice rippling with invitation. 'They'll never tell you – your uncle, the Professor. They don't want the secret getting out. But you can find out, Sophie. Here and now. Behind that door.'

She didn't know where the strength came from but she stepped out from behind Arthur and advanced on Will. For a moment he seemed determined to block her way, to keep her from entering. And part of her wanted him to.

Her heart hammered at the inside of her ribs, ready to shatter them, and her throat squeezed itself tight around what little air she still had in her straining lungs. The song was back. It pounded through the ground, reverberating up through her body, surging with her blood.

'Will?' she said, amazed that the voice which emerged, so sure, so certain, was really hers. 'Let me in.'

He froze there, indecision making the years fall away. She saw the boy she had loved, who had tried to stop her before, who had tried to help her. She reached out her hand and he took it, his fingers threading between hers, shaking now.

She squeezed his hand, begging him silently to trust her, even if she wasn't sure it would do any good. It didn't matter, not now, not when she could finally discover the truth.

She released him and at the same moment Arthur's hand closed on Will's shoulder. Something changed in the air, something like electricity and the smell of old ashes. Will's eyes went wide for a moment, focused on her in betrayal.

Then he slumped down, dropping to the ground at her feet.

'What have you done?' she asked. 'What was that?'

Arthur smiled. 'Oh that? Art. That's what we call it. Everyone else just says magic.' He shook his hand as if ridding himself of cobwebs. 'He'll be fine. Just sleeping. We don't need him right now. He'll only get in the way. He's a crappy guardian anyway. Open the door, Sophie. Let's find out together.'

'But Will—'

Arthur shook his head and grabbed her shoulder, spinning her around. Before she knew what was happening he seized her hand and shoved it onto the wood of the door.

The door opened. Sophie sucked in a breath as the air within swept out carrying the scent of earth, rich with peat, foliage and water, sweet forest scents that stirred a thousand memories she didn't know she had.

Sophie froze, indecision making her unable to move one way or the other. But the same tug in her chest pulled her, dragging her onwards, and she took the steps she suddenly wasn't sure she wanted to take. Reality rippled over her, the air changing, as if she was passing through something invisible. Into another place, another time.

In the room beyond there grew an immense tree, exactly like the one in the garden. And at the same time not. Nothing so mundane as that.

Its branches soared overhead, the leaves golden and glittering. The silver paper-like bark peeled in places from the slender trunk, far too slender to support something that size. Its branches curved like a work of art.

How was this possible? It didn't make any sense. How was this here? Under the library? Or maybe… maybe she wasn't under the library any more.

The music came from the tree. From the golden leaves. It came from the roots beneath them.

This was the tree from her many dreams. Since she was a child, all those dreams she had been told were not real, all those images she had been told to disregard.

Sophie gasped, unable to keep the air in her body any more. It escaped in a wild rush, and the leaves shimmered, shaking above her in response.

All around the base of the Tree another garden spread out, nurturing it, cradling it. A stream ran through the centre, and she could see fish in the water, leaping, darting around. Where it came from or where it went, she didn't know. There was no sunlight here, only the light that radiated from the Tree. She looked up but couldn't make out any sky or ceiling through the branches and golden leaves.

'The heart of the library,' said Arthur, exaltation in his voice. 'It has many names, the Axis Mundi, the Between World, the Thin Place. It is where the divine and the mundane meet, where if we are lucky we can catch a glimpse of God. Each of our souls reflects a facet of it. You know this. You are part of it, Sophie. Just as your mother was. And this is the Tree that grows in its heart.'

Sophie struggled to find words, any words. The scene before her just seemed to swallow them up before she could say them.

'It's the tree from the garden up above us,' she managed at last, and instantly regretted it. What a stupid thing to say. It was clearly not the tree from the garden. It was so much more. It glowed with life, with everything. It made the air around them tremble with expectation.

'Well.' He smiled a slow, self-satisfied smile. She didn't like the expression. It was snide and cunning. It harboured so many secrets and she was sure he was making fun of her, if only for his own benefit. '"As above so below", as they say. But it is not that tree. Not exactly. Fairer to say that mundane little sapling is a reflection of this one.'

'I… I don't understand. The Thin Place? The Between World? What *is* it?' she asked.

'The Tree of Knowledge, of course.' Arthur cursed softly and shook his head, gazing at her as if she was an idiot and he was forced to use very simple words. 'This is the very Tree from which Eve ate the fruit, from which Odin hung, from which… Did he really teach you nothing at all?'

She frowned, suddenly defensive. 'He?'

'Your father. Why was that, do you think?'

What was he implying? Her father hadn't told her about the library because it broke his heart to think of it. Every single time. Because it had taken everything from him. Because it was dangerous. Was it this place? Had the Tree somehow taken her mother?

'My father was trying to protect me.'

'Was he?'

The way he twisted everything into a question made her grit her teeth together. How dare he imply anything else?

Thinking of her father, she stood beneath the library, down in its deepest place, in its heart, beneath the spreading boughs of a vast tree with leaves of gold. A tree she had thought existed only in her own imaginings. One her father had always refused to speak about.

'Is this real?' she asked.

'Of course it is,' said Arthur.

She stood her ground, strangely calm.

'I want to know what happened to my mother.'

'*This* is what happened. This place. The magic that surrounds it, permeates it. It sucked her in, devoured her, made her part of it. Look at it. Isn't it beautiful, Sophie?'

He looked like a child at Christmas.

And it was beautiful. More than beautiful. It was beautiful and terrible, and it had taken her mother from her. It had taken everything from her. There was so much power here. One false step and it would swallow her whole. Just as it had her mother. And it had been her fault. That thought was like a spear of ice through her, a line of agony she wasn't ready to confront. Not yet.

What could she do? Turning and running away was always an option, she supposed. It felt like something the old Sophie would do. And she didn't want Arthur to have the satisfaction if she did. It would prove to him that she was a silly little girl, scared of anything unusual, sheltered and cosseted and… And she wasn't sure she'd be able to anyway. Something had drawn her, and was holding her here. And it wasn't Arthur Dee.

That same something swept over her again, and she caught a sense of the stained glass and the angels moving in it, the song that had called her down here, and the movement in the walls and the carvings, the way the building lived and breathed… all the sighs, whispers and murmurings she'd heard in the library since she came back.

Sophie sank to the ground, kneeling in the soft dark earth. With her palms pressed on the flat rock at the base of the tree, she could feel the vibrations deep within it now, slow and steady, like a resting heartbeat. The roots of the Tree tangled around the stone, as if at any moment they would crush it to dust, and plunged into the earth around it. The whole place was alive with an otherworldly vibration, even the air around her.

It was trying to talk to her. Not talk exactly. Sing. Commune.

'Sophie?' Arthur's voice sounded so very far away. 'What are you doing?'

She didn't know. She didn't care. It was all too much. And somewhere in here, somewhere she could hear a voice calling to her, reaching for her, trying to warn her.

'*I need you to be strong now. For me.*' A force gripped her, rippling over her and forcing Sophie's gaze up to the Tree. A thousand new questions drifted out of her consciousness before she could ask them. The Tree reflected in the water below her, its leaves glowing, the light in them turning incandescent, lines tracing through them, burning. A host of voices rose up around her, a chorus of singing and crying, screaming, all in a wave of sound and nightmares.

She couldn't help herself. Lost in the maelstrom below her and around her, she felt everything she was sweep away.

'*It's the language of the birds. The Tree will tell me…*'

Words flared up in the back of her mind and, unable to stop herself, she spoke them out loud.

Chapter Seventeen

Will lay in darkness, dust in his mouth and nose. When he tried to breathe it was a great agonised gasp, as if he had never drawn breath before. He opened his eyes, and the cat stared back at him. Titivillus. Just a misty image of the cat, but one that was gradually becoming more real right before his eyes.

'You will go ahead to save your comrade.'

The voice sounded like Edward's – not Edward now but Edward long ago. A bell rang and he said something else. The words he spoke weren't English. They hadn't been spoken in thousands of years. The air shivered at the sound of them, and so did Will.

'You know the way to protect your friend.' It was Tia. She sounded the same, but then, she always did. He knew these words. Dreaded them. They gave him nightmares. When she had told the story of the guardian in the pub, it had been all he could do not to run out the door. No one else would have known what they meant. But this was long ago…

Another bell sounded.

'You will take the road to guard the Tree.' A third voice. Elizabeth. Unmistakably Elizabeth… But Elizabeth was gone. Years gone.

A candle flared into life and he could see them, the three of them. Elizabeth and Edward were young, younger than he and Sophie were now. Tia looked the same. She always looked the same. They stood around him, towering over him, and their eyes were full of pity.

'And now we draw you back,' Elizabeth went on, clearly the one leading this bizarre ceremony. 'I take you and I bind you. I fix you here and sever you from the power within you. I bid you be our protector, our faithful sword, two parts, two lives, and a guardian to protect this place.'

Titivillus blinked at him, the green eyes so bright, so much like his own, but not his own. They knew each other. More than that…

Will reached to the shadows within him. Normally as familiar and easy to summon as breathing. But now they eluded him.

He cried out, a child's voice. 'No, you can't do this to me. No, no, no…' But it was already too late. The connection, the feral power inside him was gone.

'It's for the best, my pet,' said Tia and her voice cut with sobs. 'I promise. It's for the best.'

The sense of loathing, of wild rage, of despair that welled up inside him made him scream. But there was nothing he could do now. He was just a child.

'Wake up, Will,' Elizabeth whispered. Not then. Now. Whenever and wherever now was. 'You need to wake up. You have a duty. You have a purpose.' But Elizabeth was gone.

The sound came from the walls and from the floor beneath him, a rippling hum which shook the air itself. A moment of pure chaos later, it shook itself into a melody, and from there into a massed choir of harmonies.

It was the Special Collection. He knew the sound from his dreams, from his waking hours, from the moments when he lost track of where he was, when he drifted into daydream. It was the library itself, and it was afraid.

The world around him seemed to break apart into a thousand pieces and then reform. He shook his head as the song rattled around inside his skull.

'Enough,' he hissed but the library wasn't listening to him. This was chaos unbound, ideas and rumours swirling, wild and untamed. For a

moment he felt like it would sweep him away entirely. 'Stop. I'm coming.'
The air around him vibrated in warning but the noise did, however,
quieten to a bearable level. 'What is it? What is happening?'

He heard a sound of leaves rustling, of branches creaking, and the
howl of wind, but that was all he needed. And the world around him
shifted, changed.

*

Everything was hard and cold beneath him, the air rumbling above him
like a volcano had erupted. His shoulder ached like it had been frozen.

He dragged his eyes open, the pain behind them reminding of
reality. He had come down here. He had seen Sophie, and Arthur.

Arthur had done this to him.

He could feel the library now, wondrous and terrible, all his nightmares and every desire he had ever experienced. Its music deafened
him, and colours blinded him. It was everything.

All at once.

It was Sophie. It had to be Sophie. He didn't know what she had
done or why, but it had to be Sophie. It was too much like what had
happened all those years ago. And that had almost ended in complete
disaster for them all.

They had lost Elizabeth. He wouldn't lose Sophie too.

Who else would cause something like this? Who else was innocent
enough to make something like this happen?

Something potentially this disastrous.

The wildness buried deep inside him tried to tear itself out and he
could barely keep it in check. The library was calling and the creature
in him wanted to respond. Rage made it worse. So did fear.

The door was closed.

Light poured through the cracks around it, bright and golden.

But it didn't open for him.

That had never happened before. Whatever had possessed the library, it didn't want Will in there, didn't want him interfering.

The sound grew louder, singing voices that could drive the sanest person to insanity.

Securing a lock was a simple enough Art. It was just persuading something inanimate that it couldn't move. Unlocking it, however, was a whole different problem.

The door was old wood, hard as iron and bound with iron. It was made to keep out invading armies, to stop those who would desecrate the most sacred of places. He couldn't get through. He would batter himself to death before that door gave in.

There was only one way then. He drew in a breath, his hands balling into fists at his side. He could do this, he had to do this. If Sophie was in there, he didn't have a choice. The havoc that could be unleashed was unimaginable. All he had to do was let go. Let it out.

He closed his eyes and felt the darkness inside him begin to unfurl.

'Will,' said another voice from the shadows. 'Stop.'

'Tia?'

She stepped out of the darkness, her long hair loose like blood on either side of her pale face. 'Let me,' she whispered. Her voice was as strained as the lines around her eyes.

He stopped, placing himself between her and the door. She had always been there for him. But right now, that probably meant nothing. He'd failed to stop Sophie. He couldn't afford to let Tia in there too.

'I can't. You know that.'

Did she though? Tia had that wild look in her eyes, that dark and dangerous look. 'I won't go in,' she told him solemnly. 'But it will open to me. Arthur has locked it against you. Nothing can lock it against me. Not if I command it.'

'But you can't command it, Tia. Not any more.'

Her smile drew itself across her face like the blade of a knife. 'Can't I? Once I could tear the whole Axis apart if I wanted to, you know that. Just by setting foot in there.'

'Sophie's in there.'

At her name the smile faltered. 'With Arthur?'

'Yes.' He didn't have time for this. Sophie didn't have time. He needed to get in there. He needed to stop her before it went too far. Before—

'Of course. The scheming little bastard. Does Sophie know what it is? Does she know anything?' The fierce light in Tia seemed to falter. Will shook his head and suddenly Tia seemed more herself again. 'She doesn't remember anything. Not what happened fifteen years ago. Not what happened to her mother.'

She sighed and shook her head. 'You like her, don't you?' Her voice was little more than a whisper. 'You like her far more than you should. She calls to you, in the same way the Tree calls to her. Don't you know how dangerous it is? She's in there right now, ready to tear our world to pieces because of her ignorance. If you can't stop her… What will you do then?'

'I don't know.' It was the only answer he could give. 'Please, Tia…'

She nodded solemnly, and the wildness Will felt inside himself faded completely. 'Let me open the door. The rest will be up to you. I will not enter. I swear it on the library.'

What else could he do? He had to trust her. He didn't have anyone else except her and the Keeper. And maybe Sophie, if Sophie survived that long.

Will stepped aside and Tia walked forwards. She wore black, which made her look part shadow, only the blood red of her hair standing out in the blinding light ringing the door, pouring through the cracks at the edge.

With a slim arm, elegant as a dancer's, Tia reached out and pressed her hand to the wood, fingers splayed wide.

It felt like a concussion, a wave of nothing and everything. It burst from her palm and twisted the air around him. He could hear no sound. Instead it felt like the absence of sound, as if everything slowed to silence before a sonic boom that made no noise, or was beyond his mortal hearing.

He knew what Tia could do, or at least he had been told, warned, at length, in detail. He had only ever seen glimpses and, to be honest, he'd thought the wild stories were nothing more than exaggeration. This was beyond expectations.

The door opened as if wind had thrown it back and she stood there for a moment, staring in. Light drenched her face and she lifted her chin as if drinking it in.

As if longing for it.

And then, to Will's amazement and disbelief, she turned away. As he rushed by her he caught a glimpse of her stricken face, the pain etched into deep lines around her eyes and mouth which aged her beyond reckoning.

Inside, in the light, Sophie knelt beneath the Tree and golden leaves whirled around her, dazzling with their light. Everything else was cold and empty, a void of damp stone. A cell, a dungeon. The garden was gone, sucked into the vortex of the Tree.

It was worse than he had imagined. Far worse.

Will sprinted across the space, dodging the leaves which swarmed around him, desperate to escape their touch.

Arthur sprawled on the ground, stunned, entranced by what was happening around him. Will didn't give a damn about him. He'd caused this. Again.

And Sophie… his Sophie… knelt in the centre of it, her head tilted back as the light of the tree rushed towards her.

Someone screamed. No, something. Many things. It wasn't human. Shrieks and howls rose in a spiral of panic and pain. Will looked up and saw the leaves burning, an inferno whirling over his head. For a moment all he could do was stare. They were wild, frenzied, and the air shook with rage. Flames shimmered through the air and he couldn't tear his eyes away.

The air around him was boiling, and he could feel his skin shivering. Magic, raw and unadulterated, was loose and feral. He'd seen it before and it never ended well. Until it was earthed and brought back under control it was dangerous.

'Will! Step back.'

The Keeper stood beside him. He hadn't heard her approach, hadn't even seen her enter the chamber. All he could see were the leaves and the flames arcing between them. The frenzy above…

She looked so small. Desperately small.

'Professor…' he tried to say, but his voice drained away.

'Take the girl and go. Get her out of here before it—'

And in that instant he knew it was too late. Light lanced towards Sophie but, before it could strike her, the Keeper stepped in the way. She raised her hands, welcoming the raw magical power. Light wreathed her outstretched fingers, and flowed like static electricity down her arms. She threw back her head in a gasp that could be pain or joy. Maybe both. It ran through her body and into the ground beneath her. For a moment she was illuminated from within, and she stood there like

Da Vinci's Vitruvian man, her arms spread wide. There was so much energy, swallowing her up, until she almost seemed to fade into it, to become part of it. For a moment he thought, he was certain, that it would be too much, that they would lose her too.

And then she seemed to surge back into reality, a shadow against the light, eclipsing it with the force of her presence alone.

The golden leaves fluttered silently to the ground. Within them, the Professor wilted, her body wrung out. Will had to catch her before she fell.

'I'm fine,' she whispered, but her face was white as parchment. She didn't look fine. Far from it. She prised herself free from Will's grip and advanced on the spot where Arthur lay.

The stillness fell like snow around them. And Arthur stirred, looking up at her, stricken.

'Will, get that girl out of here before anything else happens,' the Keeper hissed through her pain, without taking her eyes off Will's brother.

'Professor,' Arthur began. 'Let me explain. Think about what this could mean, what we could—'

'Be quiet!' Anger filled her now, rebuilding the strength she had expended on containing the tree. The ground trembled with her rage.

Will helped a dazed Sophie to her feet, turning her so he could look into her eyes. She glowed with light. It spilled like molten gold down her cheeks and for a moment, a terrible moment, he thought he was too late.

Elizabeth's eyes glowed with light, and then she was gone.

Then Sophie blinked. The light faded, leaving only tears behind. He brushed the pad of his thumb gently against her soft, wet skin, trying to banish the tears.

'Sophie? Talk to me. Please.'

As she struggled to focus on his face, to recognise him, a tiny line appeared between her eyebrows. Her mouth parted and for a moment it didn't seem possible for her to form words. Had it broken her mind completely? Was she gone?

She swallowed hard, blinked again. 'Will? The voices…'

He pulled her against his chest and this time she didn't resist. She leaned in against him, breathing hard, her heart hammering so violently in her chest that he could feel its echoes in his own. He thought he'd lost her. Just after getting her back, he thought she was gone.

Even if she wasn't *his* to begin with. It didn't matter. He felt the fierce need to protect and cherish her, to keep her from harm, as surely as he felt his own heartbeat.

'I heard.'

'They said so many things, so many… strange things. They told me… if I let them in, I could do anything. I heard her…'

Impossible. Surely that was impossible. And yet… she had understood the grimoire. She had been able to read the words in it. Or at least, that was what he had thought.

But it was Professor Alexander who asked the question. 'You understood the language? The same way you understood the grimoire?'

'Of course she did,' Arthur hissed. 'She knows the language of the birds. Elizabeth told her so, years ago. She can understand it, read it. She can interpret it for us. It is even more natural for her than it was for her mother. She was born here. The library is in her blood. That's why her father took her away. He knew. It sings to her. They sing—'

'Enough, Arthur,' the Keeper interrupted, her voice harsh. 'Do you even realise what it could have done to her? Will?'

Will half thought they had forgotten he was there. He still held Sophie, but she had started to tremble with exhaustion now and he knew he was probably the only thing keeping her from falling.

'Yes, Professor.'

'Why are you still here?' she asked. 'Take her back up to her room. Watch over her. Now. And tell Margo I need...' She swayed on her feet and a new alarm filled him.

'Professor? Are you sure you're okay?'

Arthur caught her arm, holding her up. 'I've got her,' he said and all the defiance drained away. The Keeper looked so old, all of a sudden. And she was precious to them both. 'Get help.'

'But I...'

'Now, Will,' his brother snarled, the enormity of what he'd just done, and what the cost might be this time, hitting him. 'For God's sake, get the girl out of here and send help.'

Will lifted Sophie off her feet and carried her out of the chamber, and the sound of the tree's sobs followed them, echoed in his chest. He couldn't understand the words, not as he feared Sophie could, but he didn't need to. Will could read the tones, the feelings. He might not be able to read the language of the birds but he could feel the emotion behind them. His own empathy, Arthur had once told him, was his curse.

Sophie passed out as they went through the doorway, which was probably for the best. There was no sign of Tia on the other side, not now. She had retreated, the better to avoid temptation, he suspected. Also, probably for the best.

It was a long climb, especially carrying an unconscious woman, but he managed. She didn't weigh that much. How could she? She was all skin and bone.

He needed to get help. He needed to find someone else.

Titivillus was waiting in the Rotunda and Will gave him a pointed glare. A warning would have been nice, but then, the little demon did what he wanted. Always had done.

Will also knew that he wasn't alone.

'Tia?'

She had to be around here somewhere. She would want to know how this played out. He knew her well enough.

'Tia, come on. I need help.'

'With her? How can I help with her?' She was sitting in the shadows at the turn of the stairs, her knees hugged in against her chest.

'It's the Professor…'

'I felt it. Haven't felt anything like that since… well… since before *she* left.' She looked shaken, afraid and so strange in the half light. There was no doubt which 'she' she meant. She glared at Sophie. A singularly dangerous glare.

'Tia,' he said, the tone a warning. 'They need you. Down there. Professor Alexander…'

And like that, she was gone. He didn't doubt she'd be there for the Keeper. She always had been. No matter what the cost.

Will found the door to Sophie's room standing wide open, and he laid her down on her bed, smoothing her hair back from her face.

The fierce sensation rose in him again, a protectiveness, the thought that she didn't deserve any of that. It wasn't fair. All he wanted to do was make it better, make it stop. Protect her.

But she knew the truth now. The truth of the Special Collection. Or she would do very soon. The Tree had woken for her, accepted her. She was a true Binder, born from it, bred for it. She had walked into the Axis Mundi and the light had filled her. She would want to know more, ask all her questions and this time no one would deny her. Soon enough she would know the truth about him.

All he wanted to do was kiss her again. At the same time the thought of doing so terrified him. He would be revealing too much. Far too much. All his secrets were on the line. He wanted to trust her, he really did. And after all she had seen tonight, all she had experienced, he couldn't burden her with anything else.

Chapter Eighteen

The morning came too soon. Peeling her torso off the bed, Sophie sat up, trying to make her head stop swimming. The building murmured to her, the same siren song which had summoned her down to the vaults. On the edge of sleeping and wakefulness, she could hear them, all those voices that were buried in the walls, in the glass, that rose from somewhere impossibly far beneath her, that clustered around the tree. Trying to get her to return.

She couldn't. She didn't dare.

She had heard the noises of the library, the building with its whispers and sighs, all through the remains of the night. As dawn came, she could hear something outside her room, pacing back and forth, like a black dog guarding her. A dream, that was all.

Or a nightmare.

She dragged herself out of the bed and into the shower. She scrubbed her scalp, blow-dried her hair and got herself back on her feet.

Because she had to.

Sophie kept the necklace around her neck where it belonged, touching it for comfort every so often. It was warm and familiar, a weight she knew. She promised herself she wouldn't take it off again.

She had heard her mother in that room underneath the library, the room that couldn't physically be there. In the light of the tree.

She made her way down to breakfast. Margo dished up porridge with cream and fresh fruit. The aroma itself made Sophie's mouth water and she ate in spite of her churning stomach and pounding head.

'How is the Professor?' she asked.

Margo gave her a strange smile, half bewilderment and half reproach. 'She's resting. She works too hard, you know? They all do. And you should be resting too, young lady.'

Will wandered in, but he seemed distracted. When she asked after the Professor again, she didn't like the hunted expression she saw on his face.

'I'm going to see her now.' But he didn't elaborate on that. Nor did he stay to talk to her.

He had rescued her last night, she knew that. And still, she didn't know how to talk to him. Not about the kiss. Not about all that madness in the vault or wherever she had ended up. Not about anything. Magic, Arthur had said. A thin place between worlds...

Tia and Hannah joined her, sitting down without preamble. Titivillus strode in as well, as bold as brass. He jumped on Sophie's lap without hesitation and curled himself up, purring furiously as she began to pet him, an instinctive action. Suddenly he liked her? This was different.

'It's all a bit weird at the moment,' Hannah said. 'Everyone's up in arms. What on earth happened?'

Sophie met Tia's impenetrable gaze. She was giving nothing away. If Hannah didn't know all the details, Sophie wasn't going to enlighten her. She probably wouldn't believe her anyway.

She burrowed her fingers into the cat's fur and the purring got even louder. It was a strange comfort. Tia poured some coffee for each of them.

'I'm not entirely sure myself,' Sophie said. It wasn't a lie. The images of last night were still seared onto her mind, what she could remember, but that was the problem. It was a kaleidoscope of images with no connection, whirling leaves, fire in the air, writing which glowed and burned, the Keeper standing there with her hands outstretched, so very small against the immensity of the chaos.

Sophie flinched, memories flickering… Another woman's form, a woman who stood in the same place, caught in a maelstrom of leaves and unearthly noise, her arms spread wide above her head, feet rooted in the dark earth, her form mirroring the tree while light swallowed her up.

But there was something else superimposed on that. Her mother. A memory, something she had seen long ago. And again last night.

Something was wrong in the library. Something was terribly wrong. Sophie knew it even if no one would let her in on the secret. She could feel it in the air, in the walls, in the floorboards.

The cat yawned and stretched before rubbing his head into Sophie's hand again, determined to regain her attention. 'I never thought I was a cat person.'

Tia smiled softly. 'He tends to decide that for himself, don't you, Villus?'

Her obvious affection for the cat touched Sophie.

'It's an unusual name,' she said, scratching under his chin, an act of which he clearly approved as the purrs got even louder, a rumbling in the air. 'What is it? Eastern European?'

'Latin, I think,' Hannah replied, munching on some toast. 'But it could be older. Hang on.' She fished her phone out of her pocket.

'It seems familiar.'

'Well, he is,' Tia cooed. 'He's *my* familiar. Although the little traitor seems to prefer you at the moment.'

Sophie almost snatched her hand back guiltily. 'I'm sorry. I didn't…'

Titivillus eyed her balefully and made a soft '*mhyr*?'

'No, it's fine,' Tia said with her strange soft laugh. 'I'm joking. He's not mine. He doesn't belong to anyone, just himself and perhaps the library.'

'Titivillus was the name of a demon,' said Hannah, putting her search skills to excellent use. 'But not the scary kind. He was the patron demon of scribes. Like a patron saint but, you know, for the other side. So the poor old scribes would slave away in the scriptorium all day, finish, and when they returned in the morning they'd find all these mistakes. Or even bloody great paw prints all over their work.' The cat turned that glare on Hannah now and she grinned, leaning down to give him a scratch. 'Yeah, that sounds like you, all right.'

'Someone had a sense of humour when they named the library cat that,' Sophie sighed.

Hannah excused herself, but Tia lingered at the table, watching her. Whatever Tia wanted to talk to her about, Sophie wasn't letting the opportunity get away.

'Is the Professor okay?'

Tia drew in a breath and then let it out again in a long, low sigh. 'The Professor is… resting. That's the company line. I don't know, Sophie. She worked a great Art last night and that has a cost. It could have swallowed her up entirely.'

Sophie swallowed. She had to ask.

'And… the Tree?'

'The Axis Mundi will be fine. It's not really a tree, Sophie. It presents itself as such, because that's how a mortal brain can understand it. And it's dangerous. It always has been. We've lost too many people who have tried to bring it to heel. Especially when it's wild like that. That's what Art is all about. There's always a risk.'

It was the way they all said the word – *Art* – as if it had much more weight than it should.

'And by Art you mean…'

'Magic.' There wasn't a flicker of humour, no trace of a lie or a wind-up. Tia meant it. Clearly, she had decided it was time to level with Sophie, especially after what she'd seen.

A wave of cold fear washed over her, through her. It was madness, but she didn't doubt it, not really. Even if she wanted to deny it and pretend.

'Tia… was it real?'

The archivist paused before answering, carefully formulating her reply.

'What is "real" anyway? Reality is such a fickle notion. Especially here.' The smile on her lips was fleeting as Sophie glared at her. 'But yes. I'm afraid so. For as much as anything is "real", what you saw was real. But the good news is you aren't losing it.'

'Magic.' Her own voice sounded flat to her, sceptical, and yet she could not deny what she had seen, what had happened, everything she had felt.

'Books and magic have always gone hand in hand. And the library is probably the reason why.'

'But a tree…'

'What else would it be? They'll explain it all. Eventually.'

'Can't you?' The thought of sitting down with the Professor and having her speak of wonders in that dry, calm voice was too embarrassing to think about. But first she'd have to be able to sit down with Professor Alexander and everyone seemed to be freaking out about her health right now. It didn't sound like that would be happening any time soon.

It had been Sophie's fault. She should never have opened that door. What had she been thinking? It was all her fault.

But Tia shook her head. 'If I tried, I'd blow your mind. You could ask Will. He likes you, you know?'

Sophie remembered the expression on his face, the rage. No, Will didn't like her. Or at least not any more.

'I don't think so, Tia. He was… last night…'

'I know him better than anyone, Sophie. If he was angry it's because he was scared for you. He was trying to protect you, and the library of course. That's what he does. He's our guardian. It's his whole purpose in life.'

Tia smiled at her, a curiously gentle smile for her. 'He always held a torch for you, Sophie Lawrence. You two know each other better than anyone else on this earth. Sometimes it's simply like that. Don't overthink it. Look, when anyone leaves the library, memories of it grow fuzzy and drift away. It's a fact of life here and we're used to it. But you didn't forget Will, did you? You don't remember me from when you were young, do you? And yet I was here. You could see marvels within these walls but, if you leave for too long, they seem unreal. Like dreams. Your father knew that. He counted on it. Philip was… he was broken. He blamed us. It was a petty vengeance, taking you away, but maybe he believed he was protecting you. The magic of the library faded in your memory. It's a self-preservation thing, but whether it comes from the library itself or the human brain is anyone's guess. There's probably a paper in it. But who would ever remember enough to write it?'

*

Everything was quiet, peaceful. From a perch in the sun-flooded windowsill in her studio, the black cat opened one eye and gave her a speculative glare.

Sophie decided not to ask how he got in there. He seemed to have taken it upon himself to keep her company, maybe even to act as her guard. It was a curious thought, and one which wasn't entirely offensive. While everything seemed sane and in perfect order today, she was reluctant to probe beyond the surface.

Everything else was exactly as she had left it. Except that another phase box like the one into which the Professor had put the grimoire sat on her desk.

She stared at it for the longest time and then decided to simply get on with her own work. She wasn't going to open that. Yes, ignoring it and hoping it would go away might not be the most mature reaction but at the moment it was about all she could manage. She didn't want to open it. She didn't want to see what another small blue-grey box would hold.

Shortly before lunch, Edward arrived, in an explosion of indignation and concern.

'Sophie, are you okay? What a way to—'

'To find out about all this?' she interrupted, caustically. 'Yes, a heads-up in advance would have been nice. Don't you think?'

He retreated, almost recoiling, and she couldn't believe she had said it out loud. She had never spoken to anyone that way in her life. But, God, it was a relief.

He should have told her. He should have told her everything right from the start.

'I'm sorry, my dear, but...' He sighed and closed the door behind him, shutting the two of them away from the rest of the library. 'Would you truly have believed me if I had told you back in London?'

Would she? Would she really have believed that the library was magic, that there was a chamber beneath it with an enchanted tree and the voices of a thousand spirits? Or whatever they were...

No. Of course she wouldn't have.

She put down the tool with which she had been trimming the prepared leather. She was making a new cover for one of the eighteenth-century books in her care. Clamped in place, with the leather cut into the required size already, she had spent the morning on it and was almost finished. Some things she couldn't do in the Great Hall. And without the Professor, she wasn't sure she would want to.

The cover would have to wait now.

'I'm sorry,' she said. 'I just… I had dreams about this place for years and my father said it was all my imagination. The psychologists said it was trauma-related due to losing my mother, same as the memory loss. And now… now I find out it's all true?' Her voice was getting louder. She let it. 'What happened down there? What is this place?'

'No one bothered to explain? Typical.' He didn't seem too happy about that. Neither was she. And it didn't change the fact that he should have told her at some point himself. 'All right, come for lunch with me. Away from here. We can talk.'

She nodded, grateful for the invitation, for the excuse, grateful to get away for a while, ask her questions and get some actual answers that hopefully she could understand… that would be a blessed relief.

He was family. He owed her this much.

*

Her uncle drove a brand-new Jaguar, because of course he did. It was state of the art, electric and a thing of beauty. She sat cradled in a soft leather seat, exhausted. If she allowed herself, she might sleep for a week. She tried to focus on the countryside flashing by but that wasn't helping. Edward turned on the radio but it was playing something soothing and classical. In the end Sophie fiddled with the air vent until she could get a cool breeze flowing right at her face, which helped.

They drove for a little under an hour until Edward pulled into the car park of a traditional inn with nothing around it for miles but fields and hedgerows. Sophie wasn't surprised to see several awards proudly displayed over the door. She was coming to understand the vast expense of her uncle's tastes by now.

He walked in like he owned the place and Sophie followed, watching the way people instantly fawned over him. He ordered without even consulting a menu, either so familiar with the kitchen or entirely used to demanding what he felt like at the time and being immediately accommodated.

Or maybe this was magic too.

'Sophie?' he prompted and she couldn't help but shrug, so he ordered for her as well. It was easier anyway. She was used to it. Victor used to do it all the time.

'*Think of it as a surprise*,' he would say. She shuddered at the thought.

They sat in a quiet corner, away from everyone else, in a bay window. Sophie nursed her glass of water and waited.

'The library…' her uncle began and then paused, as if choosing his words with care.

'Are you sure you want to talk about it in public?'

He glanced dismissively over at the other diners. 'Oh, they won't hear us. And even if they do, they won't understand. That's the nature of the library, its innate Art. In order to learn about it, about the heart of it, you need to already know it. As you do. Even people living there, like the scholars and some of the employees, will never know the whole truth.'

Sophie nodded as if she understood and wished that she actually did. 'Tia said when people left it they forgot about it.'

'Something like that,' he said and took a sip of his water before continuing. 'A lot of this is metaphysical so bear with me. I normally wouldn't attempt to explain without a lot of brandy, but as it's only lunchtime and I'm driving…' It might have been an attempt at a joke but Sophie didn't smile and he went on, the ice unbroken. 'Well, then, I should start with the tree. Once upon a time, as the tradition goes, or in the beginning, because that's how far back we need to go…'

'You're stalling,' she said, matter of factly.

He didn't argue about the accusation. 'Wouldn't you? I'm trying to collect my thoughts. So, the Tree of Knowledge…'

'As in the Garden of Eden?'

'In a way. That's an interpretation, if you like. You could also go back to Norse legends of Yggdrasill and the Asvattha in the Upanishads, its roots in the sky and its branches covering the earth. The Tree of Life, or the Tree of Knowledge of good and evil, or simply Knowledge itself, they're all the same. And this is what you saw.'

'Under the library.'

'Yes. Oh, it's not an actual tree but that's how it manifests. The easiest form for it to take, one which the human mind can construe. It isn't really under the library either. Think of it like a doorway to somewhere else. In reality – in its own reality though, rather than ours – the Tree is raw inspiration, and the falling leaves are the ideas that—' He caught the dubious look she hadn't bothered to hide. 'I did warn you it was metaphysical. The Tree is a manifestation of that thing from which we all come.'

'God? Are you seriously talking about *God*?'

He shook his head adamantly.

'No. At least not in the way religion understands God. The tree exists only in the in-between world you entered beneath the library. The leaves that fall are inspiration, ideas that could escape into the world and seed countless fertile minds.' He paused as the waiter arrived and served them.

How could he just talk about all this like it was normal, like it was an everyday conversation? Maybe it was to him. It had always been part of his life, she supposed.

'And the voices?' she asked, when they were alone again.

'Ah yes, they sang to you, I believe. And you understood them.'

'It was more than singing. It was… overwhelming. Nightmarish. As to understanding…' She shook her head. 'As much as anyone can understand a thousand voices screaming different things at once.'

'Well, yes. Control comes with practice.' He poked a fork at the salad that had arrived and speared some asparagus, which he ate with relish. 'Some believe they are angels.'

She waited to see if he was pulling her leg, but he seemed to be deadly serious.

'Angels?'

'Yes. Arthur and Will's ancestor studied it in the 1500s, and made quite the name for himself as well. Mainly as a madman. The family has continued the study down through the years. They're obsessed. Especially Arthur. Say what you must about Will, but at least his mother gave him a modicum of sense in that regard.'

'What I heard didn't sound like angels. And I don't… I can't remember what they said. But I thought I heard my mother, Edward. I was sure of it.'

It hadn't just been hearing voices, either. It had been more. So much more.

Something had flowed through her, filled her. At any moment it had felt like it would overwhelm her and explode. A chill ran down her spine and she pushed the last remains of her salad away.

Deftly, without a moment's interruption, the waiter came and took it from the table. Sophie hugged her arms around her chest and closed her eyes, breathing slowly.

When Edward spoke again, his voice was brittle, the pain in it undeniable.

'Elizabeth is gone, Sophie. Yes, that was the last place she... the last Art she worked... but she is gone now. Something of her may remain in the Tree but... What you heard aren't angels as people think of them today. Nor are they demons, or ghosts, or anything like that. Spirit is probably the best description. Voices from other worlds, other times, and other places. The daemons of Plato, or familiar spirits. Some people, like the Dees, believe the voices can teach us magic, that they are a source of power. Others, like Paracelsus, Ashmole and Forman – our School of Night ancestors – believed in *Magia Naturalis*, that we must learn from them but not seek to control them. Both views are a trifle fanciful, to be honest.'

Their next course came and Sophie ate the delicately spiced chicken on a bed of saffron risotto while trying to take in what he said. In that time, she managed to get her emotions back under control. Now he was finally talking, she didn't want Edward to stop.

'Plato and Dee, I've heard of. And Ashmole of course. He founded the Ashmolean Museum in Oxford... The others...'

'Great healers, the fathers of modern medicine, in many ways. And alchemists, of course.'

'As in turning lead into gold?'

He laughed at that, clearly relieved to be on safer ground. 'Hardly. If we could do that, I'd be a happy man long since retired. And the Special Collection would not be a giant sucking hole for funding either. It's a common misconception. What alchemy is truly about is a study in itself, of nature and the world, of aspects of the soul, but in the end it all comes back to the Tree. And the attempts to understand it. Or, by the foolish, to use it.

'At first there was simply chaos. That's what every creation myth will tell you. "The earth was without form and void, and darkness was on the face of the deep."' He had that type of voice you wanted to listen to, soft and compelling, musical. 'And so the story of the Tree goes. There was a goddess, long ago, chaos incarnate. But nothing can thrive in chaos. Creativity is born there but it cannot take shape there. It cannot grow, and that is what it longs to do. Our forebears were the servants of that goddess, in all her glory, but humans knew that we couldn't survive without order. Which is where the Tree comes in. We begged the goddess to help us and she sacrificed herself to do so. We formed the Tree from the Art she taught us and it burst into being, spilling out dreams and nightmares, thoughts and inventions, all the wonders. And she paid the price, giving up her power, a final sacrifice.'

'The goddess… became the Tree?'

'No. The Tree is the Axis Mundi, the point where creative energy flows into the world, the birthplace of thought and inspiration, of everything. The Tree of Knowledge can spin out of control in a heartbeat. The library came into being to bring some order around it. All those spirits, running wild, well… you can imagine. And then there are the leaves.'

She remembered them, whirling around her, golden and glowing. She remembered her dreams where she had tried to catch them and they had slipped through her fingers or turned to ash in her hands.

'They seemed alive in their own right.'

'They are, in a way. They are raw inspiration. They exist in a state of agitation and creativity, but unchecked and untempered. Wild. They are why the Special Collection came to be, to contain them and tame them. Chaos may be the natural state of the world, but it is not sustainable. Eventually it will tear everything, even itself, apart. Order is the only way existence can be maintained and the library brings that order.'

Everything. This place, this strange, idiosyncratic place, was the lynchpin of reality. She sucked in a breath, trying to stop her mind spiralling out of control and losing herself to the tsunami of emotions that threatened her.

'How?'

For such a small word it encompassed a world of questions. Edward chose to interpret it as simply as possible.

'Such leaves as survive their fall are gathered up and bound together as very special volumes, kept in our vault. But only by one who knows the Tree, who understands it. With anyone else they burn.'

Ashes on her hands…

She knew then. She'd tried to bind the leaves, as a teenager. And she had failed.

'But once they are contained, the ideas can filter out into the world in a controlled manner. The scholars who work here act as a conduit in some cases. In others… well… Let me ask you, how is it, do you think, that two philosophers would have the same idea at the same time even though they are on opposite sides of the world and have never spoken? Or how inventors create devices to serve the same purpose, or fulfil the same need without knowing about each other's work? It happens all the time. Inspiration courtesy of the Special Collection and, ultimately, of the Tree. Ideas wrought from stimuli which come directly from the Axis Mundi, springing to life, the work of a muse.'

A muse. The Axis Mundi. The Tree at the heart of the library. She filed these things away to study later. 'And who binds the leaves? You?'

He smiled at her and she knew his answer before he said it. 'No. Gods forbid. That would be you now. The Keeper too, of course. That's her talent. Your mother was especially gifted. I would be a poor substitute, which is why I moved to acquisitions. I can find the ones we've lost over the years. And there have been many. Through fire and war and destruction. I only have to walk into a library and they call out to me. I bring them home, here, where they can take their place and the Special Collection can filter their secrets out into the world as intended. Otherwise that knowledge would be lost, trapped in a library vault with no way out. Stifled and forgotten. Worse than forgotten, unknown.' He sounded forlorn at the idea. In that moment she realised the joy he took from his role here, the purpose it gave him. 'But I can't bind them, I can't create them. The Tree does not talk to me. Doesn't even let me into its presence on my own. *You*, on the other hand... have the potential to be phenomenal.'

Sophie shook her head. She had finished her food now and she had so many questions it left her queasy. 'Is that why you brought me here?'

'To the restaurant? No, the risotto was the reason we came here. Did you enjoy it?'

That same dry humour, the same deflection. He meant it to be disarming. She'd have to watch that.

'I meant to Ayredale.'

'The *train* brought you to Ayredale.' She gave him a stern look and Edward laughed. 'You're very like your mother when you do that, you know? She didn't get my jokes either. All right, all right.' He raised his hands in surrender. 'I brought you here to the library because it is your home. Your true home, your family home, a home that will welcome and cherish you. And I was worried about you in London on your own. And finally because we need you. There, is that what you wanted to hear?'

She nodded absently. But was it? Was it what she wanted to hear?

Having a home and being needed was good, wasn't it? Better than the alternatives anyway.

'And my father?' He'd died. He'd had a brain tumour and died raving.

'Ah.' Edward had the grace to look subdued now.

'If he'd stayed here, would he have died? Did leaving kill him? Was it Art or...? And what about my mother? Your sister? How did she die, if the library protects its own?'

A mask of pain and sorrow came over his features, so complete a change that her breath caught painfully in her throat.

'That is another matter. I don't know everything that happened that night. I never will. And those involved... can't tell me.'

'Wait? People know what happened? Who knows?'

Edward tugged at his collar now.

'When you stood under the tree, do you remember what happened? What you felt?'

'I felt... I felt power. Energy. I could feel that it was alive and that it wanted something.'

'It wanted you, Sophie.' She remembered the way it had felt, the light pouring through her. The way the Professor had stepped in the way and for a moment, for a terrible moment, Sophie had thought she would vanish in that light.

'Why me?'

'You were there before, Sophie. The tree, the leaves, reacted with such power to you that it risked tearing itself apart for you. And your mother...'

A dreadful sense of foreboding swept through her. Sophie balled her napkin up in her hand and tears made the table blur in front of her.

'She stopped it.'

He nodded slowly. 'You were all so young. You didn't know what you were doing. No one blamed you.'

Except her father. He had clearly always blamed her.

And he was right, whether he ever found out the truth or not. Her mother was gone because of her.

Chapter Nineteen

The staircase leading down towards the vaults yawned below Sophie, the whole effect still reminiscent of an open mouth in the middle of the library. But this time light streamed in from the high windows, highlighting motes of dust in the air like fireflies. The place seemed alive and potent.

Even if there was no one else there.

Two days had passed since the night she'd gone into the Axis Mundi. Two days since the Professor had been taken ill. She'd been in her rooms ever since, resting. That was what they said and no more information was forthcoming. Two days, during which time Sophie threw herself into her work, spent time with her uncle and tried to work out what on earth she could say to Will to broach the subject of her mother's disappearance. And their apparent involvement in it. And what had happened that night after the pub. After their kiss.

She didn't know where to begin.

And how did you bring up something like that? *I think together, you and I, had something to do with the most traumatic thing that ever happened to me, that caused me to have a breakdown. The thing that drove my father away and destroyed my relationship with him. I suspect we were responsible for the disappearance of my mother. And you said nothing.*

She couldn't. And if Will noticed that she pulled away from him, he didn't let on. He was too much of a gentleman to bring it up. Professor Alexander was still unwell, so Will seemed preoccupied anyway. He rarely sat still for more than a few minutes, constantly finding something else to do, always distracted.

Besides, with Edward here she was finally getting some answers, and with the answers came so many more questions. He seemed to have taken it on himself to educate her on every aspect of the Special Collection. Sophie barely had a moment to herself.

'This particular location came into being in the seventeenth century,' said Edward. 'We wanted somewhere new, away from London. The fire was an unfortunate by-product of course, but libraries and fire are old enemies.'

'The Great Fire of London? The library caused that?'

'They botched the unbinding. Just a bit. Occupational hazard, I suppose. They considered Oxford and that was Elias's first choice but in the end—'

'Elias?'

'Ashmole. He picked up leadership of the School of Night after Rudd.'

She grasped for the thing she recognised, the familiar. 'Elias Ashmole? As in the Ashmolean Museum? You mentioned him before.'

'The very same.'

She glanced over her shoulder, just in case. 'Is he lurking around here too?'

'Very funny. His great-great-something-or-other nephew calls in from time to time. He's a chemist, quite a good one too. It's fitting. Alchemy is a forgotten pursuit. Or almost forgotten. It is a study of metaphysics, the interconnected science of the entire universe.'

Lights ringed the staircase and, on each level, Sophie saw a number of doors which she was certain had not been there the other night. They reminded her of the main entrance, but each one was a different colour. The very bottom of the staircase was lost in the darkness but she could almost feel it calling out to her. Her pendant was heating up. Sophie shuddered, and followed her uncle.

They had only gone down two floors when Edward left the stairs and made for a door painted dark blue and withdrew a large ring of keys from a pocket in his jacket. The door unlocked with a decisive click and he swung it open.

The familiar grey metal shelving on rails stretched out on either side, large wheels on each row end to move them by. Sophie couldn't see how far back they went. It was a common way to save space in libraries and archives all over the world, packing many shelves into a smaller space. But this room just seemed to go on and on.

She thought of all the doors, all topped with a different light, all different colours, floor after floor of them.

'How many…' she started to say but her voice failed her.

'Countless,' said Edward. 'Truly countless. Now, grab that stool.'

It was a squat grey metal cylinder with a rubber top and base, the kind that anchored itself down when you stood on it and wouldn't slip. So utilitarian, so common. It almost felt like she had been dreaming everything else and here at last she had found reality.

Edward grabbed the nearest handle and began to turn it. The shelves opened up like a magic door.

'Always take a stool in with you in case someone doesn't know you're there and tries to close the shelves. Blood is difficult to get out and we've lost too many assistants that way.'

'No you haven't,' she replied automatically because in every library she had ever been in, someone told that joke about rolling stacks. But everyone still brought a stool in with them, especially when working alone. Just in case.

He grinned. 'One or two perhaps. Come on. I want to show you this one.'

It wasn't the Mortlake grimoire, although the box was of course identical. Pale blue-grey, cut to hold the book it contained exactly, cradling its precious contents.

Edward carried it back out and up towards the entrance where Sophie saw a small wooden table, and a lamp with a by now familiar green glass shade. Edward turned it on, took out a cushion from under the desk somewhere and opened the box.

He lifted out an ancient book and placed it reverently on the white cushion, nestling it in as if making sure it was comfortable. He opened it and turned a couple of pages before stepping back and offering her the seat.

'Tell me what you see, what you can read?'

The book had to be hundreds of years old. Handwritten, the script slightly faded now, but that didn't matter. For a moment Sophie wondered again if he was pulling her leg, but he wasn't. She knew that instinctively. Edward had not lied to her yet, had he?

He'd omitted things, maybe, but she didn't think she'd caught him in an outright lie.

She sat and tried to fight down a wave of panic at the thought of sitting there trying to read something while he watched. Her dyslexia wasn't the worst case, she knew that, but reading was never comfortable for her. She glanced at the page and saw only squiggles and shapes that made no sense at all. Wincing, she was about to say so when the page seemed to shiver in front of her eyes, the letters changing, reforming, sliding around in that way they did when she was probably going to end up with a massive migraine shortly.

'I can't,' she tried to say. 'It's just—'

But suddenly, she could.

It was like last time. Words shimmered into view, the ink moving like a living thing, words that formed and reformed like watching something living slither beneath the surface of the page. The leaf, she realised. The book was made of the same material as the grimoire she had seen. And the language was the same, the language of birds.

'Four kings there are who rule the air, each in their castle with their troops arrayed before them. Their names are inscribed in the circle and they can be called thus—'

Edward cut in, stopping her. 'No need to read the whole thing, my dear. I don't think we want the company of the kings right now.'

The company of the kings? What kings? Kings of where? Sophie decided she didn't want to know. She felt a wave of icy cold sweep over her, like standing at the open door of a walk-in freezer.

Magic. It was real. She knew it was real. She'd half hoped he was making it up, that suddenly everyone else would burst in and laugh, their practical joke complete. She would be embarrassed but the world would be back on its axis once more.

'How can I read this?' she asked and glanced down at the page again. The letters were still moving, the words reforming into something else. There were pictures, diagrams, designs. She could read it all.

'Art,' he said. He reached out and took the book in careful hands, closing it and putting it back in the case. 'And a connection to the source. The Axis Mundi. It sees you as a conduit. Just like Elizabeth was.'

'I have dyslexia, Uncle Edward. I mean I…' She gestured at the books. 'None of this should be possible.'

'It's not dyslexia, not really. It's just that your mind is trying to read in its native tongue first of all so it takes a moment longer. It's like you were reading in a second language all your life. Elizabeth always said that you knew it instinctively.'

'Do you?'

'Lord, no. It's all Greek to me. Worse, because my Greek is actually excellent.'

She frowned. 'What about the others here? Will and the Professor?'

'Will has a strange relationship with it. He doesn't so much read the books as… hear them, I think. He has an empathy with the library that I have never seen matched. He is its guardian in many ways. The Professor… She has many secrets. She's learned not to share her knowledge easily.'

Had she? She had been nothing but open with Sophie. Or maybe that was the way she wanted it to appear. She hadn't told her about Will, Arthur and Sophie being down in the Axis Mundi, or Sophie's mother coming to help them and being lost. No, she hadn't shared that. But she must have known. Just like Edward.

Sophie wondered how he felt about that, about losing his sister that way. And then lying about it. For years. Being part of that lie, even to her.

Oh, she'd been wrong when she said he hadn't lied to her. Almost all he'd done was a lie. Omissions were still lies.

But he wasn't even the worst. That was the tragic part. 'My father didn't tell me anything. In fact he hid it from me, all of it, and forced me to repress it as well.'

'I think he was trying to protect you, Sophie. You were traumatised afterwards. When he came back, you couldn't tell us what had happened and Elizabeth was gone. We had to protect the library, but he blamed us all, insisted on taking you away. By the time you recovered, your memory had faded. Well, it was his decision.'

He wasn't there. He didn't know everything. But he must have guessed.

'And after he died, you decided otherwise?'

'I thought you deserved the truth. I think everyone deserves to know the truth about their own lives. Don't you?'

Of course she did. Having had so much hidden from her, the truth was increasingly important to her. She nodded, which seemed to please him. Or maybe relieved him.

But there was still someone she needed to speak to. She just dreaded the idea.

Will had lied to her as well.

*

Sophie's work consumed her. With Professor Alexander ill, she spent more time with Edward in his office, discussing the disaster preparedness plan they were drawing up. The work of the library had to continue, he'd said. She had finished most of the work the Professor had already set aside for her. So she persuaded her uncle that documentation was the way to go. Edward had seized on the idea. Perhaps he just loved the mundanity of paperwork.

It had been strangely quiet in the library. The others should have been here too, going over the paperwork, but neither Will nor Tia had arrived. Sophie fidgeted nervously. She knew the Keeper was not improving. No one said it. No one dared. But Sophie could feel bad news approaching with the inevitability of winter.

'Right, next section, flood,' said Edward. 'Probably the most urgent given the river. Of course, we have our own protections.'

Sophie rolled her eyes. 'You can't put "magic will take care of everything" in an official document.'

'I don't see why we have to have an official document to begin with,' he replied with a soft smile. 'We never have before.'

'Well the ISO says differently. International standards are standards for a reason, Uncle Edward.'

A peremptory knock on the door made both of them look around. 'Enter,' Edward said curtly.

Delphine opened the door, her face very white, her eyes wide in uncharacteristic panic. 'I'm sorry, Dr Talbot, but you need to come now. It's Professor Alexander.' The beautiful library assistant glanced at Sophie, and her words seemed to dry up in her mouth. She still didn't like her. Perhaps even more so now.

'What's happened?' he replied, clearly as confused as Sophie.

Delphine looked up at him again, Sophie forgotten. 'They want you to come at once.'

Will had told her the Keeper had her rooms on the top floor of the west wing but Sophie had never been there. Edward knew where he was going. He strode ahead of her, his long legs carrying him up the stairs and down the corridor so quickly Sophie found herself almost jogging to keep up, mainly because she didn't know what else to do.

The far end of the landing was dominated by an arched stained-glass window, depicting another angel, this one playing a trumpet. Underneath it on an ancient wooden chest topped by a red velvet cushion sat Will, his head in his hands, his knees splayed on either side of him, a picture of devastation. Sophie slowed her pace, uncertain. This wasn't good. It couldn't be good.

Will's shattered gaze met Edward's.

Sophie's uncle broke into a sprint she wouldn't have imagined he was capable of, tearing down the final stretch and almost skidding on the plush carpeting as he ran into the Keeper's bedroom.

'What happened?' she asked, coming to a halt in front of him. 'Will?'

'She's dying,' he replied, his voice broken, defeated, and so very lost.

'What do you mean, she's dying?' Sophie blurted out and then clapped her hands over her mouth. She couldn't be dying. He couldn't mean Professor Alexander. This couldn't be happening. 'Will? Talk to me.'

She reached out and took his hands. She could feel him trembling even as he closed his fingers around hers, that strong, dependable grip that normally was so reassuring.

'I don't know what to say,' he whispered.

Sophie sat down beside him, not willing to let go of his hands. She rubbed his palm with her fingers, and tried to soothe him, to comfort him. It wasn't working, but at least he didn't pull away.

'What happened?' she asked again.

It was a stupid question. That seemed to be all she could come out with at the moment. She knew what had happened. *She* had happened. She had arrived at the library and woken everything up. She had started asking questions about her mother and about her past. She had followed the call down to the Axis Mundi and caused all that chaos to escape. The Professor had done everything she could to save her. Too much. It was all her fault.

Was that what happened fifteen years ago? That was her fault as well. Edward had all but said it out loud. Elizabeth went in there to save the three of them, whatever they had done. Whatever *she* had done. Sophie knew it. It was the only thing that made sense. She'd gone into the Axis Mundi, woken the Tree, and then...

And now...

She had done the same thing again.

'It's because of me,' she whispered.

'No,' he said, and his voice changed, becoming fierce and bitter. 'It's because of Arthur. And he's in there beside her, waiting for her to name him her successor, because that's what he wants more than anything. If he is the Keeper, he can do what he wants with the Axis Mundi. He's been rallying the other warders of the School of Night to put him in control. He's just waiting for her to die, and it's his entire fault.'

Sophie didn't know what to say. Will gave a broken sob and folded in on himself again. The Professor had always been kind to her, as much as she could remember. To Will... she was all the family he had. Sophie knew that. Whether they were related or not, it didn't matter. The Keeper had raised him as if he was hers. She had been his grandmother and maiden aunt, his sponsor and his friend. She had been everything.

'When I was little,' he said when he had control of his voice again, 'I was all alone. And she took my hand and walked me around the place. She told me this was my home and always would be.'

'What happened to your family, Will?'

He shook his head. 'They aren't... they don't want me. But she did. And your mother.' He looked up suddenly, his green eyes glistening. 'And you.'

He fell silent again, looking lost in thoughts about the Professor, about his childhood, about everything he had lost. He glanced towards the door through which Edward had vanished. His grip on her hand tightened abruptly, the anger in him palpable.

'I have to get out of here,' he said. 'I have to get out of here right now.'

Sophie got to her feet, pulling him with her. Will didn't resist, following her, even though he was the one saying he wanted to leave. They bundled up in their coats against the winter chill, left the building. Sophie led him out into the gardens and from there down to the river's edge where it was quiet. They sat together, and she wrapped her arms around him and held him close.

Her mother hadn't drowned, she thought, staring at the water as it roared past. At least, not in the river. She'd drowned in the light of the Axis Mundi.

If they expected the earth to shake and crack or the skies to open when the Professor died, it didn't happen. The winter's sun beat down on them, glistening in the flowing water of the river, and a bird sang in the nearby skeletal willows.

For a moment a cloud passed over the sun, plunging them into shadow, and Sophie knew. She just knew. Will's entire body stiffened against her and then wilted.

There was nothing to say, nothing at all. It wasn't like when Sophie's dad died. It wasn't like that at all.

It was quiet and still, a very private tragedy, and even so the low winter sun shone brightly and the river flowed on.

Chapter Twenty

The funeral took place on a Tuesday. Will couldn't actually decide how long it had been since her death. It felt like forever. It felt like no time at all.

At least he had Sophie. She hardly left his side and for that he was grateful.

Tia had retreated into hiding. Margo was devastated, Hannah and Meera were trying to hold everything together for the others and Delphine seemed to have suddenly assumed that she was general manager of a library without a Keeper. Arthur held court in his office, ringing around the School of Night, rallying support to his cause. And Edward?

He had been with the Professor at the very end. Whatever she had said to him, he had left that night and headed up to London. He had only come back yesterday and had locked himself away. The warders of the School of Night descended this morning.

Immediately after the funeral, they would meet to choose a new Keeper.

There was no hanging around. No delays. The interregnum had gone on long enough.

Will knew it would be a disaster. Factions and squabbling and debates about the future and the past which meant nothing. They hadn't elected a Keeper in fifty years. Not one of them had been involved in that before. This was their moment. This was their reason for being, the reason the School of Night continued to exist.

The little church in the village was full when they arrived. Frost clung to the bare trees and the grass outside. In a black suit that felt like it was going to crush him alive, and an overcoat he had fished out of the back of his wardrobe, Will knew he looked like he could be the funeral director rather than a mourner.

He couldn't believe she was gone. It wasn't fair. He knew Sophie felt responsible but it wasn't her fault. Arthur on the other hand... Well... Will had other thoughts there.

And then there was his own fault. He had failed her.

Would the School of Night demand an investigation? Would they quietly move on? Would they, worst of all, choose Arthur to take over?

That was unthinkable. Will didn't know what he'd do if that happened. Leave? Where else did he have to go? Leaving the library would be like losing a loved one all over again.

But he couldn't stay. Not with Arthur in charge. He just couldn't.

The music washed over him. She'd picked the oldest hymns. Oh, he didn't doubt the Professor had chosen every element of her funeral right down to the last details. Even the flowers on her coffin, blue water lilies and papyrus, spoke of her family history, of her legendary status. Where someone had gone to get them, especially in flower, he didn't know. Maybe they weren't real at all. Maybe it was one final act of Art to honour her.

Edward. It had to be. Who else could do that? Who else would?

Arthur stood near the front on the other side and didn't so much as glance at Will, only spoke to the warders of the School of Night standing with him.

Afterwards a stream of dignitaries filed past, offering condolences, and Will nodded, shook hands and tried to force himself to say something in return. It all sounded so banal.

'Where now?' he asked no one in particular when it had finished.

'Uncle Edward said there's a reception back at the library,' Sophie said. 'But we don't have to—'

'No, it's okay. Let's go.'

They walked back, even though there were cars that would take them if they wanted. The river was high and as they crossed the bridge he paused, leaning over the low stone wall to stare down into it.

'Are you okay?' Sophie asked.

'Sure,' he lied. She gave a half-hearted smile and stared down into the water alongside him.

'What happens now?' she asked.

'They'll pick a new Keeper. Someone else to run the place. Or at least try to. It won't be the same. She's irreplaceable.'

'Who do you think it will be?'

He shrugged. He had no say over that and he didn't want to contemplate what might happen if the wrong person took on the role.

'Arthur?' she asked and he could hear the fear in her voice. He didn't blame her either. If Arthur was in charge, what would he ask of Sophie? She knew the risk as well as he did. Arthur was young, charismatic and well connected. He worked the room, as they said, made contacts and forged alliances. He used people.

What would he do with the library? And what would he ask of Sophie and her ability to commune with the Tree? She was a Binder, he was sure of that, in more than the mundane sense. The whole library responded to her. He would charm her like he did so long ago, persuade her to help him. And then what? Will didn't know. And he dreaded the possibilities.

His brother didn't care about the library, not truly. He cared about renown, fame, and his own prestige. He cared only about the Dee legacy and the birthright he felt was his due. He would pillage the library to get what he wanted.

And what did he want? Even Will couldn't really answer that.

'Let's hope not,' Will said.

*

The group of men in the lounge looked around accusingly as Sophie entered and Will gritted his teeth. They stared at her as if she was a creature to be examined. Given that Edward and Arthur were there too, he had no doubt everyone had been fully briefed on who she was and what had happened. She shrank back against him, instantly seeking an escape. He didn't blame her but it was too late.

'Excellent, here she is,' said Edward. 'And William as well. We were wondering where you had got to.'

The warders of the School of Night sat in various seats, some with refreshments, some in discussion, seven of them. He knew the Sidney brothers, of course, and Theodore Fludd. Not a woman among them, not now.

The only one not sitting was Arthur. He stood with his back to them, staring out of the window, but turned as they entered, a dark look on his face. So the warders had made their decision and clearly Will's brother wasn't pleased. His gaze scoured across Will and then Sophie, who folded her arms over her chest defensively. If Arthur noticed, he didn't care how nervous she was. He strode across the room, grabbing his coat from the back of a chair as he went, ignoring the others.

'Who?' Will asked, softly, as Arthur reached them. He had no choice but to pass them to leave. Arthur hesitated, bit back a reply and cast a scathing glance at the others. They were gathered around Edward and Will winced, knowing what was coming. It could be worse, he told himself. It could be much worse. It could have been Arthur.

'Edward Talbot?' Will asked.

Arthur nodded. A single jerk of his head. But he hadn't left yet. He was waiting to see Will's reaction, wasn't he? And maybe Sophie's too. Will was too dumbstruck to think about that too deeply now.

Edward Talbot as Keeper. Right where he had always wanted to be. Tia wasn't going to like it either.

'Has anyone seen Tia?' But no one answered. Sophie met his gaze. She looked as concerned as he did. Tia… no one had thought about her, as usual. Will frowned. 'We should find her. She's going to be upset.'

If Sophie understood what that meant, she didn't let on.

'I didn't know Tia wanted to be Keeper,' said Sophie.

'Oh, she doesn't,' Arthur said with a bitter laugh so unlike Will's own. 'But she won't like Edward being her boss. None of them will. Especially not our precious Will.'

She frowned at him, clearly not liking his tone. Something of the old, fierce Sophie crept back into her voice, defending him. 'What does that mean?'

Arthur didn't reply to her. As always, when thwarted, he directed his barbs entirely at Will.

'I mean, she's a crap mother, Will, but she's the only one you've got, isn't that right? Not that she remembers half the time. Elizabeth was more of a mother to you than Tia ever was.'

'Jesus Christ, Arthur,' Will snapped, his voice too loud in the quiet room. All the murmuring voices went silent.

All the warders turned, staring at Will as if he had committed some kind of mortal sin. And in the middle of them Edward stood triumphant. Will didn't like the look on his face one bit.

He started to apologise and then realised Sophie was gone.

'Drama still runs in the family then,' Arthur sneered. God, he was a bastard through and through. How had Will ever admired him? 'Edward won't last long, I guarantee it. He has his own agenda. Besides, Mummy dearest is going to be pissed as hell, isn't she?'

*

It took Will longer than he thought to find Sophie and Tia. But they were together. Of course they were. Sophie had sought Tia out the moment she left the reception. Had she asked her about Will? What had Tia said?

He didn't dare ask.

They were most of the way into a bottle of red wine, tucked away up in Sophie's room, and he was pretty sure that if he hadn't arrived Tia's next move could have been a rather surprising seduction. He wasn't sure how that would have worked out for either of them. But he knew her too well.

Tia was sprawled elegantly on the floor, her back against Sophie's desk which could not be as comfortable as she made it look. Sophie, on the other hand, nestled in the chair beside her.

'There you are!' Tia raised the wine bottle to him in a toast.

Sophie frowned. He could still see the tear stains on her face, her eyes washed out. 'Sophie... I'm sorry. My brother is an asshole. Always has been.'

'I can testify to that,' Tia chimed in. 'So was his father. We've been drinking to Hypatia the way she would have wanted us to. Well, not exactly because there wasn't enough sherry in the world. But I thought a good red would do.'

For the moment he ignored Tia. 'Sophie? Are you okay?'

She held a glass of wine in her hands, cradling it. Tia was the one swigging from the bottle.

'Yeah. Fine,' she said, in a tone which implied quite the opposite. 'Why didn't you tell me, Will?'

'Which bit?' He'd kept so much from her. It was nothing personal. He kept it from everyone, even himself sometimes. It was more like a habit at this stage. He sat down on her bed, trying not to think too hard about the idea that he was sitting on *her* bed, stretching his legs out in front of him. It was the furthest he could sit from her, and he knew at once she noticed that as well. Carefully, he shed the suit jacket and tugged off the constricting tie. Then he rolled up the shirtsleeves until he felt almost himself again. Sophie waited until he was finished, refusing to let him distract her.

'Tia's your mother?'

'Oh, he doesn't like to talk about that,' Tia interrupted. 'Neither do I. Ugh, Roland Dee, what was I thinking? A terrible mistake. Apart from Will, of course. Wine, Will?'

He gave her a stern look. 'How long have you been drinking?'

She couldn't have done a better impression of a belligerent teenager if she tried. 'Dunno. Started last week. Stopped counting.'

'Will,' Sophie said again, drawing his attention back to her. 'What did Arthur mean?'

'He's a bastard, that's all. Always was. It took me a long time to realise it. I idolised him. I'd do whatever he asked. I was an idiot.'

'Typical Dee,' the archivist murmured. 'A manipulative, power-hungry bastard, like his father. So is Edward, when you get down to it. All men are, especially in this place, except Will. He's special. What? I'm not an idiot. I know what Edward is. I know better than anyone. I've always known and it didn't stop me. I made the same mistake with Roland over thirty years ago, thought he loved me. He was handsome though, as handsome as Will is, and so charming. So determined. I've always had the *worst* taste in men. I've made the mistake all over again with Edward. I thought he adored me. That's what he said. And now he's got it all, hasn't he? He's the Keeper. What do you reckon he'll do? With the library? With the Tree?'

Will shook his head. 'At least it isn't Arthur?'

'There's that, I suppose,' Tia agreed softly. 'One blessed relief. I don't know. I couldn't have borne it if…' For a moment Will thought she was going to cry. She sat there, staring at the wine bottle and her eyes misted over. She swallowed hard and then shook her head. 'I'm tired. I'm taking my wine to bed. Will's just going to tell me off and say I drink too much anyway. It doesn't matter. Not to me. Not any more.' She levered herself up off the floor and swayed towards the door.

'Do you want a hand?' Sophie asked, although she didn't move. She knew as well as he did Tia would never allow that.

'No. You two need to talk. And shag. Preferably shag. It's quicker.'

'Tia!' Will exclaimed. He couldn't say Mother, because he never called her that and he wasn't about to start now. She'd never been a mother to him, not really. She had never grown up at all. His father Roland Dee had taken advantage of that but faced with the consequences of his actions, with a flesh and blood child, he'd rejected them both.

Will hated him for it.

He wondered if Edward had been any better.

'Oh, I take it back, Will,' Tia groaned. 'I'm sure you'll last for ages. If only you'd ever get started. Goodnight. May tomorrow be infinitely less shit for once in our miserable lives.' She lifted the bottle in a toast to them both. 'It won't be though.'

She closed the door firmly behind her.

Will let his breath out in a long rush and closed his eyes.

'Sorry,' he told Sophie. 'She doesn't mean it.'

'Yes she does. She's been telling me about it for almost twenty minutes. She was…' Sophie cleared her throat. 'She was most insistent about the sex, by the way. And fairly graphic too. She had all sorts of advice. It's okay. She's drunk, that's all.'

'I didn't think she could actually get drunk. I've seen her polish off bottles and be fine. She must have been drinking non-stop for—'

'Days.' Sophie drew in a shaky breath. 'I guess no one ever dared to stage an intervention for her. Will, is she really your mother?'

'Yes. For what it's worth. My biological mother. She's not great at the rest of it. Not in her nature.'

'Wow,' she murmured. 'And my mother… Will, Edward told me something…' She rubbed her hands together, fidgeting to avoid saying more.

Will felt that bad feeling return. 'About what?'

She stared at him, like she was trying to see into his soul. 'Do you know what happened to my mother?'

Gods, it was like a punch to the stomach. It drove the air out of him. That was the last thing he'd been expecting. But of course she'd found out. Arthur had told her. Edward must have filled in any blanks. Gleefully, probably.

'Sophie, I—'

'It's okay if you don't remember. I don't. Just snapshots.'

He had to tell her. He knew that. He couldn't keep it from her any longer. But he couldn't bear for her to think the worst of him. Even now. Even if he deserved it.

'It was… I don't remember it all,' he replied cautiously.

Sophie was unrelenting. 'Does Arthur remember?'

Will tried to shrug nonchalantly. He had blamed Arthur, Arthur had blamed him, but that didn't help, then or now. All was confusion, that night. He remembered the light, the fire, the noise and then nothing.

You did everything you could, Will.

Elizabeth's voice. Gods, he had loved her voice. Now it haunted him.

Our guardian. Let go, love… Let me go.

The light. And then nothing but darkness and rage.

'Will?'

He opened his eyes again, stared into hers, that soft blue grey. 'We should never have gone down there, but it was a dare and we could never resist a dare.' Especially when it came from Arthur. Neither of them could. And where had it landed them? 'He said it was all going to be ours one day so why wait to find out. So we did. We were idiots. And it all got so out of control.'

He swallowed hard. 'The tree reacted to you, like it did the other night, and you tried to hold it back. You were lost in it, Sophie. You were glowing. When I tried to pull you free, it knocked me out. The next thing I knew, Arthur was gone, Elizabeth was there, taking over from you. I thought she could do it, bring it under her control again. You ran for help and when I went back to try to get her out… there was so much light. And fire. The whole Tree was singing. I couldn't… I couldn't save her.'

Suddenly he became aware he was sprawled on her bed, his face wet with the tears he had never shed before, and she was sitting forward on the chair, staring at him. Studying him. Waiting until he finished his story.

Sophie got up from the chair, left the wine glass on the table and came to the bedside. She sat down beside him, and wiped his face tenderly with her fingertip, her touch trailing over his skin in a frighteningly effective way.

He never wanted her to stop.

'I'm sorry, Sophie.'

'For what?' Her voice was low and soft, but without a trace of hesitation.

'I should have saved her. I should have—'

Slowly she lifted his hand to her face and kissed it, lips brushing over his knuckles, finding skin he never realised was so sensitive. The apology fell to a sigh. Will closed his eyes, drawing in the deepest breath he could manage. He couldn't remember when he hadn't wanted this. Just this.

Not just this. More. Everything.

But he didn't deserve it. He had failed her.

'Have you blamed yourself all along?' she asked. When he gave a halting nod, the most tragic of smiles flickered over her sensual lips. 'Me too. But we were just kids, Will. We didn't know what we were doing. Maybe it's time we forgave ourselves.'

He returned the smile and pressed his hand to her face. She leaned into him like a cat and looked up at him, her pupils wide and dark. Waiting for him.

Still, he hesitated.

'Sophie? This isn't… this isn't because Tia said that… is it?'

Will wouldn't be able to bear it if she said it was. Or if this came from pity. He felt her smile, her lips pressed to his palm, so soft, so gentle. Then he felt her shift on the bed and her lips touched his at last.

It wasn't the time or the place. It couldn't be. Not with everything going on. Not with the abyss of things they still needed to talk about.

But it was.

'No,' she whispered, her words falling into his mouth. 'This is just about us. Kiss me, Will. Please?'

How could he refuse?

Chapter Twenty-One

The next couple of weeks were an unexpected whirlwind of activity. Edward was taking the 'new broom' approach to the workplace and everything was in uproar. Sophie's work continued, but Edward kept saying he had new plans in the pipeline which made it hard to focus. She pressed on with the work Professor Alexander had left behind, now Sophie was the only binder at the library, and the sole conservator they had. She would just have to manage, she told herself, until her uncle decided to share whatever it was he had planned. Sophie's evenings were spent with Will, nights in his arms and all thoughts of anything else fell away.

She knew it was moving fast. That didn't seem to matter. It was more like picking up where they left off all those years ago, extending the relationship they had then into their adult lives. And if she still didn't have answers as to what happened, she knew more than she had before. Perhaps she'd never know everything. Something had happened at the Tree, deep within the Axis Mundi, and it had been her fault. So perhaps not knowing was better after all.

She could have asked Arthur, but Arthur had not come back to the library since Edward became Keeper. Delphine said he had so much leave saved up and losing the Professor had devastated him. He needed the break. Meera, more quietly, added that he'd left with his nose out of joint and might quit altogether, which Sophie thought might be closer to the truth. But then, she wasn't sure Arthur Dee was the type to give up so easily.

The argument took everyone by surprise. Sophie didn't know what triggered it, only that one evening they were sitting in the lounge and raised voices made every head swivel around to the door to the Rotunda.

'I can if I want to,' Tia yelled, furious, devastated. 'You can't stop me.'

'Tia, please calm down.' Edward was trying his best dad voice and it wasn't working. 'You're being completely unreasonable.'

Will and Sophie made it to the door first. Edward stood at the bottom of the stairs while Tia leaned over the banisters halfway up.

'"Unreasonable"? I'll show you "unreasonable", Edward.' The ground shook, the air heating and something rumbled deep underground. 'I'm not the one being unreasonable. You won't even touch me.'

'I can't. You know that. You know why. Tia, please calm down. Everyone's listening.'

'Well we can't bloody have that, can we? People might hear something! Gods, the horror! They all know anyway. And they know we're finished. And they know why! You! You and this job. Your damned *ambition*.'

Will pushed past Edward and bounded up the stairs towards her. 'Tia, please.' He stretched his arms wide and she stared at him as if he was betraying her simply by being there. 'Come on, you don't want to have this out here.'

'Why not?' she snarled. But then she seemed to wilt, sobbing, and Will gathered her in his arms. 'It's not like I need him anyway.' Will led her away carefully.

'Are you okay?' Sophie asked Edward. Blood had drained from his face and his hands were balled into fists at his side. He looked dreadful. 'Uncle Edward?'

'Fine,' he said through gritted teeth. 'I'm fine, Sophie. Personal matters which had no place... It's over anyway. It has to be.'

'You broke up with her?'

He glanced at her and she was certain that his eyes glittered with heartbreak. He was barely holding it together. The despair came off him in waves.

'I had to. Rules. Old ones.'

Edward met her gaze for just a moment and then turned away. Not the Keeper, not her uncle. Just a man who, even as he appeared to have won, had instead lost everything.

*

Sophie had forgotten entirely about the box in her workroom until, late on the following Tuesday, she was searching for some marbled paper and noticed it once more.

It had been sitting there since before Professor Alexander died.

The thought sent a shudder through her. She pulled it to her and untied the string holding it closed, just as Will arrived with coffee.

'Break time,' he said. 'What have you got there?'

'I'm not entirely sure,' she said. He put the coffees down on the bench nearest the door, knowing she wouldn't want them anywhere near her actual work. Whatever it was had been wrapped carefully in tissue paper and Sophie opened it with the utmost care.

The box was full of leaves.

Not just any leaves. These were huge, a pale golden hue, and the writing on them was elaborate and impenetrable. The colours glowed, illuminated sections in the most vibrant tones, lines more intricate than anything she had seen since the Mortlake grimoire.

'Are they...?' Will began.

As Sophie touched the top one, the letters inscribed on it seemed to glow. 'She must have left them here for me to bind.'

'It's a huge job,' said Will. 'We'll need to tell the Keeper. He'll want to know.'

Will always referred to Edward as the Keeper now, Sophie had noticed. Whether it was a way of putting some distance between the two men, or between the fact that he was both their boss and her uncle, she didn't know. Edward's elevation could have driven something between Sophie and Will, but so far the nascent relationship was holding on. Will was attentive in a way that Victor had never been. And he didn't crowd her, or quiz her endlessly about what she was doing or why. Victor had wanted to control everything she did. But Will seemed content to share daily life with her. And he made love to her in that earnest, focused way of his.

Sophie knew she was in love, and that she had fallen hard. Even when she had thought she loved Victor, she had never felt like this, never experienced this sense of contentment, of joy.

For the first time in her life she began to dread when it would all fall apart.

When Edward arrived, Sophie opened the box again and gingerly took out the fragile leaves. Her uncle's eyes went wide for a moment and then narrowed as he tried to read them.

'Hmm,' he said. 'Clearly not meant for me. Sophie? Can you?'

She read the first few lines, something about divining the soul within the currents of a pool which frankly made no sense at all to her but Edward seemed satisfied.

'The Keeper—' Will stopped, embarrassed. 'I mean… Professor Alexander must have gathered them. After the last time she was at the tree…'

Sophie felt a spear of regret and misery lance through her. Her fault, her conscience said again. She had made these leaves fall. She had made the Professor take charge of too much magic and bring it under control, more than her system could stand. And it had cost her everything.

'You'll have to bind them, Sophie,' Edward said. 'That's your role now. Since the Tree woke for you...' He paused, looking around the bindery. 'Use whatever you want, the finest materials. Make it a work of art. We're going to have to make some changes, I'm afraid. The Special Collection needs to move on and there are some financing issues to address. Arthur has actually been helpful in that respect.' A chill ran through Sophie. Edward's gaze was cold and she didn't like the way he looked at Will. Arthur apparently had found a price that suited him in order to support Edward.

'What do you mean?' Will asked, suspicion colouring the words.

Edward pinched the bridge of his nose. He looked tired, Sophie thought. 'It is possible we will need to raise funds in a variety of ways, develop services, offer our expertise more widely, and perhaps sell some of our more mundane items.'

Will was shocked, but didn't seem able to argue. When his eyes met hers, he looked away in a strange sort of shame.

Suddenly she felt as if she didn't know either of them. 'But, Edward—' she began.

He couldn't mean this book. He simply couldn't. And he had been the one to impress on her the importance of keeping the many items in the Special Collection secure. Now he was willing to send them out into the world for the highest bidder? She could picture Victor salivating and it sent a wave of revulsion through her.

Edward used that tone, no-nonsense and not to be argued with. 'It's for the best, Sophie. We have a duty to protect you and to protect the library, isn't that right, William? But we can't do that with debts hanging over us. Hypatia had her own ways of dealing with it. I have mine.' He pored over the leaves once more, as if they offered solace from the realities of his job. 'I can't wait to see what you make of this, my dear. It will be beautiful, I'm sure. Worthy of the Professor.'

*

Sophie cut a length of the finest linen thread and ran it across the block of beeswax. It was an act of meditation, and an act of homage to Professor Alexander. She couldn't bring herself to work in the Great Hall, even if it had been practical. Instead, she shut herself away in the studio, tuned the radio to a classical music channel, and told Will she needed to do this alone. He didn't argue and to be honest that should have concerned her.

Something was wrong with him. She didn't know what, but there were so many possibilities at this stage. He had lost the woman who was as good as a grandmother to him. He blamed himself for not being able to save her. And now his whole world was changing.

She tried to tell him that it wasn't his fault but he wasn't listening. She knew the truth.

It was her fault. It was all her fault.

Sophie pushed the thought away, trying to dampen the rising panic attack. She needed to do this. Otherwise what had been the point of the Professor's death? Well, no, there had been no point. No point at all.

The old woman had gathered these leaves up for her to bind. That was why she was here, after all. The repairs, the care and maintenance of the collection, that was secondary to this. Binding something new. Binding something unique. Something for Professor Alexander.

Sophie had already blocked the leaves that would become the pages, trusting Professor Alexander had already put them in the order she wanted, and used an ancient but viciously sharp awl to make the holes, marvelling at the touch-smoothed wood of the handle. Who else had used it? How many hands had pressed it through pages like this?

She could feel the weight of centuries clinging to it. She could almost feel her mother's hands guiding her. The Professor's as well. Countless others. Sophie closed her eyes and breathed as she sewed, connecting the leaves into quires and the quires into a block. She wove the threads together, looping stitches in an intricate cat's cradle until she had constructed a book. Not a finished book. It felt ragged and feral, still straining against her control.

She couldn't bring herself to use the guillotine to cut the pages to shape. Instead she used a trimmer, shaving the edges of each page in turn, a laborious task but one that kept her focused. Once she had finished, had carefully glued layers of Japanese tissue over the spine with wheat starch paste, followed by a strip of fine linen, she slid the new volume into one of the huge book presses for the night, winding down the screw at the top to lower the weighted plate onto it.

When she finished for the day, she fell asleep in Will's arms, exhausted.

She dreamed of the tree, but it was a gentler dream this time. Not the wild insistence. Not the demand for her attention. This time it sang to her. It was a hymn, a lament for the Keeper. The whole library was its chorus. It glowed with the touch of sunrise, warming her skin. She could feel it calling her and even as she woke up the next morning, all she knew was the need to finish the book. It was only because Will insisted that she ate breakfast.

'Are you sure you're okay?' he asked.

'Of course,' she told him, but he didn't look convinced.

For the cover she chose rich blue leather, decorated with a stamped roll which made her think of the woodcarvings on the main stairs. She treated the title area and the spine with the thin egg wash known as glair and added the title in gold leaf with hot type, pressing the irons into the gleaming surface one after the other, slowly, carefully. She added decorations as well, swirls of gold, flowers and leaves.

She knew what it was called, not because she read it. The book seemed to whisper it to her as she worked – *The Dream of Hypatia*.

At the end of the day, with Titivillus purring on her lap, she sat there, staring at the finished book. The cover, lush and perfect, her finest work, fitted perfectly around the book block, a cradle for the leaves. A treasure chest. She used marbled pages for the end paper in peacock colours, and then she was done. It would need time to rest now, its sitting time, her father called it. She wrapped it up and placed it back in the press, where the glue would take and the compression would firm up the book. Where, finally, it would transform from a number of disparate objects into one, unified whole.

It was beautiful, her finest work. She knew that objectively. But it felt like something more. The sense of achievement made something glow within her, warm and satisfied, a feeling of having done something she was always meant to have done. A feeling of rightness.

When it was ready, she brought it out and laid it on the workbench as she set about making a phase box for it. Every so often, she brushed her fingertips over the cover and smiled.

What secrets did it hold? She hadn't tried to read it, not while she was working on it. And perhaps she never would. She was coming to understand now that the Special Collection allowed her to read only what it wanted her to. But this book, stored away, hidden within the vaults, would seed so many minds with wonders, filtering through the subconscious of the world until whatever secret knowledge it held found its perfect home. It was where it belonged.

Will stared at it for the longest time, his eyes misting.

'I've never seen anything like it,' he told her. 'Wait until Tia sees it. You're a wonder, Sophie Lawrence.'

Sophie had never felt that kind of pride before. Never.

Which was why what happened next made everything come crashing down in an avalanche of ruin and regret.

*

Friday after lunch, Delphine arrived with word that Edward wanted to see her in his office. Sophie didn't think twice about it, but she didn't like the frown Delphine gave her either.

Edward hadn't taken over Professor Alexander's rabbit warren of rooms on the upper floor but rather had installed himself in the impressive office off the Reading Room on the ground floor which she had only ever used for meetings. She wondered, perhaps unkindly, why her uncle felt the need for a setting so grand and impressive.

'He's very busy,' Delphine said. 'He's drawn up all kinds of new funding models. It's very exciting. He wants to drag this place into the twenty-first century.' She was quite the acolyte all of a sudden. 'You'll see. We were talking, Dr Talbot and I, about digitisation and how we could create online access to everything we hold here.'

Sophie thought about some of the books in the vault and the magic teeming within their pages. That sounded like a terrible idea. Even if they would deign to be scanned. He couldn't mean that surely.

'*Some* people,' said Delphine with a snide edge to her voice. '*Some* people want to live in the past.'

'Which people?' Sophie wasn't sure she wanted to hear the answer.

Delphine laughed, a pretty trill of a laugh that wasn't as attractive as she clearly thought it was. 'Well, *quite*.' She leaned on the word with meaning. 'Tia isn't the apple of his eye any more. She is in *such* a sulk about it.' She said it with a little too much venom. Sophie frowned but Delphine didn't appear to notice. On one hand, at least she seemed to have moved on from her fixation on Will, but Sophie wasn't sure this new obsession with her uncle was an improvement. 'I told him the other day, that's just *so* unattractive. Don't you think?'

'I'm sure she isn't sulking,' Sophie replied softly, not even sure Delphine was listening. 'She's grieving. We all are. Sometimes it comes out in strange ways.'

'Oh, of course. It was awful. But life moves on, doesn't it?'

Sophie sucked in a breath, shocked at the callous way she said it.

They reached the door and Delphine stopped, holding the handle, even though Sophie was pretty sure she could manage opening a door herself. But Delphine was clearly relishing the power of being in control of this situation.

'There are going to be some changes around here. But I suppose as his niece you'll be fine anyway. We should have a coffee sometime. It would be nice, wouldn't it?'

'Sure,' Sophie replied, although she was pretty sure she would be busy whenever she asked. She'd make sure of it. Delphine had no intention of befriending Sophie for anything other than her own advancement. Sophie knew the type too well.

Delphine smiled broadly and opened the door, sweeping inside. 'Here she is, Dr Talbot,' she chimed.

Tia was there, but she didn't turn around as Sophie came in. She stared out of the window, as if she wished she could be anywhere but here right now. Will, on the other hand, was pacing back and forth at the back of the office, agitated, seemingly intent on wearing a track in the exquisite carpet that had been newly installed. Arthur Dee was there too, along with two other, younger men in their late twenties, brothers from the look of them. Sophie vaguely remembered them from the funeral.

And one last man, sitting right in front of Edward's desk, the one in a suit almost as fine as her uncle's, who turned and smirked at her, a shark's smile, one she knew all too well.

The world around her spun and contracted, her skin tightening against her skeleton as all the heat drained out of her.

'Hello, Sophie, my darling. So this is where you've been hiding.' He sounded so smooth and confident, like nothing had happened at all. He rose to his feet, crossing the room and reaching out to embrace her.

Sophie recoiled, just managing to evade him. He stopped short of hugging her, as Edward pointedly cleared his throat. Her own voice came out in a strangled gasp of shock.

'Victor? What are you doing here?'

Chapter Twenty-Two

For a moment Sophie couldn't breathe, she couldn't think. All she could do was stand there, staring. It was only when she felt someone touch her arm, she realised she could still feel at all. Will, it was Will. He linked her arm with his and stood beside her.

Victor saw it, saw their closeness, and his eyes narrowed a little. Just a flinch really, hardly noticeable at all. But she recognised it. He wasn't happy.

That wasn't a good sign. It was never a good sign.

'Your uncle invited me,' he told her. 'To discuss some sales of rare books from the collection. It's a very exciting proposal.'

She felt Will stiffen beside her. 'You didn't mention sales.'

'Everything is on the table,' said Edward. 'I thought you understood that, Will. Sit down, everyone. Please. We have been eating through our budget for years. The Academy and the various universities that fund us have been most understanding but the money can't continue forever. I have assured the School of Night that I will take care of it.' Arthur and the two brothers nodded their agreement, one of them giving her a helpful smile which did nothing to actually help. 'Sophie, you remember Henry and George Sidney. Sit down, all of you. Let's discuss this like professionals.'

It wasn't like anyone had a lot of choice. Sophie took a seat between Will and Tia, and as far away from Victor as she could get. She stared at her uncle, trying to work out what he was doing. And why? Why bring Victor into this? Why *him* of all people?

'Modern times call for modern methods,' Victor said smoothly. 'As I told you, I have collectors lined up who will take anything from the Special Collection and pay any amount of cash. This place is legendary. Your secrecy is your own undoing. In the past, the odd item escaped you…' He laughed at his own joke, but only Arthur joined in. 'But over the last two or three hundred years…'

'We were more careful, yes. With good reason.' Henry Sidney cut him off. Maybe he wasn't as keen on the idea as it appeared. Arthur gave him a look. 'But perhaps overcautious. Not everything here requires such secrecy. Some of it, certainly, but not everything. Don't you agree, Keeper?'

Tia shook her head, leaning forward. 'This is not a good idea, Edward. This is dangerous. You know that.'

'Not at all,' Arthur replied before Edward could. 'So long as we are cautious about what books are released and who they are released to, it will be fine. George?'

George Sidney opened a file on the desk in front of him. 'We have an arrangement with Mr Blake here that will ensure the utmost security. Anyone buying an item from the Special Collection will have to sign a fully binding non-disclosure agreement. They won't even see one of our volumes before that. A single sale will fund us for at least a year.'

So that was it. They had already decided. They had arranged everything and they had brought in *Victor* of all people. It made sense.

There wasn't a rare book dealer like him, no one with the contacts. The people Victor sold to were like dragons with their hoards. It didn't matter if they were legal. It didn't matter if anyone else would ever know that they owned them. It didn't matter how they came by them either. They would lock them away and the world would never know. It was all about possession.

Just like Victor.

And what would happen to their magic then? The Special Collection filtered those ideas and innovations out into the world. Lock them away in the wrong vault, with the wrong intentions, and it would stifle them forever. Wasn't that what Edward had said about the ones which found their way into other libraries around the world? It was the reason, as Head of Acquisitions, he had travelled to reclaim them.

Stifled and forgotten. That was how he had referred to those lost books he went and found. *Worse than forgotten, unknown.*

But this would be worse still. Knowledge previously available would be removed, torn from the whole fabric the Special Collection offered, leaving only a gaping hole. How could he agree to this?

'The Professor would never have agreed to this,' Will said.

It was the wrong thing to say. Edward gave him a warning glare and his voice became glacial. 'Hypatia lived in the past. Time to move on, William. Arthur is right. We have to make accommodations to living in the modern age.'

Will shot Arthur a glare, which Arthur contrived to ignore, but he didn't suppress the smirk of triumph he wore. Will pushed himself out of his seat and stalked to the back of the room again, as if to distance himself from whatever happened next.

'The School of Night are fully behind this,' said George, his money-grabbing little hands folded in front of him. 'The Special Collection needs to move forward. We can't continue to bankroll this money pit with no returns. That isn't the way of the world any more. I know you agree, Edward. So… this first item…'

A plain blue-grey box sat in the middle of the desk but Sophie knew it the moment Edward placed his hand on it.

'I haven't agreed to—' Edward began at the same moment as Sophie gasped.

'No,' she whispered. 'Please, I've only just—'

'All the more reason,' Victor cut in. 'It's new, unique, original. And some of your finest work. You've flourished here, Sophie love.' The endearment slid over her skin, leaving an unpleasant sensation trailing after it.

'When did you see it?'

He didn't answer her question but smiled that awful, knowing smile again. 'When I tell them that this book was bound by Philip Lawrence's daughter, they'll be impressed already but when they see it—'

The title was picked out in gold, the title she had read in the glowing letters in the leaves, the title this book had given itself when it separated itself from the Library Tree. *The Dream of Hypatia.*

She had made it the most beautiful thing she could imagine, because Professor Alexander had died for it, and because it would serve as a tribute to the Keeper. Here, in the library, where it belonged. It didn't matter what was in it, what secrets it held. It didn't even matter that its knowledge would never join the whole if they sold it. It was special because it was Professor Alexander's book. Her last book, even if Sophie had bound it for her.

And she had done it for nothing. All for nothing. For some billionaire somewhere far away to buy it and for bloody Victor Blake of *all* people to profit from it…

Sophie got to her feet. Tia had tears in her eyes but sat there defeated. Whatever Edward had said to her before this meeting, she didn't have any fight left in her.

And Will? Oh, he wasn't happy, but Edward was the Keeper now. Will wouldn't say a word against him, would he? He stood there, at the back of the room, his arms folded behind his back. The good soldier, standing to attention, ready for orders he wouldn't argue against.

This was wrong. And if no one else was going to say it, she wasn't going to be a hypocrite. Even if she was the only one.

'I can't believe you're going to do this,' she said to Edward, her voice choking. 'After all you said—'

'*Miss Lawrence*, that's quite enough. Control yourself. We are all professionals here.'

Victor smirked at her. Positively smirked.

He was loving every minute of this. He probably asked specifically for her work. He'd want all of it. Everything she had repaired, everything she had rebound, everything to come. If he couldn't have her, he'd take everything she cared about instead. Just to spite her.

That was how he worked.

She had made him a lot of money in the past. Now she was going to make him rich, whether she liked it or not.

Oh yes, she got it now.

Sophie couldn't believe her uncle was falling for it, that he was willing to do this. She wanted to slam her hands on the desk, scream at him, tell him that Victor was using them and that this undermined everything the Special Collection stood for. But it was pointless. Edward didn't care. Victor had already inveigled his way into the library. Now he was going to force his way back into her life.

If he couldn't have her, he'd still make his living from her. He'd still manipulate her and control her.

And Edward was giving her no choice at all.

Sophie had thought she was safe here, or as safe as she could be. That she wouldn't be used. It was her home, the place she had last been happy, and she had thought that maybe she was reclaiming some of that happiness again. She had found out what happened to her mother. She had found Will. She had found a place here for herself, following her mother's footsteps.

Arthur and his schemes were stripping everything away from her.

But it was just one thing after another.

Her mother died to protect the Special Collection, died because Arthur had wanted control over the Tree, and here he was again, wheedling his way back into power, manipulating Edward into making a terrible decision and undermining everything the Special Collection stood for, everything her mother believed in. They were going to destroy it all, little by little, take the precious volumes away and hoard them for the rich alone, people who couldn't even recognise them for what they were. Her mother died to keep the Tree from collapsing into chaos, gave herself up to keep the Special Collection intact. So had Professor Alexander. Now Edward, dear, stupid, gullible, heartbroken Edward, bowed by the pressure of it all, was putting everything they cherished at risk. For money. Because Arthur had wormed his way into the mind of the School of Night and brought all that pressure to bear on him. And her uncle was buckling.

Disgusted and helpless, Sophie turned her back on them all and forced herself to walk rather than run from the office.

*

Will came to find her sitting at the bottom of the stairs to the vault, staring at the door to the Axis Mundi, listening to the humming air behind it. She held her pendant, gazed at the symbol and tried to figure out what the library wanted from her. The Tree called her but she hadn't tried to go in. It was probably locked anyway. It ought to be locked. Especially with a mercenary shit like Victor on the grounds.

Besides, she was too angry to go in there now. There was no telling what would happen. If the Tree picked up her emotions she might trigger another disastrous cascade of power. If there truly was sentience in there, it might realise the magnitude of the betrayal being foisted on it and then she feared they really would see an eruption of outrage.

No, she just sat there, trying to make her body stop trembling, trying to fight back the tears. She hated this. Hated it. They were tears of anger, of impotent rage, not of grief now. But there was absolutely nothing she could do about it. She didn't own the book. She didn't own any of them, even if she poured her heart and soul into their binding and repair. They weren't hers even if they felt like a part of her.

Had Elizabeth felt like this? Had she realised the only way to save the Special Collection was to sacrifice herself? Sophie didn't even have that option. It would do nothing to help her now.

'They're leaving,' Will said, as he sat beside her, his long legs folding up against the stairs.

'*He'll* be back.'

'Yes.' At least he didn't try to lie to her. That was the good thing about Will. He knew exactly who she meant. 'But you don't have to see him again.'

Sophie shook her head. 'You don't understand.'

'Do you… do you *want* to see him?' The suspicion in his voice stabbed at her. Will was staring fixedly ahead, but she could tell he was dreading the answer. Did he honestly think she wanted Victor? After all they had shared, the two of them?

'*You don't understand*,' she repeated more forcefully, because what was the point in arguing? She didn't understand it herself.

'You were in a relationship for years. Until quite recently. You never really broke up with him, just took the job here and vanished.'

She could hear the echo in his voice, the echo of what Victor must have told them. 'Is that what he said?'

'Sophie, talk to me.'

'There's nothing much to say.' She pushed herself back up onto her feet, walked forward before he could stop her and pressed both her hands on the door to the Axis Mundi. She could feel it through the wood, singing, sighing, its hypnotic murmuring trying to comfort her. Even now it was reaching out to her. 'I left him because I had to. I thought I was safe here. I was wrong.'

God, she wanted to go in. She wanted to shut herself away in there, curl up at the foot of the tree and let it take her away. Anywhere.

She could find her mother, stay with her. Lost in the light of the Tree, in that other place, deep within the Axis Mundi. Walk in there. Give up.

'Sophie…'

Will didn't move, didn't try to hold her, or crowd her, or pull her away.

'He'll wreck everything, Will. He's already wrecking things. It's what he does. He must have moved in on Arthur the moment he heard about what happened here. Or earlier. I thought I saw them together in the pub that night. But I… it doesn't matter. He'll influence us all and it'll all seem so reasonable until suddenly I'll be isolated and I won't have any choice but to turn to him. It's what he does. It took me so long to see it. I won't let it happen again. I won't.'

A wave of cold swept through her and goosebumps rose on her arms. She wasn't going to let him. She wasn't. She couldn't do it again. She wasn't going back to him. Never. If she had to, she'd leave the Special Collection. Which would mean leaving Will.

Will's hand rested lightly on her shoulder, a tentative gesture, but comforting nonetheless. 'It's a time of change. We all go through them. We'll work something out, appeal to the School of Night to find someone else or – I won't – I won't let him hurt you, Sophie.'

The words stopped her racing thoughts. No one had ever made a promise like that to her before. Not one she believed.

With her heart in her throat, she wrapped her arms around his neck and pulled him down into a kiss.

She didn't want to leave this place. Or him.

'Will they listen? Victor's waving a solution to all their money worries in their faces. He's offering to make this place pay for itself at last. They won't want to hear what I have to say. Trust me.'

'You know I do,' he murmured into her skin. 'I'll talk to Arthur. Maybe we can work something out, limit Victor's access to the library and… And you will have to trust me. Please, Sophie.'

She wanted to say yes, of course, yes she trusted him with her life, with everything. And she did, in her heart. But her rational brain had too many questions, too many doubts.

Will kept too many secrets.

*

It was getting dark by the time they made their way back upstairs.

'Do you fancy a walk?' she asked and Will nodded. They fetched their coats and headed out the main door, Will pausing only to close it behind them as Sophie started down the drive.

Victor was waiting. He stood by his flashy car, in his flashy suit, flicking through something on his phone while Delphine flirted with him. Meera stood to one side, looking embarrassed, her eyes growing wide as Sophie appeared. Delphine carried on, oblivious.

Sophie had been sure Victor had gone but no. He'd just been biding his time.

When his eyes met Sophie's, she stopped dead in her tracks.

'Sophie,' he called, leaving Delphine standing there alone and open-mouthed. 'I'm so glad you're okay. I was worried about you.'

'You were? The last time I saw you, you called me—'

He sidled in against her, blocking Will who had to take a step back. 'I was an idiot, wasn't I? You know I lose my reason where you're concerned. I always have. Look, let's have dinner and sort this out. I'm staying in the hotel on the other side of the village. It's not far. Let me treat you and I can explain.'

'I don't want—'

'You have to give me a chance, love. Please.'

Meera opened her mouth but no words came out. Delphine whispered something, her gaze never leaving Sophie, judging her. The jaws of a trap seemed to close around Sophie, crushing her. A lifetime of being told not to make a fuss, not to cause trouble.

She opened her mouth to say no but something else came out. 'You really hurt me, Victor.'

His voice was a purr. 'I know, sweetheart. I know. I took you for granted but I only want a chance to make it up to you.' He moved closer and she heard Will step back. The sound rasped against her heart.

No, this couldn't be happening. Victor was not allowed to do this to her. She steeled herself and tried again. 'I have a job here, a life.'

He took her hand, turning it over in his so he could caress her fingers the way she loved. Will flinched. She caught it out of the corner of her eye and winced, pulling her hand free. But she was too late.

'I think you need to leave Sophie alone,' Will said.

Victor smiled at him. 'Oh, so he's the new man, is he? You've never been good at being alone, have you, Soph? She was like that in college, flitting from one boyfriend to the next. A classic serial monogamist.' He laughed, actually laughed, as he lied about her.

She'd had friends in college, the odd date, but nothing serious. Victor had always read more into that. He'd wanted their names and asked all about them. He was only interested, he said.

Now she understood the truth. He'd been jealous. He was jealous now.

But Will didn't look happy. In fact, he looked like he was buying this crap. And he was getting angry too. She could feel it in the air, shimmering around him like an aura, that sense of threat growing all the time.

'Sophie and I are old friends, that's all,' Will told him and Sophie frowned. She'd thought they were more than friends. What had the last few weeks been? 'When we were kids.'

'Oh well, yes, she's good at having *friends*. But not so good at keeping them, are you?' Victor laughed and slid an arm around her shoulder. She froze, not sure how to get out of this without making a scene. Which she didn't want to do. Not at work. Especially not because she had made one in Uncle Edward's office. 'Come on, in the end, you always forgive me, don't you, Soph? We belong together.' He squeezed her skin, right down to the bone, his old familiar claws digging in.

She felt cold, standing in the patch of winter sunlight with Victor winding stories around her again, winding his grip around her too. He was charming. He always had been and people always believed him, no matter what she said or did. He was the one everyone trusted. The one with the crazy girlfriend. How did she get away from him? She'd only managed before by leaving absolutely everything and walking away. She didn't know what to do, or what to say. The problem was, he wasn't actually wrong. She did always forgive him. She ignored his transgressions and the words he said that hurt her. He usually had a reason anyway. Or at least his own reason, even if it didn't make sense to her.

'Victor, please...' she muttered. 'I need to...'

'Oh no, I get it,' he sighed and withdrew abruptly. 'You'll figure it out in the end. I get it. They want to keep you here. You're so talented, Sophie. Your work has grown, far beyond your father's now. I guess they'll do anything to keep you here, given what you can do for the library. They probably aren't even paying you enough. We should talk to Edward about that. I'm going to be part of the furniture around here, Sophie. We need to come to some sort of agreement, don't we?'

Part of the furniture? Oh God, he planned to be here all the bloody time, didn't he? He was going to make life impossible for her.

'We should talk, I guess,' she admitted. If only to lay some ground rules about work.

Victor beamed at her as if she had said something else entirely. 'I knew you'd get there in the end.'

'No, I mean...' What did she mean? She felt so strange, so lost. Victor closed in on her again, pushing his luck. He was always pushing his luck. Always crossing one line or another.

But someone else was watching.

'Enough,' Will snarled, and the feral shadows she had seen in him from the start burst out. His eyes were dark and endless, wild. One moment he was standing there and the next, he grabbed Victor and shoved him away from Sophie. 'Leave her alone. Sophie doesn't want to go anywhere with you.' Victor's designer shoes scraped on the gravel as he tried to anchor himself. Will was taller and broader, and suddenly looked so unlike the gentle man Sophie knew. He dwarfed Victor.

But Victor wasn't cowed. 'I don't think you get to say what Sophie wants or doesn't want, do you?'

'Will,' Delphine chimed in. Right on cue. 'Will, calm down.'

But even as he mimed defending himself, Victor leaned in and hissed something at Will. She didn't know what, didn't catch it, but she saw Will's face go white with rage.

Sophie knew what was going to happen seconds too late to stop it. As Will's fist swung at Victor's face, she heard shouts from behind them, Edward and the Sidneys emerging from the door in time to see it all. Victor went down in a heap, cradling his face, and Will was on him.

The scuffle was violent and vicious. Victor kicked and tried to give as good as he got, but Will was bigger, stronger and fitter. And it looked bad. It looked so bad.

'Will, please,' Sophie shouted. 'Stop.' He was going to get fired. He was going to get charged with assault. She launched forward, trying to grab him, trying to pull him off when someone's elbow came back and slammed into her shoulder, throwing her back with a cry. Her head cracked off the ground as she did so and she lay there winded as everything dissolved into shouting all around her.

Tia helped her up, Tia who trembled as if she was trying to keep herself from shattering, but still attempting to help Sophie. Will and Victor had been separated and Delphine bent over Victor, hands fluttering in apology, while Will... oh God, Will...

Will was standing there, still bristling while the Sidneys held him back. They looked livid, as did her uncle.

'Walk it off,' Edward said, pointing in the opposite direction. 'Walk it off now. Meera, go with him. Make sure he doesn't come back until he's calmed down. I'll talk to you later when you regain your senses and there will be repercussions, William. Serious repercussions.'

He sounded furious. Beyond furious.

When Sophie glanced at Victor again, even through the mask of blood and snot on his face, she could read his triumph.

'Shit,' she whispered. 'Oh Will, oh God...'

'What is it?' asked Tia.

'Will's going to be fired. Victor will press charges just to make a point.'

'They can't fire Will. He belongs here. I'm sure Edward will—'

'Tia, I know Victor. He did it on purpose. He'd going to insist and they all saw it. They'll make him fire Will.'

'But Will wouldn't hurt a fly. He isn't like that.'

Sophie knew that. Or at least she thought she did. But she also knew there was something in him, something buried deep inside, a need to protect the library and those associated with it which didn't know reason. It rarely came out but it was there. Which told her that, yes, Will could very much be 'like that'. And Victor had spotted it too. And used it.

That was what he did.

'Well, Sophie,' he said, the white handkerchief at his face turning red. 'We certainly have a lot to talk about now, don't we?'

Chapter Twenty-Three

Will had never felt so lost. He couldn't even say what had come over him. He'd lost it, seeing that smug bastard smarming over Sophie. And then he'd leaned in and said those words.

'Hope you screwed her already. Arthur tells me you're not going to be here much longer. The old bitch was the only one keeping you here anyway, you half-breed bastard.'

Just like that, Will had lost his reason. The monster inside him slipped loose.

It only ended with Sophie trying to stop him, with her falling back, that noise as she hit the ground...

It was like a nightmare. His worst nightmare.

He'd done that. He'd hurt her. The one thing he had sworn to himself that he would never do.

Beside him, Meera was jumpy and nervous. Well, who wouldn't be? Will's temper had acquired a near mythic status. They knew it existed, but he'd never let them see it. None of his peers. It was part of his nature but he usually kept it under tight control. He'd learned how, over the years. Letting it out never solved anything. It came from the library, from being its guardian, from having his whole family line tied here to protect it. And something else, far greater. Something that came from Tia.

Arthur jogged across the lawns to the riverbank. 'What were you thinking?' He glanced at Meera. 'You can head back. I'll deal with him now.' He waited until they were alone at least. 'You're going to be lucky if he doesn't have you charged with assault. They're talking about firing you, Will.'

Of course they were.

'Where's Sophie?'

'Sophie? I don't know where the bloody girl is. She went off after Blake. Damn it, Will, you need to focus on you right now.'

How could he focus on him? Sophie had gone after Victor. He had screwed up everything. Absolutely everything. The air felt like it had been sucked from his lungs and his head swam.

He swore loudly and Arthur took a step back. 'Take a damned breath and calm down. You're hardly a child so leave the tantrums here, will you?'

'I'm sorry. I ... What did they say?'

'Mostly things about a lack of professionalism and tarnishing the reputation of the Special Collection. Edward is probably going to suspend you from duties without pay. But if Blake brings charges...' He left the warning hanging.

Victor was going to bring charges. Of course he was. This was what he had wanted. Sophie had tried to warn Will that he'd try to isolate her. He was succeeding.

And yet she was the one running after him now.

Well, why not? Will had sent her flying. Or one of them had, but he had no idea which of them actually hit her. All he knew was it was his fault. If she never wanted to see him again, he wouldn't blame her.

Tia found them some time later, Will sitting in silence, mulling over his own mistakes, and Arthur on the phone to one of the warders, trying to rally support for his errant little brother.

'He's a guardian. You know how they are. Yes of course. Well, he felt there was a threat. She's the binder and the library has already suffered a loss… yes, yes, I understand.'

He hung up and dialled another number.

'There you are,' said Tia softly. 'Edward's furious.'

'Edward's always furious these days. With all of us. Sucks to be the boss, I guess.'

'I suppose so,' she replied, glancing at Arthur as he wandered off, arguing with someone else. 'He isn't handling this well, is he?'

'I embarrassed him. That's the worst sin.' Will let his head fall forward, cradling it in his hands. 'Is Sophie okay?'

'Just winded. She's fine. You didn't hurt her, Will.'

Didn't he? He was pretty sure he had. Or at least frightened her. 'I'm a monster, Tia.'

She hugged him suddenly, her long arms around him, her head on his shoulder. 'Aren't we all, my darling? Aren't we all? Come back now. We need to sort this out and quickly. You need to talk to Edward. Now.'

'So he can fire me?'

She drew back, tried to smile. It wasn't convincing. 'It won't come to that. The Tree won't allow it. You're tied here like me, remember?'

'Has anyone told him that?'

She hugged him again. 'It will be okay. I promise. Won't it, Arthur?'

His brother was back, standing over them with disgust all over his face. He shrugged, unconvinced.

*

There was no sign of Sophie back at the library, and no sense of her either. Will hadn't realised how she permeated the place until now, how much more comfortable he was within the walls when she was here.

But she was gone. It left an emptiness in the air he couldn't define. He tried to ring her but the mobile went to voicemail. He left a message, an apology that didn't feel like enough.

And then Edward summoned him.

It was what he had been dreading and he knew it was going to be bad. He stood in the office waiting, fidgeting like a kid hauled up in front of the headmaster.

'Take a seat please, Mr Rhys,' Edward began, closing the door behind him. Not even the obnoxious 'William'. This was bad. Very bad. Will sat. It wasn't like he had any choice. 'Your brother has made an appeal on your behalf.' He had? It was a miracle. 'So has Tia, naturally. I appreciate there has been a large amount of stress in our workplace of late. The loss of Professor Alexander had a profound effect on all of us. Especially on you. I *do* understand that. How close you were...'

He cleared his throat and then pinched the bridge of his nose as if warding off a headache. 'But you assaulted a guest. I know your role here is a unique one, William, but that cannot pass. However, Ms Matthews has also made a statement in your defence and she was a first-hand witness.' Delphine? Wonders really would never cease. Will thought she was still mad at him for not being the romantic hero she desperately wanted. 'She thought you felt Miss Lawrence was threatened in some way?'

'Yes.' Felt it, knew it, had no doubt about it whatsoever.

'And yet Miss Lawrence was the person who ended up hurt.' Anger simmered in Edward Talbot's eyes. Oh, he had never liked Will, but he had put up with him, so long as he stayed in his place. Professor Alexander had protected him, but she was gone now.

'That was an accident.'

Where was she? He should have made sure she was okay. And here he was, sitting in Edward's office wishing he knew where on earth she was. All he wanted to do right now was find her and grovel in apology.

'We need to talk about some anger management therapy, but for now I'm suspending you without pay for three weeks.'

'What?'

'You heard me. If you're going to argue about it I can make it permanent.'

Will opened his mouth to reply but then thought better of it. Right now, he was only going to make matters worse and he knew it. 'Where am I meant to go?'

'Take a break, William. When was the last time you had a holiday?'

Never, that was when. Holidays weren't in his nature. He and Arthur had gone away with family sometimes. He'd visited his grandparents before they passed away and that had been a nightmare. He'd taken Tia away a couple of times but she wouldn't leave for more than a night or two. The longest he'd ever been away from Ayredale was when he was at college. His life was here. His duty. Everything.

And maybe that wasn't healthy either.

'Look,' Edward sighed, and the change in tone of voice brought Will's head up in shock. 'Things will settle down. I'll sort out Victor Blake. He's easily bought when you get down to it. I peeled him off Sophie once and I will again if needs be. No matter what it takes. I have no qualms about that. Trust me.'

'Yes, Keeper.' What else could he do? Edward was in charge now anyway.

'Good man.' Edward sat back in his chair, his fingers threaded together in front of him. 'We'll get through this, Will. And we'll make this library great again.'

'By asset-stripping it?'

Edward didn't like that description and it showed in the tight lines of his face. He felt as bad about this as the rest of them. 'That's a crude way of putting it.'

'And whose idea was it? Victor Blake?'

'Arthur's actually. We move with the times, Mr Rhys. A few items. That is all. Nothing dangerous, nothing of true value.'

'What about that?' Will nodded to the newest book.

Edward shook his head. 'That was a mistake, I see it now. Your brother's suggestion, something to really get Blake hooked.' He sighed. 'We don't even know what's in it, what secrets the Keeper left for us. I had no idea Sophie would—'

'React like that? She poured her heart into it, for Professor Alexander. You asked her to.' His throat tightened. He could feel the love that emanated from the book, the respect. It was an echo of his own. 'We have to tread carefully with that man, Edward.'

'I know. Not this book. I'll see to it. But... there will be others, Will.'

He might not like it but he had no say in the matter. The School of Night had decided, and even Edward didn't have the means to deny them. Will supposed he was lucky to have a job to come back to. But then, he was a legacy, the guardian. Dee's son, though Roland Dee himself had been ashamed to admit it. Tia's son, which was probably more of an issue. They couldn't throw him out. He was the guardian of the library.

Will knew there was no way in this world that they would let him leave forever. For the time being, Edward just needed him out of the way. Safely tucked out of sight until he could smooth it all over.

'I'll get Delphine to book you into a hotel somewhere, how about that? Cornwall maybe? You'll like it. It's very relaxing. Go and pack, tell Tia that you're going, and I'll have something sorted by the time you're done. Dismissed.'

Like he was a soldier. Which, in a way, he was.

Under orders, and in disgrace. And now dismissed.

*

'What do you mean you're going?' Tia asked, her eyes wide. 'You can't just go. You belong here.'

'I wasn't given a lot of choice.' He shoved more clothes into the rucksack which was the only bag he had suitable.

'But where are you going?'

'Cornwall. On holiday.'

'Cornwall? That's the end of the world! What is he sending you there for?'

'It's hardly the end of the world, it's a few hours' drive, that's all.'

'And then some. It'll be past midnight before you even get there. Why now? Why is he sending you away? He can't do that.'

'I don't know, Tia. He's your boyfriend. You tell me. Could it have something to do with the assault charges his niece's ex-boyfriend is threatening me with?'

She slammed the door to his room and Will jumped, but she was still there, only now they were closed away from the rest of the library. Her eyes burned. 'It has more to do with stripping the library, me, *and* his niece of our guardian, and you know it.'

Will's hands closed into fists. He couldn't help himself. She was right. 'He could try to find another guardian, Tia.'

Will had always thought that was impossible. But then he had never thought anyone connected with the library would contemplate what Edward was doing. Except perhaps Arthur. Everything was changing. He couldn't keep up with it. No matter how he tried to hold things together, they crumbled in his grip like sand.

'Well there isn't one. Not one that will be acceptable. Arthur's rubbish and always was.' She raised her hands before he could protest. 'Oh, it's true. We all know it. Your father knew it. That's why he was also such a bastard to you. The *other woman's* son. You. The library chose you, Will. And it chose you for a reason. Edward can't get rid of you now. He made you part of this, him and his sister. I'll talk to him. I'll make him see sense. We may not be together now but he'll still listen to me.'

'Don't worry about it. It doesn't matter any more.'

Will picked up the bag. He still hadn't managed to get Sophie on the phone but he'd keep trying. He'd explain. He had to.

But Sophie had taken off after Victor and he didn't know where he stood now. She'd seen the monster in him. The people of the library might have called him the guardian, but he knew what he was.

Will wasn't under any illusions. He had let himself dream a little too long. Because of Sophie.

He drove away, down the narrow lanes and into the night, promising himself he'd stop somewhere for a coffee and a rest once on the motorway. But he didn't want to. How long was it they recommended? Every hour and a half or something? Maybe two. He could push it to two.

The phone started ringing before he even got to Kingsford, ten minutes down the road.

Chapter Twenty-Four

Sophie drove Victor back to the hotel. It was some way out of the village on the far side from the library. Victor couldn't possibly drive himself and while she didn't think his nose was actually broken it took a long time to stop bleeding. They had pulled into the car park before he even tried removing the blood-soaked handkerchief and dabbed tentatively at his face.

It was dark outside. They sat in the pool of light under an ornamental lamppost.

'Are you feeling better?' she asked, not moving.

'Yes. I'm so grateful you're here. Not back there with that animal. What were you thinking, Sophie?'

She frowned, but didn't answer. Her phone had rung a couple of times as they drove and she hadn't been able to check it.

'We are finished, Victor,' she reminded him. 'I left you. You were merrily screwing your assistant or whoever she was, if you remember.'

He hung his head. 'Sophie, this all started when your uncle sent you that letter. He's done this, hasn't he? Manipulated you. Arthur told me all about it.'

'No.' But... he wasn't wrong, was he? This had all started with Uncle Edward, with his letter. And she knew now that magic was real. Edward could do it, and had no qualms about using it. She couldn't tell Victor that. She could only imagine what he'd do with that knowledge. It was bad enough that he was after the books. He couldn't be allowed to know about the Tree.

'You know how easily swayed you can be,' Victor said. 'You've been so lonely, especially since your father died. I'm sure Edward was a father figure to you, but he's manipulative. He wants to use you.'

Did he hear himself? No, enough. She wasn't listening to Victor any more.

'I need to get back. It's late.'

'Come inside and talk to me, please, Sophie. At least give me that much. Maybe you can explain to me why I shouldn't press charges against your boyfriend.'

'He's not my—' The words came out before she could stop them. And anyway, Will had said they were just friends. Friends with benefits maybe. But nothing more.

Boyfriend was too small a word for the way she felt about Will. But if she could persuade Victor not to press charges she might be able to save Will's job. Because right now she knew that it was in danger. He was at risk of being thrown out of the library that he loved. The only home he had. The only one he had ever known.

Victor sighed, his voice calm and reasonable, making himself patient while she was the one getting upset.

'I only want to talk, Soph. That's all. You never even gave me a chance to apologise. I want to make this up to you, clear the air. Come on, for old times' sake.'

Old times' sake? What the hell was that? But if she could persuade him to leave Will alone, that had to be worth something.

'Fine. But we're sitting in the bar. You have twenty minutes and then I'm leaving.'

He opened the door and got out, waiting for her in the car park. Damn it, she didn't have any choice here. Sophie heaved in a breath, willing herself to be strong, and opened the door.

Victor held out his hand for the keys. It was his car, after all. She'd have to get a taxi or walk back in the dark. She hadn't thought of that. At least she had her coat.

Great.

Inside, the hotel bar was quiet. It wasn't late but obviously it hadn't been a busy night. The barman looked bored, and they were alone apart from him and a waitress who took the order while never making eye contact.

Well, Victor's order – a bottle of red wine and a steak. He charged it to the room, making sure Sophie heard the room number.

'Or we can take it up there, Soph, if you want. Have a bit of privacy?'

'No, thank you. We're fine here,' Sophie told the waitress, in case there was any doubt that she wasn't planning to go anywhere with Victor. 'Just a coffee for me please. I won't be staying long.'

If that disappointed him, Victor didn't show it. 'You want to help your boyfriend, don't you?'

'What do you want now, Victor? You have your deal with Edward and the library, you have the books and my work. What else?'

He leaned forward. 'Apart from you?'

She stared back at him, loathing him. She got it now. She only had value to him when he couldn't have her. He couldn't see her as a person, only a trophy. That was all she had ever been. So she needed to take that off the table.

'Apart from me.'

Victor sat back, still smiling, still so self-confident. She hated him for it. And for everything else. All the times he'd manipulated her, made her think something was her idea when actually it was his, every time she had given up something because he wouldn't like it.

'Let me eat first, love. I'm ravenous. I can never talk while I eat, you know that.'

Sophie drank her coffee and Victor ate his steak, bloody and rare. Every so often he offered her a chip which she refused. He held it out like she was a pet, expected to take it from his hand. But she could see through him now. All the affectations and superficiality. All the tricks.

The waitress refilled her coffee and Sophie drank again. She wasn't going to be able to sleep tonight at this rate. His time was up. She'd given him more than twenty minutes already.

Outside, the wind was howling, and she could hear rain hitting the window panes. Great. If she did have to walk back to the library she was going to get soaked now. And the moment she got up to leave, he'd tell her not to be so silly as to go out in this weather and he'd delay and defer yet again. It was exhausting.

When the door behind her opened and a rush of freezing wind tore through the bar, she knew who it was. She knew without even having to turn around.

'I was worried you might have taken off already,' said Arthur Dee. He took off his wet coat and shook it out, hanging it over the back of the chair. 'There's a storm brewing out there. Took an age to get away. God, I hate the bloody countryside, don't you? Now, Soph, we have a lot to discuss.'

She glanced from him to Victor, who was grinning at her like this was all some nasty practical joke and she was the brunt. Whatever was going on, they were in this together and she didn't like it one bit.

'What are you doing, Arthur?'

He laughed, actually laughed in her face like she was an idiot. 'I'm going to be the Keeper.'

'Edward is the Keeper. The School of Night decided.'

He shook his head. 'The Keeper of a brand-new library, back in London where the action is instead of isolated out here in the middle of nowhere. Edward can preside over the rubble of this place. And you're going to help me.'

Like hell she was. 'Why would I do that?'

'Sophie,' Victor cut in, intent on explaining it to her like a child. 'Think about it. He can tell you what happened to your mother. He knew her. He was there.'

She scowled at him for a moment and then turned her attention back to Arthur. He'd been conspicuous by his absence since Edward told her the truth. Or maybe he had just been avoiding her. It was his fault they had been down there in the first place. He'd dared her to go to the Tree. He'd wanted to take over the library even then. And it had cost everything. Her anger boiled beneath her skin but she needed to keep her wits about her.

'What about her?'

'I can show you. But we have to go back to the library. We have to go down to the Tree. And you need to take me there. She's still there, Sophie. Waiting for you.'

No. She wasn't listening to him. Not now. Charm and manipulation were what Arthur did best. Her mother was gone. Sophie knew that, had always known that. What she had heard were just echoes. Ghosts. Dreams.

All the desperate hopes of a broken child.

She pushed herself up onto her feet. 'I've had enough of this. I want nothing to do with either of you.'

Arthur scowled. An ugly and vicious expression on a face enough like Will's as to make it a travesty. His hand shot out, closing on her wrist in a grip so tight and painful Sophie couldn't move. Something settled over her, like a black shadow closing all around her, stealing her breath and making her head swim in a fog.

'Sit down,' he said, his voice reverberating against her. Sophie's knees buckled and she sank back into the chair, unable to resist. 'This is Art. This is what we do. With it, we can command the world and you're the key to that, Sophie Lawrence. You, those spells knocking around your pretty little head from Dee's book, and that Tree. You will be working for me from now on. Understand?'

The pendant around her neck had turned icy cold and she shivered. But still she couldn't move. Arthur could do magic and he was using it on her.

'Will won't let you do this,' she said, desperately trying to cling to her own will.

'Will's loyal to the library. And now we have a way to control him and Tia. He'll do what he's told.' A way to control Will? What on earth did he mean?

A thousand questions she didn't dare ask...

'I don't want to,' she tried, one last desperate attempt.

'You don't get a choice, Sophie,' said Victor, pouring himself some more wine. 'It's about time you accepted that. We're going to be back together, love. Maybe we'll stay here, get a little house in the country? Nice and quiet. It'll all go back to normal, exactly as it was. You'll see.'

Sophie tried to lever herself up again, the thought of a life with Victor in complete control of everything giving her enough strength to try. But her body was rooted to the chair. She was trapped.

No, she couldn't accept this. She wouldn't.

Tears stung her eyes and Victor stared at her while he drank, smiling, loving it.

'It was you in the pub, wasn't it? You were meeting Arthur there?'

'Yes, and he was not happy when you all rocked up, were you, Arthur? Do you know he can do magic, Sophie? Amazing. You didn't even recognise me. I looked right at you and—' He curled his hand almost into a fist in front of her face and then flicked his fingers out like a firework going off. She flinched back. 'You didn't know me at all. Magic.' He laughed. 'I bet with enough time I could learn it too.' The nasty thin smirk was back, the knowing gleam in his eyes. 'That would be fun, wouldn't it? Even to have the ability to get you to do as you're told like Arthur can, that would be some trick.'

The threat seeped through the words.

Please, she thought as panic surged within her blood and pounded in her head, *please no. I've got to get out of here. I've got to—*

The pendant around her neck turned suddenly hot, like a fire against her skin. Something shot up through her, something wild and dangerous, out of the earth itself. The door to the bar burst open and the wind filled the room, the storm outside tearing through the room. Arthur cursed loudly, turning, while the waitress gave a scream of alarm.

And suddenly Sophie could move. She threw herself out of the chair and straight for the door, wind whipping around her as she made it outside. The rain lashed against her face but she didn't care. The only thing that mattered was getting away, getting out of that room and back to the library. She had to warn Edward and Tia. They'd know what to do. She had to find Will.

She didn't have a car, so she took off running up the road. Maybe she could flag someone down. Maybe she'd have to run the whole way. It didn't matter. She had to get away.

Rain lashed down in her face, blinding her, soaking her. Behind her she heard Victor shouting and a car started up. They were coming after her. They had to be. Almost blind in the darkness of the country road, she tried desperately to get her bearings. It wasn't far back to the library, it couldn't be. She'd only driven Victor because he'd been hurt and didn't want to leave his precious car there.

The bridge over the river up ahead reared out of the darkness.

Sophie lurched forward. She could hear the river roaring ahead of her, and the car from behind. She was out of options, nowhere to go. The car accelerated towards her and she tried to throw herself to one side. But she was already on the bridge. The wall hit her middle and the next thing she knew she was falling, arms flailing. The river, freezing and turbulent, closed over her, swallowing her up.

The world turned violent and bewildering. She tried to scream and her mouth filled with water. She hit the riverbed, her body bashing against the slick rocks, and came up for air again, gasping, trying to find a handhold on something, anything to stop her.

Someone yelled her name and she went under again.

Strong arms grabbed her, hauling her up onto the muddy bank and her thundering heart deafened her. As the arms tried to roll her onto her side, she fought back, lashing out, kicking.

'Sophie! Sophie, it's me. It's me. Sophie! You're okay. I have you. You're safe.'

Slowly the words made sense again and she recognised the voice. His voice. Will. It was Will.

She grabbed him and clung to him, desperate, unable to bring herself to let go.

Her voice strained against the sound of the storm. It grated against her throat, faint and broken. 'Will, it's your brother. Your brother and Victor.'

'I can't hear you,' he replied, his own voice almost drowned out by the storm. 'It's going to be okay. Just hold onto me. I'll get you back to the library.'

She could see the outline of his car, pulled in on the edge of the road from the library, the engine still running and the lights still on. The back seat had a rucksack and some other belongings. His things. Where had he been going?

Will bundled her into the passenger seat and fished a blanket out of the rear which he wrapped around her. It smelled of him, of his musk and his body. Once he was sure she was safely inside, he struggled back around the car in the wind and rain, and then climbed in beside her. He shook his wet hair, trying to get the water out of his eyes.

'Will, please listen.' Her voice sounded thick and slurred and her head pounded. It was almost quiet now, though the storm raged on outside. It shook the car but Will threw it into reverse and started turning around. The cold was getting to her. The shock too. She couldn't stop shaking. At the same time a terrible sluggish heat crept up her body, stealing her consciousness a little at a time.

He drove back down the dark country road. The phone rang, the screen lighting up the dashboard, illuminating his face.

He didn't even look like himself. Focused, haunted, broken.

'Arthur? It's okay,' Will said. 'I found her. I've got her. I'm heading back to the library.'

Chapter Twenty-Five

With the heat turned up full and her treacherous body hanging on the edge of consciousness, Sophie struggled to focus, not to give in to panic. Whatever was going on, she needed to keep her wits about her. But she couldn't stop shaking, and she couldn't forget what she'd heard Will say, or who he had been talking to.

'How did you find me?' she asked.

Will glanced at her, just for a moment, and then returned his attention to the narrow road, treacherous in this weather.

'Arthur called, said you'd run off from Victor. I was worried.'

'Worried.'

He gritted his teeth, his jaw firming up. 'Terrified, actually,' he replied as if reluctant to admit it. But she didn't doubt him either. 'And then… I saw you in the river. I thought… I don't know what I thought.'

'You were leaving? Just like that? I thought you had a duty to this place. I thought… I thought… Weren't you even going to say goodbye?'

He blinked, and then frowned. He was soaked too, and exhausted. Water dripped down his face.

'I wasn't given a lot of choice, Sophie.'

'I saw Arthur…'

'I know.'

'He wants the library. He wants to be Keeper. He wants to move it to London and run it from there.'

Will turned up the drive she now knew so well, the headlights picking out the library building in the distance.

'*I know,*' he repeated. 'And that will mean the destruction of everything here. Possibly all of Ayredale. He threatened Tia, Sophie. He's going to do something to her. You asked me to trust you, Sophie. Now I'm asking the same thing. Please trust me. Can you walk?'

'Of course I can walk,' she snapped, her patience at an end now. 'I need to see my uncle. Now.'

He parked the car and she threw open the door, stumbling out into the storm before he had a chance to help her. Or stop her. Or whatever he was planning to do. Sophie didn't know which side Will was on any more. Half an hour earlier she would have said, without a shadow of a doubt, he was on hers. And that he would do anything to protect the library.

Now she didn't know.

Will came up behind her as she reached the side door, and she jumped, turning on him. He stepped back, his hands held high. 'Have you got a key?' he asked. 'Because I have.'

All the same, he looked like she had slapped him in the face with her reaction.

It wasn't as late as she had thought. Edward was still in the lounge, sipping on a whisky in a cut-glass tumbler. It hadn't been the first one from the looks of it. There was something dishevelled and wretched about him. He'd taken his jacket off and flung it over the back of the chair. Even his tie was loosened. Only the gleaming brocade of his waistcoat still hugging his white shirt, and the rich golden watch chain, reminded her of her debonair uncle.

'What on earth is going on? You're like drowned rats. William, I thought—'

'That I'd left. I know. We don't have time for that. Edward, it's Arthur. He's making his move. He's after the Tree.'

Sophie's uncle looked from one of them to the other. 'Nonsense,' he said.

'He wants control of the library,' Sophie protested.

'Well of course he does. He always has done, just like his father. *And*, apparently, his brother too. But he doesn't get to choose that. Only the Tree does.' He got to his feet, advancing on Will. 'I thought I told you to leave.'

'I have a duty to the library. And it is in danger. They've got Tia, Edward. I don't know how or why but Arthur phoned me. He told me to find Sophie and bring her back here or he'd use Tia to uproot the Tree and move the library. You know what that means.'

Edward's face turned pale. His mouth worked, but only one word came out. 'Tia?'

'I think she's still in the archives,' Will said and Edward nodded.

With Tia in danger the bedrock of his world seemed to have fallen away. For a moment Sophie thought he wasn't even aware the library was under threat as well.

The ground beneath her quaked, like a huge animal turning over in a restless sleep.

'We don't have time for this,' Sophie said. 'We need to go to the Tree. Something is happening. Now.'

For once they didn't argue with her, or dismiss her. Edward put the glass down with a clunk and took out his phone, bringing up a number. 'Follow me,' he told them.

Whoever he rang didn't answer. Edward cursed as he made his way through the Reading Room and into the Great Hall itself. The vaulted ceiling soared over them and their footsteps echoed around it. Outside, the wind and rain buffeted against the building and it felt like a great ship in a storm, timbers creaking, the only thing sustaining them against the tempest and the deep. As Edward turned on the lights, the books rustled and whispered. At the top of the steps, a figure sprawled on the floor, very small, very still. Will rushed forward, leaving Sophie with her uncle, and knelt down.

'Meera?' The younger woman groaned, blood leaking from a wound on her head.

'Will? I was just…' She tried to focus on Sophie and Edward and went white. 'Dr Talbot… I came down for coffee and I heard something in here. It was unlocked and I…'

'It's okay,' Will said. 'Take it easy, okay? It's going to be all right.' Even as he said the words, Sophie knew Will wasn't convinced. He glanced up at Sophie, and then at Edward. '*Now* do you believe me?'

'We need to find Tia, quickly, and get her to safety.' Edward was already heading for the stairs. 'Meera, you have to raise the alarm. Dial zero on the phone in my office. Tell them Arthur has betrayed us. Possibly the Sidneys too. Will,' Edward snarled his name and Will seemed to flinch before snapping to attention. Sophie barely recognised her uncle. The suave man in a suit wasn't there any more. This new Edward looked murderous. 'If you truly want to prove yourself, now is the time. I need to find Tia. You and Sophie need to find out where Arthur is and report back to me. Stay together and stay safe. Do not engage. Understand?'

Meera levered herself up and ran for the Reading Room and the phone system in there. Edward was already down the stairs to the archives, only a floor or so below, and soon out of sight. Will stood, poised at the top, ready to follow, but he stopped, waiting for Sophie.

She heard it again. Not the song of the library this time. Something else. A lamentation rose through the cracks in the floorboards, echoing up from the massive stairwell. And with it a deep, reverberating thud, like a heartbeat. She stood on the edge of the precipice.

'Will?' she gasped.

But he lifted his finger to his lips. No noise. Whoever was down there didn't need to know they were coming. At least that was what she hoped he meant. He held out his hand to her, an invitation, a plea.

Will said they'd done something to Tia. Arthur had said they had a way to control him. Sophie couldn't see Edward any more. He'd peeled off somewhere, searching for Tia in the archives one floor down.

'Listen to me,' Will whispered. 'Tia's down there with them and we could have a real problem. If she thinks the Tree is in danger...'

'She's with them? You lied to Edward? What's going on?'

'I didn't tell him because he's safer if he's looking for her in the archives. Just stay with me, and stay quiet. I won't let anything happen to you.'

The promise did it. He'd protect her. Telling Edward that Tia was already in danger was not going to help. She followed Will.

Down and down the stairs wound and they followed. As they descended, she could hear it more clearly. A banging noise. A rhythmic thud. Someone, or something, pounding on the door. It sounded like they were using a battering ram.

'They're trying to break in,' Sophie whispered. Trust Victor to use brute force where charm failed.

'But it won't work. The Axis Mundi has to allow you in. Arthur knows that.'

She closed her hand around the pendant hanging around her neck, her mother's pendant, part of what connected her to the Tree. It would let her in. That was why Arthur wanted her in the first place. To open the door.

'Sophie,' Will whispered, as if realising what she was thinking. 'I won't let them hurt you. He has Tia. He's going to… to hurt her. She's my mother. And if she gets angry…'

So Will was bringing him Sophie instead. The Axis Mundi opened for her, the Tree would respond. She had almost destroyed the whole thing. Only the Keeper had saved them. And at what cost?

Oh, he was good at making promises, Will was. She suddenly wasn't so sure he was good at keeping them. At least, not to her.

Tia meant everything to him. She was his mother, the only one who really cared for him. He'd do anything for her.

Make any sacrifice. Even Sophie.

She stopped, feet rooted to the step.

'Oh God, Will, what have you done?'

He turned, dismay making his mouth open, his eyes wide, and reached out his hand for her, to stop her, to grab her.

Sophie ran, tearing back up the staircase so fast she used her hands as much as her legs. She needed to find Edward, to warn him. Will called after her, his voice panicked, but he didn't pursue her.

As she emerged back into the vast space of the Great Hall something hit her hard, slamming into the side of her head and dropping her like a sack of potatoes.

Victor stood over her, rubbing his fist, his face leering at her as it swam in and out of focus.

'Where do you think you're going, Soph? Come along, let's get you down to Arthur. I've got to get to work emptying this mausoleum.'

*

Victor carried her down, slung over his shoulder. There was no sign of Will on the way, nor down at the bottom. She didn't know where he was, as if he had just vanished into the shadows. Her head ached and her vision distorted. The Library whispered all around her, sounds of alarm and fear, and Arthur stood at the door, waiting, his face a mask of distaste. Tia stood very still, her eyes closed like a statue's. Whatever he had done to her had to involve magic. Sophie could feel it, like slime in the air.

Victor dumped Sophie unceremoniously on the stone floor in front of Arthur.

'Where's Will?' he snapped, but Victor just shrugged. Arthur swore to himself and spoke rapidly into a handheld radio. Five men surrounded them minutes later, all of them dressed in black and armed. They moved like soldiers, like special ops out of a film. This was far bigger than Sophie had thought, some kind of military operation. Arthur worked with the Ministry of Defence, she remembered. Had he brought them in? They didn't look like the army, but they moved like them.

Arthur handed Victor a ring full of keys. 'Start in the Great Hall. Take your pick. The lorries will be outside in half an hour so load them up. And find Will. I need him taken care of.'

'Edward and his people could still be up there.'

'Edward, an old woman and a bunch of girls. Right.' Arthur clicked his fingers at the mercenaries. 'Help him. You know what to do.'

Victor blew Sophie a kiss from the foot of the staircase. 'The disaster preparation plan you worked on was most helpful, Sophie. Tells us exactly where to look for the good stuff.' And then he was gone, back up the stairs, the soldiers trailing after him.

There was no sign of Will. Sophie pulled herself towards Tia but the archivist didn't move. Her eyes remained closed, like she was sleeping. Pale ribbons of green light flickered around her body. Arthur had said he'd figured out one spell from the grimoire when they had studied that single page in the display case. An age ago, it seemed now. *To Bind*. She remembered the bright green vines lacing through the text. Clearly it worked.

'Let her go,' Sophie said. This was why Will was doing what Arthur wanted. Because of Tia. But where was he now? What was he doing?

'Let her go? Right now she's alive with power so I would not advise that. No, Tia will stay where she is for now. We don't want her losing her temper. To say she goes off like a volcano is a bit too on the nose. The Axis Mundi is being unhelpful. Make it cooperate.'

'I can't—' she started to say but Arthur grabbed her by the back of her shirt and dragged her up onto her knees. The pendant was heavy around her neck. 'I'm not helping you,' she spat.

His radio crackled and a voice came out, distorted and unintelligible to her. But Arthur bared his teeth in a grin.

'Oh I think you are,' he told her and let her go. She sank back against the door, her chest heaving as she tried to calm her breath and failed. Waiting. Dreading.

Moments later a struggling form was dragged down the stairs by two of his guards and she saw Will. Blood flowed down the side of his head and his arms hung limp at his sides. He staggered as they shoved him forward, and fell to his knees. He must have put up a fight, but there were far too many of them, even for Will.

'Go up and help Mr Blake coordinate the extraction,' Arthur told the soldiers. 'I'll deal with this.'

They didn't even argue. She wondered suddenly if they knew what they were doing, if they were enchanted as well. Or simply excellent at following his orders.

Will shuffled towards her, trying to put himself between her and his brother. But Arthur missed nothing. Flicking back one side of his jacket, he pulled a gun from the holster under his arm, pointing it at Will who slumped down, staring back at him, so defeated that Sophie couldn't stand it.

'He's your brother,' Sophie protested.

'*Half*-brother. And a complete waste of effort as far as the family are concerned. He could have delivered all of this to us months ago, perhaps *years* ago, but no. Not the great and noble Will Rhys. He took some persuading but in the end, well, blood will out, as they say. He's her child, after all, whether she realises it or not.'

'Leave them alone, Arthur,' Will gasped through the pain. 'Let them go. Please. I told you, I'll do what you want.'

'Enough,' Arthur said, in his low ominous voice. 'We don't have time for this. I'm taking the Tree and starting again. Somewhere else. Somewhere better. Doesn't matter where. With Tia, the Axis Mundi, and Sophie, we can do that. You can still be the guardian, but you'll be taking orders from me, understand?'

He was trying to steal the Library Tree. Edward had said they'd moved it here around the time of the Great Fire of London. Was that what had caused it? All that destruction? Just from moving the Axis Mundi? Where else had it been moved from, leaving devastation in its wake? She thought of the Villa dei Papiri in Herculaneum buried beneath the ash clouds of Vesuvius, of the fires devouring Alexandria while the Christians rioted, the destruction of the library at Ephesus by earthquake and fires, the looting of Constantinople during the Fourth Crusade… all those precious ancient libraries lost in time to natural disasters or acts of mankind. They could all have been the Special Collection. How many times had this happened and history hadn't even recorded it? How many times had they managed to move it without destruction? How many times had they failed? How many deaths had the Special Collection and its mismanagement caused?

Arthur was going to destroy Ayredale…

Her home.

'You brought the whole place alive by being here when you were a kid,' Arthur said. 'I'm amazed you don't remember, but you've done it again by coming back, made it ripe for a move. Eager for it. You're going to open that door and take me in there, you're going to unbind the Tree for me, or make Tia do it – however it works, I don't care – or I'm going to take Will apart piece by piece, understand?'

He kicked Will in the stomach, to punctuate his point.

'You'd give away the whole Special Collection to Victor? Why Victor?'

'Hiring mercenaries doesn't come cheap, not even when half a dozen special ops owe you big time. But it's not about money. It's about power. Victor doesn't get that. He thinks it's about you. And the money. He always was a mercenary. I told him all about you, where to find Philip and how to get himself into your life. But he couldn't keep it in his pants and Edward exploited that to get you back.'

So when Victor had first come into her life… his intentions had always been to manipulate her. To use her to get to the Special Collection. That's all it had ever been. Arthur's plan.

Sophie tried to grasp the enormity of it and she couldn't. Arthur Dee had wormed his way like a cancer through her whole life.

'You can't do this,' she protested. 'You'll burn the whole library. The Special Collection will be scattered, if it even survives. All that knowledge, the entire function of the place. Arthur, think about this…'

He rolled his head back as if she was the most boring thing in the world and he couldn't bear to have to explain this again.

'The books up there don't matter. They're old and dead, even the unique ones, just fallen leaves. If Victor gets them out, fair play to him. He can have them. In there…' He waved the gun towards the door between them and the Axis Mundi. 'That's what matters. That Tree. It can do anything. It can remake the world, turn back time, creation itself, Sophie. And you're going to help me take it.'

Will found his voice again. 'Arthur, please, you have to stop. Don't do this. It's too dangerous.'

'Oh, stop playing for time. Edward and his motley crew up there aren't coming to help. What does he have? Please. I have my own fucking army up there, Will.' He glanced at Sophie again, but kept the gun unshakingly on Will. 'Do you know what happens to the human body when you shoot it, Soph?'

He waited for an answer. He wanted to hear her say it.

'It… they die.'

Arthur contemplated her answer with a grunt. 'Sometimes. If you aren't careful. It doesn't have to kill. Not right away. Shock sets in quickly but it doesn't kill. Kneecaps, fingers, that pretty face as well… Shoot him in the stomach and he'll bleed to death slowly and in agony. We have all manner of fun ways to make him suffer.'

'Sophie, don't,' Will said. His eyes were clear and bright, absolutely determined. He was waiting, she realised, biding his time. Maybe Arthur was right and he was stalling. But for what?

Arthur cursed, muttering something under his breath, and fired.

The noise was deafening, echoing all around the stairwell and rebounding like a physical assault. Sophie screamed and Will doubled over as if he'd been punched in the gut. But it was worse than that. So much worse. He folded and slumped to the floor. Sophie flung herself at him, ignoring everyone else. She didn't even know how she got there. No one else mattered. She fell at his side on her hands and knees, reaching out for him, pressing her hands to the wound and bringing them away covered in bright blood.

'Sophie, I didn't… I didn't mean…'

'I know. I know. Just… Jesus, what do I do, Will? What do I…'

Arthur seized a handful of her hair, dragging her back. 'You open the goddamned door, you stupid bitch. *Now.* Or I keep filling him with bullets until he stays down for good.'

Will's eyes fluttered closed, but his whole body tensed with pain and a sheen of sweat glistened on his pale skin. Something shook the library. All around them the walls creaked and the ground trembled again.

Tia stirred, her eyes finally opening. 'Arthur? What have you done?' she whispered, as if waking from a dream.

Arthur glanced at her and then stretched out his free hand. Sophie didn't understand the stream of words that came from his mouth but the lights around Tia grew brighter. Her eyes, however, didn't close again. She stared at him, looking so confused, but she fell silent.

When Arthur spoke again his voice was less certain. Still determined, still harsh and unyielding, but underneath it… he sounded scared.

'Open the door, Sophie. Maybe his precious Tree can save him, maybe it can't. But there's nothing else you can do. Unless you want me to finish him now.'

No. It only took a thought. If there was a chance to save Will, if only a chance, she couldn't help herself.

The door swung open and beyond it all she could see was a maelstrom of light. Arthur grabbed her again, dragging her inside with him, Tia following sedately. But once over the threshold, he faltered, stopping, and Sophie pulled free, desperate to get back to Will, to help him. She made the mistake of glancing up at the tree, and then she was lost.

This time the Tree didn't hesitate. It knew what it wanted, who it wanted.

The leaves swirled like a whirlwind, the tree alive with light and fury. Sophie felt it rush through her, all that power and energy. It raced along her veins, electricity making every nerve ending fire in pain and pleasure.

Her legs gave out beneath her but she didn't fall. Something else held her, something so much greater than she had ever imagined.

Was this what Professor Alexander had faced, what she had been able to channel and bring under control? For a time anyway. It had killed her in the end, too much for her system to sustain her. And now Sophie knew why. It was like staring into the ocean of stars and darkness, and then realising each star was a sun. Like the moment she fell into the river and it swallowed her.

The other figures, dark stains on the light around her, fell away and all she knew was the light of the Tree. Pulled to it, swept inside it, she hung there, helpless.

'*It's okay, love,*' said her mother's voice, coming in snatches, in whispers, in moments lost in time. '*I need you to be strong now... Together we can stop it...*'

Sophie uncurled her fists. She couldn't hold on any longer. Everything fell away and she gave herself up to it.

Chapter Twenty-Six

Will tried to breathe. The wave of pain swept up through him, radiating out like a sunburst. The light from the Axis Mundi drenched the chamber at the foot of the stairs with a light far brighter than the sun, the light of a thousand suns. Where it touched him, his body ached with a numb joy, but he couldn't move.

He lay alone in the dark corner, as one by one Arthur, Sophie and Tia spilled into the light and he was left behind. No longer needed. An accident, a by-blow, a mistake.

All the things that his father had called him over and over again, all throughout his life. It had never mattered to him who his father was, or who his mother was. The library had been his home. The Professor had been his family. He didn't care.

And he constantly told himself that. Even when he knew it was a lie.

Once, Arthur had been his friend. His big brother. His everything, the guiding light he looked up to and admired, the person he constantly tried to emulate.

But that Arthur was gone. He'd been gone since Will was sixteen years old and they had, between them, got Elizabeth killed. Arthur had dared them and they couldn't resist because every teenager believes they are omnipotent and that no harm can come to them. That they know best.

Arthur had used that blind self-belief and manipulated it to his own ends. Perhaps the Arthur Will had dreamed of as a brother had never existed.

And still, every time Arthur came back here, Will hoped, *prayed*, that it would be different, better, but it never was. It never would be. Every time it was another disappointment. Another heartbreak.

The gunshot confirmed it. His own brother. He didn't know who that man was now, the one who had let hatred eat away at him.

'Sophie?' He heard Edward's voice, coming down the stairs.

'She's in there,' Will tried to say but he didn't have the strength. 'He took her in there.'

Edward knelt down in front of him and cursed softly. His cursory examination was surprisingly gentle.

'Who did this?'

'Arthur.'

'He shot you? Your brother?'

'Half-brother, as he's so fond of saying.' He hissed as Edward gently peeled back his shirt to get a better look. To help, presumably.

Edward pressed his hands to either side of the wound, causing blood to well up from it, but he ignored that, closing his eyes and drawing on things Will couldn't see or hope to see. Some of the pain faded, but he'd heard somewhere that not feeling pain from a gunshot wound was a really bad sign.

Tia… where was she? She had been there, locked in Arthur's power, but now he couldn't see her. Had he taken her inside?

'He enchanted Tia, Edward. He's going to…'

'What were you thinking? He can't hurt her.'

'But he can do worse. He can release her. Make her give him the Tree, make him the new Keeper. He doesn't understand what it means. He thinks it's a prize.'

Arthur controlling Tia was bad enough. Releasing her was unthinkable. He didn't realise what she might do. He couldn't.

Will saw the blood drain from Edward Talbot's face. He knew what that meant. They both did. 'He wouldn't.'

'Sophie knows the spells from the Mortlake grimoire. She has a perfect memory. And she only had to read it once…'

Arthur's ambition had robbed him of his reason. Maybe he thought he could control Tia. He'd already used the spell to bind a goddess. But if Arthur unleashed Tia she would destroy them all. She wouldn't be able to help herself. He could no more control her than he could an inferno.

'You've got to get me in there,' said Will. 'I'm her guardian. Her son.'

'Moving you could kill you. You've lost too much blood. Absolutely not.' So now he cared if Will lived or died? That was a novelty. And completely unhelpful.

'The Axis Mundi is tilting and Sophie is lost in it. We'll lose the whole library if we don't. It'll go down in flames if the tree is uprooted. You of all people know that, Keeper. You have to do this.'

Part of him wanted to say that some of this was Edward's fault as well. He'd brought this on them, trying to work with Arthur, believing his lies. But what was the point? Edward knew. He recognised the horrible mistake he had made and knew it might cost everything. Nothing Will could say now would help to make that better. Edward could beat himself up enough for both of them. Later.

Will tried to pull free, to drag himself towards the door under his own power if he had to, but the moment he moved he could feel the bullet lodged somewhere deep inside him like a spear of fire. Blood filled his throat and he coughed it up, trying not to choke. Although choking was the least of his problems right now. He had to get through the door. That was all that mattered. That light was calling him.

He had to find enough strength…

'*I'm here,*' something seemed to whisper. So familiar a voice. He'd heard it every day, throughout his life. He shivered and he could hear her, feel her. Not just near but all around him. Tia… And not Tia. It was more than that. It felt like the Tree. Like the library itself.

He limped forward, supporting himself against Edward, getting blood all over his expensive waistcoat as he tried to stop Will falling.

Light washed over them both and Will felt his legs give out. The ground of the chamber caught him in a soft embrace, almost welcoming.

'*Let go, Will.*' But it wasn't Tia. It sounded like… but that was impossible.

A memory. An echo.

He didn't want to let go. He was afraid. It wasn't easy to admit, not even to himself, but he was.

Tears spilled out of his eyes, burned their way down his face.

'Will?' Edward murmured and held his hand, his grip tight but shaking. Even he knew it was dangerous, a risk they should never take. Will was the guardian. He was there to stop Tia if need be, that was the nature of his being, his role, the reason for his existence here.

He was the only one strong enough, with her blood in his veins.

Or not, as it turned out, in his veins so much any more. The sweet earth of the Axis Mundi drank it down.

It was too hard, too difficult to hold on. He could feel himself slipping away. Even as he tried to hold on. It seemed like everything told him to give up. To give in.

The tree was in sight, burning, leaves whirling, the air a maelstrom of light and destruction. Silhouetted against it he could see the others. His brother, his mother… and Sophie.

His Sophie.

You aren't even human. Not all the way through. How many times had he heard that? Arthur had loved throwing that at him. And Elizabeth would wipe his tears away and tell his brother that he was a bully. Not to mind him.

But Will had only wanted Arthur to love him.

His father Roland had wanted nothing to do with him from the start, and that was fine. A known quantity. Will wondered if he had ever truly loved Tia, or if it had all been for the sake of his own ambition, or an experiment which had an unexpected side effect. A second son. One which had caused his own wife to walk away, cursing him. One with the power and strength to usurp the first. One on who Tia doted. Not as a son, she could never really comprehend that. But maybe as a friend. As a person.

'I'm sorry,' Edward whispered, his voice broken and wrung out. 'I'm so sorry. This is all my fault. I should have been more help. I should have taken more care of her. I should have…'

It doesn't matter, Will wanted to say. But he couldn't find the words.

Will had been both born and made. He was a sacrifice then, now, and always.

There were other words, from another time and place, from all around him, words which sang and sighed and cried out in both harmony and terrible discord. The voices of the tree. He could hear them.

'Ancient goddess of chaos and fury, we name thee Tiamat and we summon thee. Your child's blood is spilled, your trust betrayed. We summon thee in vengeance and rage. We summon thee.'

The words dissolved in a high-pitched whine and then he heard a rush of laughter. Wild, unfettered, reckless, so very dangerous…

She'd never really been a mother, not in the way other people had mothers. But she was a friend. She was there for him. In the end, until Sophie came home, she was all he had.

Ever since Elizabeth had been lost…

You did everything you could, Will. I always knew you would. Our guardian. Let go… Let me go.

Elizabeth had tried to help him. She had managed to hold the Axis Mundi in place and it had cost her everything. Same as the Professor.

But Sophie couldn't do it. She didn't know enough. She wasn't strong enough.

'Elizabeth…' he whispered. She was near as well, waiting, subsumed into the stones of the building, into the wood of the beams and the floors, in the whispers of the books. She was part of it all, part of the Library Tree.

Edward frowned at him, his expression confused as Will mentioned his late sister. Will had never noticed that they had the same eyes. If he had explained, if he had told Edward what had happened, would everything have been different? If he hadn't felt the misguided duty to protect his brother?

His brother who tried to wake the Tree, to take control of it and become the Keeper in spite of the wishes of the library. He'd persuaded Sophie to help him. Arthur could persuade the two teenagers to do anything.

We were born for this, Will, the three of us. We can wake it. We can control it. This is all going to be ours one day. Why wait? Why not now?

But the Tree had been too powerful for Sophie and his brother had run, leaving them behind. Elizabeth had found the two of them huddled there in the heart of the chaos, terrified, Sophie trying and failing to bring it under control. It had been burning its way through her, arms stretched wide, her face tipped up, a mask of pain as the burning leaves turned to ashes in her hands. Elizabeth had taken her place, but was already too late. Will carried Sophie out and he had run back to Elizabeth, tried to pull her to safety as well.

She'd looked down at him, through all the flames and light and turmoil, through the pain in her face and the glow that had invaded her eyes. And smiled.

You did everything you could, Will. I always knew you would. Our guardian. Let go, love. It's too late. You have to protect Sophie now. Let me go.

Will closed his eyes and the last painful breath slipped out of his mouth.

A scream shook the world, tearing through him, through the library. Alarms were sounding, and somewhere he knew Meera was calling in reinforcements. Somewhere in Whitehall, a man in a nondescript office was calling in a special squad of highly trained troops who reported only to him and were largely unknown anywhere else. Once upon a time, Will had thought he might join them. Tia had disabused him of that fanciful notion immediately. *Have you turned out like Arthur? I don't think so. Besides, we need you here.*

We need you.

'*Guardian, free yourself,*' Elizabeth whispered now, her voice so real he almost felt her breath against his ear. '*The time has come. Let go, Will.*'

But that was impossible.

The light had swallowed her up, that ocean of light. The Tree had made her part of itself and by saving Will and Sophie, she was gone. She'd left her brother. She had left a widower and a daughter. A broken man and an even more broken girl who couldn't recall anything that had happened. Who had lost her mother and didn't know why.

And it had all been Will and Arthur's fault.

'*Not your fault, pet,*' she told him now. '*Destiny has no care for what we want. Let me go now. Find Sophie. Protect her. Please, Will. Now.*'

With the last gasp of strength in him, Will shoved Edward back through the door… the door which promptly slammed shut, locking him safely away. Or perhaps it was Elizabeth who did it, saving her brother one last time.

You did everything you could, Will. I always knew you would. Our guardian. Let go, love…

And he did. He let go of everything inside him, all that made him part of the library, all that made him human.

The guardian of the Special Collection was a very specific role. Tia could spin stories about ancient Keepers calling it out of nowhere, or demigods being torn apart. She could tie it to the earliest legends, to wild things tamed and given purpose. But it didn't have to be as complicated as that. The guardian was a protector, someone who loved the Special Collection so fiercely they would do anything to defend it. The library chose them, not anyone else. They had only one job: to keep the innate chaos at the heart of it in check. Nothing more, nothing less.

And Will knew that chaos intimately. It was part of him. Always had been. The Tree lived and breathed creativity. It gave inspiration to the greater world. All the thoughts and dreams that spilled out of it came from the primordial chaos. But creativity couldn't thrive in that chaos. It had to be nurtured, given the space it needed, and that was the job of the library. Protecting it was his job.

But sometimes you needed chaos. Sometimes you had to call on old gods and goddesses. Sometimes you had to set them free. Even if it meant giving up everything you were and becoming that other part of yourself, the thing you suppressed, the thing that came from *her*. Such things took blood and sacrifice.

Will slipped free in the darkness.

Tia stood like a statue in the Axis Mundi, the ripples of light still shivering over her. The shadow that was Will had only to brush against her to hear the words of unbinding rushing through the air… '*O mighty Tiamat, great beacon of destruction, brightest light of heaven…*'

He felt her wake, even as he circled their attackers, even as he gave in to the rage and the mindless need to hunt and kill, to destroy their enemy. To be her creature once again. Her shadow, her beast.

Tiamat awoke, barefoot and terrible, the earth reforming itself beneath her foot, melting and shifting, her red hair like a flame, her eyes blazing light. Raw power of creation drenched her.

She was a monster. She was chaos itself, trapped in a human form by a spell long ago. They all knew that, the legacies who lived here and worked here, but it was never so clear as now. She lifted her upper lip, exposing her teeth, and Will, whatever was left of Will, felt a shudder of fear and jubilation. And a hunger. It was fierce and terrible. But it was just an echo of what ran through her veins, a trace of it passed on to him through blood. Millennia suppressed, controlled, kept in her place. Even her smallest rebellions were nothing to this. She was free, truly free, for the first time since the beginning of so-called civilisation.

The spirit that had been Will, that was once Will but was part of her and always had been, felt her gather him in, examine him, and then release him. Suddenly her rage burned even more brightly, as bright as the Tree and its burning leaves, incandescent fury. It burned within him.

'*What have you done?*' Tia said and her voice shook the shining air around them. The twisted earth beneath them trembled again. '*What have you done to my son?*'

Chapter Twenty-Seven

The light of the Tree blazed like an inferno and Tia walked through that fire, the ground beneath her feet igniting where she walked. Sophie saw the plants kindle to flame, and the rocks begin to melt as she approached.

Arthur grabbed her arm, pulling her back against him. She could feel his whole body, muscles tensed with fear. Yes, fear. Sophie recognised it now. He was terrified.

'She isn't meant to be able to do that. That's the whole point of having spells to control her, of having a guardian.'

A guardian. Will. The man he'd shot. Sophie felt a sob rise inside her like a diamond made of ice.

'You shot him.' And then the realisation hit her. 'You *killed* him.'

He shook her as if that would make her deny it. 'That wouldn't kill him. You don't know him. It's his fault. He'd have to choose it. You don't even know what he is.'

What he is…

A shadow skirted the edge of them, separate to the glowing Tia, fleet and terrible, flowing like water from one shape to the next.

She remembered it.

In the light, in the flames, it had wound itself around her. A fleeting memory, an echo, something from a dream. It had tried to protect her…

Arthur raised one hand and his panicked voice echoed through the chaos as he tried to cast the Art for binding her once again.

'*Conjuro te, serpens antiquus, per iudicen vivorum et mortuorum—*'

'Gods, I hate Latin.' Tia's voice rippled through the air, deep and full of malice and a trace of satisfied amusement. 'A bastard language worming its way in everywhere. Besides, it won't work. Not this time. You need something primal, Arthur, something that makes the earth shake, languages only I remember. Blood has been spilled. My blood. His blood. You didn't think of that when you shot him, did you?'

But still, Arthur tried, his voice turning harsh and determined. '*Exorzizo te et constrigo te, domonstress te michi in pulcra forma humana cum omni pietate—*'

'*Pietate?*' Her scathing reply silenced him. 'Obedience? Have you *met* me recently? You cannot bind me now. You cannot command me to human form. You and your kind have bound me for too long, lied to me, used me.'

Arthur grabbed Sophie, his arm around her neck, and he pulled her back against his body. His grip was too strong, the hold expert. The gun dug into her side.

The smile on Tia's face widened, far wider than a human smile. Her teeth turned sharp and white behind her stretched lips.

'Hail, great Tiamat,' Arthur said but his voice shook and he kept Sophie between them, a human shield. Sophie could feel his heartbeat thundering away behind her. She could smell the sweat starting to bead on his skin. 'I'm here to offer you service and—'

'Very generous since your spells don't work in here. This is my place of power. Didn't you realise that, little man? You have nothing to offer me, Arthur. You killed my son.' She jerked her chin up to make her point. '*My son.*'

'He's free. Isn't that what you want, Tiamat? Freedom?'

She walked towards him slowly, step by step, reality distorting around her feet. But she didn't argue. Not exactly. 'You have no comprehension of what I want, Arthur Dee. None of you ever did. Not even your illustrious forebear. He was an idiot too.'

Arthur dragged Sophie back to shield him. The grip around her throat was too tight. He was cutting off her air. Spots of light danced before her eyes as she struggled. But the muzzle of his gun felt cold and hard, far too real in this place of unreality.

She could feel it all breaking down around her. The tree was blazing, tearing through reality and Tia tore her way through the rest. They were going to destroy it. They were going to cause everything to cascade into destruction.

'You've got to stop,' Sophie tried to say. Not to Arthur. To Tia. But she didn't think Tia could hear her any more. And if she could, she wasn't listening. The Tree would unleash all its power, undoing itself. With Tia there in her goddess form, the forces holding the Axis Mundi in place were breaking apart. Everything would come crashing down. She could feel all that raw magic and the powers of creation breaking free, cascading into chaos. Just because Tia... no, Tiamat – Tiamat the primordial goddess of disorder... because she had arrived in her full power once more.

'I want control of the library,' Arthur yelled desperately. 'You can give me that. We can do a deal.'

Tiamat stared at him for the longest moment and then she smiled again. 'Control of the library? Oh Arthur... haven't you realised? There isn't going to be a library any more. There isn't going to be a Tree. Only chaos. You brought me in here.'

'You moved the Tree before. We'll go somewhere else. Anywhere else. Start again. You can choose. There's always…'

Something dark moved at the foot of the tree, winding around the trunk, a shadow. Sophie saw it out of the corner of her eye. Swift and fluid, a hunter. It slid over the ground like a dark ghost.

Tia laughed. 'You would make a deal with me? The last time I was free I destroyed their pitiful city. It was only a Talbot who persuaded me to stop, to move the Tree here instead. And to stay. To agree to diminish again. For one of them.' She nodded at Sophie.

As if to answer her, Arthur shook Sophie like a rag. 'If you don't, I'll kill her.'

The ground shook beneath them. 'Oh, I wouldn't do that if I were you, Arthur. You're in enough trouble as it is. Do you know what *Sophía* means? Wisdom. Kill wisdom and where does it leave you?' Tiamat's voice rang with that hollow bitter laugh, not the laugh Sophie knew. Something so much worse.

'She's just a girl. She knows the words that will destroy you. I can make her say them.'

'I won't,' Sophie said, loud enough that they both looked at her in surprise. Her defiance had not been expected. Tia might kill them both. But Sophie was not going to betray her. Not now, not ever.

Arthur tightened his grip around her throat again. If he crushed her windpipe she wasn't going to be saying anything. Didn't he realise that? No, he was terrified. And not thinking. Not any more. Arthur Dee was way out of his depth now.

Tiamat's voice softened to some semblance of reason. She tilted her head to one side, studying them. 'Sophie is a Talbot, a legacy. Her family's service stretches back to the founding of the first library.'

'So is mine. I'm a Dee.'

'The Dees are parvenus in comparison. I mean the *first* library. A tree in a desert, spawning a garden, spilling life and knowledge out all around it, creating this world you're so eager to destroy. The Talbots were witness to that. You're named after a river, for fuck's sake. Names, Arthur… They all have meaning. They all have power. She's mine. Let her go.'

He didn't. If he did, Sophie wasn't sure what Tiamat would do, nothing good, and Arthur knew that too. The risk to Sophie was the only thing keeping her in check right now. And perhaps the game. Tia did enjoy playing games.

'What does Talbot mean, Sophia?' she asked.

'Talbot? It's…' She knew this. Her father had told her, ages ago. He'd laughed about it, said it fitted Edward to a tee. 'Messenger of destruction. It means—'

'Not destruction, *chaos*. *Messenger of chaos*. Your ancestor was my servant, my high priest, my beloved. That's why you can read the words. You are *mine*. Like my son.' And something in her voice broke. A sob cracked the perfect exterior and her eyes turned dark as a moonless sky. For a moment, though, it was Tia's voice, diminished, mortal. 'Like my son… my Will…' Dark veins spread beneath her pale skin and a blast of wind made her hair fly out like flames, and the endless voice of the goddess was back. 'Will means control, conscious thought and decisions, will means desire, self-discipline, restraint… All that you took from me, Arthur Dee. All gone now. William… my guardian…'

'Shut up!' Arthur yelled at her.

But Tia took another step towards him, looming over him and making him retreat. Playing with him. Herding him.

'And Rhys,' she said. 'I gave him that name too. Rhys means warrior, protector, killer.'

Panicked, Arthur shoved Sophie away from him, sending her sprawling on the ground at Tia's feet.

'I didn't kill him,' Arthur said. 'I just – I know what he is. It shouldn't have killed him.'

Her voice turned glacial. 'Maybe it didn't but the boy, the man is still gone. There is magic in sacrifice, especially here. Such magic. It unbound him. Just as it unbound me. All is unbound, unravelling, undone.'

'Stop,' Arthur yelled. 'Stop what you're doing. Now!'

But the primordial goddess ignored him. She opened her arms wide in welcome, as if she was going to embrace a child.

He aimed the gun at Tia now, ready to fire. 'Stop it, Tia. Don't make me—'

The shadow detached itself from the tree and moved like a streak of darkness. Sophie had dreamed of it, sensed it, and now she actually saw it for an instant, a cat-like shape launching itself directly at Arthur.

He turned, firing wildly at it, round after round. Claws like knives slashed through the air. Arthur Dee cried out, a dreadful wet sound of agony, and slammed back onto the ground with the creature on top of him. It all lasted only a second, the jaws on his throat tearing out his screams, and then all was silence.

Sophie shoved herself up on her elbows, ready to scramble backwards, but she couldn't move. She could only stare.

A panther, that was what it looked like. Bigger, wilder, more dangerous, with eyes so dark a green they burned, absorbing light rather than reflecting it.

But she knew it. Knew him…

'Titivillus?' The cat stared at her, daring her to admit the truth, daring her to see. Her voice, when she could use it again, was no more than a whisper, a breath. A prayer… 'Will?'

The growl was a warning. Even as she gazed into its eyes… his eyes… she could hear her heart beating so loudly, so wildly.

And like smoke in a breeze, like a ghost, he vanished.

Sophie stared where he had been, at Arthur's shredded corpse, and then turned around, searching for Tia. Or Tiamat, or whatever she was.

She stood under the Tree, her arms outstretched as light spiralled around her, a maelstrom which tore the leaves from its branches, tore the earth up beneath it. Whatever she was doing, whatever she was planning, this was wrong. The world was shaking itself apart just having her standing there.

'Tia!' Sophie cried out. 'Tia, stop. Please. You have to stop.'

'This ends, now. Everything. All this order and structure. It ends and is made anew in glorious pandemonium.'

Sophie crawled towards her, dragging herself upright against the roots.

'Tia, please listen to me. What about Edward? He loves you.' And Will, she almost said before she remembered… *Will*…

Will was dead. Will was gone. Her Will.

'Edward doesn't love me,' Tia whispered. And it was Tia's voice again, the voice Sophie knew. The vibrations of divinity dropped away but the whirlwind of power and chaos carried on, all around her. The leaves cascaded around them, screaming and crying out.

A shape burst from the darkness, running across the rupturing landscape from where the doorway had been. He looked exhausted, broken, as if he had run a marathon to reach them. Perhaps he had, across the Axis Mundi, a place now determined to keep the mortal world out.

'But I *do*.' Edward fell to the ground at Tia's feet, wretched and desperate, his clothes dishevelled and bloodstained. He barely resembled her uncle any more. 'I always have. I always will.'

She turned on him with a snarl, inhuman again. He'd hurt her. He'd abandoned her.

'You love what I can give you. You are the Keeper now. You don't even need me any more. You want to control me, to bind me. To use me. You love power.'

'No. Tia, no.' He lifted his eyes up to her face. 'I love you. Just you. Like you said about Sophie. I'm a Talbot. I am yours. But I am bound here, bound to you. I'm not leaving you, Tia. If you don't stop, you'll kill us all. The library will burn. All of it. Your library, your archives, everything you worked for, sacrificed your power for... but I will be here with you. To the end. I will always need you.' He shouted out the words, and they were like a song. '*O divina numen, Tiamat splendida, lucidissima stellarum, te amo...*'

She turned around, stared at him in wonder and devastation. These words were different, not words of binding, not words of control. They were the words that had invaded Sophie's mind since she read the Mortlake grimoire. These spoke of love, of adoration, a prayer.

O Divine Goddess, most wondrous Tiamat, brightest star in the heavens, I love you...

Because what was love if not chaos?

Sophie knew that. So did Edward.

Burning tears streamed down Tia's face, almost like mortal tears. 'It's too late, Edward. You're the Keeper. You and I... It's forbidden. You were right. The Tree is falling, dying. Bringing me here, unbinding me, Arthur has undone it all, just as he did when Sophie and Will were children. He was a fool even then. I will come undone, lose what I have become, what we have…'

She closed her eyes again and her head fell back. Light filled her, the light of a newborn sun, the light of creation itself.

'I'm sorry, Edward, my love, my own. I can't stop. It's too late. All is loose, all is broken. You need to leave. Get Sophie to safety. Before it's too late.'

Tia reached out her hands and seized the lowest branches of the tree. The light burst from them both and Sophie had to shield her eyes. Tia's body went stiff and then slumped down, all strength, all energy leaving her. Edward lunged forward to catch her, cradling her in his arms.

The tree shook, the earth quaking. The world was being torn asunder around them. Sophie could feel it dissolving into confusion and disarray. Voices filled her head, those myriad voices, screaming, crying, singing.

They're written on your soul. It's the language of the birds.

Her mother's voice from her memory, and from somewhere else. Sophie shivered, wrapped her arms around her body and held herself tightly.

Leaves falling, golden and beautiful. Her hands reaching up to catch them. The air trembling around her, and a wave of energy building within her, ready to tear itself free.

'It's okay, love. I'm here. I'll deal with it, Sophie. I need you to be strong now. For me. Get Will out of here…'

But Will was gone. Professor Alexander was dead. And Edward… Edward couldn't do it. All Edward wanted was to protect Tia.

Sophie found her own voice again, one which seemed to marry with another one from long ago. 'Edward, get Tia out of here.'

Her uncle glanced at her, opened his mouth to argue, but then stopped. Whatever he saw in Sophie's expression gave him immediate pause.

'You can't,' he told her.

'I have to. There's no one else. I have to try to bring it under control, to channel it, root it once again.'

'Sophie—'

'She said we were the oldest bloodline. Her servants, her messengers, her keepers. She said you were *hers*. *Her Edward.* Her innate chaos is unravelling the spells holding it together. You need to get her away from the Tree and then maybe I can...'

'Sophie, I can't possibly allow you to do this. I'll try. Maybe I can...' She didn't believe it any more than he did, so he didn't bother finishing. 'No.' The word was unequivocal. 'No, I lost Elizabeth like this. We lost Hypatia. I won't lose you too.'

She could hear all those voices singing, their words a symphony which flowed around her and through her.

Edward lifted Tia, cradling her against him as if afraid she'd shatter at his touch. He wanted to believe Sophie. He wanted to save the woman he loved.

There wasn't time to argue.

'Sophie... tell Elizabeth...'

'Go!' she told him and reached up with her hands. The light wreathed them, tangled with her fingers, trailing up her arms, filling her.

And then everything was light. The tree and the library, the chamber and the Axis Mundi, the world as she knew it. Light everywhere, light that sang and screamed, that whispered and sighed. She could hear all the books, all the thoughts and ideas. She drew it into herself and lived it, breathed it.

'Mother,' Sophie whispered as the light became too much, as it coursed through her veins and welled up inside her thundering heart. 'If you're there, please, help me.'

'*You were born for this, Soph*,' Arthur had said. No wonder she hated being called Soph... God, what had she been thinking? Was she so easily manipulated all her life?

'I know you can do it. Go on, I dare you.'

'We shouldn't.' Will tried to stop her, even then. He knew how dangerous it was. They all knew. But Arthur laughed at him. And neither of them wanted to look like a child in front of him.

'Scared of getting caught?'

Will blushed, and looked at his feet. 'No, it's just... it's the Axis Mundi. The Keeper said—'

Arthur's voice was full of passion, of reckless wonder. He wanted it. He wanted it all and he didn't care what got in his way. 'I don't care what the Keeper said. We were born for this, Will, the three of us. We can wake it. We can control it. This is all going to be ours one day. Why wait? Why not now?'

But it had all gone wrong. It had all gone terribly wrong and the Tree had gone wild as she tried to touch it. Burning leaves rained down on them. Like now. Uprooted, unbound, raining destruction.

Will tried to pull her free but he couldn't. His hands touched her and the tree lashed out, sensing Tia's blood in his veins perhaps. His scream surrounded her, the agony ripping through his voice. Sophie felt the power of the Tree crushing her down but she had to hold on, to hold firm. She had done this. She had to put it right.

Her mother ran through the mounting chaos, running to Sophie's side.

'It's okay, love,' she called, wrapping her arms around her daughter one last time. 'I'm here. I'll deal with it, Sophie. I need you to be strong

now. For me. Get Will out of here and find help. Do as I say now. Please.'
Elizabeth took off her necklace, that beautiful, delicate pendant, and hung
it around her daughter's neck. She could feel its cool weight against her
burning skin. 'Go,' she said.

'What are you going to do?'

'The Tree will tell me. I understand it, the language of the birds. I'll
try to hold it here until the Keeper comes. Together we can stop it. Now
go. Run.'

She'd found Will and together they'd struggled out of the chamber.
Once he was sure she was safe, he'd gone back for Elizabeth while Sophie
screamed for help, running up the stairs as fast as she could towards
the Great Hall. He had tried… tried to save her too. Tried so hard.

Sophie didn't know what her mother had said to him back in
the chamber. But she knew something had passed between them.
Something that had broken his heart.

Elizabeth's hands closed over hers, her body wrapped around her
daughter's. Sophie could recall it now, all of it. And at the same time
a ghostly presence wound itself around her. Her mother's fingers
threaded with hers.

'*Creativity is born in chaos,*' her voice whispered in Sophie's ear. '*But*
it cannot thrive there. It needs us to bring it order, so it can truly live, so it
can spread. We're the midwives of inspiration, the shepherds of new ideas.
Alone it is too much. But together, Sophie, together…'

Sophie leaned back into the light that flickered around her, gaining
the warmth and the strength she needed. She opened herself to the
waves of energy. Leaves swarmed around her, and the light of the tree
grew brighter and brighter.

Another presence joined them, another woman, her mind as sharp
as a diamond as she brushed against Sophie and her hands joined theirs.

'*A fixed point in the library, a legacy, just as you are,*' said Hypatia Alexander's voice.

Others rose around them, the others who had lived here and died here, who had served the tree and helped Tia contain the chaos she embodied. The keepers, the binders, the legacies, the warders, the guardians, all those who had given their lives for the library.

Power burst like a wave cresting, crashing over Sophie, driving her back a few feet but she stood her ground, pushing back on it, arms raised, fingers spread wide.

And then it was gone. All of it. Abruptly, like a door had been closed. So were the others.

Sophie fell forward, down onto her hands and knees. The shock of it drove the breath out of her and she sobbed violently.

She couldn't see. The light still burned inside her, the blaze in her mind too great to contemplate. She crawled forward but found only the churned-up earth beneath her. Her fingers sank into it, deep down into it, and suddenly she realised what was wrong.

Sophie blinked back fiery tears and forced herself to open her eyes. To look.

But it was too dark in the chamber. Too dark to see anything much. The Tree had vanished.

Chapter Twenty-Eight

It wasn't possible. It simply wasn't possible. It had been huge. It had filled the room, reaching to the top of the vaulted chamber. And now... now it was gone.

She dug her hands into the dirt, scrabbling through it, trying to feel the tree. Maybe it had turned her around, maybe it was behind her, or further away in the dark. Maybe she just couldn't see it. Maybe...

But it was gone.

A light blazed from the doorway and Sophie turned, startled, and then had to shield her eyes. A torch. It picked her out in the darkness and then wobbled back and forth as someone ran towards her.

'Sophie? Sophie, are you okay? Talk to me.'

It was Edward.

'I'm...' Her voice was hoarse, grating against the sides of her throat as if she had been screaming. Maybe she had. She didn't know any more. 'I'm here. I'm okay.'

She wasn't though. She felt unsteady and sick. And she had lost the tree.

The enormity hit her and she slumped back down, sobbing. Tears streamed down her face, dripped off her skin into the parched earth beneath her.

Edward reached her, pulling her into his arms and she let him, limp and helpless now. It didn't matter. Nothing mattered now. She had failed. They had all failed.

'Sophie, talk to me.'

'I'm… I'm… Edward, the Tree. It's…'

'It's gone. You stopped it destroying everything. You did that much but we have to leave. The Axis Mundi is closing in on itself. Without the tree and a guardian… without…' She stared at him, his face very pale in the torchlight. His voice was so grim.

Without Will, he meant.

'Arthur shot him,' she whispered.

And then she realised what she was saying. Arthur had shot him.

Titivillus, or Will, or whatever he was had been set free. She had seen him, the creature, Tia's son. Seen his, or *it*, tear out Arthur's throat. A demigod, Tia had said in her story, a lifetime or so ago in the pub, wild and dangerous, a monster of chaos. And the librarians had used a spell to bind him and break him in two. But they had left his heart torn between the two halves so he could never find peace…

But if that spell was broken, what did that mean for the man she loved? Sophie let Edward help her to her feet and, once she could stand, she couldn't wait another moment. She tore herself free and ran to the place where he lay.

Will's body sprawled on the ground inside the doorway, blood pooling beneath him and drenching the black soil, his green eyes wide open, gazing back at the stairs. But he didn't blink. His chest didn't move.

'No!' The word echoed back at her a thousand times, so loud she didn't even recognise her own voice, rebounding off the Axis Mundi chamber, off each floor of the vaults beyond, off the roof of the Great Hall far overhead. 'No! Please, no!'

A noise in the shadows made her head snap up and the cat stalked towards her, blinking its enormous green eyes. Not a supernatural creature now, just the cat she knew. He nudged his head against Will's shoulder and made a quizzical sound. When Will didn't move he tried again.

Sophie dropped to her knees and reached out her arms but Titivillus ignored her. And Will didn't move. Couldn't move.

Instead, Sophie took his hand and pulled it up to her face. It was so cold. Even with the blood on it. His blood.

The cat curled up against his neck, purring furiously. The sound was a rumble, an engine, and Sophie let herself slide forwards. She thought for a moment she might scare the animal off, but she was beginning to realise it took a lot more than her to scare Titivillus.

What was he? A demon, like Tia said? Some aspect of Will as Tiamat's son? Or something else entirely?

But there was a whisper. One single voice. Corporeal. Grief-stricken. It sounded like a song of lamentation from long ago.

'When he was born, I didn't know what to do. He was mine, part of me, but not part of me. A demigod. There hadn't been one of those for millennia. Something that should not be loose in this world unchecked.'

Tia sat just outside the doorway as if trying to get as close to Will as she could without setting foot back inside the chamber. She leaned against the door frame, her long legs curled under her, the same way Will would sometimes sit. Her long red hair flowed like blood on either side of her pale face. Her hands were pressed to the flagstone where it met the lifeless black soil of the room. But she didn't come in. She didn't dare.

Edward moved silently to her side, his arms encircling her, trying to pull her back to safety, but Tia was not to be moved. He knelt beside her and she leaned against him. And she spoke again, that plaintive broken voice that echoed around them.

'Elizabeth had the idea to bind him in two forms, to pull his nature apart and diminish him so that he could survive in this world. So the world could survive him. We were so careful, made sure there was a perfect balance. Edward and Elizabeth found an ancient Sumerian spell, hidden in plain sight in the carvings of Ashurbanipal's library. The poems were lost until 1849, but it was right there, ready to make a demigod into a man. It even has a goddess moving a tree. So obvious, when you think about it. Elizabeth said she just followed the breadcrumbs to find it. The first spell, the first story, the first library... And she used it, fearless, determined to help me. My friend...'

Her voice trailed off in grief, choked with memory. Edward pressed his lips to her hair and closed his eyes. He murmured something else, snatches of an old song, something ancient indeed.

He went ahead to save his comrade.
He knew the route to protect his friend.
He took the road to the Tree.

Edward fell silent and Tia's voice, when she spoke again, softened with reminiscence.

'She helped me raise him. She was so much better at it all than me, your mother. I might be a disaster but she was born to be a mother. It was as natural as breathing. But me? Not so much...' Then she laughed, a broken bitter sound. 'I wasn't meant to be a mother. He should never have existed, and yet he did, and I loved him. I loved him like a fire.'

'Can't you help him?' Sophie asked.

'Do you think I haven't tried?' she snapped. The tone changed in that instant and Sophie could hear the vengeful goddess again. To be honest it was better than hearing her broken heart flowing through the words. 'Edward tried too. There is no one else. Do you want to call all the king's horses and all the king's men, because they're going to descend on us at any second, I'm sure. They're dealing with your bastard ex-boyfriend and his cohorts up there right now.'

She'd forgotten about Victor. Arthur had been prepared to give him all the treasures of the library so long as he could get the Tree. He didn't care about the Special Collection or what it might do. What those billionaires might use its contents for. Perhaps he never intended Victor to get away. If it was true, if moving the Tree would destroy the library, he never would have been able to anyway. Had Victor even realised that he had been used as well? Anyway he didn't matter now. Perhaps he never had. How strange to realise that…

Only one person mattered.

And he was gone.

Titivillus gazed up at her, his eyes so very bright, so very green. She reached out with her free hand and touched his fur, stroking him gently, feeling the vibrations rumble through her. Through the earth. Through Will's body as well.

'Sophie,' Edward said, reaching out to her through the door, stretching his hand towards her. But she didn't take it. She held Will, rocked him, buried her face in his hair. 'Sophie, please, come out now. Before it's too late.'

'No,' she said, shocked at how firm and unshaken her voice sounded. 'I'm staying here with him. I'm staying.'

Here, in the darkness. With Will. That would be enough. She'd stay.

Something stirred in the earth beneath them, where Sophie's tears mingled with his blood. Edward cursed, a word more of shock than horror. Tia shot to her feet, clinging to him before he tried to plunge inside and pull Sophie to safety. But Sophie couldn't move, and wouldn't move. She held Will, crushed him against her, and stared.

The ground stirred beside them and something uncurled. Something impossible.

It was slender and pale, glowing with a nascent iridescence that seemed to throb like a heartbeat. Its stalk gave off a watery silver light, and as they opened she saw the two flawless, miniature leaves were gold. It pushed itself up, unfurling, growing in front of her eyes.

A tiny, perfect seedling struggled up through the wet, bloody soil, through the darkness, and slowly its glow began to spread. A pool of light surrounded Sophie and Will, spilling across the ground, and with its touch other things were stirring, growing. Life was returning, as all the creativity of the newly born tree trickled out around them.

And suddenly, Will drew in a single shuddering breath.

His eyes focused on her, wild and desperate, terrified. But they were his eyes, green as spring, and he was alive. He was breathing.

'Sophie?' His voice sounded brittle, but it was his voice. 'Sophie, what's going on?'

'You're alive!' she gasped. 'Will, how are you alive?'

Sophie scrambled around the sapling and pulled him closer again. Tentatively, she kissed him, a kiss he returned with a passion that overwhelmed her. His hand came up, his fingers in her hair. Her hands explored his body, checking for injuries – not subtly but he didn't seem to care. He was dazed, lost in her.

The gunshot wound was gone.

'Come on,' she told Will. 'Let's get you out of here.'

'But the Tree...' he protested.

'Later. I want to make sure you're okay. The Tree is fine. It has to be fine. I mean... I have no idea what happened, but I need you to—'

He let her help him to his feet, although if she was honest she leaned on him as much as he did on her, and together they staggered out of the chamber and into the bottom of the stairwell beyond.

Tia gave a howl of raw emotion and threw herself at them as they appeared from the light and stepped through the door into the stairwell. She pulled him free of Sophie and fussed over him, asking a million questions, framing his face with her hands while she by turns berated him for recklessness and told him how relieved she was to see him alive.

Edward and Sophie watched, unwilling and unable to intervene, and she felt the energy drain out of her again. Whatever she had done in the chamber, whatever power had filled her and empowered her, it was gone now. She was exhausted.

'Edward?' she whispered. He caught her elbow, steadying her. 'What happened in there?'

He gazed back at the sapling, still growing, but more slowly now, pale and slender, like a shaft of light in the twilight-shaded chamber.

'I don't know,' he replied at last. 'Magic is often born of sacrifice. Perhaps Will's blood and your surrender to it allowed a new seed to germinate, another tree to be born. I'll have to find the right volumes to research it. I'll have to...'

He gazed up towards the library and its vaults, the endless collection of priceless and unique volumes.

'There might be an answer in here somewhere,' she said.

Edward smiled. 'Then we'll find it.'

As they turned to go, a sound echoed around them, a little trumpet trill of curiosity and greeting, a sound Sophie knew too well. The black cat strutted out of the shadows, tail held high. He stopped, looking up at Sophie with those bright green eyes, and then leaped straight into her arms. Before she could stop him, he had clambered up to her shoulders and settled there like a fur collar, purring loudly.

Edward smiled at them. 'I guess he survived as well then.'

'Nine lives,' said Sophie, as she reached up to stroke the cat under his chin. 'Of course he did.'

Chapter Twenty-Nine

When they emerged from the vaults, yelling filled the air. Soldiers appeared from everywhere, decked in tactical gear, with huge guns that frightened the life out of Sophie. Not Arthur's men. These guys were even more terrifying.

Edward shoved his way to the front, hands up and spread wide, shielding them all.

'I am Dr Edward Talbot, the Keeper of this library. Stand down. Now! I need a full report. Where is your commanding officer?'

Victor and the other mercenaries Arthur had brought in had been rounded up already. There hadn't been any kind of a struggle. For all their weapons and menace they had been expecting library staff and an easy heist. Sophie could hear Victor loudly protesting his innocence as he was led away – that he had been lied to and used, that it had all been Arthur Dee's idea, that if they asked Sophie Lawrence or Dr Talbot they would tell them who he was. She kept walking until his voice faded and vanished from her hearing and her life.

There was no dreadful misunderstanding here, and Sophie only had to take one glance at Edward's dark expression to know that Victor would be paying for all this for a very long time.

Sophie didn't want to be vindictive, but she was glad. More than glad.

He deserved everything he got.

Will was whisked off by an army medic on Edward's orders and she made her way quietly back up to her studio. Her sanctuary. Victor and Arthur's goons hadn't made it this far. She sat down at the workbench, staring out of the window as dawn rose and turned the river to gold, trying to remember how to breathe.

The cat slipped off her shoulders and down into her lap. She stroked his fur idly, wondering about the connection between him and Will. And if whatever it could be was still intact.

That was when she saw it. Another book.

Of course there was another book. But who could have left it here? When?

She unfolded the phase box and examined it.

Was it new? No, it couldn't be. It was already bound and that wasn't her work. It wasn't her mother's either, or her father's. It was far older. Delicate and careful, a practised hand, it could be a thousand years old or more. Incredible. Even after all she had seen, it was a wonder.

She brushed her hand along the spine, feeling the luxurious red goatskin, running her fingertip over the delicately tooled panels of geometrical decoration with a two-stranded design like the patterns of an illuminated manuscript. Cords ran horizontally across the spine beneath the leather and she knew the threads holding the text block together wound around them.

The pages inside were the same smooth and soft materials as the leaves of the Tree. She knew instantly what she was looking at.

The first page was a riot of colour, a carpet page of elaborate decoration from which the title of the book emerged for her.

A Treatise on a New Sapling, being an examination of the nature of the Axis Mundi, and the opening of a new doorway into the Otherworld.

Even as she studied it the words appeared. It wasn't a struggle now and there was no sense of strangeness. The words simply unwound themselves before her eyes, almost as if something was speaking to her.

Greetings to you, Keeper, for only the eyes of a true Keeper will have the ability to read these words, and when you have brought forth a new sapling, a new incarnation of the Axis Mundi, it will reveal itself to you here.

Keeper? The library was declaring her the Keeper?

Sophie winced. What was she going to say to Edward? Maybe she shouldn't say anything. She didn't want this, not at all. This was her uncle's dream. She closed the book carefully and reached for the phase box to put it away.

'Sophie?'

It was like she had summoned him with her thoughts.

'Uncle Edward. How's Tia?'

He leaned against the door frame, and it was only now she realised how unkempt he looked, so unlike the urbane man she had met in the Academy. His hair was a mess, his sleeves rolled up and who knew where the waistcoat had gone. But he looked younger and more vibrant than she had ever seen him. Even in her memory.

'She's resting. I think she… she's fine. I hope.' It was in the way he said it, the relief on his face.

'You honestly do love her, don't you?'

A smile flickered over his lips. 'Yes. I do… which presents me with a dilemma. One which I believe you can help with, or am I wrong?'

His glance flicked over to the book in front of her.

'What dilemma?' she asked, determined to play dumb as long as possible.

'As Keeper, I am bound by certain rules. Strictures, if you will.'

'As Keeper, you can't be with Tia. That was why you left her.' She couldn't keep the tones of accusation from her voice and he flinched back, guilt written all over his face.

'I was a fool. I put my duty to the library above her, forgetting who she is, what she is. I hurt her. I could have lost her completely. I realise that now.'

She remembered the way he had changed and Tia – poor Tia – had been broken-hearted. He had been trying to follow the rules because a Keeper couldn't be romantically involved with Tiamat, not and keep control of the library that imprisoned her. Or rather in which she had imprisoned herself. Because that was what she had done. So many years ago. And again today. It was a conflict of interests.

'What do you want, Uncle Edward?'

'Would you believe I want my old job back? Or preferably another one. One that will keep me here with her. Librarian, perhaps? You are the Keeper now, whether you like it or not. You held back the Tree's magic, Sophie, you kept the Axis Mundi intact long enough to give the Tree a chance to regenerate. You brought forth the new Sapling and rooted it here in Ayredale. You and Will together. Keeper and guardian. Through blood and tears, through sacrifice, through love. You know, don't you? It always comes back to love, ever since Tiamat first gave up everything for our ancestors.'

She put the book away carefully. It had far too much to say about her new life and she wasn't ready for it yet.

'I can't be Keeper. I don't know what to do, how to run a place like this.'

He laughed, a soft, self-deprecating laugh. 'Oh *that*. You think I do? We can work that out. But I knew from the moment I met you again what was going to happen eventually, from the moment you stepped into the room, that the library would love you. That you had a destiny.'

'You lied to me. A lot.'

He had the good grace to look guilty, just a little. 'I… bent the truth. I'm sorry for that. But Sophie, I spent my whole life knowing that my sister would become the Keeper of the library and I would help her every step of the way. And I was free to love where I loved, to love Tia as I always wanted to. Because I loved her as soon as I knew how to love. When I thought all that was gone… I never realised how much I needed her. Or how badly I'd treated her.'

'Shouldn't you be telling *her* that?'

'I have, and I will. Every day from this moment on. Listen to me, the Keeper isn't the person who runs the library. Day-to-day administration is my absolute forte and I can keep doing that for you as long as you want me to. The Keeper is the heart of the library, the one who can channel the Axis Mundi and maintain it. Keep it healthy and strong. Love it. The one who cherishes the Tree, cares for it. The one who binds it all together.'

There didn't seem to be a way out of this. But all the same, she felt like an imposter. She hadn't been alone.

'I heard their voices. My mother, and Professor Alexander, and others. All of them. The previous Keepers. They helped me. I wouldn't have been able to do it without them.'

He smiled. 'That's exactly what I mean. They didn't speak to me. They never did. I would never have been able to do that, Sophie. It would have burnt through me like I was dry straw in a volcano.'

'But what about Will and me? If I become Keeper…'

'There's no becoming, Sophie. That book told you as much.'

'Did you leave it here?'

Edward laughed again. 'As if I have the power to do that. The library itself sometimes nudges us in one direction or another. That's how. It's been helping you, guiding you.'

The library itself… and the Tree, and all the voices she heard in its song. She sighed.

'My mother is there, in the Tree somehow. Arthur said she would be.'

'Perhaps that's true. But Arthur never understood the Tree. Not the way she did. Not the way you do. He never loved it. He thought of it as a thing to be controlled, to be brought to heel. When I think of what he would have done to Tia if he'd had the chance. He almost won. He almost took her from me, through my own fault. My own idiocy.' He shook his head, as if dismissing a nightmare. 'I would have killed him myself if I could.' And, to Sophie's surprise, he laughed, a brief bitter laugh. 'I'd probably have made a mess of that too.'

He hadn't killed Arthur though. That had been Will. Or whatever Will had become in those moments. Which brought her mind back to the issue of a Keeper and a guardian. Of the two of them being together.

'You never answered about Will and me.'

A smile flirted across his lips. 'Will is not the same as Tia. He's her son, not part of her, but his own person. He is the guardian of the library, and of its Keeper. That is all he has ever wanted to be, no matter what I thought. I was wrong about him, Sophie. There are no rules governing that.'

A weight she didn't know had settled on her shoulders seemed to lift.

'Now,' Edward went on. 'Margo has made a most delicious breakfast, all the trimmings. Her speciality. Come along. You can't hide away in here forever, Keeper.'

But when they went down to breakfast, there was no sign of Will at all.

*

The Sapling grew faster than any normal tree. Sophie watched it, visited it every day and talked to it. And the voices spoke to her in return. Calm now, soft whispers, content, soothing, spilling out the secrets of the library, from all throughout history, and beyond.

Tia was right. They weren't angels or demons, or anything in between. They were something else entirely. Some had lived here, some in other locations, all of them tied in some way to the Special Collection and the Tree. They spoke of long ago and far away, of seconds and moments, like the whisper of Will's breath against her bare skin. That never-forgotten, longed-for sensation.

But she hadn't seen Will in weeks. Not for more than a few minutes, never alone. Oh he was polite, and he was deferential but he was avoiding her.

She couldn't even begin to define how much that hurt. After everything, after all they had been through, after everything they had done… After that kiss in the chamber, that kiss when he came back to life…

But she was through running after anyone.

Tia and Edward were enraptured with each other, blissful. It was almost sickening. They spent their nights together and most of their days as well. He took her out to dinner in all his favourite expensive places and in return she made him eat pizza and visit the chipper. He was devoted to her and determined to show it all the time. He made her laugh and she loved to shock him, especially in public.

'Disgusting really,' said Delphine in the refectory one day – after Tia had dragged Edward out by his tie, clearly intent on taking him upstairs to do divine things to him – and went back to texting her latest boyfriend. 'Old people shouldn't act like that.'

It all served to drive home to Sophie what she had lost by their exchange.

Because although he had magically survived his brush with death, Will was a ghost.

And yet she didn't know what to do. She didn't know how to reach out to him or what she would possibly say if she could get him to listen.

'*What would you want to say?*' Voices like the singing of birds, like the chiming of bells surrounded her.

'I don't know,' she replied. And the music of the spheres swirled around her. She was growing used to it now, familiar with its tones and nuances. To be honest she knew she was spending too much time down here, with the Sapling, but where else did she need to be?

Who else wanted her?

Edward ran the library on a day-to-day basis, Tia by his side causing her own particular brand of chaos. Everything was ticking along exactly as it should. Delphine, Hannah and Meera were all content, although they sometimes eyed her like they would a miracle worker.

And Will was avoiding her.

She was more comfortable down here anyway.

Once Sophie had thought she might break out of her shell, that she might actually begin to live the life she had always intended to live. But that clearly was not to be. After Victor was arrested, after some rather imperious people from the military interviewed her about what had happened as well and the School of Night gave up trying to reinstate Edward as Keeper because neither he, nor the library itself, wanted that, Sophie had found herself at a loss. It wasn't a feeling of being trapped or anything. She was content here. Fine. Comfortable. But she also knew what was missing.

Oh, Will was polite and as kind as ever. But he didn't meet her eyes. And he didn't smile at her. And he stayed near her as briefly as possible, never close enough to touch her, even by accident. He called her Keeper in that quiet and deferential way. She was starting to hate it.

'What are you doing down here again?' Tia asked from the doorway. She didn't come in. She didn't dare and didn't want to. Unleashing what she had been was not her plan and never had been. She was, she had declared, entirely at peace being the archivist here, in *her* library. The emphasis on the word 'her' didn't escape anyone's notice but it seemed to be a mutually agreed upon decision not to broach that subject.

'Just checking,' Sophie told her.

'It's fine. It's a tree. It'll grow. It's magic. You need to get out a bit.'

She didn't. It was the last thing she wanted. But Tia wasn't going to back down. She did this daily, to make sure Sophie emerged for light and air. She'd made it clear the first time that if Sophie didn't cooperate, she'd send Margo down instead.

Sophie followed her up from the vault and ate food she barely tasted. Then she made some excuses and went for a walk.

The snow had come down and there were Christmas lights up in the village. Sophie bundled herself up and walked along the silent road, her feet crunching through the snow beneath her. It was dark by the time she got back and the whole place seemed to be deserted.

The library whispered to her, sang to her, and she knew she was never truly alone here. It just felt that way. There was a part of her heart that even the wonders of this place couldn't fill. And never would.

Will had come back to life for her. He had kissed her.

And now he wouldn't even acknowledge her.

*

Sophie woke in the night with a terrible dread – the whole thing unfolding in front of her again, the gunshot, Will's blood – her eyes wide open in sudden shock. She wasn't in bed. She wasn't even in her room. For a terrible moment she thought she might be outside in the snow.

But she wasn't cold. And the stuff fluttering down around her wasn't snow.

She put out her hand and caught one. It lingered for a moment before melting like a mist.

Blossom. Haunting, ghostly blossom.

Sophie recognised her location now, the soft light, like moonlight shifting through water. She was in the Axis Mundi, in front of the Tree. It had grown again while she had been gone. Now it was taller than she was and it was decked in white flowers, more like cherry blossom rather than the catkins of the aspen it resembled most of the time. But this was no normal tree. She, of all people, knew that.

'What are you playing at?' she asked it, as more tiny petals rained down on her. They floated through the air and vanished before they reached the ground. Like it was trying to make the Axis Mundi beautiful for her. Like it was trying to set a scene.

'Sophie?'

His voice took her completely by surprise. She'd thought she was alone. Whirling around, she found Will sitting on the old boulder on the far side of the chamber, where the original tree had once grown.

'Will, I didn't know you were here.'

'I…' His voice faltered, and then remade itself in formality. 'I come here most nights.' When she wasn't here, he meant. Watching over the Tree the same way she did by day. The very thought of it stabbed through her like physical pain. 'I didn't mean to disturb you, Keeper. I apologise. I'll go.'

Sophie swallowed hard on the sudden lump in her throat. The formality was a shield, but it was a weapon as well, pushing her away. She watched as he uncurled his long legs and made his way through the rain of blossom and shifting moonlight, heading for the door without looking at her. He was dressed as usual, in black jeans and a T-shirt, and she felt strangely vulnerable barefoot, in her nightclothes. But how could she feel vulnerable around Will, especially now?

He was thinner, paler. He looked lost.

'Will, don't go,' she whispered, terrified he'd ignore her. 'Not again. Talk to me.'

It wasn't a request, certainly not a plea. Because if it had been she knew he might have made an excuse and left. No, it was an order, and Will couldn't resist that. Perhaps it was unfair. But he wasn't being fair either.

He shuddered, his lips tightening as if he wanted to defy her even in that one small thing. But he couldn't. Not for long. 'What do you want me to say? What *can* I say?'

Sophie frowned at him. She didn't want anything in particular. Only him. 'Talk to me.'

'Keeper, I—'

She drew in a laboured breath. That was all he did now, call her Keeper and avoid her. She was sick of it. It was infuriating.

'Sophie,' she reminded him sharply. She walked towards him, blocking his escape, and stood in front of him, her chin jutting out as she stared up into his face, defying him. 'My name is Sophie.'

'I know that.'

'Then why won't you say it?'

'Because you're the *Keeper* now. You're the Keeper and I—' He finally met her gaze and she realised his eyes were glistening with tears. 'I betrayed you.'

'Will…' His name was a breath she couldn't quite catch. The pain in his voice undid her.

'I did. I brought you back here, to Arthur. When he called me and said I had to bring you back or he'd hurt Tia, I thought I could do something, I could stop him. I meant to protect you, Sophie. Always. But I had to get close enough to reason with him and I used you to do that, and it all… it all went wrong.'

A massive understatement, there, she thought. Well, he probably wasn't expecting his brother to be a psychopath.

'He shot you. You couldn't help that.'

'Yes. And you saw what I am. A monster. I can't help that either. I killed him. And I… I wanted to.'

The pain in his voice showed on his face as well. It broke her heart. 'Will, you saved me. Without you there, he would have…' Well, she didn't know what Arthur would have done. He wasn't going to get his way and she didn't know what he would have done in that case. Probably shot her as well, and she was fairly certain there wasn't any divine blood in her veins that would have saved her. Or would she have spent her whole life a prisoner, bound to him or passed over to Victor, to make sure Arthur's power over the library stayed intact? Will had killed him because he had no choice and she had no regrets about it. 'You did what you had to do.'

'I'm a monster. A thing. Not even human. Not really.'

It wasn't fair. He was so much more than what he feared. To her, especially.

'You're Will. Just Will. And I love you.'

Sophie reached up to touch his face. His skin felt warm and the stubble grazed against her fingertips but she didn't care.

'What happens now, Sophie?' There was so much weight in those words, so much longing. She felt it too. He wanted her to decide.

'I don't know. But I think we should kiss again. Don't you?'

A fleeting, desperately hopeful smile flickered over his lips, lips she wanted to do so many other things but, for this moment anyway, she was content to see it there.

'I love you, Sophie Lawrence. I just need to tell you that. I love you and I always have. I always will. I'll do anything to make it up to you. I—'

Sophie pulled him down towards her and claimed his mouth with her own. She felt his arms slide around her, pulling her closer, and nestled into the curves and hollows of his body, matching it to her own. They belonged together. They always had.

The air whispered around them, a sigh, a soft laugh, a sense of her mother, watching over them.

And here in the heart of the library, Sophie finally felt as if she was at home.

A Letter from Jessica

Dear reader,

I want to say a huge thank you for choosing to read *The Bookbinder's Daughter*. If you did enjoy it, and want to keep up to date with all my latest releases, just sign up at the following link. Your email address will never be shared and you can unsubscribe at any time.

www.bookouture.com/jessica-thorne

Libraries have been important to me, all my life. From the little local library we used to visit when I was a child, where the shelves were folding units in the town hall which could be closed up and tucked away when the hall was used for other things, through the magnificent ones I have visited all over the world, right up to the one I work in to this day. I remember the absolute thrill of getting my first library card, and then, not very much later, getting a special pass to use the adult library because I'd read my way through the children's one.

Magic and libraries have always gone hand in hand for me. The amazing art and craft of the bookbinder is a constant fascination. Storytelling is as old as humanity and books are our way of capturing those stories, of preserving them for all time. Opening a book, any book, means you are opening a door to another world, and stepping into an adventure which comes to life through your imagination. And in many ways, this story is my love letter to everything related to libraries, books and bookbinding.

Many thanks to all my writing friends, Lady writers and the Naughty Kitchen, my editor Ellen and my agent Sallyanne. Thanks also to my many library friends and colleagues all over the world.

I hope you loved *The Bookbinder's Daughter* and if you did I would be very grateful if you could write a review. I'd love to hear what you think, and it makes such a difference helping new readers to discover one of my books for the first time.

I love hearing from my readers – you can get in touch on my Facebook page, through Twitter, Goodreads or my website.

Thanks,
Jessica

JessThorneBooks

@JessThorneBooks

www.rflong.com/jessicathorne

CPSIA information can be obtained
at www.ICGtesting.com
Printed in the USA
LVHW020813271021
701667LV00003BA/410

9 781800 198579